The Last Wolf

David Shaw Mackenzie

TP

ThunderPoint Publishing Ltd.

First Published in Great Britain in 2018 by
ThunderPoint Publishing Limited
Summit House
4-5 Mitchell Street
Edinburgh
Scotland EH6 7BD

ISBN: 978-1-910946-38-1 (Paperback)
ISBN: 978-1-910946-39-8 (eBook)
Printed and bound in Great Britain by Clays Ltd, Elcograf S.p.A

www.thunderpoint.scot

Dedication

For Rachel
and in memory of my best teacher
Mrs Carolina Macritchie (1903 – 2009)

“El original es infiel a la traduccion.”

(The original is unfaithful to the translation.)

Jorge Luis Borges

Contents

PART ONE

That Awful Business with McRone

McRone placed his twelve-bore shotgun in its new brown leather case on the back seat of the Land Rover.

'Might be a hare up by Ardkaig,' he said to his wife.

She smiled briefly.

'Hare soup, eh?' he said. 'That'd be good.'

'Hare soup,' she said quietly. 'Yes.' She was standing in the open front door of their cottage. She had a small green canvas haversack in her hands. 'Don't forget your lunch,' she said. She raised a hand to her head and pushed a stray lock of her short brown hair behind her ear. Although she didn't know it, this tiny action was one that he loved to see.

He walked back the few steps to the cottage and took the haversack from her. 'Thanks,' he said. He leaned forward and kissed her lightly on the lips. This act of affection seemed to take her by surprise.

He got into the Land Rover and put the haversack on the front passenger seat, next to a case containing a pair of binoculars. He rolled down the window. 'Home by five,' he said. 'Six at the latest. Frank's off today so there's just myself.' He closed the window.

She waved goodbye.

At the end of the short rutted driveway he turned left onto the road that led him quickly down to sea level and the junction with the bay road. To the right was the promontory of Swordale Point with the castle, stately and dominant, on top. He turned left. Ahead of him lay the village of Ardroy with its stone pier. Beyond, the curve of the bay led to Glass Point. It was a warm, bright and calm day, the sea unable to decide whether its colour should be grey or blue. The hills of Cnoc Mhabairn, Cnoc a Mhargadaidh and Meall an Tuirc rose from the haze on the mainland shore, eight miles away. There were patches of purple on their grey-brown slopes.

Soon McRone reached the turn-off to Ardkaig but he ignored

this and drove on into Ardroy.

There were very few people in the short main street. McIndoe, the postman, was loading his van for his first delivery of the day. McRone slowed as he passed and drew a wave. McKechnie hadn't opened his garage yet and there was no one on the pier, or no one he could see, anyway. It was well known that Richborough, the harbour master, sometimes spent the night in the pier office which was a single storey wooden structure about half the size of McRone's cottage, situated near the pier end. From the village pub, 'The Old Scots Pine', to this office was a walk of about a hundred yards whereas from the pub to Richborough's home was the best part of half a mile. 'No contest,' he would say, 'no contest, eh? Keeps the wife happy when I've enjoyed the evening a bit too much.'

A mile beyond the village McRone turned off left, away from the sea, and followed a dirt track for about a quarter of a mile. He parked the Land Rover in a narrow, graveled passing place. He took the binoculars from the passenger's seat and slung them, still in their case, round his neck.

He got out of the vehicle and walked up the track for a further couple of hundred yards before climbing over a fence into a field. Cattle turned their heads slowly and regarded him with indifference. Small black beasts with a thick white band round stomach and back. This was McEwan's herd of Belted Galloways moving languidly in the early morning.

Before him was a low hill with a copse of a dozen Scots Pines on the top. Several of the trees had lost their western branches to the on-shore winter gales and looked as if they had been constructed from odd pieces of jagged, angular timber. He followed a contour round till he was on the other side of the hill from the village, then he strode up towards the trees. He had to climb over another fence and fight his way through bracken before he reached the outcrop of rocks among which the pines grew. He crouched down and made his way forward until he was able to lie flat out on a slab of rock which overlooked an estate cottage very similar to his own.

This was the cottage where Frank Millwood, his assistant, lived.

McRone took the binoculars from the case and focused on the front of the cottage. A few yards away stood Frank's open-backed

Ford truck. So, he was still at home. It was just a question of waiting.

But not for long. Within a few minutes Frank had come out of the cottage and was in his vehicle, manoeuvring it round the small parking area until he got it pointing in the right direction. Then he was off, down the hill, dust rising from the dry gravel of the drive.

When he reached the main road he turned right, in the direction of Ardroy.

Unhurried, McRone made his way back to the Land Rover. He turned it round, drove back down to the main road again and set off towards home. But ten minutes later, when he reached the drive that led up to the cottage he'd lived in with his wife for four years, he didn't turn in but drove past, slowly. He couldn't see Frank's Ford but then he didn't expect to. A hundred yards on, he pulled into a lay-by.

He reckoned there were three places where Frank could have parked. He drove on again for a mere twenty yards before branching off onto a dirt track that quickly turned at a right angle on to a small clearing surrounded by birch trees. On one side of the clearing there was a pile of sand mixed with salt used by the council snowploughs to grit the roads in winter. On the other side sat Frank's Ford.

McRone got out of the Land Rover. From the floor by the back seat he picked up a light chain which was used, in normal circumstances, to cordon off Forestry roads, including the rutted and often water-logged track that led up to Ardkaig where he was supposed to be working that day. There was about fifteen feet of chain, complete with a couple of padlocks. Halfway along its length, fixed to it by wire, was a small rectangular metal sign. NO THROUGH ROAD was printed in red on a white background. The chain was looped up. He slipped it over his head and carried it over one shoulder like a bandolier.

Then he reached in to the back seat and drew the shotgun from its leather case. He loaded it with two cartridges taken from his jacket pocket. He didn't cock the gun but carried it broken over his forearm. He set out for his cottage.

He couldn't use the road. He needed to get to the front door but from the other side of the building. It was a bit like stalking a deer, keeping downwind and hidden at all times. He used the birch grove as cover for the first fifty yards then moved above the cottage. There was a small rise which ensured that he could only see the roof and someone looking from the cottage couldn't see him at all.

Finally, after climbing two fences, he was in the grounds of the cottage with the bedroom on the far side. He stepped carefully across the small, scrappy lawn that had dried up in the recent heat, ducked under the living room window, though he was sure there would be no one there, and reached the front door.

The door was unlocked. He even managed a smile. Was this stupidity, laziness or indifference? Or sheer neglect in the haste to get on with the principal activity of the morning? He opened the door as quietly as he could and stepped inside. He was in the short, wood-lined corridor that led to the kitchen at the back of the cottage. The bedroom was the second door on the right.

He stood close up to the bedroom door and listened for a full minute. The noises he heard were much as he expected. He cocked the shotgun with as quiet a click as he could manage and raised it to vertical. Facing the door, he took one step back.

He booted the door hard, just by the doorknob so the jamb splintered and the door was propelled inwards. Immediately there was screaming.

'What the fuck!' This from Millwood.

McRone said, 'Good morning.'

'Alan, Alan…Christ…' McRone's wife, Ella, was shaking, holding her right hand out towards him, her left arm dragging the sheet up to her throat.

'Alan, please…'

McRone raised the shotgun to his shoulder and pointed it at Millwood.

'No! No! No! Jesus!'

McRone moved his aim three feet higher and let off one round. Through the density of the detonation, the sheer roar of it, his wife screamed once more, unheard. Bits of plasterboard and dust were sprayed over the room and a ragged hole appeared in the wall above the headboard of the bed.

Ella was now on the floor, curled up, still screaming, 'No… no…' in a series of extended syllables.

Millwood seemed incapable of speech.

'Well, Frank,' McRone said to him, 'why don't you tell me it's not what I think, eh? That's the usual story, isn't it? It's just not what it looks like, eh? Eh?'

Millwood found his voice and said, 'Alan…Alan…I mean, you've got to…'

'Oh, just be quiet,' McRone said. 'You see, I understand, I understand completely. Give me some credit, eh? No, no, you were just passing and it's a hot day and you were feeling a bit tired so…so Ella said, why don't you lie down for a bit? In fact, it being so warm and everything, why don't you take your clothes off and…well, look, I'm a bit tired myself so I'll lie down too, next to you in fact…Is that it, eh? And then she said that, for the sake of equality and all that she'd…well, she'd take her clothes off too. Only fair, after all…'

'Alan, look…'

'Oh, you're going to explain everything now, are you?'

Millwood shook his head. 'No, look, I'm sorry, I'm really sorry…'

'Like fuck you are,' McRone said. He broke the shotgun, ejected the spent cartridge, loaded another in its place and cocked the gun again. 'OK,' he said, 'now just get down onto the floor.'

'What?'

'On the floor, now. Face down.'

'Alan, no, wait. We can sort this…I mean, we can sort this without any…sort it easily…'

'Precisely what I'm going to do. So get on the floor.'

'Alan, please, just listen for a minute…'

'Please don't hurt him, Alan, please…' This from Ella who was now sitting on the floor on her side of the bed, squeezing the bedclothes with tight, frantic fingers.

'You just be quiet,' McRone said to her. 'And as for you…' He looked at Millwood. '…be thankful you're still alive but take care because that condition could change dramatically if you don't do what you're told.'

'No, no, come on, Alan, for Christ's sake, let's just be calm here…'

'Calm? Calm? I'm perfectly calm. Really. And I don't really want to kill you unless I have to. So…let's put it this way, if you stay on the bed and don't do as I say then I'll definitely kill you. But if you get down on the floor we move from certainty to mere probability. I think that's clear, isn't it?'

Millwood said, 'Christ…' but didn't move.

McRone let off another round. The hole this produced in the wall was a foot lower than the previous one, barely eighteen inches above Millwood's head. Ella began screaming again. Millwood, his hair whitened with plasterboard dust, slid off the bed and onto the floor on the opposite side from where Ella sat hugging her knees to her chest with an intensity that made her fingers and forearms white and bloodless.

McRone leaned forward to peer at the bed. 'Well,' he said to Millwood, 'looks as if you've pissed yourself. Is that right?' He leaned further forward. 'Piss or sperm? No, I think it's piss. Well, there you go. Now you two, I want you both to listen carefully. Are you listening?'

Millwood said, 'Yes.'

'And you?' McRone said, raising his voice for the first time, 'you pathetic excuse for a wife. Are you listening?'

'Oh, Alan, please…'

'Are you listening?'

'Yes, yes, but please listen to me first, Alan, please. I can explain…'

'No!' McRone shouted. 'Don't ever say you can explain. Don't ever say that. Don't even think about it. Right now just shut up and listen. So…' This outburst over, calmer tones returned. 'It's like this. Right now I don't particularly want to kill anybody. But that's purely for selfish reasons. I mean, I'd wind up in jail for a while, wouldn't I? Of course, it probably wouldn't be for too long, even if I killed both of you. Crime of passion and all that. But…well, actually, come to think of it, maybe it would be worth it after all. But then, just the one, or both of you? Difficult decision, I think you'll agree…'

'Alan, look…' Millwood twisted round, his face pressed into the pale grey pile of the bedroom carpet which was now lightly dusted with bits of detritus from the plasterboard wall.

'Hands together behind your back,' McRone said.

'Christ, Alan…'

McRone rested the barrel end of the shotgun on the left cheek of Millwood's bare backside. 'This gun is cocked, you know,' he said quietly.

'OK, OK,' Millwood put his hands together behind his back.

McRone broke the gun and laid it down carefully on the empty bed. Then he took the chain he'd been carrying and threw it on the floor next to Millwood. He took one end of the chain and bound Millwood's wrists together tightly, securing the bond with one of the padlocks.

'That fucking hurts!' Millwood complained.

'Get used to it,' McRone said.

'Please, please don't hurt him,' Ella said. She was still sitting on the floor, holding her legs tightly to her body, her forehead resting on her knees. She seemed to be overcome by total dejection, only intermittently participating in what was happening. She was sobbing quietly.

'The only way you can be released from pain completely,' McRone said, 'is if I blow your head off. That's an option that's still available, by the way.'

'Fucking hell, Alan...'

'Now, just you stay there,' McRone said when Millwood's hands were secured to his satisfaction. 'Remember, I've still got the gun.' He picked up the shotgun and stepped out of the bedroom, across the corridor and into the living room. Working quickly he opened the top drawer of a sideboard and found some cash and a cheque book. He pushed these into an inside pocket of his jacket.

When he got back to the bedroom all was as before, Millwood lying face down on the floor and, on the other side of the bed, Ella huddled and inert. But she started to speak again. It was difficult for McRone to separate words from tears as Ella had begun to shake with fear but he found that she was saying, 'Please don't hurt him, Alan. Please don't hurt him...'

'Think of yourself,' he said to her. 'Think of yourself and think of me. And you...' he said to Millwood, 'on your feet, you. We're going for a walk.'

'What?'

'Up! Come on, up!'

'Christ...'

'Come on, get up.' McRone jerked on the chain that bound Millwood's hands.

'All right! All right!'

Millwood struggled onto his side and then up onto his knees.

'Hold it there a minute.' McRone put the shotgun down on the bed once more. He picked up the chain and, standing behind Millwood, stretched it from Millwood's wrists up, over his left shoulder, round his throat twice and back over his right shoulder.

'You're fucking choking me!'

'Exactly right. But if you keep your hands as high as possible, that should reduce the pressure a bit.'

'You bastard.'

'Oh, getting a bit bolshie now, are we? Not a good move for a man in your position. Now stand up.'

'Jesus!' With difficulty, Millwood got to his feet. 'What the hell now?'

'Front door. Oh, and by the way…' He had the shotgun in his hands again. 'The gun's cocked, all right? So, any sudden movements from you and, goodness knows, I might just pull the trigger accidentally, you know? Just pure accident. And then you'd lose your arse or your balls or your head. Understand?'

Millwood nodded.

'Say yes.'

'Yes, damn it!'

'Good, good. Now you…' He turned to look at his wife. 'You just stay sensible, right? Stay inside and don't speak to anyone, OK? Hear me?'

'Yes, yes…'

'If anyone comes after me in the next half hour I'll kill this bastard. Understand?'

Her sobbing intensified and then abated.

'And I might just kill him anyway. Now,' to Millwood, 'let's go.'

'Go? Where the fuck to?'

'Out.'

'What? Christ sake, let me put some clothes on at least. Jesus…'

'Nice warm day,' McRone said. 'You'll be fine.'

'Oh, come on now. Just hold on a minute…'

McRone yanked on the chain which pulled hard against Millwood's throat. With a yelp from the pain he fell to the floor and sprawled out from the bedroom into the corridor.

As Millwood struggled for breath, McRone loosened the chain round his neck. Then he leaned over and spoke quietly into Millwood's left ear. 'Just listen to me, you little shite, you've got only one chance of survival, right? One chance, and that's to do exactly as I say. Exactly. Right? So get up and start walking. No clothes, no shoes, nothing. Just you and me and this chain and this shotgun. OK?'

By this time Millwood's gasping had reduced to merely breathing heavily. He struggled to get back onto his knees. He nodded. 'OK, OK.'

'Right. Get up.'

A few moments later Millwood was standing at the open front door, looking out at the dusty yard of the little cottage. McRone left him to go quickly through the kitchen to the back door. He locked this from the inside and drew out the key. As he walked back he passed the telephone which was on a small table in the hall. He wrenched the telephone wire from its socket, pushed the phone onto the floor and kicked it towards the kitchen. At the front of the cottage once more he pushed Millwood outside and locked the door behind them. He put the key in his pocket.

'Come on, then,' he said to Millwood. 'Move it.'

'Where's the Land Rover?' Millwood asked.

'The Land Rover? Don't need it.'

'So where are we going then?'

'I thought a wee walk down to the village, eh? Fine day like this. Enjoy the scenery.'

'Enjoy the scenery? Are you fucking mad?'

'Well, you'd better hope not. After all, I'm the one with the gun. So let's go.'

Millwood didn't move. 'Come on, Alan, this has gone far enough. Let's just stop now. Let's be sensible here.'

'Sensible?'

'This has got to stop. Right now.'

'We're going to sort this out down in Ardroy,' McRone said.

'No, we're not. I'm not going anywhere.'

'No?'

'No. Not for you or anybody.'

'I see. Not for me or anybody. Well, let's just think this through, shall we…'

'You fucking think it through,' Millwood said.

'Well, I will…'

Stumbling in his bare feet on the gravel, Millwood turned to face him. 'Do whatever you want but I'm not moving.'

'You've made that clear. So…not for me or anybody. That what you're saying?'

'That's it.'

'And for Ella?'

'What do you mean?'

'Would you move for Ella?'

'What the fuck are you talking about?'

'Would you move to save Ella's life?'

Millwood was silent for a few seconds then said quietly, 'Alan, for fuck's sake, stop this, OK? Stop it.'

But McRone ignored this. 'Simple,' he said. 'If you don't agree to do as I say, I'll go back in there now and shoot Ella.'

'Mind games, Alan. You wouldn't do that.'

'No?'

'No.'

'Sure? I mean, absolutely sure?'

Millwood was tense and uncertain. He was blowing hard, too, not so much from exertion as from the pressure of the moment. McRone looked relaxed and confident.

'Well,' McRone said at last, 'I think you've made your choice.' He took a grip on the chain and pulled Millwood, stumbling and close to falling over, across the yard to where there was a rowan tree about twenty feet high. Its flowers were gone, its berries not yet red. McRone wrapped the end of the chain round the trunk several times, drew the end through in a crude granny knot and headed off back to the cottage.

Millwood called after him, 'Alan, don't be stupid now. Alan!'

McRone reached the front door, took the key from his pocket.

'Alan! Stop! Now!' These three words progressed from a tone of command to one of fear and alarm.

McRone opened the door.

'Alan, stop it now. I'll do it. Anything. I'll do it.'

McRone turned to look at him. 'Too late,' he said and he went into the cottage, closing the door gently behind him.

For half a minute or so, Millwood heard nothing. He was trembling and breathing more quickly as the silence continued. Then there was a scream, followed by a gunshot. Millwood tried to wrench himself free from the tree he was bound to but he couldn't. He stopped again to listen. There was another minute of silence, followed by a second gunshot.

From a small stand of pines on the hill above the village came the cawing of crows, more indifferent than angry as, for the second time in as many minutes they were disturbed by a gun report and rose into the air to circle languidly their roosting place.

McRone came from the cottage. He left the front door open. Without saying anything he walked up to Millwood and began to unwind the chain from the rowan tree.

'Christ, Alan, what've you done? You didn't kill her...tell me you didn't kill her, for Christ's sake...I mean, you couldn't...'

'No,' McRone said as he finally separated Millwood from the tree. 'No, you're quite right. I didn't kill her.' After a few moments he added, 'You did.'

'Me? Me? What do you mean? I didn't...'

'No, no. No, of course not. I killed her. That's it, yes. I killed her, but with a little help from you, don't you think?'

Millwood began to shout. 'Ella! Ella!'

No sound came from the cottage.

'Ella! Come on! Speak to me!'

Nothing.

McRone shrugged. 'Well, there you are,' he said.

Millwood was shaking his head. 'No,' he said, 'You couldn't do that, not even you. No, Christ...' Then he shouted out, 'You're fucking mad!'

McRone said, 'Let's go, shall we? I mean, I've killed Ella so obviously I could kill you right here too. But I'm not going to. We're going down to Ardroy so that I can humiliate you. That's the plan, OK? And just bear in mind that the longer this goes on, the more chance there is of you surviving. Well, there's a slim chance, anyway. Or...or would you prefer it if I killed you now? What do you reckon?'

'Christ...' Millwood looked down at the worn earth and gravel at his feet. 'Do what the fuck you like,' he said.

They began to walk slowly towards the road. Millwood complained that his feet were already beginning to bleed.

McRone said, 'It's odd, isn't it. You're still expecting me to be sympathetic.' He smiled. 'Just keep walking. The first mile's the worst. After that your feet'll be so numb you won't feel a thing.

Anyway, tarmac soon. You'll be fine.'

They reached the end of the drive and turned towards the village. The road was mostly single track with passing places every fifty yards or so. Millwood, stepping carefully, was in front of McRone who had loops of chain in one hand and the shotgun in the other. At one point McRone transferred the gun to his chain hand and took from his pocket the front and back door keys of the cottage and the keys of the Land Rover. He dumped all of these in a ditch.

It was three or four minutes after they began the gentle descent to Ardroy that they encountered the first vehicle. The post van laboured up the hill towards them. It squeezed past and then came to a halt a few yards behind them. McIndoe leaned out of the window, looked back and shouted, 'Christ, Alan, what's going on, man?'

'Just a bit of societal readjustment,' McRone called to him.

'He's fucking mad!' Millwood shouted. 'Get the police, for Christ's sake!'

'Alan, what...' McIndoe got out of the van and advanced towards them. 'What the hell's going on?'

'I'm taking him down to the village to execute him,' McRone said.

'What?' McIndoe took off his postman's cap. 'You're what?'

'He's mad!' Millwood yelled out again. 'He's completely mad! He's going to kill me!'

'Alan, Alan...' McIndoe began. 'You can't...'

But McIndoe's response was interrupted by the sound of a car as it climbed the hill towards them.

'Better shift the van,' McRone said. Then he turned away from McIndoe and prodded Millwood in the backside with the shotgun. 'Move,' he said. 'Move.'

McIndoe retreated to the post van at a run. The car arrived at speed and the two men drew a bewildered look from the driver as he passed. McRone didn't recognize him but gave him a cheery wave anyway.

McIndoe had to drive to the next lay-by to let the car behind him pass. By the time he'd turned the post van round and driven back to where he'd encountered the two men, they'd disappeared.

They'd gone through a gate into a field which allowed them to take a short cut to the village. Below them lay the bay with its narrow ribbon of flat land. The low hills, with their splashes of purple as the heather came into bloom, rose in a ragged arc which began at Swordale Castle and ended at Glass Point. The sky was untroubled by clouds and in the quiet of the field they could hear the broom pods in the hedgerows popping in the heat.

'Take care you don't step in any cow shit,' McRone said. 'Lot of it about and I wouldn't want you to get your feet dirty.'

'Take care. Oh aye, fine,' Millwood said. Then he came to a stop. 'I'm fed up of this,' he said.

'That a fact? Well now...' McRone yanked the chain and Millwood landed on the grass, struggling for breath again. McRone leaned down and looped another length of chain round his throat. 'You just don't understand, do you,' he said quietly. 'I could strangle you right now. Very slowly. Maybe that's what you want, is it? Is that what you want?'

Millwood couldn't speak. Nor could he breathe. McRone waited till the redness of Millwood's face suggested he was about to pass out. Then he loosened off the chain.

Lying on his side on the grass, Millwood coughed and gasped for nearly two minutes. His face remained red, though not as red as before. His cheeks were wet with sweat and tears. 'You're a fucking maniac,' he said when he was able to speak. 'You're a fucking homicidal maniac.'

'Just as long as you don't forget that,' McRone said. 'Now, get up.'

When Millwood managed to stand, they set off again.

Soon they were walking in awkward tandem down the main street in the village of Ardroy. Millwood began to shout in a voice that was hoarse from the ministrations of the chain against his throat. 'Help! Please! Call the police! Help! Come on...'

'Interesting, that,' McRone said to him. 'I mean, you calling for the police and all, because you and I know – and everyone else, too – that the nearest police are ten miles away and eight of those miles are water. Should be here in a couple of hours, eh? What do you reckon?'

Millwood said, 'Fuck off.'

'Anyway, let's say they're really quick and get here in twenty minutes. Well, it'll still be too late. You'll be long dead by then.'

Now, from the post office and the village shop, both just opened, from half a dozen of the houses, from the one small hotel and from the side door of the Old Scots Pine pub there began to emerge, cautiously, villagers and a few others who were at first curious, then bewildered and shocked, appalled at what they saw. Millwood and McRone knew every one of them, except for three who were guests at the hotel.

Forbes Kendale, a local councillor and the owner of the village store, was the first to approach. 'What the hell are you doing, Alan?' he said and his tone was a blend of caution and authority. 'What's going on?'

'Public retribution,' McRone said, 'for crimes committed in private.'

'What?'

'He's mad,' Millwood said. 'Look at me, I'm half dead already. Jesus...'

'Half dead?' McRone said. 'Well, any more shite out of you and I'll be happy to supply the other half. No problem at all.'

Kendale said, 'Let me at least cover him up, man. There's women here.'

McRone laughed. 'My god,' he said, 'my god. I mean, here's a man that's just about to be shot and all you're interested in is the fact that he's naked. Don't you think you might...you know... you might have got your priorities wrong?'

'You're going to shoot him?' Kendale asked.

'Of course I'm going to shoot him. And he's staying naked for the time being. While he's still alive, at least. Oh, and another thing...' His voice rose as he looked round at those who were beginning to assemble close by. 'Keep your distance all of you, right? This thing's loaded...' He raised the shotgun above his head. 'And I don't mind using it. Now, I'm not going to shoot any of you. No, no, I wouldn't do that, no, but...if any of you get too close, I'll be happy to shoot this bastard here...'

The seven or eight people who were witness to this strange procession of McRone, Millwood and now Kendale, each took several steps back.

'You keep your distance too,' McRone said to Kendale who also retreated a few yards.

Kendale spoke again. 'What's all this about, Alan?' he asked.

'What's happened?'

'Caught him in bed with Ella,' McRone said.

No one responded to this information, nor did Millwood himself make any comment. The slow progress down the main street continued.

'So where are you taking him?' Kendale asked.

'To the pier. Ferry's due in a few minutes. Let's go and see it coming in, shall we?'

Millwood said, 'Christ almighty.'

'Can't you let it be, Alan?' Kendale said. 'I mean, I know nothing can make up for what he did...'

'Tell me about Janice,' McRone said.

'Janice? What about her?'

'How would you feel if you got home one day and found her in bed with this bastard, eh?'

'Oh, come on, Alan...'

'No, no, no, I'm serious. Couldn't possibly happen to you, could it? Janice is a fine woman, pillar of the Kirk, faithful, honest...No, she'd never do anything like that, would she? No, well that's what I believed about Ella. So I'll tell you how you'd feel in my position.' McRone's voice began to rise. 'You'd feel betrayed and humiliated and dirty. You'd feel that nothing much mattered any more. You'd feel...I don't know...you'd feel that all you wanted to do was kill the bastard that's done it to you. And knowing you I'd say he'd probably already be dead. By god, he's getting off lightly with me, I can tell you. So far, that is.'

'He shot Ella,' Millwood said.

'What?'

'He shot Ella. He killed her.'

'Alan, god almighty...'

'Oh, for Christ's sake don't be ridiculous' McRone said. 'Of course I didn't kill Ella. She's up at the cottage and she's trussed up like a turkey. Bloody uncomfortable, maybe, but she's fine. Don't worry about her. Worry about this bastard here, OK?' McRone's voice was still loud, almost shrill. 'This is my way of dealing with it, all right?' he said, looking round at Kendale and the other silent bystanders. 'You can watch if you like,' he went on, 'but by god I promise if anyone gets too close I'll unload both barrels into this bastard's arse. Now, someone go onto the pier and tell them all to stay out of my way.'

Kendale said, 'That'll be me.' He turned and set off briskly ahead of them onto the pier where the harbour master and half a dozen men were preparing for the arrival of the MV Glen Coyne on its first crossing of the day from the mainland.

Millwood, now limping, and McRone made their way down the centre of the pier towards the harbour master's office at the pier head. The men who worked there, warned by Kendale, formed a kind of ragged guard of honour, standing on the outer edges of the structure, regarding with astonishment the progress of the two men. They all knew McRone and they all knew Millwood. One of them, from a nervous need to break the silence, said, 'All right then, Alan?'

'All right? All right?' McRone said. 'Does it look as if I'm all right? Christ...Tell you one thing, though,' he added, 'I'm better placed than this man here.' He walked on.

The Glen Coyne, with its capacity of twenty-five cars and eighty-five passengers, was already in sight, rounding Swordale Point, the mass of grey granite on top of which the castle had been built. Despite its square, turret-like tower, Swordale wasn't really a castle, it was a huge, early Victorian country house. It was the property of Major Maurice Redburn who was McRone's boss.

There had been much talk on the island about the replacement of the Glen Coyne by a new ferry with greater capacity. Few on the island could see the need. This morning there were only nine cars, so far, waiting to board. McRone had counted them as he approached the pier. Nine drivers who had watched his and Millwood's stuttering progress and wondered what the hell was going on. They all stayed inside their vehicles.

The men on the right hand side of the pier decided to cross over to the left because McRone and Millwood were heading towards them in order to go round the waiting room and the harbour master's office. As they passed the office, McRone could see Kendale in apparently intense discussion with Richborough, the harbour master. There was a tall lamp standard halfway between the office and the end of the pier itself. At its top, some thirty feet above the pier deck, was a cluster of floodlights.

McRone told Millwood to go and stand up against this tall metal column. Millwood was now dazed and seemed to have travelled beyond any ability to differentiate one act from another. He stumbled forward and leaned his left shoulder and the left side of his chest against the lamp standard.

'Turn round and put your back against it,' McRone said, 'and face the sea, not the island.' Numb from what had happened to him over the past half hour and unable to argue, Millwood did as he was told.

'McRone!' This was a shout from the harbour master's office. McRone turned round and saw Richborough striding towards him. Kendale was further back, standing at the open office door.

'What the hell's going on here?' Richborough shouted.

'None of your business,' McRone said.

'What happens on this pier is my business.'

'Not today, I'm afraid.'

'Now look here...' Richborough stepped forward and pointed at McRone. 'I'm in charge here and you do as I say...'

McRone shook his head slowly. He said nothing but was smiling faintly as if he were witness to some strange species unacquainted with the world.

'I want both of you off this pier now,' Richborough went on. 'The ferry's due in ten minutes and I'll not have everyone treated to the sight of this...of this nonsense. So just get off the pier right now.'

McRone had let the loops of chain fall from his hand. They were lying on the deck at his feet. But there was no question of Millwood escaping. In his exhausted and traumatized state he had slipped down and was now sitting at the foot of the lamp standard, elbows on knees.

McRone cocked the shotgun and slowly raised the butt to his shoulder. He took aim at Millwood's head.

'No, no, Alan. Wait, for Christ's sake. Please...please...' During these few words Richborough's tone shifted from authoritarian to alarmed to merely pleading. 'Don't do anything stupid, now. Please...'

McRone quickly raised the shotgun high, took aim and fired. He blew away one of the cluster of four floodlights thirty feet above them.

'Christ, man!'

Pieces of metal and glass sprayed down onto the far edge of the pier and the sea beyond. Millwood yelped as a piece of casing and a small shower of glass shards fell on him.

McRone ejected the spent cartridge from the shotgun and reloaded. Once more he pointed the shotgun at Millwood's head. 'What you have to understand,' he said to Richborough, although he wasn't looking at him, 'is that if you don't go back into your office right now I'll blow this bastard's head off. I don't really want to but...well, no, you see, over the past few minutes I've... well, I've started to change my mind. I'm at the stage when I don't really care any more. Do you know what I mean?' He turned briefly to Richborough who said nothing so he went on, 'Think of it this way. It's a balancing of probability. If you go back into your office as I asked you to, then I won't shoot this man, or at least not straight away. If you don't go back to your office I'll kill him now. So what's it to be, eh?'

'OK, OK,' Richborough said. 'I'm going. I'm going right now.' He began to walk backwards, away from the two men.

'Into the office,' McRone said. 'And just sit down. Have a chat with Forbes if you like but don't communicate with the ferry. Just let it come in. Let everybody land. OK?'

'OK, OK. I'm just...'

'Go!'

The harbour master turned and ran.

McRone smiled. 'OK,' he said to Millwood. 'On your feet.'

Trembling, Millwood undertook the great effort that enabled him to stand.

'Back against the post.'

Millwood stayed still as McRone walked round him, paying out the chain, winding it round his upper body, waist, thighs and calves, binding him to the post. The little sign which read NO THROUGH ROAD was pressed against his left hip. McRone then placed the shotgun, broken, carefully at his feet, took the second padlock from his pocket and locked the chain in place.

The ferry was only a couple of hundred yards from the pier. McRone said to Millwood, 'I think it's time, eh? What d'you reckon?' He picked up the shotgun and walked to the pier edge. Then he turned and, with his back to the incoming ferry, he cocked the gun. He looked at Millwood, raised the gun to his shoulder and took aim. Some of Richborough's men who were within sight of this called out, 'No, Alan, no, no...' Millwood began to whimper.

But there was no shot. McRone relaxed his aim and broke the gun. He walked over to Millwood and whispered in his ear. 'There you are,' he said. 'Now you can relax because I'm not going to shoot you. Good news, eh? So smile, why don't you. Smile! Smile for all the nice people on the ferry. Might be some with cameras, who knows.'

The Glen Coyne was close in now. Passengers were congregating on deck, ready to disembark. McRone could see fingers being pointed as they took in the scene below them on the pier.

He walked away. He ejected the two cartridges which he put in his pocket. As he approached the harbour master's office he called out, 'All done, all done. You can come out now.'

Richborough appeared at the door with Kendale standing behind him. 'By god, Alan,' he said. 'By god...'

'God had nothing to do with it,' McRone said. 'He was a long way away on far more important business. As he always is. Anyway, I'll be off now. You'd better take this. He presented the shotgun to Richborough who accepted it with some reluctance. 'It's not mine, anyway,' McRone continued. 'It's the Major's. He'll be wanting it back. But I'll keep the cartridges for the time being. Anyway...'

The harbour men had secured the ferry hawsers to the capstans and the Glen Coyne was being drawn in to the pier. Within a couple of minutes the front ramp would be lowered to let the vehicles off and the gangway would be in place for the passengers to disembark.

'I suppose I'd better go,' McRone said. 'After all, you'll be quite busy, what with the ferry arriving and all. Oh, by the way...' He put his hand in his pocket and took out two small keys. 'These are the keys,' he said, 'to the padlocks.' He nodded towards Millwood. 'But you don't really need them, do you? If you're desperate, the estate'll have copies, I'm sure.' He turned and threw the keys over the side of the pier and into the sea. 'I'll say goodbye then.'

McRone set off back down the pier, walking purposefully rather than briskly. He passed the line of now thirteen cars that were waiting to board the ferry. He knew some of the drivers and gave them a wave. Some nodded an acknowledgement. No words were exchanged. When he reached the main road he turned right, away from the village, and headed off round the bay in the direction of Glass Point.

News of what was later referred to as 'that awful business with McRone' reached the castle nine minutes later. During these nine minutes, Richborough was a very busy man. He got two men to stand in front of Millwood to shield him from view, halted the placing of the gangway to delay disembarkation and sent two other men in search of a tarpaulin. This large, heavy sheet, discoloured and smelling of seawater, was wrapped round Millwood, covering entirely the man, the chains and the lowest eight feet of the post. 'I'll fucking suffocate in here,' Millwood called out as the men were encasing him in the foul-smelling rough material. 'You'll be fine,' Richborough said to him. 'Just keep quiet for the next ten minutes or I'll suffocate you myself.'

'What do we do now?' one of the men asked Richborough.

'Leave him, ignore him. Just keep folk away from him, I don't want them seeing him, that's all.'

'They've already seen him,' one of the other men said. 'They've all seen him.'

'Just keep them away,' Richborough repeated. 'He's not there, right? We'll sort it out in a couple of minutes when everyone's off the ferry.'

'Has McRone gone clean daft or what?'

'How the hell would I know? Just forget about it. You've got work to do, haven't you?' He looked hard at the four men in front of him. 'Haven't you?'

'Aye, right…'

'Then get on with it. And act normal.' In a quieter voice, to their departing backs, he added, 'Difficult for some of you, I know.'

He went into the office and rang the castle.

It was Major Redburn's son, James Redburn, who answered the phone. He told Richborough that the Major was not available. He was in the castle grounds, probably tending the water garden. Richborough then recounted what had happened on the pier.

'McRone?' Redburn said. 'Now, which one is he?'

'Your keeper.'

'Oh, the gamekeeper. Yes, of course.'

'His father was keeper before him.'

'Alexander McRone. Yes, I remember him clearly. So...so you're saying that this McRone – Alan, isn't it?'

'That's right, yes.'

'...you're saying he took this Millwood chap hostage?'

'If you want to put it that way. Dragged him down to the pier without a stitch of clothes on him, shackled him to a post, made as if to shoot him...'

'He shot him, you say? You mean he's dead, this Millwood...'

'No, no. He's fine. Well, no, he's not fine but at least he's alive. McRone only threatened to shoot him. He didn't actually do it. Just an exercise in humiliation, I'd say. Anyway, he handed the shotgun over to me and then he left. It's been quite an interesting morning so far.'

'So what are the police saying? Are they there yet?'

'The police? No, there's no police.'

'But you have called them?'

'No, I haven't.'

'You...you haven't called them?'

'No.'

There was a pause on the line and then James Redburn said, 'Why not?'

'Well, there's two reasons, really, Mr Redburn. First, there's no police on Glass so they've got to get here on the ferry which isn't due for another hour and that's only if there's someone available to come over here. And then...'

'Yes?'

'Well, I thought your father would probably want to sort all this out straight away and not involve the police if at all possible.'

'I see. So that's what you think, is it?'

'Well, yes. Remember that both McRone and Millwood are his employees, so...'

'Actually,' James Redburn said, 'as I'm now managing the estate they're my employees and if either of them has broken the law, then it's a police matter. So I suggest you call them straight away.'

'Well, you know, I'm not sure to what extent the law has been broken,' Richborough said. 'A bit of public humiliation certainly, a bit of damage to the pier...'

'What damage?'

'He took a pot shot at one of our floodlights.'

'Well, there you are. It's quite clear to me that you have to call the police and let them handle it.'

'Mr Redburn...'

'You are going to call the police, aren't you?'

There was a pause of about ten or twelve seconds before the harbour master said, 'No, Mr Redburn, I'm not going to call the police and I strongly suggest that you don't either. Or at least, speak to Major Redburn first. See what he thinks. He knows all the parties involved and I'm sure he'll know what to do.'

With what might be called rather strained formalities, the phone call ended.

Richborough resented James Redburn's tone which was that of someone who thought he had authority but in fact had none. And James Redburn resented Richborough's audacity in telling him what he should do. At the end of their conversation Redburn called the police and explained, as well as he could, what had happened on the pier. Then he left the castle and walked down, across the descending terraced lawns, to the water garden where his father, with a wooden rake, was clearing some blanket weed from the pond.

'McRone, you say?' the Major said.

'That's right. The gamekeeper.'

'Well, I know who he is.' He began to disentangle some weed from the head of the rake. He dropped a handful of thick green strands on the grass at the side of the pond. 'Little creatures, you see,' he explained. 'Water beetles, caddis larvae, that sort of thing. Leave the weed here at the edge and they...they get the chance to get back into the water.' He turned to his son. 'So what's McRone done, exactly?'

'Apparently he found someone in bed with his wife.'

'Really? In bed with Ella? Well, not too surprising, I suppose.'

'What do you mean by that?'

'Very pretty. You haven't met her yet, have you?'

'No.'

'Very pretty,' the Major repeated. 'Oh, I'm not saying it's her fault. No, not at all. No, but...well, I half expected something like this, you know.'

'You did?'

'Yes, yes. So, tell me, was it Millwood by any chance? In bed with her, I mean.'

'Well, yes, it was. How did you know that?'

'Lucky guess,' the Major said. 'Saw them together once a few weeks ago. Together a lot, of course, since he's McRone's assistant. Anyway, just a look, a certain look between them. Just made me a bit suspicious, that's all.'

'Well, it seems you were right.'

'Yes. Pity. I'd imagine that most of the men on the island envy McRone his...his choice of wife. Anyway, what did he do when he found them together?'

'He marched Millwood down to the pier and tied him to a post.'

'Did he, by god.' The Major leaned over to place the rake carefully on the bank of the pond. As he straightened up he was smiling. 'Did he, by god,' he said again.

'And apparently Millwood was naked.'

'Ha!' This time the Major laughed.

'I really don't think this is a laughing matter, you know,' his son said.

'No?'

'No.'

'Well, I suppose not. But tell me, what would you have done?'

'What do you mean?'

'I mean...not now of course, no, but when you first got married...How long ago was that, again?'

'Twenty, twenty-one years.'

'Right, well, let's say that you came home from the office one day and found Marina in bed with one of your colleagues – oh, I'm not implying anything about Marina, of course not, no. Purely hypothetical. But...but what would you have done, d'you think, in that situation?'

'Well, I think I can categorically say that I wouldn't have gone round the neighbourhood terrorizing people with a shotgun.'

'Is that what he's done?'

'According to the harbour master, yes.'

'Ah, Richborough,' the Major said. 'A man much given to exaggeration. But to be fair, mostly after six o'clock in the evening.'

'And the shotgun is, of course, estate property.'

'Well, it would be.'
'I'm thinking of the damage.'
'Damage? What kind of damage?'
'To the island. To the reputation of the island and the castle.'
'Reputation?'
'When we finally open the place up.'
'Ah.'
'Something like this could put people off.'
'Well, I suppose it could...' The Major turned to the pond again. Although referred to as a pond, it was more like a small lake, fifty yards long and fringed with rushes. At the far end there was one willow overhanging the water. Its leaves brushed against an area of lily pads which spread across from one bank to the other.
'Used to be four, you know,' the Major said.
'Four? Four what?'
'Willows.' He pointed. 'And now there's only one. Five years ago now, or was it six? Very hard winter, anyway. Killed three of them off. Great shame, really.' He turned to his son. 'Do you remember them?'
'Actually, I don't. No.'
'Ah well, why should you, really...'
'Father, please, can we get back to what's happening now. We really need to sort this out.'
'Yes, yes, of course.' The Major leaned over to pick up the rake again. 'More important things to think about, I know. Let me go down to the pier now and see what I can do.'

By the time the Major had driven down to the pier in his fifteen-year-old Land Rover, Millwood was sitting in Richborough's office. He was wearing the only outfit the harbour master could offer – a pair of yellow waterproof over-trousers and matching jacket. The stiff, heavy material, which smelt of fish and seawater, was particularly uncomfortable as Millwood had nothing on underneath.
'Took us ten minutes to cut through the chain,' Richborough said.
'Chain?' the Major said. 'What chain?'
'He was chained up,' Richborough explained. 'Chained to a post on the pier. I'll show you in a minute if you like.'
'Well, yes...'

'We spent twenty minutes searching for a bolt-cutter. I mean, you'd expect McKechnie to have one at least, but no. Couldn't find one anywhere. Had to use a hacksaw instead.'

'I see. And you?' the Major said, looking at Millwood. 'What have you got to say about all of this?'

In his smelly yellow suit Millwood was sitting on a wooden chair which was painted blue. He had a mug of tea in his hands. Both Richborough and the Major could see that his hands were trembling.

'Man's in shock,' Richborough said.

Millwood spoke for the first time. 'Shock? Bloody right I'm in shock. And you'd be too if you were paraded naked through the village at gunpoint and then chained up to a post. I thought the bastard was going to kill me.'

'But he clearly didn't.'

Millwood took a sip of tea. 'There's bits of me feel dead. My feet...'

'I've patched them up as best I can,' Richborough said. He pointed to an open first-aid kit on his desk. The Major looked down at Millwood's feet which were heavily bandaged.

'I'll take you over to Dr Loughlin,' the Major said to Millwood who nodded but said nothing.

'So, how did all this business start?' the Major asked.

Millwood didn't respond immediately so the harbour master intervened. 'It seems that Frank here...' he began.

But the Major put his hand up to terminate this explanation. 'I'm sorry, Mr Richborough,' he said, 'but, if you don't mind I'd prefer to hear Mr Millwood's side of the story directly from him.'

'He found me in bed with Ella,' Millwood said. His hands were still shaking.

'Well, you get ten out of ten for honesty, at least,' the Major said. 'And how long has this been going on? This affair...'

'A few weeks.'

'I see.' The Major looked round the office. 'Couldn't find me a chair, could you?' he said to Richborough who pulled the red swivel chair from behind his desk and offered it to the Major.

'Thank you, thank you. Old bones, you see,' he said as he sat down. 'A lot of bending down this morning. Not good for the hips. So...where were we? Ah yes...' To Millwood he said, 'So what would you have done?'

'What do you mean?'

'If you'd found him in bed with your wife.'

'I'm not married.'

'I'm aware of that. I'm speaking hypothetically.'

'Well, I wouldn't have done what he did.'

'No?'

'No. I certainly wouldn't have shot my wife.'

'What?' The Major got to his feet. 'He…he shot Ella?'

'Yes.'

'Good god, you…' He turned to Richborough. 'You know about this?'

'I'm a bit sceptical,' Richborough said.

'Sceptical? What does that mean?'

'We both know Alan, Major. He wouldn't do a thing like that.'

'For Christ's sake, he shot her!'

The Major turned back to Millwood. 'You saw him, did you? You saw him shoot her?'

'I heard the shot…'

'We've been through this,' Richborough said. 'He didn't actually see it. I've sent a couple of the lads up to the cottage to check. Haven't heard from them yet.'

'Ring them,' the Major said. 'Ring them at the cottage.'

'He tore the phone out,' Millwood said. 'Didn't want her to call anyone.'

'But…but you said he shot her. How was she supposed to use the phone if she was dead?'

'He went back into the cottage. I mean, after we'd left, after he'd torn the phone out. He changed his mind, decided to kill her. So he went back inside. I heard the shot. Two shots, actually.'

'Two shots?'

'Yes.'

'But you didn't actually see him killing her.'

'No. But he did, I'm sure of it.'

The Major sat down again. 'Well, I'm not,' he said. 'I'd say he just wanted to scare you out of your wits. Which he's clearly achieved. Two shots? No, no.'

'He gave me the gun,' Richborough said. He picked up the shotgun from the desk and passed it to the Major.

'Is it loaded?' the Major asked.

'I've no idea.'

'What?' The Major's tone took on a note of irritation. 'You're handing me a shotgun that's cocked and primed for use and you don't know if it's loaded or not? Good god, man, don't you know the damage one of these things can do?'

'I...actually, yes, I do,' the harbour master said as he watched the Major break the gun and check the barrels.

'Empty,' the Major said with some relief. He held the gun, broken, on his lap. 'Sorry, what did you say?'

'You asked me about damage.'

'And?'

'Well, he blasted one of the floodlights.'

'What floodlights?'

'At the end of the pier.'

'And showered us with glass,' Millwood said.

The Major seemed unimpressed by this last comment. 'Expensive to replace?' he asked Richborough.

'A couple of hundred pounds, I imagine. Maybe three hundred.'

The Major shrugged.

There was a knock on the door.

'Who is it? Richborough called out.

'It's Mickey, Mr Richborough.'

'Ah, one of the men that went up to the cottage.' He went over to the door and opened it. 'Come in, Mickey, come in.'

Mickey was seventeen. He was wearing sea boots and a heavy blue jacket. He came into the room and said, 'We found Mrs McRone...' Then he saw the Major. 'Ah, Major Redburn,' he said. 'Good morning to you, sir.'

Richborough said, 'Mickey, for crying out loud, what about Mrs McRone?'

'She's fine.'

'Fine?' This from Millwood.

'Well, I mean, there's no injuries, like. She's a bit shaken up, a bit teary...'

'She wasn't shot?' Millwood said.

'No, no, nothing like that. I mean, she was all tied up, with her mouth taped and everything and, as I say, a bit shaky, right enough.'

'But physically unharmed?' the harbour master asked.

'That's right, sir. A bruise or two maybe but no injuries as such.'

The Major said, 'Good.' Then he added, 'So where is she now?'

'Well, once we got her untied and she…well, she put on some clothes…we took her over to my mother's house.'

'Mrs Osbourne,' the Major said.

'Yes.'

'Good idea. Yes, very good idea. Took care of me once, you know. Did she ever tell you about that?'

'She has mentioned it, sir, yes.'

'Oh, long time ago. Before you were born. She was still a nurse then and I was in hospital for some…some minor thing. Can't for the life of me remember what it was…' His gaze strayed to the office window through which, if he had focused, he would have seen the Glen Coyne on its second run of the day, halfway to the island. 'Anyway…' He dragged his attention back to the matter in hand. 'So let's see where we stand with everything, shall we? You,' he said to Millwood, 'you're all right, aren't you?'

'All right? All right?' Millwood said in a tone of distaste bordering on disgust. 'Depends how you define it.'

'You're alive,' the Major said. 'All that business on the pier… people will forget.'

'Will they?'

'Yes, they will. And your feet…well, Dr Loughlin will sort out that problem. Maybe go over to your cottage first and get you some clothes.'

'I'll have to leave,' Millwood said. 'Leave the island, I mean. Can't stay here any more.'

After a few seconds the Major said, 'Might be best if you left, yes.'

Millwood smiled. 'I see,' he said. 'So it's all figured out already.'

'Aiming for the best solution all round,' the Major said. 'The best solution for everyone, including you.'

'Including me?'

'Yes. If that's what you want to do – leave the island, I mean – then I'll give you every assistance.'

'Get shot of me.'

'You were the one who mentioned leaving,' the Major said.

Millwood didn't respond. The Major went on, 'So we've got…

who's left? Ah, Ella, of course. Mrs McRone, I should say. Well, she's in good hands, I'm sure of that. So that just leaves Alan. Where's he off to, d'you think?' This question was directed at Richborough.

'Well, after he left here he was off round the bay, towards Glass Point.'

'Walking?'

'Yes.'

'He's got a boat there,' Millwood said.

'Yes, I know,' the Major said. 'Probably a good idea to avoid the ferry. But that means he could be anywhere.'

'Over to the mainland, abandon the boat somewhere...' the harbour master offered.

'No, no. He won't abandon the boat. Or at least he'll leave it somewhere in plain sight.' The Major looked at Richborough. 'Not his boat, you see. It's the estate's boat.'

'And why should he care about that?' Millwood asked.

'Well, he cared about the shotgun.'

'Because it's estate property,' Richborough confirmed. 'His very words.'

'We'll find the boat,' the Major said. 'I'm sure of that.'

Richborough looked out of the window. 'Ferry'll be here soon,' he said.

'Ah.' The Major stood up. 'Stay here for the moment,' he said to Millwood. 'I'll be back shortly.' To Mickey Osbourne he said, 'Thank you for your help, Michael. Please remember me to your mother.' With the shotgun in his hands he left the office and walked with Richborough the few yards to the end of the pier.

'Is this the floodlight that was damaged?' the Major asked, looking up at the top of the post.

'That's right. Glass all over the place. And a few bits of metal as well, of course.'

'I'll pay,' the Major said. 'Get it fixed and send me the bill.' He looked at the foot of the post where two lengths of chain were coiled up on the floor. The NO THROUGH ROAD sign lay on top. 'I'll not charge you for damage to estate property, by the way,' he said.

'Now you've lost me, Major.'

'The chain. You cut it in half.' He smiled. 'I'll let you off.'

The Major went back to the office to collect Millwood. The two men made their way to the Land Rover, Millwood stumbling in over-sized sea boots which were the only pair Richborough could find that were big enough to accommodate Millwood's bandaged feet.

Fifteen minutes later, when the ferry docked, the first vehicle to disembark was a police car. There were two policemen and they immediately went to the office to speak to the harbour master.

'You rang the police?' the Major said.

'I certainly did, yes.'

'But whatever for? Why on earth would you want to involve them?'

'Well, it was clearly a police matter,' James Redburn said. 'I mean, a hostage, firearms…someone nearly murdered…'

'Murdered? Don't be ridiculous.'

'Look, from what Richardson told me…'

'Richard…you mean Richborough.'

'The harbour master, yes. From what he told me…'

'Richborough had no idea what happened,' the Major said. He was struggling to control his irritation. 'All he had to go on was what Millwood said and Millwood was scared out of his wits. And anyway, I know McRone. Known him since…well, since he was born. Incapable of murder, even in the heat of passion. Two shots, you see…'

'Two shots? What are you talking about?'

'Millwood said that McRone went back into the cottage to kill Ella, but then he heard two shots. Now, you don't need two shots, do you, eh?'

'You know, I've never actually tried to kill anyone,' James Redburn said, 'and I doubt if you have either.'

'Oh, I'm afraid I have,' Major Redburn said. 'Killed a few, I'm afraid.'

'Ah, yes.' James Redburn shook his head. Then he added quietly, 'Yes, well that was different, father. That was…very different. We're talking here about someone catching his friend in bed with his wife…'

'McRone wouldn't waste a shot, you see, even in a situation like that. These things are...well, a form of conditioning, if you like. A very disciplined character, McRone. Very controlled.'

James Redburn made a gesture which wasn't quite of dismissal but more of resignation. He said, 'I acted in accordance with information received. What else could I do? In any other place I'd be thanked for doing the right thing.'

'This isn't any other place.'

'Well, that's quite clear, certainly.'

Father and son were standing on the polished parquet of the third floor landing. A few feet away was the open door that led into what James Redburn hoped would become the Polar Room, an exhibition devoted to his exploits in the Antarctic twenty-two years before. All this was speculation but he was determined to reverse the fortunes of the castle which had been in decline for decades. Now that he was back, after a long absence, he could see that change was necessary. This was a view shared only grudgingly by his father.

Beside them on the landing there was a large glass case containing a stuffed animal, a wolf, its mouth slightly open, lips peeled back in the semblance of a snarl.

'By the way,' James Redburn said, placing a hand on top of the display case, 'when did this arrive?'

'Last week sometime, I think.' The Major stepped back and looked down into the glass prison that enclosed the wolf. 'It was McRone brought it over from your uncle Christopher.'

'Really?'

'A gift for you, I think?'

'For me?'

'I think so, yes. He knows about your plans, you see. Opening the castle and all that. Thinks this might be something people would like to see.' He crouched down and peered at the small brass plate on the wooden cabinet base. '"The last wolf killed in Scotland by Sir Ewan Cameron, 1680"' he read. 'Quite an antique, don't you think? And it was the inspiration for his book, I suppose.'

'Have you read it?' James Redburn asked.

'No. And no intention of doing so.'

'I see.' James Redburn examined the case and its occupant again. 'I'm not sure. Might be a place for it somewhere, I suppose.'

The Major grabbed hold of the banister and pulled himself up again. 'Anyway,' he went on, 'what I can't understand is why you didn't talk to me before you rang the police. I was here, after all.'

'You were in the water garden.'

'Less than a five minute walk away.'

'Time was critical.'

'No it wasn't,' the Major said. 'They have to come from the mainland so they have to wait for the ferry. Five or ten minutes was neither here nor there...'

James shook his head. 'I can't believe that you're upset with me for reporting a crime, and a crime committed on this estate using estate equipment.'

The Major waved this away. His voice softened, not so much from subsiding irritation as from fatigue. 'It's just that all this might have been avoided.'

'All what?'

The Major sighed. 'The consequences of police involvement. They don't come all the way over here to return empty-handed. They'll charge McRone with something.'

'And so they should do. If they find him.'

'Oh, they'll find him. Or he'll hand himself in.'

'You think he'll do that?'

'More than likely. But then they'll charge him with...with all these petty little things...'

James said, 'Threatening to shoot someone, discharging a shotgun in a public place, destruction of public property...'

'A couple of floodlights that needed replacing anyway.'

'Grievous bodily harm,' James went on. 'How about that one?'

'What on earth do you mean?'

'Frank Millwood.'

The Major shook his head. 'No, no, no. A few cuts on his feet, that's all.'

'But look what he went through. I mean, he thought McRone was going to kill him.'

'Brought it on himself,' the Major said.

'You believe that? Really?' James smiled.

'Yes, I do.'

There was a short silence and then James continued, 'You think that Millwood's the guilty party here, don't you. Not McRone.'

'Is Millwood innocent?'

'In terms of the incident on the pier, yes, of course he is.'

'But it's not just that, is it,' the Major said. 'There's what went on before. It was what Millwood did that started off all this nonsense.'

'You think so?'

'Well, yes. It's obvious, isn't it?'

'I disagree. It certainly isn't obvious. Remember...I mean, if you want to examine what happened before then remember that there's always two sides to a story. And in this case, perhaps three.'

'What do you mean?'

'Well, this Ella woman is the key, surely. And maybe... obviously I don't know for sure, but...maybe her marriage to McRone wasn't going so well. Along comes Frank Millwood who's young, good-looking and she begins to flirt with him...'

'Ella wouldn't do that.'

'No? How do you know? I mean, if they were having an affair, then clearly she was a willing partner. And what about McRone himself? If there was something wrong with the marriage, maybe it was his fault. All I'm saying is that you're making assumptions without any basis in fact.'

But the Major wasn't convinced. 'Making love to another man's wife is wrong,' he said firmly but without anger. 'There are rules,' he added. 'There are laws and that's one of them.'

A couple of days later Alan McRone walked into the police station in Craigton and gave himself up. He wasn't exactly sure what he was giving himself up for but he'd seen a copy of the local paper and read a report of the incident on Glass. He knew he was in trouble – there was some suggestion of attempted murder – and that the police would find him sooner or later. Better to give himself up now and start the process of getting past this mess.

Twenty minutes after arriving in the police station he found himself being interviewed in a small box-like room – a table, three chairs (one empty), no windows, a constable standing by the door. The interviewer was a young detective inspector who, to McRone, looked about sixteen which, if true, would have made him half McRone's age. He must have been in his mid-twenties – so McRone argued, anyway. But perhaps the detective inspector knew how young he looked for he had tried to grow a moustache. It was slight and wispy and reminded McRone of a schoolboy's first attempts to grow facial hair. If anything, it made the man look younger.

'What exactly are you charging me with?' McRone asked.

'First, I need to offer you a lawyer,' the detective inspector said. 'Do you want a lawyer?'

'Do I need one?'

'You certainly do.'

'So what am I being charged with?'

'That hasn't been decided yet.'

'Am I being charged with anything?'

'Nothing's been decided so far.'

'So I'm free to go then?' McRone said. He stood up. He was aware of movement behind him. The constable by the door preparing to thwart an escape attempt, perhaps? McRone turned and said, 'Don't worry, I'm not going to run away.'

'Sit down, Mr McRone,' the detective inspector said.

McRone sat down again.

'You're not free to go.'

'But you can't hold me without charge, can you?'

'Oh yes, we can. Up to twenty-four hours. But forget about that. The point is, you're in serious trouble.'

'So serious you don't know what to charge me with?'

'You threatened to kill someone.'

'Maybe I did. But then the man was fucking my wife. I got, you know, a bit angry. You might have got just a wee bit upset yourself in that situation.'

'You tried to kill him.'

McRone smiled. 'No, no, no. If I'd tried to kill him, he'd be dead.'

'He says you fired at him but missed.'

'My god.' McRone began to laugh. 'Actually, I fired twice and missed both times. Look,' he said and he leaned forward with his elbows on the table, 'I'm the keeper on the Swordale Estate... OK, OK, maybe I'm not any more but that's by the by. I'm the best shot in the district and I had a twelve bore and the guy's head was three feet away from the end of the barrels. I did not fire and miss. I deliberately fired into the wall above his head. Christ...' He sat back in his chair. 'Christ, if I'd wanted to kill him, I'd've killed him. I just wanted to scare the hell out of the bastard and then humiliate him. And then scare the hell out of him again. That's all.'

'Really? Well, what about his injuries?'

'Injuries? What injuries? I didn't shoot him and I didn't hit him.'

'He needed medical attention.'

'Oh yeah? Sunburn on his cock, was it?'

'Lacerations to his feet.'

McRone laughed again. 'My god, the pathetic bastard.'

The young inspector's response to this was to look down at his notes. On the table before him was a clipboard with half a dozen sheets of paper untidily held together. He leafed through these for a few moments and then, without looking up, he asked, 'Where have you been for the last couple of days?'

'None of your business.'

The inspector looked up. 'Oh, I'm afraid it is. You see, it's quite clear you've been staying somewhere, been looked after...'

'Is that a fact?'

'Your clothes are clean, you've had a shave this morning...'

'Quite the young Sherlock, eh?'

'...so this isn't how someone looks who's been sleeping in a ditch. So where were you?'

'Once again, none of your business.'

'And once again, it certainly is our business. Whoever helped you could be in serious trouble too. Harbouring a felon...'

'So you've decided then, is that it? You've already found me guilty of something but you're not quite sure what it is I'm guilty of?'

'There's plenty in here.' He placed a hand on top of his notes.

'If you say so.'

'Look,' the inspector said and he leaned forward as if to speak in confidence, 'a bit of advice. Now I know you don't particularly want advice, especially from me...'

'You're not wrong there...'

'...but I'll give it to you anyway. Co-operate. Co-operate with us and it'll be better for you in the long run.'

'Will it?'

'It will, certainly.'

McRone sighed. It was close to being a sigh of resignation. The inspector noticed this. 'Judges like co-operation,' he went on.

'Might make a difference of six months or a year on your sentence. And that might not sound much right now but when you're inside it'll mean a hell of a lot.'

'When I'm inside,' McRone said quietly.

'Yes. Just...just think about it.' He stood up. 'So, shall I get you a lawyer, then?'

McRone shook his head. 'Not yet.'

'When we charge you, you won't have the option. We have to make sure you're represented.'

'Let's wait till then, shall we?'

'Well, if that's what you want. So...anyone else you'd like to see? Your wife?'

'Ella? You're joking. No, I certainly don't want to see her, even if she wants to see me, which I doubt. No...' He folded his arms and sat back in his chair. 'No, I'd like...I'd like to see the Major,' he said. 'Major Redburn.'

'Major Redburn? Now, let's see...' The inspector began again to sort through his papers. 'Let's see...yes, yes, here we are... Major Redburn. Well, you're in luck. He's asked us to get in touch if you turn up. So I'll let him know you're here.'

The Major disliked leaving the island and did it as seldom as possible. But estate matters sometimes dictated that he make the trip by ferry across the eight miles of Atlantic Ocean that separated the island from Craigton, the nearest point on the mainland. Sometimes he even ventured as far as Glasgow or Edinburgh but rarely stayed more than a night or two. He had nothing against these cities other than his belief that they were places for young people or, at least, younger people. He was nearing eighty and, although he didn't consider himself to be very old, he knew he was no longer young.

There were times when even the Island of Glass with its population of barely fifteen hundred seemed too busy, too crowded. At such times he wanted to get away to somewhere more remote where the levels of noise and disturbance would be dictated by nature – the commotion of seabirds, the impact of an Atlantic storm, the call of a raven in still air – rather than the busyness of people in pursuit of ill-defined and often irrelevant aims. He feared that one of these people might be his son, James.

Some years before, shortly after his seventieth birthday, there had come up for sale the Island of Grannich, off the west coast of Glass. It was a small island, barely half a mile in length. Ten miles separated it from Glass but on its western coast, three thousand miles of ocean lay between it and Labrador.

The occasionally fierce nature of the weather on Grannich was the main reason that it had been uninhabited for decades. In the eighteenth century it had had a population of about a hundred people who reared sheep and chickens and collected sea bird eggs. And when the weather allowed them to put their boats in the water, they went fishing for cod and ling and horse mackerel. But Grannich was a place to leave, not to migrate to. By the late 1920s the population had dwindled to forty and, on August 29th, 1930, they all arrived in Craigton, having realised that they couldn't live on Grannich any longer.

Now the island was host to some wild sheep, a huge gannet colony, a village of forty ruined houses and a church of which only a stump of the east wall remained.

The Major decided to buy Grannich. When he told his wife, Alice, of his plan, she said he was mad. When he said he would go as far as selling Swordale Estate in order to buy Grannich and build a house on it, she told him he was completely mad. But he made enquiries anyway. The island's owner wanted two hundred thousand pounds which was more than the Major could raise without selling Swordale. He began to realise the enormity of this step. Perhaps his wife was right. But it wasn't so much the money, it was his growing realisation that this was an old man's dream – seclusion, a quiet retreat from the world. Surely life at Swordale could be managed to satisfy this need. He decided to make do with what he had. He told Alice that he agreed with her, up to a point. Not completely mad, he assured her, just a little bit, perhaps.

But something of importance did arise from this short-lived interest in Grannich: the Major got as far as having Swordale Estate valued. Unfortunately this involved a trip to the mainland. Marcus Brunt was the estate agent recommended by MacRae, the Major's accountant, and he was based in Craigton. The Major took the first ferry and was in Brunt's office by 10am.

He described his estate. There were about seven hundred acres in all: five hundred acres of hill land – mostly deer forest; one hundred acres of woodland; sixty-five arable. The castle and grounds came to twenty-five acres, more or less, and there were a few acres of foreshore.

'And what profit does the farm make?' Brunt asked. He was a man of about fifty-five and had been an estate agent all his working life.

'Profit?' The Major was surprised, not so much by the question itself but by the fact that it was the first question to be asked. 'There isn't a great deal of profit,' he said.

'Could you be...a little more specific, perhaps, Major?' Brunt said. 'I mean, the annual turnover?'

'Ah. Don't actually have the figures with me,' the Major said. 'Should've brought them, I suppose.'

'But the farm is viable?'

'Yes. Well, just about.'

'Just about?'

'I keep it going mainly to keep McEwan in a job.'

'He's the tenant, I take it.'

'That's right, yes. Family's been on the farm for...well, decades. Took it over from his father. I'd want assurances from any buyer that McEwan's position was secure. Goes for all my staff, of course.'

'I see. Well, Major, is there...is there any chance that McEwan would want to buy the farm himself?'

'McEwan buy the farm? What would be the point in that?'

'It's a question of disposing of the main asset of the estate. I'm guessing at this stage that this is probably the farm. Is he a good farmer, this McEwan?'

'As far as I know, yes.'

'But he's barely making a profit.'

'Well, that's right. But you know as well as I do that farming is hard, especially these days. It's a hard way to make a living.'

'And that's precisely my point, Major Redburn. The only way we could sell the farm would be it if were a profitable enterprise and demonstrably so. Not just getting by but thriving.'

The Major thought for a few seconds and then, in a voice a little jaded from this intrusion of reality, he said, 'Hardly thriving, no. Not thriving.'

'I see.'

'But why are you so interested in the farm?' The Major asked. 'After all it's only a small fraction of the estate.'

'As I said, it's probably the most marketable part.'

'But what about the castle?'

'Ah, the castle,' Brunt said.

'You've probably not been inside but you've seen it, haven't you?'

'Oh, you can't miss it. I always look out for it when I take the ferry over to Glass. Wonderful location.'

'Commands the Sound,' the Major said. 'Dominates it.'

'Yes, well, you see, Major, the important...'

'Fifty rooms,' the Major went on. 'Well, about fifty. Not actually sure any more. Been some changes over the years. Steeped in history, of course. The gardens...'

'Major...'

'...the gardens are quite wonderful...'

'Major...'

'Yes, of course. I'm sorry. Getting a bit carried away...'

'Major, I'll give you my honest opinion...'

'Well, I hope you wouldn't give me anything else.'

'Quite. Well, in my opinion, Major Redburn, and I'm truly sorry to have to say this, I think that the castle, in terms of the current market, is not worth very much.'

'What?' The Major took a few moments to think about this. 'Not worth very much? But how can you say that? I mean, fifty rooms...three acres of gardens...'

'Yes, but who would want to buy it?'

'Well, I don't know. That's your job, isn't it?'

'Well, yes, and I can advise you that it would be almost impossible to find a buyer.'

'But surely...' The Major's incredulity slipped towards resignation. 'I don't understand,' he said.

'Well, you see, Major, what you've described to me – the size of the castle, the extent of the grounds and so on – these are no longer assets, they're liabilities. I mean, for example, how much do you spend each year on the upkeep of the building?'

'Oh, it varies, varies a lot. Sometimes a few thousand...There's always something that needs fixing. The roof will need some attention quite soon, I know that.'

'And rates? What do you pay in rates?'

'Oh, prohibitive.' The Major shook his head. 'Prohibitive. I'm appalled...'

'I'm sure you are. So, do you see what I mean? Anyone buying the castle will immediately be presented with further costs. Substantial further costs. You've said you've got some staff?'

'Well, there's a gamekeeper plus an assistant, there's Grindall, the factor, a couple of...what shall we call them...general factotums about the house. That's about it, I think.'

'And what about the gardens? You said you have three acres.'

'Yes. Well, we had a gardener, but he's retired now. Still lives on the estate of course. These days I do most of the gardening myself. Mowing the lawns and so on. My wife helps out from time to time.'

'You've got a retired gardener who lives on the estate?'

'Yes, and Mrs Niven, retired housekeeper. They've each got a small cottage.'

'Ah, so there are other properties on the estate?'

'Five cottages in all, yes.'

'In good repair?'

'Not bad, I'd say.'

'Well, we could certainly sell some cottages. I'm pretty sure of that.'

'They're all occupied,' the Major said.

'By staff or retired staff, I take it.'

'Yes. So they're not for sale separately. By that I mean that anyone buying the estate would have to agree to allow these tenants to stay in the cottages for as long as they wanted.'

'Right.' Brunt thought about all this for a few moments. Then he said, 'Major, I'll be honest with you...'

'So you've said.'

'This past year there's been one castle sold on the West Coast that I know of.'

'Ardruie.'

'Yes, that's right.'

'I read about it,' the Major said. 'But I don't know how much it went for.'

'Well, I do.'

'Really?'

'Yes. I wasn't directly involved in the sale but I know the estate agent who managed the deal and he told me it was bought for one pound.'

The Major looked at Brunt in astonishment. 'Did I hear you correctly? One...did you say one pound?'

'One pound, yes.'

'Surely you can't be serious. I mean, it's a huge estate. Magnificent...'

'And greatly in debt. You see, it wasn't a case of making money on the sale, it was an attempt to avoid spending even more money, which the original owner didn't have.'

The Major said, 'Matchwell.'

'I'm sorry?'

'Lord Matchwell.'

'Oh yes, that's right,' Brunt said.

'Met him a few times,' the Major added.

'Ah, so you know him?'

'Not well, no. More of an acquaintance than a friend. Didn't realise he was in financial straits...'

Which was a circumstance that didn't apply to the Major. No, his financial situation was sound. Or at least fairly sound. He had inherited funds from his father, mostly tied up in overseas stocks, which afforded him a regular income. Not enough to spend two hundred thousand pounds on the purchase of an island but enough to keep the estate going, for the moment. He was aware, however, that in recent years he'd had to subsidise the income from the estate by selling some of these investments of his father's. But he was confident that this would not be necessary every year. Things were picking up, after all, and if the estate wasn't exactly thriving, it was just about paying its way.

Nevertheless, as he left Brunt's office to make his way back to the ferry and home to Swordale, he couldn't stop repeating to himself, 'One pound...who would have believed it...one pound...'

The visit to the estate agent had taken place eight years before. Since that time the Major's interest in visiting the mainland had reduced further. Because these visits were so infrequent, he always saw changes, particularly in Craigton itself. As he walked from the harbour into the centre of the town, not that this was any great distance, he saw new businesses with bright new shop fronts and garish signs. Bright green, red and yellow replaced the more restrained, more comfortable dark grey and racing green. On this particular occasion he saw the blue banner sign of the New Craigton Café. There was a large plate glass window at the front allowing him to see everything and everyone inside – bench seats at the walls, white Formica-topped tables, bright orange wallpaper. It all looked rather vulgar. He struggled to remember what had been there before. Was it Crerand, the Gunsmith? No, for there was Crerand next door and still in business. So what could it have been? He couldn't remember.

But there was no doubt about the Police Station, the solid Victorian sandstone building on the corner of Shore Street and Wellgarth Road. And this is where he was heading now, having left behind the busy harbour with its fishing boats and its seagulls in constant complaint.

Soon he was sitting at the spare wooden table in the station interview room and seated opposite him was Alan McRone who looked very tired.

'Thank you for coming,' McRone said. 'I appreciate it.'

'Oh…' The Major shook his head. 'Nothing…it's nothing.'

'I know how much you dislike leaving the island.'

'Do I make it that obvious?'

'You've mentioned it once or twice.'

'Have I?'

'Once or twice.'

'I see. Well…I'm here to see if I can help you in any way.'

'I suppose you'd like to know what happened.'

'No, I wouldn't, actually. I mean, I think I've got the gist of it. You found out that Ella was having an affair with Frank Millwood, is that right?'

'Yes. Caught them in the act, in fact.'

'Yes. So I heard,' the Major said. 'Very unpleasant.' After a pause he added, 'No, unpleasant is hardly the right word. It was dreadful, I'm sure.'

'I'm afraid I made a bit of a mess in the cottage.'

'I saw it. And the pier.'

'Yes, the pier too. I'm sorry about that.'

'Nothing that can't be fixed,' the Major said.

'I'll pay for the damage,' McRone said.
'Already taken care of.'
McRone said nothing for a few moments. Then he said, 'I don't expect you to pay my debts, you know. I've got savings.'
'Keep your savings for your solicitor. No doubt he'll be expensive enough. Have you got a solicitor?'
'Not yet, no.'
'You'll need one. I can make the arrangements, if you like. Do you want me to do that?'
'If you think it's necessary.'
'Oh, it's necessary, I'm afraid. Yes. They'll charge you with something, even if it's only discharging a firearm in a public place.'
'What about menacing someone with a shotgun?' McRone said. 'That's been mentioned. I imagine Frank will be pushing for that.'
'No, I don't think so.'
'No? You sound very sure.'
'I've had a little talk with Frank.'
'You have?'
'Yes. We discussed various options.'
'What kind of options?'
'For him, I mean. What he does from now on. He'll be leaving Glass, of course. In fact, he's already left.'
'That doesn't surprise me.'
The Major shrugged. 'He needs to get away. He knows that. We all know that. But, anyway, do you know Archibald Corkindale? He's a solicitor.'
'I don't know any solicitors.'
'He's a good man,' the Major said. 'Known him for years. I'll ask him to come over. Give you some advice if nothing else.'
'That would be very helpful, Major. Thank you.'
'Oh, don't mention it. Anyway…'
'Why are you doing this?' McRone asked. 'I mean, why are you helping me out like this?'
'Well, let's see…' The Major placed his right hand flat on the table before him and began tapping the Formica surface lightly with the side of his thumb. 'There's several reasons, I suppose, some to do with you, some to do with your father. He and I were quite close, you know.'
'I'm aware of that, yes.'

‘And he got on well with my father, too. Loyalty, you see. That’s a quality my father valued very highly.’ He made a gesture, opening his right hand briefly towards McRone. ‘Well, I do, too, of course.’

‘Of course.’

A short silence followed. Then McRone said, ‘I still have the hunting knife.’

‘The hunting knife?’

‘After the General died, my father was given his hunting knife as a token of their…of their friendship.’

‘Oh, yes, yes, that’s right. You know, I’d forgotten about that.’ The Major smiled briefly and then went on, ‘Well, anyway, when your father got sick and it was clear he wasn’t going to recover, he asked me to…to…not to become your guardian exactly, no…I mean, your mother was still alive and you were into your teens…’

‘I was sixteen.’

‘Yes. Sixteen.’ The Major withdrew his hand and placed it on his lap. ‘So…keep an eye on you, that was the idea. Help out if you needed help…’

‘Which I do now.’

‘Clearly.’

‘I see. And the other reasons? You said there were several.’

‘Well, to an extent it’s because I sympathise, not so much with what you did, exactly, not with the detail, no…it’s more with your situation, how that might have driven you to do what you did. I mean, I ask myself what I would have done if I’d ever found myself in that situation. You know, finding someone in bed with my wife and…and I can’t help thinking that I might have acted in a way rather similar to how you handled it. Something like that, anyway. Something like that.’ He paused. ‘Tell me,’ he said, ‘do you regret what you did?’

‘Only in terms of the consequences for myself,’ McRone said. ‘After all, I might go to jail because of it and that’s not a prospect I particularly relish. But other than that, well no, I don’t regret it one bit.’

The Major nodded. ‘Good,’ he said. ‘That’s what I was hoping you’d say.’

PART TWO

Maurice

The Major could no longer remember how many rooms there were in his castle. He was sure that he had known once, fifty or sixty years before, or perhaps even seventy, when he was a child and ran along the cold corridors of the huge, draughty building, his stiff leather shoes with the buckles on beating out a racket on the wooden floors. He knew the castle then. He understood it as a child understands such things, marvelling at the sheer size of the doors, their weight, struggling to push them open to reveal the heavy furniture inside and the acreage of fabrics – tapestries, bedspreads, awnings, carpets – in bright rich colours as Victorian taste and fashion gave way to Edwardian. The rooms seemed too numerous to count. But he had counted them, badgering his nanny, or it might have been one of the chambermaids, to accompany him on his tour of the castle, grabbing her by the hand and dragging her, laughing, along the corridors, ground floor to fifth floor and not forgetting the tower, while he counted, one, two, three. And he had reached a number, he was sure, a number which now escaped him but which probably lay somewhere between forty-eight and fifty-four.

It had been easy then. As a child it was easy because the world was fixed and certain and he was assured in his ability to examine it and understand it. There were no problems, for example, of definition – when was a room a room? When was it an ante-room, a walk-in cupboard, a pantry? The answers were easy because he had that clarity possessed by children which allows them simply to point and say, 'one,' to point and say, 'two,' to point and say, 'three, four, five, six.'

And forty-eight or fifty, fifty-three or fifty-four. There were plans, in one of the thirty-seven large cardboard boxes of documents in the study where he was now, plans of the castle which, if he could find them, would allow him to arrive at a number. But it would be the wrong number. The plans were old and had not been kept up to date. He could think of rooms that had been added – the small extension at the side which now formed the living quarters for himself and his wife – and other rooms that had been partitioned. So the plans were really of little help. There was nothing to be done but revert to his childhood method of simple arithmetic; he would have to visit all the rooms and count them and be as rigorous and single-minded in his quest as he had been over seventy years before. And it wouldn't take long. Five floors and the tower – half an hour? Forty minutes at the most. But he knew he wouldn't do it.

He knew he wouldn't do it because there was one room he had sworn never to enter again; there was an entire floor – the fourth – that he had not visited for fifty years.

Major Maurice Arthur Stephen Redburn was in his study now, standing at the round window, looking out to sea. The study, in the top of the tower, was reached by a trap door from the floor below, the fifth. A set of rickety wooden steps was used in the ascent. At one time there had been a more substantial structure, a staircase, albeit a moveable one, with handrails to either side. His father, General Arthur Redburn, had had them made, for this had been his study too and he had also enjoyed the seclusion offered by the relative difficulty of access. But the staircase, it was discovered, had not been well made or, perhaps, had been made from inferior materials because two of the steps had broken and the entire structure had been discarded. So the Major now used a stepladder which was not particularly safe but ensured greater privacy than the staircase had offered. Sometimes his wife would climb up two rungs and strike the underside of the trap door with a broom handle but he usually ignored her. He offered the occasional half-hearted excuse that he was going deaf, which was a lie.

The study was square, with windows on every side bar one. Two windows were rectangular; the third was round. The round window faced the sea and the Major preferred to stand there because he felt as if he was on a ship. He could see the grey waves of the Atlantic through the round porthole of the window and he might be on a ship. He might be on a particular ship, one he had travelled on forty-eight years before, with a view of the

Mediterranean, not the Atlantic. Small things like this – the shape of a window, a prospect of the sea – could manufacture the past and bring it close.

But not close enough. The Major left the window and approached one of the many boxes of papers on the floor. He pulled out a file, scanned the first few documents and then tore out half a dozen pages, one by one. He crumpled each one into a ball which he then flattened by stamping on it. He took the small discs of creased paper and stuffed them into a crack in the wall to the side of one of the three bookcases that the room housed. The crack was nearly half an inch wide and allowed a draught to enter from outside. Surveyors had informed the Major that the tower was unsafe, that it was in danger of splitting in two. The crack had been getting wider and the surveyors had installed gauges to check its growth. They warned the Major that he should stop using his study immediately. He responded by tying a rope round the tower. Two men on ladders spent the best part of a morning wrapping the rope round several times and tightening it. It was as if they were binding a wound. The surveyors shook their heads as they rushed to their gauges. 'What are you doing now?' the Major asked. 'Checking its growth,' they replied. 'I've done that,' the Major said, and he laughed.

And in fact the gap did not grow any wider. But everyone knew – even the Major – that repair work was essential and could not be postponed for very long. The Major reckoned that time was the problem. Time was against him, pushing him away from things and people he wanted to keep hold of but couldn't and rushing him towards a future that held no appeal. He would freely admit he was a man of the past. And the past, he knew, was a dear thing, full of treasures to be savoured, but essentially useless. He knew too that he could no more change his feelings about the past than he could change the past itself. As for the future, there was the possibility that he might influence it but this depended on his will to do so. He felt increasingly ill at ease with what was going on around him. There was the tower, in danger of falling down at any moment, his son with his grand ideas about investing in the castle's future and there was his brother, Christopher, who had died only a few days before and whose death had prompted so many things he did not wish to think of, not least of which was his recent trip to the mainland to buy a pair of black leather shoes for the funeral which was to take place in a few minutes' time.

The Major was tall and his bearing could accurately be described as military. The top of his head was hairless but he had two tufts of white hair high on his cheeks, the bottom edge of each linked by a definite shaving line to his sideburns which extended to mid ear. His face was covered in a fine network of veins, his nose especially, which gave the impression that he might be a heavy drinker, which he was not.

The fastidiousness with which he shaved and cleaned his body was rarely apparent in his dress. Of course today was an exception, in that he was dressed for the funeral. He had found an old black suit he had forgotten that he possessed. And there was a black tie, too, that he had promised to throw away after the last funeral he had attended. But he had not done this. He hadn't done this because some time ago he realised he had reached the age when he would have to go to funerals. There would be more and more of them as his friends died out and then a space, perhaps, when there was nobody left to die but himself. But in the meantime he had to wear this wretched suit and these new shoes that were beginning to pinch his feet.

He usually wore a checked shirt, frayed at collar and cuff, and a dark regimental tie that had been tied too often and whose knot was small and hard. His jacket and trousers were from different tweed suits; the jacket was green, the trousers pale brown. He had several pullovers but the one he usually wore was green, almost but not quite matching the green of his jacket. There was a hole at each elbow of the pullover and the general tiredness and dilapidation of the wool had rendered the whole thing baggy and without discernible shape. At the back it hung down below the hem of his jacket.

Before his recent trip to the mainland, his footwear had been reduced to a single pair of brown leather boots whose condition ranged from dry and scuffed through to damp and muddy, depending on the season. However, he could not escape the influence of his initial military training, now more than sixty years in the past. This determined that his boots were cleaned and polished regularly to keep them in good condition and thereby prolong their life. He undertook the care of his boots himself. No one else could be trusted to complete the task to his satisfaction.

He was less fussy about the condition of his outer clothing. His efforts in the garden were largely responsible for this. His trousers were baggy at the knee, the creases long gone, and displayed a degree of staining whose precise colour depended on the nature of his most recent activity. This might be green from grass cutting or kneeling on the edge of a flower bed, or brown (repotting, weeding), even yellow (cutting willows laden with pollen), or just wet (kneeling on the frosty ground to retrieve a trowel from beneath a hedge). His trouser turn-ups often harboured grass clippings and leaf mould, soil and seeds, and some among his acquaintances joked that it was there that he germinated his most delicate plants.

His jacket was not garden free either. Its pockets contained elastic bands, string, seeds, plant name tags, a trowel and secateurs. The considerable strain exerted by the pocket contents, coupled with the continual kneeling, bending and leaning of the jacket's occupant had resulted in the loss of buttons. The normal procedure was for the top one to disappear first while the threads which bound the remaining two or three to the jacket front became stretched to breaking point. The middle one (of three) or the third from the top (of four) usually held on to the last, distancing itself slowly, extending on longer and thinner threads until it too became detached and landed in shrubbery or rose garden or herbaceous border.

Most unusually, the Major's garden jacket now possessed all four front buttons neatly and firmly sewn on. This was not because it was a new jacket – in fact it was at least eight years old – but because of an incident that had taken place a week or so before.

One morning, as he had set out, rake in hand, for the water garden, the Major found that there were no buttons at all left on his jacket. It was a cold, blustery morning so he tied a piece of string round his middle to hold the jacket in place close to his body. In fact what he used was a piece of twine from a roll he kept in the garden shed. Some oil had spilled over it but that hardly mattered.

As he passed by the kitchen at the back of the extension, he was spotted by his wife, Alice, who rapped sharply on the window. He didn't hear. He had advanced half way across the first terrace before she reached the path and shouted after him. He still didn't hear. In fact he was at the water garden itself before she caught up with him and demanded that he take off his jacket. He looked at her as if this request was quite odd, which in fact it was, considering how cold the wind was that was coming off the sea. 'Take off my jacket?' he said. She answered by producing a pair of kitchen scissors and snipping through his string belt. The Major was bemused. 'Take it off!' his wife demanded in a tone that lay somewhere between earnest and shrill. 'Take it off!'

He shook his head but complied. His wife had a sewing basket with her. He watched, amazed, as she sewed on three buttons which, surprisingly, were all the same. She began to shiver as she did this and was clearly very cold by the time that she handed the jacket back to him. But her voice was quite firm when she said, 'No string.' As she picked up the piece of binder twine that had served as his belt for all of six minutes, she repeated, 'No string.' She quickly coiled up the twine and put it in her sewing basket. 'You are not a tramp,' she said as loudly as she could manage before she turned and set off back towards the castle.

He had one hat. It was on his desk right now, sitting beside three documents all of which were linked to his son – a newspaper article about his son, an obituary of his brother written by his son (yet to be published) and a brochure advertising the castle also written by his son. The Major had a theory about words which was that they were tricky things which could lead to great trouble if they were misused. Unfortunately there were those who deliberately tried to misuse them and these were dangerous people. He realised that denying such people words would be very difficult – binding their eyes and ears and mouths and taping their fingers together to forbid them the use of pens – but he believed that constraints should be placed upon them. One of these people might be his son. He picked up the brochure. He glanced at the photograph of the castle on the front and then replaced it on the desk, covering it with the hat.

It was made of brown felt, the hat, with a wide brim which was uneven and battered. It was an old hat, grimy and dirty, and it had been doffed so often that the point at the front of the crown, where the sides and top were grasped by the thumb and first two fingers of his right hand, had worn away to leave a hole with three little flaps which moved in the breeze.

There were four more holes in the crown, made by the teeth of a dog.

Two years before, when the Major was out walking along the shore by the castle, a strong gust of wind wrenched the hat from his head and set it bowling along the shingle just above the incoming tide. He sent his Labrador, Jack, to fetch it but the dog, already well into old age, had difficulty keeping up with the hat as the wind propelled it along like a child pushing a wheel with a stick. At last a stronger wave scrambled up the stony beach far enough to strike the hat whose careering flight was halted long enough for the dog, now panting heavily, to catch up. But as he opened his mouth to take hold of it, the wind flipped the hat over and set it rolling again. Then, when he finally did manage to trap it he held it in his jaws for several seconds and shook it violently as if dispatching a hare, concerned perhaps that a further escape might be attempted. When the Major recovered the hat it was considerably changed; it was crushed out of shape with four teeth marks in the crown and had soaked up a deal of seawater and some Labrador saliva. He merely brushed it against his knee, punched out and reconstructed the crown and put the hat back on his head, pressing it down a little harder than normal to ensure it did not get blown off again.

It had begun to rain and he could see that the squall, coming across the Sound of Ardroy, might be short-lived but would certainly be intense. He pulled the hat even further down over his forehead and then pushed his hands deep into the pockets of his oilskin jacket. The castle was no more than a few hundred yards away and he arrived there within ten minutes. He opened the back door and held it ajar, expecting Jack to push past him into the relative warmth of the conservatory. But there was no dog.

He closed the door again and returned, in the now driving rain, to the head of the path that led down to the shore. The wind was so strong that the waves out to sea were being flattened, their spray driven along above the surface of the water like white horizontal rain. On the foreshore strands of seaweed were being stripped from the rocks and hurled like tattered black ribbon across the shingle. The Major made his way back to the place where Jack had caught up with the hat and found the dog still lying there, too exhausted to rise. He leaned over and patted the sodden fur on Jack's head and back. He pushed his hands underneath the body of the animal and tried to lift him up but the dog was too heavy. He took off his oilskin coat. The wind almost tore the coat from him but he managed to lay it down on the pebbles and fix it there with a couple of stones on collar and shoulder. Then he knelt down again and, taking hold of the front legs of the tired old dog he dragged him across onto the coat. He managed to construct a kind of sling, knotting the arms together and tying the hem into a bunch using some twine. And so he carried Jack back to the castle, stopping many times on the way and tiring himself out for, although the distance was not great, the dog was heavy. He reached the conservatory in just as bedraggled a state as Jack, his pullover and shirt soaked through. But he dried off the dog first, rubbing him down with an old towel, noticing as he did so that Jack appeared to have lost the use of his hind legs.

This discovery upset him greatly, though all he said was 'You poor beast,' as he patted Jack on the head. He transferred him over to his basket and then fetched a heater from the sitting room to warm up the conservatory a bit more. Later, when relating the incident to his wife, he said, 'It's time I had him put down.'

Swordale Castle is by far the most impressive sight to greet the traveller who makes his way by ferry to the Island of Glass. The five-storey, sixty-room building with its magnificent Wester Tower has dominated the Sound of Ardroy for the last hundred and fifty years. During this period many heads of state, members of the Royal Family and countless prominent politicians, including Sir Winston Churchill, have been entertained here.
The terraced Italian Gardens are a feature which no visitor to the island can afford to miss. The warm waters of the Gulf Stream, gently washing the shores of Glass Island, allow many tropical and subtropical plants to flourish in the rich soil.
Now Major Redburn, whose family has owned the castle during its entire history, has decided to open it to the public.

This presents an outstanding opportunity for visitors to the island to sample the truly unique atmosphere of a castle which combines the splendour and fascination of its long history with the charm of a family home. It houses a wonderfully rich art collection, including the work of Gainsborough and Turner. Also on view for the first time is the impressive Polar Exhibition. Using a display of photographs and artefacts as well as a short film, this exhibition brilliantly captures the difficulties, tragedy and ultimate triumph of an expedition to Antarctica undertaken by Major Redburn's son, James Redburn, in 1956.
The castle's outstanding features include:
Fifteen public rooms.
Twenty-five acres of grounds including woodland, a loch, a water garden, the Italian Statuette Walk and two acres of terraced lawns.
An outstanding art collection including works by Gainsborough, Turner, Maclehose and Crawhall.
The Polar Exhibition.
The Game Room, displaying sporting trophies from the mid-nineteenth century, including one of the largest salmon ever caught in the British Isles.
A delightful tea-room with spectacular views of the Sound of Ardroy and specialising in home-baked scones and pastries.
You will be enchanted by Swordale Castle. A visit will ensure that your trip to the Island of Glass is truly unforgettable.

He undertook the rereading of the brochure with reluctance and some distaste. He turned the small folded leaflet over in his hands. It was quite decently produced and the photograph on the front was good though it hardly did the castle full justice. Not his castle, at any rate. But his main problem, as ever, was with the words, their effusion and their treachery. They strove too hard, these words, there was too much hyperbole, too many capital letters, at least one tautology. And, among the several examples of stretching the truth, there was one glaring inaccuracy.

'Sixty?' he had said to his son some weeks before when first presented with the brochure.

'Yes, that's right, isn't it?'

'No.'

'Less?'

'Fewer.'

'I see. Well. It's about sixty, anyway, isn't it?'

'I don't know. Fifty-two or three. I don't know, and neither do you.'

'I guessed.'

'Obviously.'

They were standing in a large, bare room on either side of a wooden crate from which James Redburn was unpacking a number of framed black and white photographs. He turned one towards his father. 'What do you think of that, eh? Look at that iceberg. Two hundred feet high easily. Totally dwarfs the ship.' He held it up against his chest. 'What do you think, eh?'

The Major looked at the photograph. 'Gainsborough,' he said quietly.

'Gainsborough? Oh, Gainsborough, yes. The piglet.'

'No one in their right mind would call it a major work.'

'Neither do I.'

'Perhaps not, in so many words, but you give the impression that we have a great painting here. I mean, that's what you're inferring.'

'And who's to say it isn't?' He placed the photograph of the iceberg on the floor, propped against the wooden crate. His hands went inside the crate again. 'Ah yes!' he said with obvious delight as he pulled out another photograph. 'Ah yes, look at this.'

'I could paint better myself,' the Major said.

'Well, that's not the point, is it. I mean, you didn't paint it and Gainsborough did. A genuine Gainsborough's worth a lot of money, even if it does look more like a pig than a lapdog.'

'It's atrocious. And it's tiny.'

'Size has nothing to do with it. Take some of Dali's paintings. Tiny. Tiny. And worth millions. You know I can't believe I actually climbed that mountain.' He was inspecting this new photograph which showed a snow-covered mountain in the distance and, in the foreground, advancing towards it in single file, a line of ten or a dozen men roped together. 'What I need to do,' he said, talking to himself or the picture but not to his father, 'what I need to do…'

'And the Turner,' the Major began.

'The Turner?' He moved away from the crate, from the Major, and walked across the bare floorboards to the far wall. The wall to the right held two great curtainless windows from which could be seen the sea, dull grey and forbidding and, working its way laboriously across the pock-marked surface, the car ferry to the island.

'We're not even sure it is a Turner.'

'Aren't we?' He placed the photograph on the floor, leaning against the wall. 'I need to get an idea, do you see? Place them around the room. Space them out.'

'It's only attributed to Turner.'

'So? That means, to all intents and purposes, it's a Turner.'

'No, it doesn't.'

'No?'

'No.'

'Well, it means that it's more likely that Turner painted it than anyone else, and that's good enough for me.'

'It's a drawing taken from a notebook. It's another one that's very small. Very small.'

James Redburn walked slowly back to the crate. 'You seem to have this fixation about size,' he said, 'as if a painting's only valuable if it's ten feet square. I mean, what about Holbein's miniatures? Nobody complains about the size of them, do they?'

'No, but they're meant to be small. I mean, come on, there's no comparison. If someone says Turner to you, you think of The Fighting Temeraire or something like that – big canvases. You don't think of a scrappy bit of paper with a very ordinary tree on it...a shrub...I mean, it's just a scrawl.'

'Well, maybe so.' He had already drawn out the next framed photograph. Ten men stood in a ragged line, snow at their feet and behind and above them only sky. 'God, there's the whole lot of us on the top.' He looked hard at the photograph. 'There's poor old Meadway.' He replaced it in the crate and pulled out another photograph. This was of a dog, a husky, sitting in the snow. 'Oscar,' he said, and he shook his head. 'Oscar.'

'And it's not just that,' the Major went on, 'it's...it's the whole tone of this thing.' He held up the brochure. 'I mean all this stuff about the Gulf Stream gently washing the...the shores...this, this wonderfully rich...splendour and fascination...'

James Redburn put down the photograph of the dog, leant it against the crate. He looked at his father for the first time for several minutes. 'It's marketing, father,' he said. 'Selling.'

'I don't like it,' the Major said.

'I know you don't. You've made that perfectly clear all along but what I've tried to explain is that we really don't have a choice. If this place is to survive at all, it needs an income. It's just not going to work any other way. Opening to the public guarantees an income and that brochure is there to ensure that they come. God knows I can't stand the great unwashed any more than you can but unfortunately we need them and we've got to be certain they'll come. I mean, if we said to people this is quite a nice place, it's by the sea, it's got nice gardens, a statue or two and a few reasonable pictures, oh and we'll give you a nice cup of tea...I mean, would you come?'

'I don't think...'

'You and I know...' James went on, and his tone took on an urgency that had not been there before, '...we both know that this is the most beautiful spot on God's earth...'

'Well, yes...'

'...but, but we know that because we've been here a long time. This has been your home for nearly eighty years and your love for the place has developed over that period of time. The problem is that we don't have eighty years to convince people to come and visit. We've got half a minute, maybe five seconds, maybe only a glance in which to do it. That's why the brochure is written the way it is. The purpose is to get them to come. Once they're here they'll love it. You know they will. And they won't give a stuff that Gainsborough's lapdog looks like a pig. A pig!' Suddenly he laughed out loud. Then he stepped over to look out at the grey sea, the hills beyond, some of them with early autumn snow on their summits. 'The view from this window alone is priceless,' he said.

The Major agreed. About the view from the window. The view from the round window in his study was very similar, being on the same side of the castle but three floors higher. But he wasn't convinced that people would love the view. Superficially they would, of course. Just about any juxtaposition of sky and sea and hills would elicit admiration. But would they understand? Would they appreciate its real value? He thought this was unlikely. He understood and he appreciated because he had so many years' experience of this view in all its permutations of colour and tone. It had expressed all its moods to him, from joyful to sad, from bright to sinister, from gentle to violent and occasionally very violent indeed. Only four or five years ago, from this window of his study and in the full knowledge that there was absolutely nothing he could do to change what was happening, he had watched a ship founder and break up. He had seen three crewmen winched to safety up into a helicopter and four swept overboard to drown. Two days later, Jack, trotting along the foreshore on a bright, calm, warm summer's morning, had found the bloated body of one crew member and the left leg, severed at the hip but complete with sea boot, of another.

The Major had seen body parts before, in the trenches, during what he still referred to as the Great War. Three of his men – he'd been a captain then – had been killed by a shell. They'd been standing close together and the shell had blown them into pieces. In the sudden silence following the blast, there had been a little rainstorm of blood and bits of flesh, he remembered. And then, after what was surely far too much time, a leg had hit him on the shoulder and bounced onto the uneven ground in front of him.

That leg, shredded and bloody, bore no resemblance to the one he found on the foreshore which was fat and pink and perfect, albeit separated from the rest of the body.

Happily such incidents were rare. The Sound of Ardroy was mostly a thing of beauty and tranquillity and few people would deny this.

But frequently he had doubts; he had doubts almost all the time. Perhaps he was being unkind and selfish keeping all this to himself, depriving others of the chance to share in this splendour. But he decided he was right; after every deliberation he decided that he was right to want to keep it to himself. In the past he had travelled. He had visited well-known and not so well-known places and admired the views, expressed his pleasure at the recognised sights. But this was superficial, he realised, completely superficial. No, to know a landscape, he concluded, to really understand it and come to terms with it, you had to live with it for many years, experience the subtleties of its moods and let it impose some of its will upon you. That was what you had to do. He didn't travel any more. He stood at this window and looked.

Christopher Michael Redburn, son of General Arthur Redburn and brother of Major Maurice Redburn of Swordale Castle, chose not to follow the family tradition of a life in the Army but was just as successful in the career he decided to pursue. Born at Swordale in 1903, he was too young to fight in the First War, although his elder brother Maurice saw action in Northern France in 1917. Christopher showed a keen interest in literature and went to Oxford in the early twenties where he excelled in his studies of the English and French nineteenth century novelists. A career in academia beckoned but he turned down the several offers he received from both British and French universities to try his hand at writing fiction himself.

It was in Paris that he did what he later referred to as his "groundwork". There he met many writers who later became household names: James Joyce, Ernest Hemingway, Gertrude Stein. He was in illustrious company, and he knew it. He once said, in interview: "Paris in the late twenties and early thirties was a good place for a young man to be. There were lots of people to meet and lots of things to learn. I tried to concentrate on the latter."

However, it was to be some time before his first novel was published. Disaffected by his early attempts at novel writing, he began writing articles for respected journals, although he did produce some short stories as well. (The "Collected Stories" was published in 1962.) By 1932 he was back in London where he settled in Pimlico. He remained there for several years, building up a reputation as a talented and entertaining columnist. It was during this period that he met Maureen Nant and they married in 1940.

But Christopher Redburn's settled and comfortable life was to come to a sudden and tragic end. In 1949 he and his wife were involved in a car accident. Maureen was killed instantly and Christopher himself spent nearly a year in hospital recovering from his injuries. His brother Maurice Redburn, himself no stranger to tragedy, having lost his first wife when she was only

twenty-four, recalls: "When Maureen died, Christopher of course was devastated and it wasn't just his personal, domestic situation that was irrevocably altered; he found that he was forced to review his whole life, in particular its purpose."
Christopher gave up his work in London and moved back to the Island of Glass. He spent two years writing what many believe to be his finest book, "The Last Wolf". Published in 1952, it was an instant success and has been in print ever since. Although he was to admit that the actual writing of the book was not easy, the idea on which it was based was a very simple one. From an interview in 1954: "I couldn't believe that no one had thought of it before. The last wolf in Scotland was killed in the Highlands in 1743 by a man called MacQueen. Two years later we had the '45 rebellion which ended in ignominy at Culloden the following year. I have no idea whether Bonnie Prince Charlie knew of the fate of the wolves but I realised that here I had the very stuff of which romantic historical novels are made – some things ending, new things beginning and general tragedy all round. It was a mixture that couldn't fail, and it didn't."
Many more books followed and sales were always good although none matched the selling power of what Christopher came to refer to as "The Old Dog".
Although the invitations for lecture tours and visiting professorships were many, he never left his home on the Island of Glass. In fact, in later years he was even reluctant to make the trip across the Sound of Ardroy to the mainland. "I have lived in cities," he said. "I have lived in great cities and enjoyed my time there but there is little to attract me back."
Christopher Redburn's works total twelve novels, all but three of which are still in print, and one collection of stories. Of his journalism he once said: "I spent twenty years as a jobbing wordsmith and not a sentence of all that output remains, which is probably just as well." He always had a very critical eye, especially for his own work. With his death we now realise that his work was of immensely greater value than he himself rated it.

Christopher Michael Redburn, author, 1903–79.

'I was sorry to hear the sad news about your brother,' MacRae said.

'Oh,' said the Major. 'Thank you. Yes.' In fact he wasn't sure what to say. He thought for a few moments before adding, 'We didn't really get on, you see. But I expect you knew that.' He waited for MacRae to make some response to this but he did not. The Major continued, 'But even so, it's a loss, yes. Yes, it's a loss to all of us.'

He was standing, as he often did when in MacRae's office – though his visits there were less and less frequent – by the window that gave on to the street. Before and below him he could see the harbour area of Craigton and beyond it the Sound of Ardroy and the Island of Glass. On a clear day it was possible to see the castle, or the tower at least. Even pick out the crack down the side with a good pair of Zeiss.

'Do you have a pair of binoculars?' he asked MacRae.

The other man shook his head slowly.

The Major turned back to the window. It was a small, square sash window with a white gloss frame and it was set rather high in the wall as if the bricklayers had forgotten all about windows until three or four courses too many of bricks had been added. A fenestral afterthought. He put out a hand and rested his fingers on the white shiny sill. He liked this window. As with the window in his study, it reminded him of a porthole. It was the wrong shape, of course, being square rather than round, but perhaps the shape was of less importance than the height.

Without turning from the window, he said, 'I need some more money. In the region of twenty-five thousand.'

'Ah,' MacRae said. And then, after a few moments, 'I would advise caution.'

'You always advise caution. I mean, it's your job to advise caution. You're not about to advise rashness now, are you?'

MacRae smiled.

'So, is there a problem? I mean, a real problem?'

'There's a potential problem,' MacRae said.

'Oh yes? And what's that?'

'It's a question of depletion of capital. You see you're...you're reducing your regular dividends and interest payments by eating into the base investments on which these payments are made.'

'I am, am I?'

'Well, yes. I mean, if you needed an extra few hundred a month, say, then I'm sure I could arrange something without breaking into any of your major accounts, albeit there'd be a greater element of risk involved, but...but a lump sum...'

The Major continued to stare out of the window. 'See the tower from here,' he said. 'Pity you've no binoculars. Damn thing's the cause of all the problems, really. Falling down. Got to get it fixed before it falls down. So they say. Dangerous, they say. Well...I...' He turned from the window and looked at MacRae. 'I'm rather in their hands, you see. Sort of...what's the expression...safety requirement. Can't open the castle until the work's done on the tower – well, started at least. Got to get a scaffolding up and so on. Dreadfully expensive. You see the difficulty.'

'I do, I do.'

The Major was in his green tweed suit, still not too baggy at the knees. MacRae was wearing a black suit, white shirt and grey tie, looking more like a hotel manager than the financial adviser that he actually was.

'So they're saying twenty to twenty-five thousand. James reckons we'll recoup it all within three years or so...'

'From the castle visitors.'

'Yes. Done all his sums. Studied everything. I mean, could be even better, could be worse, but he's gone for some in-between figure. So...so there we are...'

MacRae gestured his reluctant acquiescence. 'Major, it's your money.'

'Yes,' the Major replied, regretting a little the haste with which he said it.

Then he began to wonder why he was bothering to explain all this. He employed MacRae, didn't he? Was it really necessary to explain? In the past...in the past he commanded, he didn't ask; he instructed, he didn't suggest; he gave orders, he didn't prevaricate. 'I...' he began. He said, 'I...' again and then stopped. Why was he finding this so difficult? He was seventy-nine years old. He had survived two world wars, events which rendered most other things insignificant. He refused to take the issue of money seriously. Maybe that was the problem. The man in front of him did.

'Just...just make the arrangements, would you?' he said at last.

'Of course, Major. Twenty-five thousand? Or just the twenty?'
'Better make it the twenty-five.'
'Fine.'
The Major looked out of the window again. He could see the sea and, coming gently towards him, the island of Capri, the uneven rows of whitewashed houses by the harbour, the steep ascent to the main village, the clamouring of gulls.
'Must be a herring boat on its way in,' MacRae said.
'What?'
'The noise of those gulls.'
'Oh.' The Major focused on the harbour again, Craigton harbour, not Capri. 'Herring did you say?'
'Yes.'
'No, not herring. Mackerel maybe. No herring now.'
'No?'
He turned to face MacRae again. 'Over fished,' he said. 'Limitations. Government quotas. Everything's changed now. Didn't you read about it?'
'I think I must have missed that.'
'Really? Got to keep abreast, you know, man in your position. Don't have any fishermen among your clients then?'
'No, I don't.'
'Surprising. Anyway...' He stepped forward and stuck his hand out to be shaken. 'Better be off.'
As they shook hands MacRae said, 'I'll see you on Thursday.'
'Thursday?'
'The funeral. I'll be over for the funeral.'
'Oh yes, yes. The funeral.'
'A sad business,' MacRae said. 'A very sad business altogether.'

The Major had experienced sadness – on more than one occasion great sadness – but he managed to survive it. He had very little understanding of the concept of sadness, believing only that everyone had bad experiences which took time to heal and perhaps he had had more than the average number of these. But he had never concluded from this that fate had some grand, ignoble design for him; he had just been unlucky, that was all.

But some of these things had been hard to bear. The death of his first wife had been particularly difficult for him. She had died in childbirth at the age of twenty-four and for five weeks he had been more wretched than he would have guessed it was possible to be. It was the only period of his life when he had drunk heavily. But he got over it. He woke up one day in a strange room with no recollection of how he had got there. He also had a fearsome hangover. He recognised that it was time to make up his mind about his future. He could continue his dissolute existence or sort himself out. It was 1932. Lying on top of his uniform, which had been dumped on a chair, was his service revolver. He contemplated loading it with one bullet, spinning the barrel and letting something or someone else decide what would happen to him. But contemplation was as close as he got to this method of solving his troubles. He got dressed and decided that to prove to himself that he was finished with drinking away his sorrows he would walk back to the castle. This proved to be a rash promise as he found, when he descended the staircase to the front of the building, that he was in a hotel in Edinburgh. The castle, or rather Craigton, the nearest point to it on the mainland, was a hundred and twenty-three miles away. He got there in seven days but it took a fortnight for his blisters to heal. In later years he was to say that it could have been worse. Before his arrival in Edinburgh he had spent some time in London.

One hundred and twenty-three miles. He could not have accomplished that distance in these shoes. He looked down at the shiny black shoes he was wearing for the first time. He preferred brown but he had to wear black today, to go with the black suit which he hadn't worn for some time – or perhaps that was wishful thinking, to put out of his mind the whole question of death which he associated with this black suit. He was surprised when he put it on to find that it still fitted him, was slightly loose, if anything. He imagined he was getting smaller, shrinking. He patted the front of the jacket. There was nothing wrong with the suit but he didn't like it. He wore it so infrequently that he was self-conscious in it, a little nervous. The sooner he could get out of it the better. The sooner this was over with the better. It made him feel uncomfortable, not just the suit but the business in hand. And the shoes. The shoes he had bought two days before, the same day he visited MacRae.

As he entered the shop he took off his brown tweed cap and looked round the unfamiliar if not alien place until he saw a sign which said *Men's Department.* He went up two steps, across an area of thick blue carpet and came to a halt in the middle of the floor next to a display stand of men's slippers. A few moments later an assistant approached him. He was disturbed to see that it was a young girl. She was about seventeen, small, and had a pretty face whose smile might well have been genuine.

'Good morning, sir. Can I help you?'

The Major was taken aback. He looked at the shoes on the displays nearest to him. He was fairly sure he was in the right place.

'Can I help you, sir?' the shop assistant repeated, still smiling.

'I want a pair of black shoes.' This was delivered in rather a flat, almost rude tone.

Undeterred, the girl said, 'Certainly, sir. Size?'

'I beg your pardon?'

'What size, sir?'

'Ah...This could be a problem. I'm afraid I don't know,' he confessed.

'I see. Well...we'll just measure them, shall we? Please take a seat.'

The Major sat. The girl went to the far side of the shop and returned with a foot gauge. She sat before the Major on one of those special stools with a sloping shelf for the customer's foot.

'If you'll just put your foot here, sir.'

The Major did so.

'I'm afraid it's necessary to measure your foot, sir, not your shoe.'

'Ah.' He leaned over and began to unlace his right boot. It laced up beyond his ankle so this took quite a long time. At last he freed his foot and placed it, wrapped in its plain green sock, on the foot gauge.

'Size ten,' the girl said. 'Just one moment, sir.' She rose and turned to the shelves behind her.

'Aren't you going to measure the other one?'

She turned back. 'I'm sorry, sir?'

'You haven't measured the other one.'

For a few seconds she looked quite confused. 'It's...' she began, and then stopped.

'They're not often the same size, you know. Not exactly, anyway. I confess I don't know with mine.' He peered down at his feet, the left one on the floor, still snug in its boot and the other on the foot rest. He wiggled his toes inside the green sock.

The girl paused. She seemed to be struggling to read the situation correctly. 'What about your boots?' she asked.

He looked up. 'These?'

'Yes. Are they the same size?'

'No idea. Made in London. Sent off a pattern of my feet years ago. Pair of shoes every six months, a year, and then the damn company goes bankrupt. You know the sort of thing.'

It was clear that the girl did not know the sort of thing. For a moment she looked at the Major as if examining a different species of being from herself. She said, 'The difference isn't usually enough for you to need different sizes for each foot.'

'No?'

'No, sir.'

'I see.' He looked down again at his left boot. 'You wouldn't mind just checking, would you?'

There was a three second pause before she said, 'Not at all.' He noticed that her smile had gone.

She sat on the stool and waited as he removed his other boot. She applied the foot gauge. 'Size ten,' she said.

'Ah well, better to be safe than sorry. I suppose we can take it they'll be the same width?' He smiled.

'Wide fitting I'm sure, sir,' she replied.

'Fine.'

She turned to the shelves again and selected three boxes. She displayed the different styles to the Major. He picked up one shoe and examined the instep carefully. Something was written there but he couldn't quite make it out.

'What does it say there?' he asked, handing the shoe to the girl.

'Made in Rumania, sir.'

'Rumania?'

'Yes, sir.'

'Good God.'

'We get a lot of shoes from Rumania, sir.'

'Do you? I'll bet there's lots of people in Rumania who haven't got shoes and here they are selling them to us.' He took back the shoe and turned it over in his hands. 'I'll bet you don't even know where Rumania is. Do you?'

The question appeared to come as a shock. Her mouth opened slightly. 'I...'

'Do you?'

'It's in Eastern Europe.'

'Oh, my dear girl!' The Major dropped the shoe in his lap and threw his hands up in mock horror. 'Couldn't you be a little more precise?'

'I...'

'Which countries does it border, eh?'

'I really don't think...'

'I know. You know it's got a shore-line but you can't remember which sea. That's it, isn't it? Well, is it the Black Sea or the Caspian?'

'I've really...'

'Black Sea. There. Does that make it easier for you?'

'Not really, sir, no. I mean...' She gave him a look that told him she was out of her depth. 'I've never really been interested in geography.'

'No?' The Major thought about this for a moment. 'No interest in geography. Well...' He thought again. Then he said, 'Have you ever thought that a few months ago someone in Rumania was making this shoe and he was using tools perhaps made in West Germany and leather possibly imported from South America?'

'Well...'

'The tools from West Germany might well have been made in a factory where most of the workers were Turkish. Did you know that West Germany has a large Turkish population?'

'No, I didn't.'

'Money, you see. Everybody needs it, I suppose. But no, my point is that here you are, unaware of all these little links that bind you to other parts of the world. Don't you think that's fascinating?'

'I suppose it is, in a way.'

'I mean, here you are, selling shoes from Rumania and you don't even know what the capital city is.'

The girl thought for a moment and then said, more loudly than she had planned, 'Bucharest!'

'Well done!' He reached forward and touched her elbow and she found, to her surprise, that she was smiling. 'Well done indeed,' he repeated. Then he turned his attention to the shoe again. 'Now...do you have anything like this that's British?'

'Yes.' She removed the shoes from the third box and held them out to him. 'These are British, sir.'

'Ah. Mind if I try them on?'

'Not at all, sir.'

The Major put both shoes on and laced them up properly. He walked up and down on the carpet. He seemed satisfied and when he sat down again he said, 'Fine, I'll take them.'

'Right you are, sir.'

He took them off and handed them to her. As she went over to the counter to wrap them up, he found that a pair of brown boots had caught his eye. 'Have you got those in my size?' he asked, pointing to the boots which were on a separate display by themselves.

'I think so, sir. I'll just check.' A few moments later she returned from a back room with a pair of boots in her hand.

He took the right boot and held it up for inspection. 'Don't tell me,' he said. 'Rumania?'

'No, sir.'

'Czechoslovakia? Hungary?'

'No.'

'Are they by any chance British?'

'I'm afraid not, sir, no. They're from Italy.'

'Italy?'

'Yes.'

'Hmm.' He turned the boot over and examined the heel. 'Damn fine boots in spite of that.'

'Do try them on, sir.'

'Thank you. I think I will.'

The boots were of the style that lace up from near the toe to well past the ankle, very similar, in fact, to the ones he was wearing when he entered the shop. Determined that he would test them out as they would be worn, he laced them up completely, finishing off with a smart bow, stamped the floor a couple of times and then took a turn round the small area that was the *Men's Department*. Again, he seemed satisfied. However, he said nothing and proceeded to remove them and put his own boots back on. The girl looked on anxiously while this was being done and then asked, 'Are they all right, sir?'

'Oh yes, fine,' the Major said. He thought for a moment longer and added, 'Look, despite our pleasant little chat I can't say that I care too much for shoe shops in general. No...' He paused. He began to think of how old he was and how many pairs of shoes he would require for the rest of his life. Five pairs? Ten? Fifteen? Perhaps only one pair. He was seventy-nine. He found it amusing that he could be reminded of his own mortality in a shoe shop, of all places.

But the young assistant, more than sixty years his junior, had no idea what might be going on inside the Major's head. She could not understand the wry smile he displayed as he looked at the new boots. And she was quite surprised when he said to her, 'Look, you'd better let me have half a dozen pairs of these.'

Instructive, he thought, his visit to the shoe shop. But he still held the opinion he expressed then: that it would be no great loss to him were he never to enter a shoe shop again. In fact, he would go further: he would be happy to forget about the mainland altogether and just stay on the island for the rest of his life, however long, or short, that might be.

He moved away from the round window and crossed the study to the square window in the wall opposite. From there he could see the first few houses of the village of Ardroy and the stand of birch trees on the edge of the moor which led up to the foot of Ben Fyrish. A wind seemed to have arisen from somewhere and the heads of the birch trees were being thrashed about. The window rattled and one of the wads of paper he had earlier stuffed into the crack in the wall popped out with a little sough of complaint. He retrieved it and pushed it back in where it had come from, feeling as he did so the cold draught on his fingers.

Back at the square window, he could see the first black limousine arriving, turning in through the gates nearly a quarter of a mile away and moving slowly up the winding drive to the car park which had been extended and freshly tarmacked in anticipation of the public opening of the castle.

He hadn't wanted the limousines; his wife had persuaded him.

Normal practice on the island was for a Land Rover to transport the coffin itself and for mourners to make their way to the cemetery by whatever means they could. But his wife had insisted on getting MacMillan from Craigton to handle it. She had muttered various words such as dignity and respect which meant little to him in this context. After all, his brother had never ridden in a limousine during his lifetime so why start now? It was all so artificial, he thought, and hugely expensive, though that didn't really matter. So he agreed, eventually, reluctantly, on one condition. 'When I go,' he said, 'I want Morrison's Land Rover and nothing more fancy than that.' But she would not speak about anything connected with his death, calling it unlucky. 'It'll certainly be unlucky for me,' he said, and she told him to stop joking. Then she added that he would live for quite a few years yet, certainly surviving longer than Morrison's Land Rover which was showing its age even more than he was. Well, that was comforting, he told her, very comforting. Maybe he wouldn't book Morrison's Land Rover just yet.

He found her concern endearing, the fact that she refused to talk about death and hated to hear anyone else talking about it. But he realised that she was terrified of being left alone. He was older than she was, by seven years, so it was more likely that he would go first. Sometimes he thought about her death, about her dying before he did. Losing her would be a blow, it would be difficult, very difficult, but not impossible. Nothing was impossible.

A second limousine arrived and parked itself neatly next to the first. Soon he would have to leave the tower, make his way downstairs in his new black shoes which he now believed were too tight for him, and get into one of these large black cars that he detested so much.

But he remembered that he had insisted upon them himself, forty-seven years ago, when his wife, his first wife, Hester, had died. He remembered that he thought then that it was an expression of the depth of his grief to have in the funeral cortege the biggest, shiniest, blackest cars ever seen on the island. It was the first and the only time that ten Daimlers had made their way from Craigton to the Island of Glass. Ferries were less certain then so the whole lot came over two days before the funeral. The drivers and undertakers were all put up in the castle. The day of the interment a storm blew up and no ferries would risk the crossing back for three days. The cars and their attendants remained at the castle for a week in all, during which the Major grew sick of seeing men in black everywhere with their white gloves which the etiquette of their profession demanded that they wear at all times.

They drove him away in the end, they and their cars, their black suits and top hats. But it was principally his dead wife, he knew, who was responsible for his attempt at a geographical escape. There was his wife's child, too, the one she had given birth to shortly before she died, but he could not bring himself to love it. At times he caught himself regretting that the child hadn't died too, or rather, instead of its mother. He never even saw it before he left the castle and it was only when he returned, some five weeks later, on foot from Edinburgh, that he found it was alive, well and baptised. Someone had decided it should be called James.

James

The West welcomes back to the region James Redburn who was born and brought up in Swordale Castle on the Isle of Glass. For the past twenty years Mr Redburn has worked for Grenville and Grenville in London, the last ten of these years as partner in the prestigious brokerage firm. Unfortunately ill-health has forced him into retirement at the very early age of forty-seven. He admits his decision to retire was a difficult one but he is also quite blunt on the subject: "It's a demanding life," he says, "and it's a job for a fit man. As I cannot with honesty put myself into that category any more I would be failing in my duty to a firm which has treated me admirably for many years if I did not step down and let someone else take over the reins." But his removal from the hectic financial world of London does not mean that Mr Redburn now intends to lead an inactive life. "It would be too easy," he says, "to spend the rest of my life pottering about the island doing a bit of fishing and shooting. That type of thing is fine for a month or two but it wouldn't suit me for much longer than that."
He has big plans for Swordale Castle which he is determined to fulfill in spite of occasional periods of ill-health. The castle's splendid gardens and outstanding art collection will soon be open to the public for the first time. Mr Redburn believes that the island needs a major attraction and that Swordale Castle fits the bill. The renovation of the castle, which is nearing completion, has been arranged in consultation with his father, Major Maurice Redburn, who, apart from his military duties, has lived there for most of his life. "My father fully supports me in this venture," he says. "He is as eager as I am to witness not only the opening of the castle but the revitalisation of the economy of the island as a whole."
When the castle opens in May, it will offer its magnificent terraced gardens and its outstanding art collection. There will also be a special room devoted to the "Polar Exhibition". This display includes photographs and artefacts from an expedition, led by James Redburn, to Antarctica, in 1956. "The trip was

quite unique," he explains, "as we explored completely unmapped territory and climbed the highest mountain on the continent."

The expedition was not without tragedy. "One of our number became ill," he says and, though it is twenty-three years since the events that he recounts, it is clear that they still affect him deeply. "Modern equipment might have saved him but we were not prepared for anything more than routine medical problems. We also hit a spell of very severe weather which meant that we were stuck for several days still a long way from our base camp. Peter Meadway did not survive the bitter cold. It has been one of my ambitions ever since to commemorate his life in some way and the Polar Exhibition is my attempt to do this."

James Redburn also has longer term plans for the castle. More exhibitions will follow next year. He is particularly keen to bring to the public's attention the great variety of wildlife to be found on the Island of Glass. He plans to offer residential nature study weekends at the castle and would very much like to set up an arts centre. "The more the castle has to offer, the greater the benefit to the island as there will be a natural growth in other services," he says.

And how many visitors would he like to see? On this point he is quite forthright: "As many as possible, as many as the ferries can bring to the island. Wouldn't it be superb if the ferry companies had to lay on more and larger ferries to cope with demand!"

Swordale Castle opens on May 8th. It will be open from 10am to 5pm from Monday to Saturday. For further details, please ring Swordale 2573.

I open doors for ladies. I doff my hat; I stand up when a lady enters the room. These and other marks of common courtesy are habits that were taught to me when I was a child and they're difficult to shift. I know we have liberation now and we're all equal and there are no ladies any more, just women, but what few people realise is that there is a difference between the intellectual grasp of a situation and a conditioned reflex, what I'd call a learned emotional response.

Take, for example, my drinking. I know that I drink too much and, on occasion, far too much. However, this knowledge doesn't serve to alter my behaviour, particularly when a bottle is placed in front of me. Of course what we're talking about now is an addiction; it's certainly reached that stage. I'm forty-seven but could easily pass for sixty. I'm overweight and my posture is bad – I'm pot-bellied and round-shouldered. And I know that if I stopped drinking and took a bit more exercise walking round the estate my health would improve. But I can't do it. Mainly because I don't want to.

Marina and I live in rooms on the third floor of the castle but I've kept a small flat in London which was my weekday residence when I worked for Grenville and Grenville. At that time we had a house in Sussex which I returned to at weekends. It would have been possible for me, without much difficulty, to commute daily from Sussex to my office in the City but I chose not to do this. In fact, as Marina pointed out on several occasions, the travelling time from the flat, which was in South Kensington, to Bank Station wasn't that much shorter than the commute into London Bridge. But for me the main attraction of the flat was and still is its size: it's very small. Only one person can live there in any degree of comfort. Consequently Marina very rarely stayed with me there. For me, the flat's principal use was to provide refuge from my wife.

Marina uses the flat quite a lot now. She hates Swordale. Consequently that small apartment in South Ken has taken on extra significance for both of us. Marina uses it to escape from Swordale and I use it to escape from her. With careful management I can be up here while she's down there and vice versa. In fact, were we only to meet at railway stations or merely wave at one another from passing trains, this would suit me admirably.

I loved her once, of course, a long time ago.

My wife is a large woman whose voice is just a little too loud. None of this mattered to me before, when we met. At that time her voice was a natural part of her vigour, her zest for life. I convinced myself it was actually part of her charm. I was hopelessly in love with her. There you are again, you see: intellect swamped by emotional considerations.

I can remember with awful clarity the moment I stopped loving her. It happened at three minutes past noon on Saturday the 24th of June, 1957. That was the exact time that she arrived at my side before the altar in St James's Parish Church, Beaufoy, in Kent. I turned to look at her and, for a couple of seconds I was confused because I didn't recognise her. The woman standing next to me was my bride but I didn't recognise her! I swallowed hard and the moment of panic passed. I recovered myself but I began to perspire. I could feel my upper lip beginning to moisten. Through the veil she was wearing I could see that this was Marina all right but there was something different about her, very different and dramatically wrong. She'd had all her hair cut off.

Even now, more than twenty years later, I can recall the luxuriance of her blonde hair. It was thick and lustrous. It fell to the middle of her back and was stunning in its beauty. And she'd had it bobbed. The woman by my side in 1957, about to mouth platitudes about loving and cherishing, had hair that was four inches long at its longest. I couldn't believe it. I couldn't believe she'd had all her hair cut off, just like that, without consulting me. I felt cheated.

At five in the afternoon, when we finally left the wedding party and were alone in the cab that was taking us to the station, I asked her about her hair. I tried to sound casual about it but my heart was pounding. 'Oh,' she said, 'it was becoming a nuisance and anyway, married women don't have long hair.'

Later, of course, I became angry, with myself more than with her. I felt angry that such a thing should mean so much to me. I was disappointed in myself. Surely I hadn't wanted to marry her simply because she had long blonde hair. Or had I? I was forced to the conclusion that, in part at least, this was true. And I can honestly say that with this realisation there came something that was close to anguish. It was disturbing that I'd based my love, even partly, on something as insubstantial as the colour and length of her hair. But it seemed that I had. And my love for her wasn't just reduced, it was destroyed, extinguished. Within a few days her just-too-loud voice ceased to be oddly charming, it was harsh and grating; her laugh was no longer free and joyous, it was embarrassing; and as for her body, she wasn't nicely rounded after all, she was overweight.

At that time I was a bit overweight myself but now I'm just fat. I'm forty-seven, I'm fat and bald and I drink too much. Sometimes I wonder what Marina saw in me then, when we got married. Was there some quality, some attribute that attracted her in the same way that her hair had attracted me? I suppose there must have been but I've no idea what it was. I'd achieved a bit of fame, of course, on my return from the Antarctic, and my prospects were good. Was that it? I wasn't particularly handsome then and I've hardly improved since. I wouldn't say that my self-esteem was low but I tried then and try now to be honest, to myself at least. I know that I had little ability as a lover in the sexual sense and none whatever in the emotional sense. I was conscious of this lack but couldn't do anything about it. I suppose that as time went on my preferred method of coping with this problem was to drink my way past it. Not a very successful approach.

Sometimes I wonder if Marina is just as pleased as I am that we see so little of each other. Maybe she is. Right now, for example, she's down in London while I'm up here. She won't be coming up for the funeral. Her dread of these events borders on phobia. And this suits me quite well at the moment. I'm glad she's not here. She'd only be rushing around in a highly nervous state, trying to help and merely getting in the way. She rang me a couple of days ago and said that she really should come up, shouldn't she? I said no, no, it was good of her to be so thoughtful but I wanted to spare her the pain. She decided to stay in London.

We never talk about this mutual desire for absence. I'd say that there are things we're both happier not knowing about; ignorance is less painful than knowledge. But this whole business has left me slightly troubled, not so much about our current situation itself but the manner of our arriving there. It troubles me, yes, but not enough to force me to any kind of action. It's the same with my other imperfections. I know what the problems are; I can list them accurately, one, two, three...but this knowledge doesn't in itself bring the power to make changes.

Take my drinking, for example. I couldn't stop when, about a year ago, my doctor said it would kill me. I couldn't stop even when the senior partner at Grenville and Grenville took me aside one day and told me I really would have to control my drinking or I might find myself in serious difficulty. And a month later I was drunk – well, not very drunk but not entirely sober – when the same man fired me.

But I'm not a pessimist, I'm a realist. I know what my weaknesses are but I also know my strengths. When I'm sober – and here at the castle I'm relatively sober most of the time – I'm good at organising things. I'm good at identifying potential and then turning it into reality. The castle has a lot of potential. I'm quite sure of this but I haven't quite managed to convince my father yet.

There's a particular conversation I had with him a few weeks ago that sticks in my mind. I was in the Polar Exhibition room. The photographs had just arrived that day from the framers and I was setting them out round the walls, getting an idea of where they should hang, deciding on the sequence. It was a slow job because I kept stopping to look at the photos. I'd had them enlarged before they went for framing so this was the first time I'd seen them in their new size. It was quite a revelation. The first one I pulled out of the second crate was of an iceberg.

I remembered the thrill, now twenty-three years old, of seeing for the first time this magnificent tower of solid crystal, the size, the mass of it, its perfection of lines, planes, curves and corners. It was white and cold and it sparkled. It inspired admiration and fear at the same time. I'd forgotten the scale of the thing; it really was immense. One of the men – Meadway I think it was – had got into one of the dinghies and rowed over to it. Not a very bright idea, actually, as these things can split apart or roll over. Very dangerous. Considering what happened later on, maybe it was a pity Meadway didn't get even closer and put himself in more serious jeopardy. No, that's an unkind thought, if an honest one.

It looks good in the photograph, anyway. There's the berg and Meadway and his little boat visible only as a tiny dark shape in front of it. My only disappointment is that the picture's in black and white. I can't recall the colours accurately but there were certainly areas of the berg that were blue.

My father arrived when I was looking at this photo. He had no interest in the berg or, indeed, in anything in the Polar Room.

'It's about this brochure,' he said. He was standing over the crate as I drew out the photographs. 'It's a pack of lies. It's just a pack of lies.'

'Oh, come on, father. It's not that bad, surely,' I said. I carried on sorting through the photographs.

'Absolute nonsense. I mean, it's just...'

'Give me an example.'

'Well, the number of rooms, for a start.'

'Sixty-two, isn't it?' I said.

'No, it isn't. It's not that many. Fifty-six, perhaps fifty-seven.'

'Do you actually know how many?' I asked.

'Not exactly, no.'

'Well then, what does it matter?'

'What does it matter? What do you mean – what does it matter? If you put something down it's got to be...accurate.'

'But we don't know, do we?'

'No, I've just said...'

'So, as you and I are probably best placed to know how many rooms there are, and we don't know, then no one can argue with what we say. What's the problem with that? And it really isn't that important, anyway. I mean, it's about sixty, sixty-two, sixty-four...what did I put down?'

'Sixty,' he said and there was a measure of contempt in his tone.

'Well then, sixty. There you are. It's a reasonable guess. What's wrong with that?'

'But you don't know,' he repeated. 'You don't actually know.'

At that moment I picked up the photograph of the iceberg again. I turned it round to show it to him. 'What do you think?' I asked.

'Fifty-eight at the outside.'

'No, I mean the photograph.' I said. 'What do you think of the photograph?'

'The what? Well, it's...' He leaned forward to look at it more closely. 'It's very nice,' he said.

'Very nice?'

'Yes.'

'I see. Well...'

He straightened up. 'The problem...the problem is that the whole thing is full of inaccuracies. I mean, take the Gainsborough...' he said.

'What about it?'
'No one in their right mind would call it a major work.'
'Neither do I.'
'But you imply it. I mean, it's a tiny painting of...of a lapdog...'
'...that looks more like a pig. I know.' I knew he agreed with me on that one. It was a running joke in the family.
'Well then,' he said.
'Well what?' I said. 'You've got to remember that it's a genuine Gainsborough. The fact that he painted it when he was six weeks old, or whatever, is neither here nor there.'
He shook his head. 'But it's hideous.'
'I agree entirely. But then so are a lot of other paintings that happen to be worth a lot of money. Take Dalí, for example...'
'And the Turner...'
'The Turner?' I propped the iceberg against the crate and drew out another photograph. Men climbing a mountain. Tiny black stick-like figures linked together by a thread and squashed against a white slab of mountain which pushed up into a pale grey sky.
'It's not a Turner,' he said.
'Are you sure?'
'It's attributed to Turner.'
'Exactly,' I said, 'and that means that, until someone can prove otherwise, it's a Turner.'
'It's a drawing from a notebook and it's very small...'
'Why are you so fixated by size?' I asked him. I stepped across the room and placed the photograph of the mountain on the floor against the wall. 'Get some perspective,' I said. 'Get a feeling of what the room might look like when they're all up.'
'It's supposed to be a tree,' he went on. 'It's just a...just a sprawl.'
'Worth a lot of money. Sell it to the National if we need to.' I came back over to the crate and took out another photograph. More snow, more sky and, linking both, the figures of ten men, in a line, facing the camera. 'My God,' I said, more to myself than to anyone else, 'there we all are, all of us. There's poor old Meadway, too. Poor old bloody Meadway.'
I could see that he was leafing through the castle brochure again. He said, 'Fancy words...splendour...magnificence...gently... gently washing the shores...'
'What?'

'…spectacular…enchanting…'

'It's advertising, father. Selling. That's all it is,' I said.

'I don't like it.'

'You've made that patently clear all along but you're forgetting that what we have here is a product to be sold. We've got something that we want people to buy and they're only going to buy it if we convince them that it's very special indeed…'

'But it is special.'

'I know that. I mean…I mean we both know that,' I assured him. I put the photograph down on the floor, leaning it against my knees. I looked directly at my father for the first time for some minutes. 'Look,' I said, 'if we're half-hearted about this in any way, nobody'll bother coming. We've got to convince them to come and that's the only way to do it. Once they're here they won't need any convincing any more because they'll see it. They'll see that it *is* magnificent, that it *is* splendid. They'll see that what's in the brochure is true.'

'Will they indeed.'

'Do you doubt it?'

He shook his head. He stepped over to the window and looked out at the distant mainland where you could clearly see a range of hills, the higher peaks still with snow. 'I know how splendid it is,' he said. 'You don't have to convince me. The view from this window alone is priceless.'

After he'd gone I stood at the same window and looked out at the same hills and remembered that I'd learned the names of them when I was a child. It had been difficult because they were Gaelic names but I'd learned them in the same way as, at Sunday School, I'd learned by heart the names of the books of the Old Testament – Genesis, Exodus, Leviticus, Numbers, Deuteronomy, Joshua, Judges, Ruth. And then, First…was it Samuel or Kings? I wasn't sure any more. I'd learned them – the books and the hills – purely as patterns of sound because the names themselves meant nothing to me. Except perhaps Numbers and Kings because these were words that were also used in other places.

I tried once again with the hills, moving from left to right: Cnoc Mhabairn, Cnoc a Mhargadaidh, Meall an Tuirc and then there was a Ben something but I couldn't remember any more. The

Gaelic words are very difficult. How many people are there left who speak the wretched language anyway? Of the fifteen hundred people on Glass, are there a hundred who speak it? Fifty? I'm not sure. Bendeallt – that was it. Bendeallt.

The distance from eye to cairn is perhaps twelve miles – a couple of hundred yards to the shore, then eight miles of water to the mainland and three or four miles of damp moorland getting wilder and craggier as it rises to the summit of Bendeallt. Father took me there once. The War had just ended and he was home on leave. We went to the mainland one day and then walked round to the village of Ardullie which sits on the shore beneath the hill we were to climb. Three miles from Craigton to Ardullie, then four miles up to the summit of Bendeallt. And then down again. I fell asleep, I remember, on the ferry back to Glass. I'd walked fourteen miles which was one mile more than the number of years I possessed at the time. I'd never felt so tired. But I can still remember my exhilaration when we looked out from the summit on that bright autumn day and saw the Western Coast and its islands spread before us like lumps of rock placed on a mirror. And father took a telescope from his rucksack. We lay down on the grass with the telescope propped up on a lump of granite and we looked at the Island of Glass.

I found the castle almost immediately. There it was, on its little hill above the sound. I could just make out the tower and though I could give no expression to it, what I felt then was wonder. It had something to do with distance and time and, intruding in both, earth, rocks, heather, sunlight and sea. I'd measured myself against the landscape, travelling over smooth grey water and then the rough terrain of Bendeallt to connect one end of this view to the other. My father, no more able than I was to identify this feeling and give it a name, said simply, 'You were over there and now you're here, at the other end of a straight line which is about twelve miles long. Tonight you'll be back over there again but by then it'll be dark and you won't be able to see this spot. Not till tomorrow, anyway.'

I'd wanted to place something on the cairn, something bright that we could identify with the telescope from the castle the next day. But we had nothing with us that was big enough and I felt disappointed. But father told me that it didn't matter. Flags were for other people. We didn't need a sign to prove we'd been there. We knew. What others believed was not important.

Having given me his opinion about the brochure, about Turner and Gainsborough and so on, my father left. I moved away from the window and carried on placing the photos round the room. Then, when they were all set out, I began to inspect them more slowly. I reached again the photograph of the ten men on the mountain. There was Woods and Linton, Heath, Liverdale and Cochran. And that was me and then Meadway of course and then the last three who were Flood, Philips and...what the hell was his name? I peered at the photo of the tenth man whose name I couldn't remember, his face half-covered by his anorak hood. Fraser. Of course. It was Fraser who had helped me dispose of Meadway's body. About the only useful thing Fraser did. Almost as useless as Meadway who had died, basically, because he gave up, and giving up is an offence.

Occasionally I think about Meadway and my main feeling about him, almost every time, is disappointment for the expedition's sake. It was sad that Meadway died, of course it was, but Meadway had become a liability. In fact, he was a liability even before he fell sick. Although I knew that it was wrong to think in that way, I felt that Meadway was no great loss. Nor would Fraser have been. Now Woods was different. And it showed because of what he became later – head of quite a large retail group. Whereas Meadway, Fraser and Linton for that matter, they were people of little value even as perhaps I was of limited value although I'd tried, I'd tried hard, which was more than Meadway ever did, the poor bastard.

I moved on. I reached the photograph of the dog called Oscar. Why do I generally find it easier to remember the dog's name than to remember Fraser? The answer to that question is simple: Fraser was in no way memorable. He was just someone who was there and did things – not very well – and came home and was never seen again. Oscar was a greater loss than Fraser would have been. Oscar was the lead dog that got sick and had to be shot. The remaining dogs in the team never worked as well after that. I shot Oscar myself and did it with great regret but with no sense of indecision. The animal was in pain and would not have survived. If it hadn't been shot it would merely have endured more pain before dying a day or perhaps a couple of days later. No, there was no problem about shooting Oscar – it had to be done. But I didn't like what happened to the dog after I killed it and I didn't involve myself in any of that.

Even now the death of the dog affects me more, in my memory of these events, than the death of the man, Meadway. I know that this feeling of mine is wrong, that a human life is to be cherished above that of a dog – surely this is what everyone would have you believe. But I can't, unswervingly, adhere to this view. I can provide a logical argument in this case: Oscar was of much greater value to the expedition than Meadway. The loss of Oscar was a blow whereas Meadway's death was a relief. Perhaps it isn't pleasant to state these facts so baldly – even to myself – but that doesn't make them any less true.

Besides, I liked the dog. Perhaps that's the key to all this. I liked the dog more than I liked Meadway or Fraser or Linton or most of the rest of them. Except Woods, perhaps. You see, I like hard work and effort and consistency and the dog was better at all that than any of the men, even Woods. Even, perhaps, than myself. And the dog liked me. That was certainly true. I was the only one of the men that could stroke Oscar, that could hold his head and his ears without being snapped at. And this turned out to be useful – stroking his head, stroking his muzzle, the top of his nose, holding it gently and pressing it down slightly to give me a clear shot through the top of his head.

Dogs have value. This is one of the few principles I share with my father. I remember how upset he was when Jack died. Even I can remember Jack from my infrequent trips north over the years. A big, bounding, jolly Labrador. Father had him for twelve or thirteen years but then, when the time came, as with me and Oscar, he knew what had to be done. No equivocation. The dog was dying so it was necessary to take him straight to the vet and have him put down.

But thrushes? I'm not so sure about thrushes. Never been terribly keen on small birds. But other people have different priorities, I suppose. Only yesterday Alice halted the building of the car park because of the danger to some fledgling thrushes in a hedge. It's the one that has to be removed in order to make a wide entrance and exit to the car park. Thrushes! Well, they'll probably fly in a few days so not that much time will be lost. There have been times, however, when I've despaired of the castle ever being ready to open up to the public. I think my father would like the delay to be permanent but then I would be the one left without any money and a huge estate to run.

Delays, always delays. A few weeks ago, one of the decorators came to find me. Said he'd found something of interest on one of the walls they'd stripped and thought I'd better see it before they went on with the repapering. At first I thought it was just an excuse to have half an hour off. Not the most dedicated of workmen, our team of decorators.

Anyway, they'd stripped off about three layers of wallpaper and got right down to the plaster. In doing so they revealed two inscriptions, two areas of writing on the curve of plaster near one of the windows. The older inscription was barely legible but it was just possible to make out a date: March 17th, 1895. There followed the signatures of several people, castle retainers with their titles. None of the names meant much to me but to one side there was another date: 17th November, 1931. Below this there were a few names, some of which I did recognise. There was Alexander McRone, described as Head Gamekeeper, J. Matheson (Mrs), Housekeeper, Murchison, the Head Gardener, and then the names of chamber maids and scullery girls. At the bottom of the list there were two names: Hester Redburn and C M Redburn. No title was given with this last name but it could only have been my uncle Christopher Michael Redburn who died three – is it? – four days ago, and whose funeral is taking place later this morning.

On the day the inscriptions were revealed, father had been on one of his rare trips to the mainland. He wouldn't say where he was going but I know for a fact it was to visit McRone – Alan, that is – in prison. I suppose his interest in McRone...no, it's more than that, it's more like guardianship...dates from as far back as the time of the second inscription because McRone's father, Alexander, got on very well with my grandfather, the old General who died, incidentally, in 1932, just a few months after this second collection of signatures.

In fact, there's a story about McRone – Alexander, that is –

walking ahead of the hearse at the old man's funeral, carrying his sword and helmet all the way from the castle down to the cemetery at Ardroy. Got soaked for his pains, so they say.

Well, I told Alice about the names on the wall and she came up to have a look. But she hadn't arrived at Swordale until 1936, so most of the names didn't mean much to her either. She could remember Alexander McRone, of course, and some of the maids. Anyway, I took a few photographs of the inscriptions before telling the decorators to carry on with the job.

And then the whole incident slipped my mind. I meant at least to tell father about it but I forgot. But now, of course, I can remember something that seems very odd indeed. I don't know of any C M Redburn other than my uncle, but in 1931 Christopher was in Paris. He didn't visit Glass from 1929, the year he left for Paris, until 1950 or thereabouts, when he came back to live permanently on the island. And he certainly didn't attend the funeral of his father in January, 1932, two months after the inscription was made. But the name on the wall is quite definitely C M Redburn. Odd. Must take it up with father some time.

Uncle Chris is a tricky subject with father and I've never fully understood why. I first met him in the early 1950s when I was about twenty. I'd already been to Greenland but it was before the expedition to the Antarctic. I'd heard of uncle Chris of course, but didn't know anything about him except that there'd been some big break between him and father. Also, apparently, he'd spent most of his life in Paris. I didn't even know he'd come back to Glass until I overheard a stray remark of father's. Alice was urging him to go and see Chris, now that he was back – had been back, in fact, for quite a while – but father was completely inflexible. 'No,' he said, 'as far as I'm concerned I don't have a brother.'

Well, I decided that even if he didn't have a brother I certainly had an uncle so I'd go and visit him. I found out he lived in Strongarve and I just went over there. Didn't consult father. But Chris wasn't there. It was about the time of the publication of *The Last Wolf* which was becoming very successful and Chris was over in Glasgow or Edinburgh doing book signings and so on. He was in considerable demand.

I left a note for him saying that I'd like to see him. It wasn't till a couple of weeks later that I got a reply. The next day I went back to Strongarve to meet him for the first time.

To be honest, I was a bit disappointed. It seems harsh of me to say that now, particularly as he's just died, but it's the truth. He was bright and amicable and clearly pleased to see me but I got the impression that he didn't really live in this world; he lived in the world of his books and his fantasies. And as to the question of his relationship with father, he made it clear – very politely – that the subject was off limits. So when I left I felt as ignorant about it all as when I'd arrived. Bit of a waste of time in that respect.

We had very little in common, you see, almost nothing, in fact. His life was dedicated to his books, to literature, which is something I've never cared for. I rarely read fiction. Why bother reading made up stuff when there's so much written about real people and real events? I'd rather read about Scott, Amundsen, Shackleton, just to name a few of the great explorers, than to waste time with all this fiction nonsense.

He gave me a copy, of course, of *The Last Wolf*, and I actually managed to read it. Bit of a struggle, though. Nevertheless he was my uncle after all and I tried hard. But even now, as I get ready to go to his funeral, I can't really describe that book as anything other than complete tosh.

But I did grow to like uncle Chris, in spite of that. Perhaps this was because I saw him rarely and when we did meet we both made a special effort to get on. He was a calmer, more relaxed man than father and he was quite funny, quite witty at times. Happily he never asked me what I thought about his book and he never offered me another one. He wrote about a dozen in all, I think. That's what I put in the obituary, anyway, the piece I've written for *The West*. I've shown it to father and, predictably, he's quite indifferent to the whole thing. 'Whatever you write will be fine,' he told me when I said I was going to write something about Chris. And although he's the person with most knowledge about Chris's life, he gave me no help at all. None. So I confess that some of the details…well, what could I do? I made them up. I'm sure Chris would have approved.

Alice

McHendrick was quite right to tell me about it and I told him so and I said stop, you must stop, even if it means we don't get the gate done and even if that means we can't open the castle on time. James was livid, of course, livid, when I told him last night. Went very quiet as he does when he's angry, though Mo's never managed to understand that, never realised, properly. A few weeks ago I overheard them talking about the opening. They were in that silly Polar Room and it got very quiet and I said to myself he's very upset and he was, I'm sure, though Mo probably never guessed. Too subtle, you see. Not that that's a criticism really, he has other qualities, lots of them, that outweigh all that but no, calls a spade a spade and expects others to and doesn't understand silence, doesn't know what it means, what it can mean. Lots of silence then and I thought better not listen any more. Tiptoed away.

So anyway, McHendrick took me down to see what was going on and I ran into that wolf on the landing, that moth-eaten old thing in the glass case that Alan dragged over from poor Chris's house. Poor Chris. I will miss him, even if not many others will. So we've got his wolf now. Ran into it on the landing. Nearly took both of us downstairs. Moth-eaten old wolf and moth-eaten old me, fetch up at the bottom like a pile of broken biscuits. No Wolf Room then and wouldn't Mo be glad. Not too bothered about the...the Polar business but not at all keen on the Wolf Room. No, not at all. And James said Yes, a Wolf Man would be better – now that would be something special and Mo said What do you mean Wolf Man? What the hell are you talking about? A joke, James said, a joke. Hmmph. That was his response. Couldn't see it, you see. No sense of humour. I married a man with no sense of humour. And James, quite witty at times, really, quite funny. Where he gets it from I don't know. Not from Mo, that's for sure, and no way of checking now if he got it from his mother.

Doesn't talk about her at all, Mo. No. Said to me when we married I will not discuss with you my first wife, it is a subject that is closed. And I agreed. The man was in pain, I could see that. Thought I might be the one to help him out of it. I agreed. I said yes. And when he asked me, I said yes. To marry him, that is. Oh, I said yes. But not too eagerly. I didn't say it straight away. I thought about it. I was thirty but not desperate. Not too desperate. He was thirty-seven and handsome and well-connected and well thought of and a victim of tragedy. A young boy to bring up without a mother and I was convenient, I suppose, and he was convenient too. For me, I mean.

And I said yes. But I had conditions, I made conditions. A month in Italy every year, I said. And he agreed. Although he said not Naples, not the islands. But that was all right. And he kept his word too, I have to say. Except during the War, of course, when it really wasn't a good idea anyway. A man of his word. Serious, honourable and good things like that but no sense of humour.

Wouldn't have laughed at me and the wolf in pieces at the bottom of the stairs. No. But then I probably wouldn't have either. But anyway, it didn't happen. Just kicked it a little bit. It wobbled too, I noticed, inside the case, but should be all right when it's set up properly. If it's ever set up properly. If Mo agrees. And why shouldn't he, really? I mean it's only a small exhibition, the Wolf Room. There's the gardens and the tea room and the Polar Room with the photos and the pickaxe and bits of rope and so on. I mean there's a lot, really. One old wolf – even though it really is old – won't make that much difference either way, will it? But it's his castle, it's Mo's castle after all, so I suppose he can decide.

So down we went. I mean McHendrick and I, not the wolf, the wobbly wolf. We went down sedately then. I try to be sedate when descending stairs; it's something my mother drummed into me. Made me practise. Book on head, walk downstairs, keep doing it till you get it right. Book falls off, go back up and start again or else no dinner. Went hungry a few times, I can tell you. But I learned. Oh, I certainly learned. Got to maximise what you've got, she said, especially if you haven't got that much to start with.

Called a spade a spade, my mother. A bit like Mo, come to think of it. Very disappointed that I wasn't pretty. Rather plain really, like herself. But she had money. To start with, anyway. I knew I'd have precious little of that since my father drank it away, most of it. Took quite an enormous thirst to dispose of such a sizeable sum, but he managed it. Plus buying drinks for his cronies, of course. One of them had a son, I remember, wanted to marry me when I was seventeen. Not pretty then either, never was, but fresh-faced, blooming, I suppose that's the best I can offer. I said no, of course. Face like a pug dog and manners not much better. Keep remembering him when I see that dreadful Gainsborough picture we've got that Mo's getting all uppity about. No thank you. Anyway, when my father had his first brush with the law over his debts, it was goodbye pug dog and thank goodness for that. Only interested in money and now we had none.

So my life's work evolved into becoming sedate. I became really awfully sedate. I could climb to the top of the house and down again with a copy of Browning's Selected on my head. Twice. Only three floors of course. And then later, two, and a bit later still, only the one floor and so no stairs to practise on. But I was still sedate, walking round the smaller and smaller number of rooms we had each time we moved. We contracted vertically first and horizontally later. And Browning, leather-bound, was sold for twelve shillings and replaced by a hymnal. I didn't like the moves at all, only a few months apart, but I was glad to see Browning go. He wrote such a lot of poems. Even in the Selected there were so many. The hymnal was an improvement. So much lighter for my poor little head.

So we were sedate. Or I was anyway, I'm sure. McHendrick's got his gammy leg and can only take a step at a time, so he's a bit slow and far from sedate. And maybe I flatter myself. Maybe sedate is a word I should avoid. Stately perhaps. Slower than sedate, I think. No movement necessary, even. It'll come to that, I suppose.

But I reached the hall first and McHendrick, puffing a bit, joined me a few seconds later and said something that was completely drowned out by this ghastly noise from the front door. Enormous van appeared. Well, that was it. Never got to the hedge at all. Well, we did, but later. Little man pops out and says Portraits? Fearful racket, right up at the front door. Switch it off, I said. Switch it off. And he disappeared and turned off the engine, came back and said Portraits? again and I hadn't the faintest idea what he was talking about. Looked at me as if I was gaga. Very small man, he was, little bald man in blue overalls.

McHendrick, getting to the point, said Portraits? You mean paintings? The little man disappeared again and came back with an oil painting. One of Mo's great uncles, in a red uniform, all very bright as if the paint was still wet.

And in they came. Must have been fifty or sixty of them. Mostly portraits but a landscape or two as well. We'd sent them away for restoration and forgotten all about them. Well, I had, anyway.

Little man had an assistant who was smaller, if anything, but very young. Looked no more than eleven, though he must have been sixteen at least, I suppose. So difficult to tell sometimes, especially with girls. Reverse with them, though, usually. Look much older than they really are, rather than the other way round. All that make-up. I wasn't allowed make-up till I was twenty-one, till the Browning and hymnal training was complete. And by then it was too late, I suppose, really. Too late to catch some young lieutenant's eye. They knew I was plain. Oh I was sedate but they didn't want sedate, after all. I was plain and I was poor. No amount of make-up would put that right.

So it was the wilderness for a few years. Till Mo came along, a Major at that, and quite by chance, and I thought well why not, will I get a better offer? Of course he told me he'd been married before. He told me about his first wife. And he told me that the subject was closed. And I said yes. I said yes when he wanted me to say yes and I said no when he wanted me to say no. Because by that time I was thirty and I so wanted something. Yes, I so wanted something.

I got them to put the pictures in the big room on the third floor, what used to be the dining room before the War, when people still used to come to dinner. I mean they still do, of course, but not thirty of them at one time. It's just along from the rooms that James inhabits with his appalling wife. Never did like her. Too loud and always dropping names as if she's the only one who's ever met the Queen Mum or the Duchess of Kent. Nobody else, just royalty. Very boring.

Don't think James likes her much now either, if he ever did. I suppose he must have done once, else why did he marry her. But there are lots of reasons why people marry. At least I liked Mo. Still do. Never really loved him, though. No, I can't with honesty say I ever really loved him. But after a while that didn't matter much. I mean, it was clear that he didn't really love me. Oh, I'm not complaining about it. What we had was a kind of agreement, a transaction, if you like. Almost a sort of contract which was made up of a number of clauses none of which was explicitly mentioned. But you got to know what they were. Little signs told you. I became very adept at reading signs.

But James, well, he's very polite to his wife. Very courteous, very formal. Obviously can't stand her. They've given up with signs, they just square off each other's territory. Seems quite likely that she can't stand him either, they spend so much time avoiding each other.

But the big dining room it was and I got them to arrange all the pictures round the room, propped on chairs or against chairs or against the wall. There were hooks on the wall, where some of the pictures had come from, witnessed by darker patches of unfaded wallpaper. But we didn't put any up. We just laid them out, round the room, and looked at them.

And I found Hester. I must say she was quite striking. Of course it's marvelous what you can do in a portrait. Even a photograph. All that make-up again, I suppose. But she looked good. In the best frame, too, an oval gilt frame, not too fancy, not trying to make up for any deficiencies in the picture because there were none really, to be honest. A bit bold, perhaps. Soft and warm, maybe, but forward, definitely a positive, not a passive look. And rather Victorian if anything. But maybe that was the hair, tied up at the back but not too tightly. Not a severe, pulled-back-tight-to-the-skull look. No, ordered and formal but not severe. Rather pretty.

The little assistant thought so too when he saw her. Came out with something like She's a bit of all right, and earned himself a cuff on the ear from his boss and a one word rebuke: Manners. But they both took a long look, concentrating on the décolletage, no doubt. Quite an expanse of pink flesh above the Empire line. Bit of artistic licence there, I'm sure. At least the little boss was a bit more polite. A very beautiful lady, he said. Well, I said, that's very kind. It's me when I was twenty-one.

I don't know what made me say it. It just came out. But there you are. Little assistant went bright red and started coughing. Little boss cuffed him round the ear again, probably to divert attention from his own embarrassment, and said: Handkerchief. And I gave them iced coffee.

Seemed like the thing to do. After all, it took the best part of half an hour to unload the pictures and drag them up to the third floor. A long way up and no lift. Little assistant had never had it before and said so rather forthrightly. What's this? he said. I've never had this before. Nearly got another clip round the ear for that but just a stern look this time, I think probably because he already had cup and saucer in hand and little boss didn't want to see the coffee, iced or not, all over the floor. But he made up for it, little assistant. I've never had it before, he said after a few sips, but it's very good. Smiles all round.

Little boss said: So, are these all relatives of yours, madam, if you don't mind me asking? Yes, I said. But that's not true. Mostly my husband's, I added. Even that wasn't true either. They're all Mo's people. Grandfathers, great grandfathers, great uncle Hector from the Boer War, great something-or-other Duncan from the Sudanese Campaign. All men, of course – apart from her – and all big men in uniform with moustaches. Dreadfully boring, the lot of them.

One of Mo, too, done in the early thirties when he was in between wives. No, I don't mean it like that, really; that was cruel. But he's there in his uniform too, with his moustache, all very aloof and independent like the others. All I can say is, he's aged well, Mo. He's still a handsome man. He's still tall and straight – military men don't seem to lose that – and he's still good-looking, even if he hasn't learned to laugh.

And then I remembered McHendrick. Goodness, I thought. Goodness. And perhaps I spoke it out loud too because I got up with a start. I'll be back, I said. Help yourselves to more. There's a flask on the table.

So it was back down in neither sedate nor stately fashion, I didn't really care, from the third to the ground floor, with a pat on the wolf's head as I passed – well, on top of the glass case, anyway. And out to McHendrick who was sitting by the hedge, sitting on one of those benches we dragged up from the Italian Gardens just after the War. Here they are, he said. Look. Just as if we'd been together all the time, nothing had intervened and I hadn't left him to fret for more than forty minutes. Here they are, he said and he parted the hedge with his hands and I looked in.

The light meant something to them, I suppose, or the movement, the sound. There was expectation, anyway. Little heads, four of them, four little mavises stretched up with beaks open. I noticed McHendrick's hands, too, that were holding back the leaves. Large hands, not too clean, with hard thick skin on them. Mo's hands are similar but he scrubs them when he gets in from the garden, always. Spends a good ten minutes with a nail brush and lots of soapy water till they're scrubbed pink and glowing. My own are like claws. I know this. Painted nails, but what else can I do? Old and veined, the backs of my hands, and bright red nails, bright red, that's right, show them off.

I said to McHendrick: They're so young. A week, he said. And how long before they fly? I said. Another week, I suppose. I'm not sure, he said. Little heads and big pink mouths straining upwards for food. I thought how delicate they were, how remarkable it is that anything so vulnerable can survive.

We'd better leave them, I said, and we both drew back. And the hedge? he asked, I'm supposed to be cutting it down. Not till they've flown, I said. I'll tell the Major, don't you worry. Aye, do that, please, he said. And Mr Redburn, too. And I did, but later on, in the evening.

I left McHendrick by the hedge. He'd already removed quite a bit of it to open up what's going to be the car park once they've got the tarmac down. I mean, I'm looking forward to it really, it's quite exciting. The place hasn't been so spick and span for years, not since we used to hold the Grand Ball here and the last one was...oh, twenty years ago at least. Twenty-five, perhaps. But I don't like tarmac much. Much prefer grass. And cars are such horrid things, but I suppose we've got to have them. Got to get the punters in, James said to me once and for one tiny moment I thought of boats, I thought he's going to put boats on the water garden.

What on earth are you talking about? I said and he said: People, Joe Public, The Great Unwashed. Tourists, if you want to be more civil. I said I preferred tourists out of all that lot. Especially not punters. A punter, I informed him, is someone who punts.

And I remembered then, only once, at Cambridge. It was in the fifties, I think, and I was on my way home from my month in Italy. Yes, nineteen fifty or fifty-one. I met Chris in London on the way back. Stayed at his flat in Pimlico for a couple of days. Never told Mo, of course. He would have been livid. I'd found out Chris's address and went to see him. Poor fellow. His wife had died some time before and he was in a bad way. We took a little trip to Cambridge. Just for a day, I think.

And we went on the river. I said: This is nice. It was early autumn and still warm and I sat back and let Chris do the punting. I said: This is nice, I feel like a little girl again and here I am over forty. Oh, he said, you can't be, surely. And he looked genuinely surprised, too. But he's a good actor, was a good actor, I know that. But he usually told the truth, that I remember as well. He was no good at deceit, he couldn't dissemble. About important things, anyway.

But he said: You can't be. And it made me feel good, even if he was lying, just this once. Thank you, I said. Thank you for that.

Then I asked him about Mo, about why he and Mo didn't get on. But he wouldn't tell me. I can't, he said. I'm really sorry but I can't tell you. Can't or won't? I said, surprised at how aggressive this sounded. Both really, he said. I've made a promise, so I can't tell you. But, even if I could, I probably wouldn't. Maybe one day you'll find out anyway. Maybe when I'm dead. Yes, that's what he said. I remember it clearly now. Maybe when I'm dead, he said. And he's dead now. Poor Chris. I did like him. In some ways I liked him more than I like Mo.

So I left McHendrick by the hedge and back upstairs it was, back up to the little man and his little assistant, past the wolf again. Pass you once again today, I said, you're becoming a pack all by yourself.

They'd finished the coffee. I've never had it before, the little assistant said, but it was great. Life's full of new experiences, I said. Lap them up. He nodded. And the other one, the little boss, asked if I wanted them to hang the pictures. It's a good idea, I said, but I don't know where they're supposed to go. May not be going back where they came from.

The little assistant asked if they were valuable and got another hard look from his boss. I don't really know, I said. Some may be. That one there is a Gainsborough. I pointed to the tiny little pug dog of a thing. A Gainsborough? the boss man asked. Yes, I said, isn't it perfectly horrid? I suppose it's probably worth a few thousand but I'd be quite happy never to see it again.

That's the one I like, the little assistant said. The one of you. For a moment I wasn't sure what he was talking about but then I remembered my lie. Yours for fifty pence, I said. His mouth dropped open and I laughed.

They left shortly after that but just when they'd reached the ground floor the little boss said Oh, by the way, how do we get to Strongarve? My goodness, I said, pictures to deliver there too? Just the one, he said, just a print, unframed. I said, Strongarve spreads out over a wide area, what's the specific address?

Well, he sent the assistant to get the print, which was rolled up in a cardboard tube. When he handed it to me and I read the name I nearly fell down. Little boss actually took my arm. Is there something wrong? he asked. Christopher Redburn, I said. It's addressed to Christopher Redburn. That's right, he said, I assumed a relative of yours. So you know where he lives, I take it?

Well, I had to sit down, didn't I. Little boss now quite worried, I think. Told assistant to fetch a glass of water. Rather pointless, really, as he didn't know where the nearest kitchen was. I'm fine, I said, I'm fine. It's just that Christopher Redburn died a few days ago. In fact his funeral's tomorrow. Oh, I'm sorry, he said. I'm so sorry. Bit of a silence then, what with little boss not knowing what to say. Just leave it with me, I said, pointing to the tube. I'll see that it's dealt with appropriately.

And later, when the picture people and their noisy van had gone and McHendrick had gone too, I told Mo and James about the hedge. Actually, it must have been much later as Mo didn't get home till late.

James was none too pleased. Spoke very quietly to me. Always a bad sign. But I said: No, and that's final. It'll be a week at the most. Meanwhile we keep away. Thrushes, James said. The opening of the castle postponed and thousands of pounds down the drain because of thrushes in the hedge. Precisely, I said, and left him.

As I say, that was much later yesterday evening. Quite a lot more happened before that. First, I went back to the third floor, carrying with me the cardboard tube the little boss man had given me. And I sat there in the middle of the room, found a chair and put it in the middle and sat there with all those faces looking at me as the light faded.

Then I got up and walked round to see the different faces, all Mo's relatives, fathers and grandfathers and great grandfathers and what not. How many of these can you have? I thought there was a limit. All looking back at me and wondering who I was. Imagination!

And I looked at her, Hester, the one I'd said was me and I put a light on to see her better, not the main light, a standard lamp, and moved her underneath and I saw how beautiful she was, not pretty pretty, not something flattering concocted by the artist. No, not like that. I've seen photos of her, that's how I recognised her. Oh, Mo doesn't know about that but I've done a bit of quiet research, I've seen photos. But I'd never seen this portrait before and I wondered where it had come from. I couldn't remember seeing it anywhere. And then I guessed, of course, and I said to myself: Right, I'll put it up now, right away, and to hell with the consequences.

So I picked it up, not too heavy, and went up to the fourth floor. Been there before, of course, but only when Mo was away, he's not keen at all on anyone going there. Seems a shame, such a waste of a lot of good rooms, seven, eight, don't know how many. Anyway, through the new door, not locked yet, that they've put up to keep the public out when they come, the punters, horrid expression, and then along the corridor to her room.

It was a bit spooky, yes it was, and I did feel a little afraid, I admit, so I said a few swearwords to build up courage. Buggeration! I said, and Buggeration! a bit louder. No one to hear it, after all, and I got there because the night was clear and the moon shone in through the big window and the end of the corridor, no curtains for God knows how long and no idea where the light switch was, if there's any light at all, never been there at night.

But I saw enough to make my way to the door, that's the important thing. I reached it. Knew which one it was. And I took hold of the old white ceramic door knob, remembered that from the last time, big round lump of cold china, put my fingers round it and turned, heard the click and the door opened. Creaked a bit, well you'd expect that, wouldn't you, and I reached for the light switch, knew where it was, and felt the dust and the old round switch that they wouldn't allow now, and I pushed and on came the light.

Rather weak. Rather pale. I was rather pale myself, I shouldn't wonder, and I stepped into the room that had only been cleaned perhaps half a dozen times in fifty years, if that, the fabrics disintegrating, the bedclothes, the floor grey with dust and not many footsteps in it. Except mine, of course, and probably James's because someone must have come in to fetch the portrait. But I couldn't see where it had been taken from. There was a rectangular patch on the wall where some other picture had been but nothing that could be described as oval, not even in my geometry.

So I stood at the end of the bed for some time, looking round the room and I thought how stupid I'd been, to go there at all. But this was the place for it, surely. I hate mysticism and all that sort of metaphysical nonsense or whatever they call it but I was moved. No, it's not too strong a word, really.

She died in this room, you see, Hester, died giving birth to James, which is why he doesn't come here any more. Mo, I mean. The whole floor is out of bounds. For him.

I looked at the walls, at the velvet curtains reduced to strips, and I saw even then past the age, the fading, the deterioration, all the way back to how beautiful it must have been then, fifty years ago, and how devastated Mo must have been by what happened.

There was a drape to one side and I could see that it didn't cover a window but a door. I pushed it aside very gently because I didn't want it to fall apart and I didn't want to get covered in dust. And then I had to take a deep breath before I took hold of the door handle. No, you don't believe in ghosts and all that rot, I told myself, though not strictly true, saw my mother at the top of the stairs a couple of years ago, trick of the light, probably, and I turned the handle.

I pushed the door open ever so carefully and allowed light from the main room to filter in which it seemed to do very slowly as if it too was on very unfamiliar territory. There was another round light switch and I reached out for it, realising that my hand was shaking. But when the light filled the room there was nothing surprising there after all. It was just a dressing room with a wardrobe – empty when I checked – a dressing table, a couple of gilt chairs with worn upholstery and wallpaper in a velvety blue colour, rather dark and gloomy, with one area on it that was even darker and in the shape of an oval.

Oh, it was for her all right. I stood on a chair – nearly went through it, in fact – and reached up and fixed the cord over the picture hook that was already there and I settled her back in her place again. And I looked round as I'd done in the bedroom, a kind of slow pirouette, to examine everything and I found a space where another picture had been, another oval, on the wall that adjoined the bedroom, the wall opposite the wall where her portrait was displayed.

Well, I thought it must be a picture of Mo, but the one in the dining room on the third floor was not oval, it was rectangular, so I didn't know the answer to that one. But I decided to go back down and check.

So I left the dressing room, and the bedroom. I made sure that I scuffed through my own footprints so that no one would be able to recognise who the visitor had been. Oh, very cloak and daggerish. And I thought as I was doing this that I wasn't a criminal so why was I acting like one? But I was, in a way. A criminal, I mean. I was disturbing the peace, you might say, moving around air and dust that had been undisturbed for years.

Well, not quite. After all, someone had come in to collect the portrait when it was sent off for restoration. James, I suppose. I think it was James who arranged the restoration in the first place. But I don't know if he knew about the picture of his mother, unless he remembered it from a long long time ago. Or perhaps he found it. Perhaps he explored the castle from top to bottom now that he's decided to live here with his beastly wife.

I went back to the big dining room and looked round all the paintings again but there wasn't an oval one of Mo. There wasn't another oval one at all. But as I looked at them I kept seeing bits of Mo, sounds awful doesn't it, bits of him – the nose and mouth especially – in some of his uncles or great uncles and so on.

I found something else, too. The tube, the cardboard tube addressed to Christopher which the little boss man had left with me. I'd forgotten all about it. I wondered if I should pass it on to Mo but then I thought, no, why not just open it right now? And that's what I did. I managed to get one of the plastic ends off and I pulled out the print inside.

It was a copy of the portrait of Hester. There was a little slip attached, with a very business-like note: One photo-reproduction, female subject, as requested. And I thought, Well!

I thought James must have decided that he wanted a copy for himself. After all, maybe he'd only recently discovered the painting. And why shouldn't he have a copy? But then, no, no…it wasn't addressed to James, it was addressed to Christopher. Now that struck me as very odd. Why did he order a reproduction of Hester's portrait? In fact, how did he know about the restoration of the portraits in the first place? Anyway, I rolled it up again and slipped it back inside the tube. Then I went downstairs and ran a bath.

And my bath made me feel so much better, more relaxed, so I went back to the kitchen and made myself some coffee. Hot coffee this time. Not good for you late in the day, so they say, but I don't really care. And then the door bell rang, not the bell at the main door of the castle – not even sure if there is a bell there any more – but the bell at our little apartment, built on the side of the castle I don't know how long ago. Didn't want to live in all those big draughty rooms, after all. Anyway, I thought it might be Mo, mislaid his key or something, but it wasn't. It was Alan McRone and I thought to myself how many surprises can I reasonably expect in one day?

He looked well, although a bit thinner than I remembered. Prison regime, I reckon. I never really blamed him that much for what he did and I don't think Mo did either. Got him that job at Ardruie. Oh, he doesn't know that I know about that, but I overheard him on the phone one day. A good man, Mo, as I've said before.

I said, you'll come in, won't you, but he said no, better not. You're welcome, you know, I said. I'm making coffee, you could have some coffee. But he said no. Said he had to deliver a letter to me and he handed me this white envelope. I said that I knew he was up at Ardruie now so surely he could have posted it but he said no. He said the letter wasn't from him, it was from someone else. I looked at it. My name on the front, typewritten. Who sent you? I asked him but he wouldn't say, just that he'd promised to deliver the letter directly to me. And he asked if James was around, which he wasn't. Have you got a letter for him too, I said. And he said yes but he'd been given the same instruction: to hand it over directly to James. Don't you trust me to hand it on? I asked him and he said he would but it wasn't up to him. So I said he'd have to come back tomorrow morning. James would definitely be around then. All of us would, because of Chris's funeral. He said that, if I didn't mind, he'd like to attend the funeral himself. I said of course I didn't mind. Then he left.

Well, I sat down with my coffee and wondered at all the strange things that had happened in a single day. So many! And some of them just a little frightening. Oh, brought it on myself of course, I mean, wandering around the fourth floor with Hester's portrait...And then Alan McRone arriving like that, out of the blue. Not frightening, no, but certainly unsettling. What next? I thought. What next? Well, there was the letter, of course.

I didn't open it straight away. I drank my coffee first. You see, I'd been thinking about Alan McRone quite a lot, ever since I met his wife – or, I suppose, his ex-wife – over in Craigton a few weeks ago.

I didn't tell Mo about this little encounter. Seemed like a good idea to keep quiet about it because what Ella told me made me think again about Alan McRone and what had happened. She was a woman scorned, no doubt about that, and spiteful, to an extent, but I'm sure there must be some truth in what she said. I know that if I passed this information on to Mo he'd discredit it immediately. Very loyal, Mo, sometimes misguidedly so. It would have hurt him to know that Alan McRone was perhaps not quite what he believed him to be. Tends to take the man's side in these matters, Mo, and I don't necessarily blame him for that, no. Just something to bear in mind.

I'd gone over to Craigton to buy some wool for Mrs Campbell who lives in that little cottage up at Ardkaig. She's not really fit enough these days to manage the ferry crossing, can't walk more than a few yards. So I promised to get her some wool on my next trip and there I was, heading for Miss Comlyn's, when someone called to me, Mrs Redburn! Mrs Redburn! When I turned I saw this young woman approaching and I didn't recognise her at first. Quite disconcerting really. She said, it's me, Ella, Ella McRone. So I said, Ella, yes, of course, and I gave her a big smile to make up for the blank look I'd started off with. Didn't recognise you, I said and it was hardly surprising really. Her hair was longer and she'd changed the colour. She'd gone from brunette to auburn. Quite suited her, I thought. My, my, you've changed, I said and smiled again. She seemed hesitant, in need of reassurance. I took hold of her arm. It's good to see you, I said. She said that not many people said that to her, these days.

We decided to have a little chat, over coffee. She suggested we went to the New Craigton Café. Where's that? I asked because I'd never even heard of it. Well, it's right here, she said, pointing. It's where old Miss Comlyn's shop used to be.

Well, I was shocked, completely shocked. For a minute or so all I managed to say was Miss...Miss Comlyn? Miss Comlyn? We were only a few yards away and there it was, the New Craigton Café. It had replaced that wonderful shop I'd visited regularly for over twenty years. The café sat there, right next to Crerand the Gunsmith with nothing in between. No Miss Comlyn.

But goodness, I said, what happened? And Ella explained that Miss Comlyn had died – oh, a few months before – and her shop became vacant and was now the New Craigton Café.

It was all so sudden – for me, I mean. I didn't even know that Miss Comlyn had died. How on earth had I not heard of her passing? Now, we weren't close, she was an acquaintance, not a friend, but she was a presence, a steadying influence, she was an assurance that some things don't change. But of course they do.

Ella said that she was well over seventy when she died. I didn't make any comment on that.

Shall we go in? she said and I wasn't very keen. I'm not sure, I said. It seems like a kind of sacrilege. I don't think she'd object, you know, Ella said. Loved her coffee did Miss Comlyn. Well, yes, I remember that too, I said. She did, didn't she. We went inside.

For a while I didn't feel comfortable. It was a bright, garish place and when we sat down I kept thinking about where the counter used to be and that exquisite bank of drawers, all polished wood and brass plates, where Miss Comlyn used to keep her yarns and skeins of wool. But the staff were very nice and the coffee was good too. Excellent, in fact. I looked round and saw that I was the oldest customer by about forty years.

Talk to me, I said to Ella. Tell me what you want to say. And she began.

Well, she admitted she hadn't been a good wife to Alan. Fine at first but after a couple of years, after they moved to Glass, in fact, things began to go wrong. Alan spent a lot of time on the estate, of course, and she began to feel a bit lonely. Their cottage is a mile from the village and a bit isolated. She got a job as a waitress in the Glass Hotel but it was a summer job only so when it finished she felt more alone than before. And Alan spent more and more time crossing to the mainland on estate business. Oh, that's down to Mo, I said at that point. The Major, I mean. Hates crossing to Craigton. But she said it happened more and more often and she began to think there were other reasons Alan made these trips.

Then she got a letter from 'a friend'. Did she know that Alan had been seen in Craigton in the company of a 'gorgeous blonde'? Despicable, aren't they, the people who write these letters. Ghastly. Unsigned of course. Well, she ignored it but a week later she got another one. Just three words in this letter: 'brunette this time'. Well, she destroyed this one too. But then she found an earring in his jacket pocket. She imagined it was a token, a souvenir, slipped into his pocket secretly, because Alan would not have kept it. Too organised, too careful. So she began to believe that maybe her husband was having affairs during these trips to the mainland and this made her despondent to the point of depression. Then Frank Millwood arrived and she fell in love with him.

She knew she shouldn't have done it – two wrongs don't make a right, I know that, she said – but she couldn't help herself any more than she supposed Alan could.

Please don't judge me too harshly, she said to me and she began to cry. I gave her a tissue, a small handful in fact – they're very generous with their paper serviettes in that café – and she managed to cheer up a bit.

Don't be too hard on yourself, I said. Sometimes it's good to learn that we're not special, that we're no different from other people. Is that how you think of yourself? she asked and if there was an aggressive edge to her tone I deserved it. I do come out with some pious twaddle sometimes. Here I am, living in a castle for goodness' sake!

But, I said, you know we're not actually that much different, you and I – oh, I don't mean the affairs...You've never had an affair? she asked and I said no, never. Never been tempted? Ah, I said, ah, now that's different. So you were tempted? she said. Her eyes were red but the tears were gone now. Yes, I said. Once, a long time ago. Nothing came of it. And do you regret that now? she persisted, I mean, not giving in to temptation? Take care, I said, bringing my firm tones to bear on the situation, take care you don't go too far with these questions. However...and I had to raise a hand to stop her from interrupting...I can quite honestly say that I don't regret it for a moment. If I'd given in to temptation my whole world would have crumbled.

So we're not the same after all, she said. Closer than you think, I said. When I was eighteen I was very poor, living in a tiny room in Camberwell. Where's that? she asked. It's in South London and it's a slum, I said. Well, it was sixty years ago and I doubt if it's improved since.

The conversation moved on to other subjects – what she was going to do now, her future with Frank Millwood and so on. At the end I asked her if there was something she wanted me to do. She said, just don't think too badly of me, that's all. I don't, I said. She said thank you and then she smiled. It was a weak little effort but I think it was genuine. Shortly after that we left the café.

So all this was on my mind last night when I sat down after finishing my coffee and picked up the letter that Alan McRone had delivered to me. I don't mind admitting that my hands were trembling when I opened it. It was just as well I was sitting down because I felt quite faint when I saw who it was from. What a shock. Please, no more, I said, no more shocks today. I breathed deeply a few times, deeply and slowly, and I unfolded the letter, its five pages, laid them out and flattened them with the side of my hand, tried to get them quite flat before I read them. And I read from beginning to end twice and then I looked round the room in astonishment and I read the whole thing a third time right through, much more slowly and carefully and if anything my astonishment intensified. It's not every day you get a letter from someone who's dead.

Christopher

I am the man my mother warned me about. This is a phrase I used a great deal at one time, many years ago. Coming from an old man it lacks any hint of the sinister. But from a man of twenty or twenty-five, with a full head of hair and blue eyes and the faintest of smiles, it was just enough to amuse and confuse at the same time. Women loved it. Well, to be fair, most women; there were two who didn't – one slapped my face and the other laughed. But the rest loved it. They enjoyed that little thrill of uncertainty that the remark suggested. How much was I joking? How much did they want me to be joking? If they stayed in my company a little longer they generally found out the answer to both questions.

And the one who slapped my face? She was an unpleasant woman but I treated her as I used to treat all women at that time – with polite deference and quite a lot of condescension. I apologised, not for my misdeed, but for hers. I was cruel to her, more cruel than if I had slapped her in return. I was so polite to her that I made her feel ashamed. This is a practice I gave up some time ago.

The one who laughed was different. More of her, later.

Dubious things can sound good in French. I used the word *flâneur* to describe myself. Said with a flourish it gives the impression of a man about town, someone who enjoys himself rather than a dedicated loafer whose chief aim is to live off the generosity of others. My father, may he rot in hell, preferred the word *wastrel*. It was suitably old-fashioned and biblical for his small, narrow mind. Wastrel, idler, sponger, layabout, degenerate – I've heard all these terms used about me, sometimes in clusters of two or three at a time, and I've never disputed them. The one person, a woman, who asked me to explain what *flâneur* meant, got the dictionary definition which is: *one who saunters about, a stroller*. 'Do you saunter a lot?' she asked me. I said yes, I did. I didn't much fancy being employed in any other way. She said, 'I've got a feeling you're a bit of a scrounger,' and I immediately agreed. I'm not afraid to admit what I am.

So, my main attributes are charm, wit, a distinct lack of application to nearly everything and, one more: complete honesty.

There's never been any moral imperative in this. If I'm honest, it's prompted by laziness. Successful lying requires a lot of hard work and a lot of planning. You've got to remember everything twice – what you actually did and what you say you did. And that's assuming you stick to only one false version of events. Otherwise you might have to memorise half a dozen mistruths about the same thing. I can't be bothered with all that. So, generally I tell the truth, though it's often got me into trouble, sometimes serious trouble.

Especially with Maurice. There were times when I should have lied to him but didn't. There was one occasion in particular when any sane, reasonable, caring person would have lied but I couldn't do it. I couldn't bring myself to begin. It's something I regret.

When I was eighteen, I didn't really want much, just a place to live, preferably quite some distance from the family, a servant or two to take care of all those tedious household jobs and a decent income, enough to live in some style. I never wanted to live modestly – where's the fun in that? I wanted to live rather than merely exist. The idea of being careful and living within my means never entered my head. The important thing, then, was to have a good time and enjoy life. I expected to be paid just for being. I admit that my views on this have changed somewhat over the years – I've had to make a few minor amendments to these basic rules of living.

As I was the younger son there was some idea in my father's perverted mind that I should pursue a vocation for the church. Even I could see that this notion had quite a lot going for it. It would have made for a relatively easy life, if a hypocritical one. But when I was about sixteen I made a rather outspoken comment about God. Didn't exist, I said. Not there. Figment of the imagination. Entire world hopelessly deluded. Well, this point of view rather closed off any ecclesiastical possibilities and my father, understandably I suppose, was furious. But then the arguments he put forward to back up his anger struck me as odd.

First there was the almost reasonable point that I was only sixteen and it was therefore unlikely that I'd already managed to penetrate the world's mysteries and so understood everything better than everyone else. I wanted to point out to him here that *everyone else* was rather a sweeping statement. I was not the only one to distrust the idea of a Christian god. There were quite a number of Muslims, Buddhists, Hindus and so on in the world, not forgetting atheists, agnostics and those who couldn't care less, so Christians were certainly in a minority. But even at sixteen, precocious though I was, I was sensible enough to know when not to argue with my father. It was when discussion gave way to anger on his part that further argument was to be avoided. I taught myself to nod, mutter a few conciliatory platitudes and leave as soon as possible. In later years, when arguing with others – not my father – I adopted a very simple strategy. The angrier my opponent got, the calmer I would become. I lowered my voice, disciplined my thoughts more carefully and presented my points in an ordered and succinct way. The more upset the other became, the more I took on a calm and relaxed demeanour. Of course this infuriated the hell out of whoever I was talking to and consequently his argument would fall to pieces. Anger is rarely a basis for progress. Curiously, this is one view I share with Maurice and it was through his use of this strategy – against me – that I learned how successful it can be and how annoying to the one on the receiving end.

But, getting back to God and his non-existence, I found my father's second point very odd indeed. What did it matter, he said, what I believed. The church would provide me with a reasonable living and keep me out of mischief.

What did it matter what I believed?

I thought about this question for days. The magnitude of it grew as the implications piled up in my mind. Although I was already somewhat of a cynic in such matters, it had never really occurred to me before that there could be such a disjunction between action and belief. Could you really order your life on the basis of a belief that you didn't actually hold? I began to wonder how many ministers of religion there might be who did not believe in God. It appalled my teenage mind to think there might be any. I actually asked an Anglican bishop this question once. Of course this was many years later, it was at a dinner party, it was late, the bishop was no longer completely sober, and I said,

'How many of your priests actually believe in God?' Clearly the question didn't strike him as being in any way out of the ordinary. 'Probably about fifty per cent,' he said as he swirled the brandy in his brandy glass, 'on a good day.'

At sixteen, then, I decided I didn't believe in God. In the years that have followed I've believed in various things – some deities (but few of them), mostly secular ideas – until I reached the point where I believed in nothing. And now even my belief in that is beginning to waver.

Thankfully, the business of a career was postponed for a few years as at seventeen and a half I was packed off to Oxford. Although lazy, I was quite bright and I got there at least partly on merit although I'm fairly sure my father pulled as many strings as he could just to make absolutely certain he had the luxury of seeing me as little as possible from one year's end to the next. I got the feeling he was trying hard to forget my name. He certainly stuttered over it on the few occasions we spoke to one another during my Oxford years.

I didn't fit in at Oxford. Most of my fellow students either took themselves too seriously or felt themselves to be special, or both. I found them insufferable and told them so. I poked fun at them and they didn't like this one bit. The only thing I took really seriously myself was developing a talent to laugh when this was least appropriate.

For example, I tittered during the Vice Chancellor's speech when he stumbled over his words because he'd obviously consumed one liqueur too many after lunch. I was reprimanded by my director of studies who unfortunately had witnessed the event. I pointed out that the Vice Chancellor had been drunk and was informed that I was wrong; he wasn't drunk, just over-tired. And anyway, I had to learn to overlook certain things in the Vice Chancellor who was an elderly gentleman with many fine books to his credit. But I continued to argue, quietly and dispassionately of course – I was already beginning to practise this technique. I said that if I was wrong – and I was sure I was not – and the Vice Chancellor was perfectly sober, then why was it necessary to advise me to overlook the fact that he was drunk? My exasperated director of studies told me I had a lot to learn about the ways of the university and even more about life itself. I replied that there were things about Oxford that I didn't really want to learn at all. He then told me to leave immediately.

I assumed that this command referred to my leaving his rooms, where our little chat had taken place, but he had a wider geographical scope in mind. The next day I received a letter urging me to reconsider my position and perhaps allow my educational needs to be met elsewhere. It appeared that they couldn't actually send me down because they didn't want any investigation to be made about the Vice Chancellor if I decided to make a fuss. They knew that I knew that they knew that I was right. The poor old man was almost permanently pickled. And this was a shame. He had indeed written several books which were highly thought of. I'd read half a chapter of one of them myself and it was quite informative, I remember, and reasonably well written, though I can't actually recall now what the subject matter was.

Anyway, the whole business ended with the usual fudge. My father wrote to my director of studies and promised my good behaviour in future – I think he still believed he was dealing with an eight-year-old. Then I had an audience with the aptly named Professor Grey, during which I was given a severe censure and then urged to put the incident behind me and stick in at my studies. I use the word "audience" because it was clear that this was not to be an interview; I was to remain silent, I was to listen and I was to obey. Well, I remained silent and I listened.

I still clung to the idea that going to university to study was a disinterested activity. It wasn't *for* anything other than itself; its purpose, if that's the correct term, was to equip you for Life with a capital *L*, not to train you for a specific job or career – unless, of course, that career was in academia itself. I still believed in the pursuit of this nebulous idea called truth and whenever I mentioned the word I was laughed at. It was clear that truth was a very personal thing. Professor X had his truth and Professor Y had his, which was very different. I became aware of academic rivalry and how bitter the competition was that it could provoke. The word *truth* was never heard so often as when rivals were promoting their pet theories. Everyone claimed exclusive rights to it and scoffed at everyone else. I found it all rather pathetic and

I steered clear of it apart from contributing the occasional untimely guffaw.

But Oxford wasn't all bad. Once I'd decided that I'd stay after all and continue to annoy people, but only in subtle ways which would not lead to another audience, I actually began to enjoy it. For the first time in my life I began to work at something with slightly more than a token gesture of effort – I studied French and discovered Zola – and I began to have a good time. I began to enjoy the company of women.

In general women liked me because I didn't flatter them. I was always tactful but honest when asked for an opinion about something of theirs whether it was an essay or a new outfit. Perhaps I should say that *some* women liked me. There were those who looked for compliments, who wanted to be petted and fawned on. They didn't like me at all. But then their first encounter with me was usually the last.

Emily was the exception. Our first meeting didn't go well. Through a mutual friend she had asked me to comment on a paper she'd written and when we actually got together to discuss it, she wasn't quite ready for the response I gave. Which was very detailed and critical but, I felt, only in a constructive way. I was in my second year then, she in her first. It was also her first paper and she'd worked very hard on it. She was not pleased by my criticism and avoided me for a couple of weeks. I believe that she made no changes to her paper but submitted it as it was, completely ignoring my few suggestions for improvement.

Then I received an invitation from her to a tea party. The tone of the invitation was formal but thankfully the tea party itself was not. It was held on a Saturday afternoon in a local tea room which had been hired specifically for the purpose. This must have been quite expensive to arrange but then, although most of my fellow students lacked wit, talent and any pretensions towards scholastic ability, few were in want of cash. Again, Emily was an exception. She was at Oxford on a scholarship and therefore had ability but not a great deal of money. I found out later that the tea party was a joint venture with friends.

Emily was not pretty. In fact she was edging towards the wrong side of plain but she had superb eye teeth. They protruded slightly and embellished her smile so much that by the end of the tea party I realised that I was greatly attracted to her. Fine detail can be so very important. By that time we'd talked a lot. We'd discussed her paper. She'd got it back from her tutor who had commented on it in much the same way as I had. Whereas I had hurt her pride, his notes had confirmed what she was already beginning to acknowledge – that she had learned a lot but still had some way to go. She thanked me for being so honest and direct in my criticism. I assured her that I wouldn't have gone to such trouble to review her paper if it hadn't been clear straight away that it was something worth spending time on. For a while we wallowed in mutual admiration. We talked about Paris and how we both wanted to go there. Even at that early stage in our relationship there was the unspoken suggestion that we might make a trip there together.

Eight months later, in the early summer of 1927, we did go to Paris together and it was not a success. We planned to stay for three weeks but came back after only a few days. Paris was unquestionably a beautiful city but it rained every day we were there. The room in our hotel on the Boulevard St Michel was not *delightful* as we had been led to believe, it was small. Its plumbing was primitive and the pipes conspired to concentrate in our little room the sound of every toilet, wash hand basin, bidet and bath in the entire building. The inhabitants of the hotel did not keep regular hours, arriving at various times during the night and early morning, each one without exception in dire need of bowel or bladder evacuation. Even to our non-medical senses it was clear that not many of these people led healthy lives.

But neither the constant rain nor the persistent night noises was the main problem. Paris was to have been the setting for our unofficial honeymoon. Up to that point Emily and I had not made love and it embarrasses me now to think back upon the awkward, if sincere, fumblings that attended our first attempts at sex. An old man can look back benignly on someone he no longer is but there's still a pang of something that's difficult to define. Something just wasn't right. I suspect that neither of us was as free as we thought we were. We were the fabulous rebels who discovered that it wasn't actually that easy to slough off the dark and dull morality that had been drummed into us during childhood and adolescence. And then perhaps I could have been kinder, more understanding, I don't know. What I couldn't do was dissemble and Emily knew that. So I said all the things that I could say that were quiet and reassuring and within the bounds of my moral code which seemed to be subject to revision by the minute. At least I managed to avoid being patronising and sentimental. Emily herself said very little but it was clear that this business of sex was as great a disappointment to her as it was to me and some of the responsibility for this was mine, though her first thought was that it was she who had failed me.

No doubt several million people have had a similar experience to Emily's and mine. But there's no doubt either that each experience was felt to be unique. For us it was as critical, as life-threateningly critical, as it was for those other millions. We walked round in a daze afterwards, trying to come to terms with all those feelings of guilt, hurt and loss. We were in shock; we spoke very little to one another; we concentrated our communication in gestures of affection and caring. It continued to rain. One morning, awakened at 5am by a toilet flushing in a distant room, Emily said, 'The pipes, the pipes are calling,' and we laughed for the first time for three days. Later that morning we packed up and left for England.

There was a letter waiting for me back in Oxford. It was from my father. It was short and inconsequential as far as the text itself was concerned but the message between the lines was clear: it would not be a good idea for me to return to Swordale in the summer. In confirmation of this implicit command there was a sum of money enclosed, to augment my allowance. The old boy rarely gave money away so I became aware just how valuable my absence from Swordale was to him.

With Maurice, of course, it was different. He was the one whose description tested the limits of cliché: the blue-eyed boy, the apple of his father's eye, the trusty first-born etc. I don't think my father loved him – I don't think he actually loved anybody – but he admired and respected those whose purpose was clear and good. Maurice's purpose was clear and good: he was a British soldier whose job it was to further the aims of the Empire. What could be clearer or better? On the other hand, my purpose was clear but not good: I was the black sheep, the thorn in my father's side, the bane of his life and so on – I had my set of clichés too.

So it gave me great pleasure to spend the money of this moral and upstanding and self-righteous bigot, my father, in distinctly immoral ways. I began to throw parties.

During the following autumn I threw two large and lavish parties, hiring rooms and a small orchestra for the purpose of entertaining a number of acquaintances, few of whom would later remember my name. I pursued two or three different women with a total lack of success and, as I partied on into 1928, I became rather depressed by the whole thing. I realised that I was dabbling in the insubstantial and shallow things of life and they were really rather dull. So I gave up parties but in April or May, in a last act of rebellion, I visited a brothel and partook, for the first and only time, of some commercial sex.

I can remember little about the incident now. I was certainly drunk and I was with two or three friends who were in the same condition. My choice of prostitute was based purely on her name which, she told me, was Emily, though everyone called her Millie. I remember no more than that, but Millie and I must have achieved some kind of sexual union because of what happened a few days later. My left testicle developed a rash and became slightly swollen. Within two days it had a red lump on it the size of a large walnut and it was very tender. The following day I discovered I needed to urinate every twenty minutes or so and the process was agony. I had a fever and I couldn't stop sweating. Of course I knew what the problem was but I couldn't face going to a doctor. Until the next day, that is, when the pain became unbearable. The doctor's surgery was only a few hundred yards from where I was staying but the walk there took me twenty minutes.

As he examined my now greatly misshapen genitals the doctor told me I was a stupid bastard. I wanted to tell him to do his job and cut out the sermonising but I didn't. I desperately needed his help and anyway, he was obviously quite right. I would have added another adjective: I was an unlucky stupid bastard. I was also very scared.

What followed was one of the most miserable periods of my life. There were other unhappy times, one in particular, later on, but this one was different in both the type and level of misery. I had to endure three months of anxiety and physical pain; I'm not sure which was worse. Modern medicine can treat most venereal diseases relatively quickly but this was not the case in the late twenties. Penicillin had not yet been invented. The treatment for my condition involved something called neosalvarsan which was better known as the *magic bullet*. I took the stuff for several weeks until it started to give me extra problems all of its own. It began to affect my liver and it gave me skin rashes as well. The doctor told me, with rather too much enjoyment I felt, that it was only a question of luck whether the magic bullet would cure me before its high level of toxicity created even greater problems than the one it was trying to rid me of.

At the time I could imagine no medical condition worse than the one I was suffering from. Even the prospect of liver failure didn't dissuade me from taking my medicine for longer than I should have. And that was when my luck changed, because I survived; I recovered fully.

Some of my classmates did not. I can think of two who did not reappear after the summer break in 1928. One of them was a very gifted student whose absence was particularly noticed. The official story was that he had been given leave of absence for a year to deal with *a personal problem*. I heard of his death eighteen months later.

During this period I was in complete turmoil. For a few weeks at the start of the treatment I really did believe I was going to die. I lost weight. I found it almost impossible to concentrate on anything for more than a few minutes at a time and I began to do all the frantic, hopeless things that people close to death do. I wrote a long confession of my misdeeds. Addressed to my father, it ended in abject apology for all the pain and misery I'd caused him. Luckily I managed to regain some self-composure after I'd reread it and I tore it up and threw it away. But the envelope was ready, I remember, addressed and stamped.

I tried to imbue myself with religious belief. I felt that if I could concentrate hard enough I could make the leap of faith and save my soul, if not my body. But, as I've said, concentration was impossible; my mind was racing and I'd lost my ability to think clearly and sensibly. I went to a few church services but had to leave shortly after or even before the start. Once I ran down the aisle weeping, pushed my way through the first door I came to and found myself in the vestry. The priest was there, halfway through putting on his outfit for the service – I remember lots of white linen and purple silk. His face turned red and I've never been sure if it was because of his sudden confrontation with a weeping man or the fact that I'd surprised him only half-robed. He managed to say, 'My God,' as I ran past him towards the outer door. Which was locked. I then had the choice of going back into the church or leaving by the vestry window which was open. To the horror of the half-naked clergyman I chose the window. I scrambled up onto a desk sending various documents flying, stepped onto the window sill, ducked my head through and jumped. I landed on a grave. I remember sitting on soft turf and looking at a very old gravestone with the unlikely name of John Smith on it. I could see the open vestry window above, with the startled face of the priest peering through. I began to laugh.

There were times when I thought I might go mad; at other times I believed I already was mad.

All of this happened while I was living in poverty in Oxford. I was poor because my neosalvarsan was expensive and I'd spent all of my extra allowance and most of my regular one. For the first time in my life I began to count pennies. There was no problem about my lodging – that had been paid in advance – but I had very little to live on. I became aware of prices. I judged food in terms of the greatest amount for the smallest sum of money. For one week towards the end of this period I survived on one small loaf and half a pound of tea. I also learned how to steal apples from a fruit stall. I only stole two whose total value might have been threepence at most but the thefts told me who I was: I was a thief. Later, when I had money, I went back to the stall and contrived to overpay the fruit seller for some oranges but this merely redressed the economic balance, it didn't absolve me from being a thief. It was about this time – the time when I stole the apples – that I wrote my confessions to my father.

Oxford was empty and I felt lonely and uncared for. There was no one I could borrow money from. Emily was spending the summer in Switzerland. We were still friends although our sexual adventures had begun and ended in Paris the previous year. She wrote to me and her letters helped keep me alive. She was walking in the mountains, she said, and having a wonderful time. The mountain air was exhilarating, the scenery breath-taking, the people friendly and hospitable. She couldn't imagine coming back to stuffy old Oxford. These were bright, entertaining letters and I struggled to reply to them but I did, because I needed her letters to keep coming. By the third or fourth letter she was doing some *proper* mountaineering, with *real* guides. She had never been to a lovelier place. Why didn't I come out and join her, for a couple of weeks at least?

Of course I wanted to but the idea was impossible. Apart from the fact that I wasn't fit enough to undertake the journey, I couldn't present myself to her as the physical and emotional wreck that I was. And anyway, I had no money for food, let alone train tickets. I managed to write back declining her invitation but promising to meet her on her return.

I never saw her again. During one of her mountaineering trips she suffered a fall and broke her leg. She spent a month or so in hospital in Switzerland, fell in love with the young Swiss doctor who treated her and married him a few months later. She never returned to Oxford and never resumed her studies. As far as I know the dissertation she had worked on with such care was abandoned.

I wasn't shocked exactly, nor even deeply hurt; it was more a sense of disappointment. This lay not so much in my own personal loss – I'd already realised that my relationship with Emily would never progress beyond friendship – but in the fact that she had so easily given up all that she had worked so hard at. She'd been determined to make a success of her career, go on to do research and a doctorate. And I've no doubt she could have done it. But then all this drive and energy and enthusiasm was thrown up for the most traditional of reasons – taking on the role of wife and mother. (I think she had four or five brats in all.) I couldn't believe that such a change could have come about so suddenly but it had and I thought the less of her for what she'd done. It was my first exposure to the fact that people can change. And then I found that I was changing as well.

By the end of the summer my health had recovered enough to persuade me that I wasn't going to die after all. Naturally enough this reprieve released in me a great burst of energy. I decided that I would make something of my life. I worked hard for the remainder of my time at Oxford, got an upper second which surprised most people and almost, but not quite, impressed my father, and I decided that I was going to become a writer. And at that time there was only one place for a writer to live. I returned to Paris.

Paris in the twenties and early thirties was a good place for a young man to be. It attracted a strange mixture of people from outside France, mostly English and American. Some came because they believed it was the cultural centre of the world. Perhaps it was, at the time. All were assured of one thing – it was a cheap place to live.

Everyone wanted a new beginning but most were running away from something – wives, mistresses, bad debts, family squabbles. A few found that their problems followed them across the Channel or across the Atlantic. There was quite a lot of pounding on doors at four in the morning. In my first few months I shared an apartment with two Americans who, on at least two occasions, left hurriedly by the fire escape at midnight, leaving me to open the door to people who were full of sorrow or anger. Mostly sorrow, as I remember.

In Paris I didn't know anyone who wasn't painting or writing or dancing or pursuing some artistic dream or other. Most of us, me included, were pretty bad at whatever we did but it didn't really matter, as long as the money held out. And anyway, if the latest novel was proving difficult to write or the play wasn't going well or you couldn't find a gallery to take your paintings, you could always talk about it, endlessly, with all the others who were in the same situation as yourself. And these conversations would take place in any of the hundreds of bars and cafés that Paris provided for the purpose, bright and airy places on the street in summer, smoky, noisy dens in winter. Things became less and less coherent as the night wore on and the wine was poured out in ever greater quantities. Some people got bigger as the party went on and some got smaller. The ones that got bigger didn't usually last long – a few months at most. They ran out of money and friends very quickly. The small people worried away at things and got bitter. They usually stayed so long that they found they couldn't exist anywhere else. There were only a few people of medium size.

It was a place where there was always tomorrow – a brandy or something similar first thing in the morning to settle the stomach, a couple of cups of black coffee to jerk it awake again and a cigarette or two. Maybe then that elusive great line would be conjured up, that particular shape or mix of colours that would fool you, for a while, into thinking that here was some kind of greatness. There were a lot of fools in Paris then.

At the beginning I was a fool too – some would say for longer – but after a couple of months I realised that if I wanted to become a writer I'd better start writing. What I needed was discipline.

From Sunday to Thursday I drank no alcohol at all, other than one glass of wine with dinner. On Fridays and Saturdays I allowed myself a freer rein and occasionally got drunk. But these occasions got rarer as I began to see what too much wine did to my friends, almost all of whom never realised their potential, assuming they had some potential in the first place. Monday to Friday I got up early and wrote for an hour before breakfast and for two hours after. In the afternoons I visited galleries or made notes for possible future use in my writing. I tried to write for an hour or two after dinner but didn't always manage to do it. However, all in all I felt satisfied with myself because within four months I'd completed my first novel. It was two hundred pages long, heavily autobiographical and a truly great piece of literature.

The initial difficulty was not so much getting someone to publish it as getting someone to even read it. Only a small percentage of those American and British Parisians who declared they were writers actually managed to put a book together but, as there were so many aiming for literary greatness, even this small percentage produced a glut on the market. However, I was lucky. The only person, other than myself, ever to read my first attempt at fiction was an English literary agent called Finch.

I was introduced to Finch by a woman called Nancy Kettleby. Nancy was quite wealthy and had lived in Paris for several years. She liked to throw parties to which she invited anyone who declared an interest in the arts. As the catering at her parties was always of the best quality – excellent food and the very best wines – everyone she met had, or instantly developed, an interest in the arts. As I had already finished writing my first novel when I met her I felt that my attendance at one of her soirées was quite legitimate. She clearly felt the same way because she told Finch, when she introduced us, that my novel was quite brilliant and that he just had to read it. It was difficult for me to guess how Nancy had reached this conclusion about my work as she had never read it. I was impressed, however, by the fact that she managed to remember its title, almost correctly. I arranged to meet Finch the following day and fully expected him not to turn up.

But, to my great surprise, he was there. When I handed my novel over to him I said, 'Look, this is my first attempt at this sort of thing and it may not be very good. I need you to be honest with me.' He said he'd see me in a week.

It was a nervous few days for me. I started writing my second novel, tore it up, started again, tore it up again and then decided to break my discipline and take the week off. After all, I had actually managed to write an entire book. Very few people could say that and even fewer in Paris where many brilliant novels were talked about which hadn't quite been written yet.

I met Finch in a café at ten o'clock on a Tuesday morning. The day was bright, colourful and quiet. The waiters were still clearing up from the night before when the café had been visited by a group of Dadaists who had started a fight and smashed up some of the furniture. A couple of tables had been wrecked. They lay on their backs with their broken legs pointing to the sky. Half a dozen wooden chairs of the folding variety were now ripped open flat, unfolded as they were never intended to be. The waiters, sweeping up some broken glass, shook their heads and muttered. When one of them brought our coffee he was indignant and apologetic at the same time. 'L'art? Pouf!' And so it was all dismissed.

Finch was a small man with slicked-back hair and bright eyes. He was very well dressed in a dark grey suit and white shirt. This put me off a bit because I had cultivated the bohemian look which was pretty much whatever you wanted it to be. My tweed jacket was old and beginning to fray at the cuffs. I could easily have afforded a new one but I wanted to look a little down at heel – but not too much – and I was determined to wait and buy a new jacket from the advance I would receive for my novel. This advance would be in the region of a couple of hundred pounds and was only a week or two away at the most. Finch was the man to arrange the details.

He ordered a café noir which he gulped down in one as if it were a shot of whisky. He ordered another. 'Look,' he said, 'I'll be honest with you.' He leaned forward and looked at the table top as he spoke, focusing on the centre of a coffee ring where he tapped out each point with the tip of his index finger. 'Your novel isn't much good. I've read worse and, as first novels go, it's reasonable, I suppose, but I can tell you now that no one's going to publish it. You'd be wasting your time to try. That's not to say that it's all bad. There's one or two scenes, maybe, that work fairly well and the whole thing does have a kind of unity – it's got a beginning, a middle and an end – but it's too long...'

'But it's only two hundred pages,' I said.

Finch didn't look up. 'It's still too long,' he went on. 'It's overwritten – too much language, too many adjectives, the sentences are too long. You've got a habit of starting sentences with "And".' He shook his head. 'And it's pretty dull, really.'

'Dull? Dull?' I said.

'Dull,' he repeated. 'It's all about you, isn't it?'

I nodded.

'First novels generally are autobiographical,' he said, 'and they rarely work. I always want to ask these people why they think they're so interesting. Anyway...' He broke off and picked up his second café noir which he sipped this time.

I was in a state of shock. My coffee lay cold and untouched before me. But Finch had more to tell me.

'You've got to have something to say,' he said. 'And you've got to be able to say it. In this book you've got very little to say and you haven't learnt yet how to say it.' He stood up. He took my typescript from his briefcase and put it on the table before me. 'My advice to you,' he said, 'is to give up any idea of being a novelist. But, if you're determined to write, then don't do it for a while. Read,' he said. 'Read lots of stuff, meet people and do a few things. Then try again. Oh, and by the way, if you do write something else, I promise I'll read it. I will.' He paused. 'If you ever want to speak to me again, that is.' Still standing, he finished his coffee and then left.

There was only one possible response to what Finch had told

me: to get very very drunk indeed. I probably started drinking straight away but I can't remember any of the detail. What I do remember is waking the next day, about thirty-six hours after Finch left me. I was in my room. The place stank because I'd been sick during the night. The sheets were sodden with vomit. My clothes were a mess. I had the typescript of my novel still, but not my wallet. I had the biggest headache in the world. It took me two days to recover, to clean up myself, my room and my head.

Finch's comments made me bitter. But I reread my book and saw that he was right. It was awful. It was predictable, it was full of clichés, it was dull. It really was dull. And Finch was right about its length. It was too long. It was two hundred pages too long. I took it out and dumped it in the first dustbin I could find.

From then on, for a while – for a long while – I became like the rest. I who was special, different, a bit above it all. I gave up the discipline I'd stuck to when I was writing. Now that I knew I wasn't a writer, what was the point? I began to go to parties and I stayed till late. I got up at noon with a hangover, had a bath, got some coffee down me and started again. It was during this time that I decided I was a flâneur and said so to anyone who would listen. I met lots of people, some of whom became quite famous later on. I had long, earnest, very important, inebriated conversations with all of them. When I had money I was popular and when the money began to run out I found myself alone.

I looked round me at what was happening in Paris. Everything was new and exciting and there was such a lot going on but I felt it was all show; there was no substance to it. And the people at first were bright and interesting and colourful but a lot of them were also greedy, selfish and spiteful. And I was becoming like that too, especially as I began to run out of money. I was still receiving money from my father but I had no independent income. I was now living well beyond my means and the little money I'd saved up in my more careful days was long gone. I fell behind with my rent and, early one morning, I got back to my apartment to find all my belongings – my clothes, my books and a few small paintings – piled up in a heap on the landing. The lock on the front door had been changed. I was annoyed but not particularly surprised. It was clearly time for me to leave Paris.

That morning I went to visit Nancy Kettleby. To my further

shame I managed to squeeze a loan out of her which covered my fare back to England. Of course this loan was never repaid. I said goodbye to Paris with little regret. To me it was mainly associated with disappointment. However, when I sat down in my compartment on the train bound for Calais, I felt very alone.

Within a couple of days I was back in Swordale. This was mainly because I had nowhere else to go. I had an idea that I might effect some kind of reconciliation with my father. It was a loathsome prospect but I desperately needed money. All the way up there on the train I asked myself if I really was such an unprincipled shit that I would crawl back to my father in the hope that he would give me a few quid. By the time I stepped off the ferry at Ardroy, the answer was pretty clear.

But things were not good at the castle. My father was very ill. He'd had a minor stroke, followed by a more serious one and was confined to bed. He was being looked after by nurses. His condition was such that he was barely able to recognize me. His speech was affected and, for the first few days, before he managed to recover a little, there was no possibility of coherent conversation. He was old and frail and rather pathetic and I almost felt sorry for him. Almost, but not quite.

Swordale was as cold, rain-battered and wind-blasted as I remembered it from my childhood. The floorboards creaked where they had always creaked and one of the windows, whose pane I had cracked with a ball when I was seven, still hadn't been reglazed. My father had let the place run down. It was Maurice, later, who launched into a programme of repairs and redecoration that effectively saved the place from falling to pieces.

But Maurice wasn't there. He sent a telegram saying that plans had changed and he was unable to return. This was not like Maurice at all. He'd been as devoted to his father as his father had been to him. Only something extraordinary would have persuaded him not to visit the old man now so seriously ill. But it didn't take me long to realise what this was.

Maurice's new wife, Hester, had arrived a week before I did. Their honeymoon over, Maurice had sent her on ahead to Swordale.

Hester was neither prim nor dull. She was very young – only

twenty-three – and I found her physically attractive but not beautiful. At that time I believed that beauty resulted from close attention to hairstyle and artificial make-up. I was drawn to women who painted their faces and made them into something that, in reality, they were not. Hester wore her hair loose or in a loose ponytail and put nothing on her face. In Paris women with freckles applied tubsfull of cream to hide them but Hester was without such camouflage. Her look was natural, easy and innocent. But perhaps she knew all along that this is what suited her best, that the sprinkling of freckles over her nose and her high cheekbones gave her a special look that powder and cream could not enhance. She was bright and organised and would take the castle staff and the rest of the islanders by surprise because she was very efficient and seemed to think of everything. She even took it upon herself to get some of the rooms in the castle redecorated to make the place more cheerful for my ailing father.

When we met she was wearing a red dress which was in contrast with the general feeling of doom that filled Swordale. And she was far from sombre. 'I've been looking forward to meeting you,' she said as we shook hands, and I believed her. She rarely said anything without meaning it, even the formulaic utterances that accompany such situations. Of course I had no experience on which to judge the sincerity, or otherwise, of her remark but her tone and her smile convinced me. I began to think, even then, that my brother was a fortunate man to have found someone like this.

A little later, as we took tea in one of the sitting rooms that overlooked the sea, she asked me what it was, exactly, that I did.

'I'm a flâneur,' I said.

'Is that so?' she replied. 'It sounds a bit devilish to me.'

I said, 'I am the man my mother warned me about,' and she laughed.

But I found out quickly that she was far from happy. A few days after I arrived at Swordale, she received a telegram from Maurice: 'Further delays; unable return yet; love M.' Six words and his name. He was being mean, not with money but with words. Hester wrote him a long letter every day; she got six words and his name, his initial, in return. I didn't understand what was going on. I was there when she received the telegram. She read it, passed it over to me and just shook her head. To my astonishment she said, 'Sometimes I wonder if I'll ever see him again.'

I could see that she wasn't joking. She decided to talk to me then. I could say she chose me because she felt I might have a sympathetic ear but I think her choice was based on nothing other than the fact that I was there and nobody else was. I expected her to cry but she didn't. She was confused rather than bitter. She told me about their honeymoon in Italy. She'd loved the sea voyage and the islands and she thought that Maurice had felt the same way, though towards the end of the cruise he had seemed restless. There had been an unfortunate incident. One of the other passengers, a man called Foster, had become ill. He and his wife had had to leave the ship immediately. This event had upset the smooth functioning of the little society that had so quickly evolved in the first few days of the cruise. She and Maurice had got to know the Fosters quite well and their sudden departure seemed to unsettle him. The remainder of the cruise had been less enjoyable. He had been preoccupied almost to the point of being morose.

When they got back to England he'd sent her on ahead to Swordale, saying that he had to report to Woolwich. This would only detain him a couple of days and he would join her as soon as he could. He still had quite a lot of leave due so they could spend some time exploring Glass. That was a fortnight ago and now she received word from him only of more delay, always more delay.

From then on he sent her a telegram almost every week but each had fewer words in it than the previous one. She felt that he was gradually ridding himself of her. She didn't understand why but this was the conclusion she'd reached. She'd written to him and sent telegrams about his father but he made no mention of him when he sent a telegram in return. She had been sure that he would come back as his father was so ill and she was amazed when he did not. I told her I was surprised myself; more than surprised, I was shocked. Maurice loved his father.

She struggled to understand it but she couldn't. Something must have happened to Maurice, something extraordinary.

It was all very curious. I suggested to Hester that I should leave right away, go down to London and find him. I said I would try to persuade him to come back up to Swordale and at least discuss with her what was bothering him. But she said no. I insisted that it was very easy; I could go down and drag him back myself; he could be at Swordale in three or four days. But she said no. Now, of course, I regret not being more insistent, or even making the decision myself, without consulting Hester. If I'd gone down to London and collared him and forced him to accept that he had to do something, then things would undoubtedly have been different and we wouldn't have landed in the mess that I was principally responsible for. Hester was responsible to a certain extent, but it was mostly me.

The winter of 1931–32 was a mild one with very little rain. I showed Hester the island. We went for walks in the hills and we went to the remoter spots by pony and trap. On fine days we arranged picnics. We crossed to the mainland and from there we took a boat to some of the other islands. As I introduced her to the beauties of the area I was rediscovering them for myself and I began to feel that perhaps I didn't really want to live somewhere else after all; I wanted to be up here. And I wanted to be up here with someone like Hester.

Rationality plays little part in these processes – I knew this even as I tried to persuade myself not to be attracted to Hester. I told myself over and over again that she was already married and not only that, she was married to my brother. And of course my logic made perfect sense. But sense had little to do with the feelings I began to have for her, especially when it became clear that she was beginning to have the same feelings for me.

For I began to understand why Maurice was staying away from the castle. He wasn't avoiding his father, nor was he avoiding me – he didn't even know that I was there. No, he was avoiding Hester. This revelation astonished me. But it was Hester who explained it to me. Maurice was a good man, she assured me. Yes, he was a good man, but he was...how could she explain it...he was rather cold. There was no spark between them, she said. Oh, he was young and handsome and she was aware enough of herself to know that she was quite pretty but...there was nothing. There was nothing between them. They were strangers and would remain strangers. Maurice hadn't said as much but then, he didn't need to.

I knew then that my presence at Swordale, the increasing friendship between Hester and myself, would only make things worse. It was absolutely clear to me that I had to go.

I decided to leave; she said yes, yes, that was the best idea and then she persuaded me to stay. I said perhaps a week more and then extended it to two. Hester's moods began to vary from joyful and exhilarated to depressed and sullen. She would order me to leave and then interrupt my packing to demand that I stay.

Looking back now, from a point decades later, my easy cynicism can call it another cliché-ridden time. I was the happiest I'd ever been and the most miserable; I was walking on air, rarely have my feet felt so leaden; I felt myself to be noble and strong and then nothing but a weak little shit. And all along I knew that I would survive this and that Maurice – even if he found out – would survive, but Hester probably wouldn't. And yet I carried on. Oh yes, I was no longer in control of my feelings, I was overtaken by something that was bigger than myself – I think I even managed to feed myself this kind of bullshit.

I have tried to persuade myself that as we lay together in the big bed with the orange velvet headboard in one of the guest bedrooms on the fourth floor Maurice walked in and found us. In fact it didn't quite happen like that. On January the sixth, 1932, about three months after I'd arrived at Swordale, my father died of a heart attack. Maurice arrived from London a day or a couple of days later.

This was not the Maurice I remembered. He had aged more than the years since our last meeting. He looked preoccupied and worried. But he wasn't a fool. He could see straight away that there was something greatly amiss at Swordale and I told him what it was. I told him that I'd had an affair with his wife. I didn't consult Hester about this, I just told him and in so doing added another example to my growing list of stupidities.

He went very quiet, I remember, and I was annoyed with him for using a tactic that was mine. He went quiet and it became my task to fill the silence which I did by offering to shoot myself or some such rubbish, or maybe suggesting that he should shoot me. Inanities poured from me and I began to shake. Maurice moved to a window and looked out over the sea. And when I'd run out of things to say or run out of breath he said to me, without turning from the window, 'Maybe you should leave.'

These were among the last words he ever spoke to me although letters, mostly formal, official letters, did pass between us at times thereafter.

However, I couldn't leave before my father's funeral.

It would be hypocritical of me to say that I felt any lasting sadness at his death.

Although he had supported me for several years, he had made no secret of his intense dislike for me. His duty as a father – to love, or at least protect his offspring – had always conflicted with the morality he derived from his religious upbringing which told him to spurn waste and idleness and those who indulged in both. So I had presented him with a clear problem of choice. It was lucky for me that he decided he was a father first and, although love never really featured in our relationship, protection did. He kept sending me money while he was alive and he made some provision for me in his will. The tacit agreement which shaped our relationship in his later years was that we should actually meet as infrequently as possible. This arrangement was fine by me. Before my arrival at Swordale in October, 1931, I hadn't seen him for five or six years.

I found it odd that duty prevailed with me as well. I had loathed my father – the word is not too strong – and, far from being grateful for the money he sent me, I enjoyed the fact that it hurt him to send it, for every time he did so he was reminded of the wasted life he had helped to produce. I despised him for his views and I despised his money even as I spent it.

At the funeral there were the usual boring platitudes from the Reverend Newarke and lots of tears, some of which might well have been genuine but by and large it was a dismal, boring affair. The only bit of light relief – if such an expression is appropriate – was during the long, slow procession from the castle down to the cemetery. Alexander McRone, the gamekeeper, who was one of the few people who got on well with my father, offered to walk in front of the hearse carrying the old boy's regimental sword and helmet. He looked quite odd, McRone, in a black suit and bowler hat when all I'd ever seen him wearing was a tweed jacket and plus fours.

Anyway, there he was, walking ahead of us all when, by the time we were half way to the cemetery it was obvious we were in for some nasty weather. The sky got darker and darker and the wind rose. Sudden storms on the island are fairly common. They creep up on you, are very violent for five or ten minutes and then just dissipate. Blue skies again. While this one lasted McRone got completely soaked and his bowler hat ended up in a field a few hundred yards away.

I remember feeling sorry for the poor man. I made sure he got a lift back to the castle in one of the Daimlers. And I persuaded Mo to give him something of father's, since the two of them had been close. A hunting knife was chosen. Mo was against it, of course – he was against almost everything at that time and I suppose I can't blame him. He agreed eventually but I had to go over and see McRone later myself to hand over the knife. Mo couldn't do it.

I can't be sure if the excellent turnout at my father's interment was because he was well known and well loved or because everyone knew there would be some largesse with the catering facilities afterwards. Like most events in this part of the world, a funeral is an excuse for a good drink.

The tables in the main reception room on the ground floor of the castle were laid out with scones, oatcakes, tea, sherry and whisky. I've rarely seen so many ghoulish, black-coated people. A few, remembering who I was, came up to me and said what a great loss my father's death brought upon the community. I noted among them men who had stolen timber from his woodland, poached salmon from his river and shot stags from the hill land on the estate. Hypocrites all of them. As my father himself had been the biggest hypocrite of the lot, I said nothing. But I could see who recognised me and wished me well – there might have been one or two – and those who wished me ill – all of the rest. And all of them scared as hell that Maurice would now rearrange everything. I begrudged them their whisky and scones. I saw one of the estate workers slipping a couple of scones into his coat pocket, the little shit, and I smiled at him. He nodded and moved on. I don't know what it was but Swordale always brought out the worst in me. I found I was formulating a plan to get him sacked from the estate. In fact I didn't carry it through. I think

Maurice got rid of him later anyway, when his light fingers strayed beyond scones.

Hester managed the whole business of the funeral magnificently. She made most of the arrangements and dealt with the stream of visitors and bearers of condolence in admirable fashion. Maurice didn't seem to have the patience himself. As for me, apart from saying hello to a few people at the graveside, I shut myself away and let it be known that I was locked in private grief. Anyone who understood the nature of the relationship I had with my father would have known this to be complete nonsense, but I didn't care. I would be leaving Swordale within hours so I was indifferent to what anyone might think about me. I knew they didn't give a damn about me and I certainly didn't give a damn about them.

So I packed and left for London. I didn't even see Hester before I left. I just packed and ran. On the ferry I stayed below and didn't venture on deck until we landed at Craigton. I didn't want to see the castle as we passed beneath it. I fancied that Hester would be there on the battlements, waving a handkerchief at me just prior to jumping to her death. Even then I could make these bitter jokes.

In London I stayed with an old friend from Oxford. Peter Marshallsea and I had never been close but I was certainly glad that I'd been able to make contact with him because I was still penniless. Throughout my life I have had the luck to find a helping hand each time I needed one. Peter had some rooms near Victoria and said I could stay there with him as long as I liked. He was surprised to find that I was about to start looking for a job. 'Thought you were a writer, old boy,' he said. I told him how things hadn't quite worked out as I'd planned. I told him that my first novel hadn't been much good. 'Oh, you don't want to worry about that,' he said, getting rid of the whole business with a wave of his hand. 'Just stick at it, it's pretty simple stuff, they tell me.'

Peter was one of those people for whom everything is easy. It was simply a matter of putting a bit of effort into something and it always worked out. Still depressed by what Finch had said to me, I was sceptical but I had to admit that Peter's attitude was refreshing and I began to think that maybe I would write again after all.

'Look,' he said to me, 'I've got a pal who's in publishing – in a small way, admittedly – but I think you should meet him. I'll fix it up, OK?'

And so a few days later I met Boyd Bankwell. Boyd was a big awkward man who was prone to knock into things. This made him very apologetic. He seemed to be forever saying he was sorry for something or other and not just when he knocked over a cup of tea in your lap – which he did to me at least twice. It seemed to pervade his entire manner, his speech and the way he constantly ducked his head when he talked. When he expressed an opinion he generally began with the words, 'Sorry, yes,' or, 'Sorry, no.' As he was a publisher, I came to wonder if he ever managed to turn anyone down. I soon found that there was quite a deal of guile behind his apparently open demeanour.

So, simply because it was Peter who introduced me, Boyd invited me to contribute to a journal of his called *Pen and Ink*. He had produced three issues so far which had sold about two hundred and twenty copies each. Consequently *Pen and Ink* was deemed to be a great success and Boyd Bankwell now had the opportunity to upset cups of tea and even glasses of champagne over some quite illustrious people. It wasn't until a year or two later that I found out that the words 'pen and ink' are Cockney rhyming slang for 'stink'. I was never very sure if Boyd knew this and I couldn't bring myself to discuss it with him. He was a sensitive man and I felt it might upset him. But I think he knew all along. He liked to be controversial and the title of the magazine, with its veiled suggestion of sabotage, fitted well with his literary designs.

Whether I had any such designs didn't seem to matter. I found out later that Peter had told Boyd that I was a writer who'd lived in Paris and was a close friend of Gertrude Stein – I think I mentioned to Peter that I'd once seen her walking in the Tuileries Gardens. He also said that I was very shy about my writing, which I took very seriously. I was very studious and would produce for him whatever he wanted. I was working on a novel right now which, even incomplete, was the talk of Paris. Any contribution I would make to *Pen and Ink* would be a massive boost to the magazine.

It's just as well that I didn't know any of this until after Peter had introduced us as I would have run a mile from Boyd Bankwell had I known. The man he actually met believed himself to be a failed writer who might just be able to put together a printable piece under the right conditions. Boyd didn't know how low my self-esteem was at that point. He told me later that he'd taken my relative silence for quiet reserve. In fact I was in rather a depressed state. The situation was helped, however, by the cup of tea that landed in my lap, urged on by a wayward swipe of Boyd's elbow. I think that after that event, for which he was effusively apologetic, he would have accepted from me just about any collection of words I managed to put together. As it was I had a fortnight to come up with a short story of three thousand words.

I wrote a story called *Light Rain* which was about the loss of a ship at sea, based on a news report in *The Times*. The bits of the actual event that I didn't like I discarded and there were other aspects that I made up. That's what writers do, I told myself, they make things up. But I kept all the names and used them, the real names of the people involved and the name of the ship. I decided that my version of events was better than what had actually happened; my version was, in a way, more truthful. That's how I justified it, anyway. I saw no inconsistency here with my general rule about honesty. Honesty was for individual people, for direct, spoken communication. This rule was suspended when it came to writing. Artistic truth, I decided, had a higher value than actual truth, though I never quite got round to defining either term. I became convinced that Finch was right: reality was dull, dull, dull. I resolved never again to write anything based on personal experience; I promised I would never write my autobiography.

Boyd liked *Light Rain* and it was published in the fourth issue of *Pen and Ink* in the summer of 1932.

Three days later, this letter appeared in *The Times*, under the heading: "Is Nothing Sacred?"

> *Dear Sir,*
> *I feel I must use your columns to express my outrage at a piece which recently appeared in what is – I am told – a well thought of literary journal called* Pen and Ink. *In issue number four of this magazine there is a story entitled* Light Rain *which is based on the loss of the ship* Marigold *two years ago, a sad event which was, I remember, well documented in* The Times.

The perpetrator of this fiction, one Christopher Redburn, a writer reputedly well known in Parisian literary circles, has seen fit to distort hugely the facts of the Marigold's *loss while blatantly retaining the name of the ship and the names of those unfortunately involved in the wreck. He suggests that mistakes were made in the handling of the rescue bid and that delays occurred which point to the culpability of the relevant authorities. This is clearly at odds with the account in* The Times *which completely vindicated all concerned.*

May I take this opportunity to reprove the editor of Pen and Ink *for his inclusion of this piece in what is, otherwise, an above average publication. Perhaps Mr Redburn would be so good as to respond by informing your readers why he took this extraordinary step.*

Yours etc,

H. Briardale.

When I saw this, I was shocked. It was clear to me that my literary life had come and gone with the publication of this little story. Who would want to publish me in future? Certainly not Boyd Bankwell, whose magazine, I was sure, I had just killed off. There was the prospect of litigation, too. What if some of the people I'd named decided to take me to court for defamation of character? I reread the story carefully, to reassure myself about its allegations. In fact I couldn't find any references at all to the culpability or otherwise of any named authorities. I decided that H. Briardale, whoever he was, had himself misinterpreted what I'd written. That evening I showed the letter to Peter.

And discovered that he had written it.

'What?' I said. 'What?' And again, 'What?'

'Marketing, Chris old boy,' he said. 'Good bit of scandal do the whole thing a power of good. But don't tell Boyd.'

'But it's...it's not even accurate,' I said, pointing to the letter.

'Oh, that doesn't matter. Better, if anything. Easier for you to refute in your reply.'

'My reply?' I said.

'That's right. You've got to write a reply, and it's got to be a long one. Make it into a kind of essay, if you like.'

'And what am I supposed to say?'

'Doesn't really matter. What's important is the tone. I think maybe start off with shock that someone's calling into question the principles of your art. Then maybe some kind of exploration of artistic truth versus facts and figures – something like that – and it's got to be sincere but not condescending. And wind up – oh, I don't know – with a statement, let's see...a statement that's forthright but not aggressive, of your aims as a writer and that you intend to stick by them.'

'I'm not even sure what my aims as a writer are,' I said.

'Doesn't matter,' Peter said. 'Make some up.'

Two days later my reply appeared in *The Times.* I'd written twelve hundred words and the letter was quoted in full. I can't recall what it was that I actually wrote – the words themselves, that is – but I followed Peter's advice and made sure I got the tone right. I was hurt that anyone should question my artistic motives, I was sincere and genuine about my art, I had principles (which I listed) and was steadfast and unswerving in my commitment to what I believed to be right.

Over the next ten days *The Times* received thirty-five letters on the subject, from which they selected half a dozen or so to print – in full – before calling a halt to the whole business. Only one of the six chosen was unfavourable towards me. Ten of the thirty-five letters had actually been written by Peter, using various pen names. As a result of all this, *Pen and Ink* lost twenty-five of its original subscribers and gained one thousand, four hundred and sixty. Issue four went into a second, third and fourth printing, selling nearly four thousand copies in all. Boyd Bankwell had paid me ten pounds for *Light Rain.* He offered me fifty pounds for another story for issue five. I received approaches from two newspapers and six other journals for pieces of my work. I wasn't sure quite where, but it seemed that I had arrived.

And so began my literary life. But I had no illusions about my talent. There's a type of boxer who is known as a journeyman. He's the kind of man who can turn up at short notice to fill in for a boxer who gets sick or gets injured in training and has to pull out of a fight at the last minute. Journeymen are competent boxers who've been around for a while but haven't fulfilled their early promise. They put up a reasonable show but aren't expected to win very often. Once they've been classed as journeymen it's difficult for them to be taken seriously as championship contenders although one or two have managed it.

I decided that maybe I was a journeyman writer. Over the next few months, following the publication of *Light Rain*, I developed the skill of producing words to order. I could never quite manage the hectic schedule of a reporter but a column commissioned a week or so before publication was a possibility. When asked for a thousand or fifteen hundred words on this or that subject I could generally do it. And if, when I delivered my typescript, the commissioner of the work said that he needed two thousand words after all, or maybe it should be cut down to eight hundred, I could do that too. I would take the typescript away and return a couple of hours later with another one. I never made a fuss about this and always did a competent job. As well as short stories I produced articles, introductions to other works, commentaries and reviews. The subjects I covered in my first year or so included Tibetan prayer wheels, the future of aviation, the demise – or was it the rise? – of the French novel, the deteriorating quality of the water in the Thames, the price of tea, and so on. As more and more journals were happy to take my work, so I was able to charge higher and higher fees for my services.

And so, in a limited way, I became successful. And the key to this success was simple: reliability. Editors knew that I would produce what they wanted when they wanted it. I was earning a reasonable living and I began to enjoy life. The idea of writing a great novel, or even any novel at all, gradually slipped away.

During the first year or so in London I received letters from Swordale and I tore them up without reading them, believing that re-establishing contact with Hester would be worse in the long run. In one of the letters, I suppose, she must have told me she was pregnant.

It was nearly two years later that I found out what had actually happened. I received a letter from a solicitor in Craigton. It was some official form to do with custody of a child. When, reluctantly, I got in contact with the man, I discovered that Hester had given birth to a boy, now called James, and that she had died while giving birth to him.

At this point even I found life hard to bear. The cynic in me died then, I believe, and one or two other things as well. I could not convince myself that I hadn't killed Hester. And this was basically because I had killed her. I had wanted her and I had got her. I had used her, then thrown her away. I had wrecked Maurice's life and completely destroyed Hester's. I had contrived to bring into the world another poor wretch who had no mother and a complete shit for a father. And I had a letter which required me to agree to a few lies.

After what I'd done, what did a few lies matter?

So I agreed to what Maurice asked. Which was basically that I gave over to him all my rights to the child and would make no attempt to advise the child of his true parentage. That pretty much wrapped it up, I suppose, though I did extract one condition which was that the child, James, had to be told who his father was at my death, or Maurice's, whichever was the earlier. I remember that a number of letters flew between us on that point but Maurice agreed eventually and communications between us ceased.

But I did get one more letter from the solicitor who, this time, was acting on behalf of my father. To my astonishment I learned that the old boy had remembered me in his will. He left me two things. The first was a small cottage that he owned on Glass but about fifteen miles away from Swordale. There was a stipulation here too – I don't think I was ever given anything after this time that didn't come with a condition or a set of conditions attached. This was that I should never stay at Swordale again – not even visit it, in fact. So, if I wanted to live on Glass, I could stay in this cottage.

The second thing that my father left me in his will was a glass case containing a stuffed wolf.

One evening in 1949, when I was walking home to my flat in Pimlico, I was knocked down by a car and nearly killed. My wife, who was walking with me, was killed. And so I record the death of this woman before even mentioning our meeting, our marriage, her name. But there's not much to tell. Well, there's lots, of course, but not to *tell*. There was nothing that was out of the ordinary, nothing that didn't happen to millions of others. Links given in detail teach us little and entertain even less. I met

Maureen at the beginning of the War, we found each other's company not unpleasant and decided to set up some kind of home together. We even agreed to marry, mainly because it made things simpler. I never really loved her but I missed her when she was gone.

Following the accident I was in hospital for three months. I decided to spend a few more months convalescing in Italy. Even by 1950 Italy had managed to rebuild itself, more or less, after the upheavals of the War. I spent a very pleasant time in the South, not far from Naples which is perhaps the most squalid and certainly the most beautiful city I've ever visited.

When I got back to London I discovered I had no interest in my work any more. Also, the newspapers and journals that I had contributed to so regularly over the years had managed to get by without me quite well. Many were reluctant to commission any more work from me. Some of my oldest friends in the business were very surprised to see me again. One or two of them thought I was dead.

I'd always had a very pragmatic approach to what I did; I knew what it was, what it wasn't and what it could never be. I churned out words. The words had to be more or less related to the subject and they had to be in some way pleasing. If they were intelligent or witty or thought-provoking, then so much the better; if, on a good day, they were all three together, then this was a bonus. But the most important thing about these words was that there had to be the right number of them. If an editor wanted a thousand words, then he got a thousand, not nine hundred or eleven hundred but a thousand. And the second most important thing was that these words should be delivered on time. This was not great literature I was composing, it was copy; it was a thousand words on the State Opening of Parliament by three o'clock. (The State Opening of Parliament didn't officially end till after three o'clock so there was no point in actually going there to witness it. The King's Speech was available in advance, the events followed the traditional sequence, so it was quite easy to report the whole thing before it happened.)

But despite all this I suppose I was like every other hack in that I believed that what I wrote was just that little bit better than the attempts of everyone else. Even cynics have to derive their self-esteem from somewhere. But now I wasn't even allowed this. The sudden indifference of many of the people I'd worked for forced me to accept that my entire output of the previous eighteen years or so was of no value whatever. During that time I'd produced hundreds of thousands of words and all that effort was a total waste. None of those words remained. Their life span was usually a day, maybe two or three at the most. So, within twenty-four hours of the publication of my last piece, my life's work was forgotten.

Towards the end of 1950 I decided to do two things, both of which scared the hell out of me: I would leave London and I would try to write something of value.

Leaving London scared me because there was only one place I could go to and that was the cottage on the Isle of Glass. My rediscovered literary ambitions scared me for two reasons. First, I might fail – I remembered Finch in Paris; I remembered the very rubbish bin into which I'd dumped my first typescript – and second, I would certainly become poor, or rather, poorer, whether I succeeded or failed.

But I packed up my things anyway, and set off north. There are two ferry routes to Glass and I took the one from Clach Liath, which sets you down on the north-east of the island. I didn't go near Craigton. I stuck to my promise. I never went to the south of the island; I never visited Swordale.

But I was back on Glass, at the age of forty-three, renewing my acquaintance with the island, albeit a part of it I hadn't known very well before. I moved into the cottage and I said hello to the wolf in the glass case. I set him up on a table in the study and I decided to call him Charlie.

James must have been about eighteen when I got back to Glass. I kept my promise and didn't try to get in touch with him. I'd had no contact with the family for about fifteen years. I considered changing my name but realised that this would be pointless. Word was bound to get back to Swordale that someone had moved into the cottage and that person could only be me, whether I was called Redburn or Smith.

So I was Christopher Redburn, I was living on Glass and I was miserable. I had nothing to do. In fact I had everything to do but didn't know where to start. In the past, in my hack days, I'd been disciplined by deadlines and numbers of words on specific subjects. Sometimes that had been difficult but it was so much easier than what I now faced. In front of me was a blank sheet of paper and the instruction to write something, on any subject, and have it finished sometime within the next year or so.

What I had to do was get back to the discipline that I'd had in Paris when writing my first novel and hope that the outcome would be better. But it was hard, much harder than that first time when my production was fuelled by the naive belief that I was a great novelist. Now I had knowledge and with it came fear of failure. Within the first three or four weeks of beginning my new life I had written the opening chapters of half a dozen novels and torn up all of them. Panic began to set in, followed by despair. It was about this time that one of Charlie's legs dropped off.

Poor old Charlie. He was looking distinctly old and worn-out, especially when he had only three legs. I decided to have him repaired and I took him to a taxidermist called Prospect, who lived in Edinburgh.

Prospect got very excited indeed when he saw Charlie. After all, Charlie was pretty old. There was a small plaque inside the glass case which said, *The last wolf killed in Scotland by Sir Ewan Cameron, 1680.* This would make Charlie two hundred and seventy years old and if he was the last wolf to be killed in Scotland, then he should be in a museum somewhere, not in a private house waiting for his other legs to drop off. Prospect said that he knew of no taxidermy that had survived from the seventeenth century and he was keen to investigate. I left Charlie with him and decided to begin some research of my own.

I discovered that if Charlie was indeed two hundred and seventy years old, then he wasn't the last wolf to be killed in Scotland. There were several contenders for this unfortunate title but the most likely was a wolf that was killed in the Findhorn area by a man called MacQueen in 1743.

1743.

It was this date, more than anything else, that prompted the idea which became the subject of the novel that I actually managed to complete about eight months later.

The last wolf in Scotland was killed two years before the

Jacobite rising of Charles Edward Stuart and three years before the battle of Culloden when that rebellion was finally quelled. Culloden marked the end of an era in Scotland; things changed radically thereafter. So there was my subject: endings and beginnings; the deaths of wolves and great causes; old worlds and new worlds mixed in with some serious romantic twaddle.

Of course I made a few historical changes, though nothing too dramatic. I decided that MacQueen would kill the last wolf in 1745, just before setting off to join Bonnie Prince Charlie's army. He presented the wolf pelt to the prince as a token of his loyalty. As a result he became the prince's right hand man and personal bodyguard. He saved the prince's life on at least two occasions but fell from favour when he expressed the opinion that the army should push on past Derby. Others advised caution and it was their advice that was heeded with the result that the initiative passed from the Scottish force to that of the English. Chased all the way back up to Inverness, the army was routed at Culloden. MacQueen was badly wounded while protecting his prince but lived long enough to be carried from the battlefield and transported back to his home in Findhorn. In his last few hours he came to realise not only that a whole way of life in Scotland was about to end but also that his destruction of the last Scottish wolf was a symbol of that passing. He asked to be buried at the spot on the hillside where he had killed the last wolf. He also asked that two pibrochs be played at his graveside, one for himself, the other for the wolf.

As far as the language was concerned, I cheated a bit there too. If I'd written the dialogue in the language of the time there would have been bits in Broad Scots, bits in Gaelic and even some in French. Looking for some sort of compromise, I read Sir Walter Scott, thinking that the dialogue in his novels, published from 1814 onwards, might help me towards some kind of authenticity. But I realised that if I adopted that policy I would be writing for a Scottish audience only and a very small one at that. So I wrote the whole thing in contemporary English, with a few Scots words thrown in for flavouring.

The result was not the great literary work I'd intended to write, but I had no problem finding a publisher for it. *The Last Wolf* came out in 1952 and received enthusiastic reviews in the more popular press and scant notice elsewhere. It began to sell modestly but steadily. My publisher was almost pleased.

Whatever its literary merit I had actually worked quite hard on the book and a few days after it came out I decided to take a break. I went back to Italy for a month and forgot all about wolves and Bonnie Prince Charlie and the battle of Culloden.

When I returned to Glass there were two telegrams waiting for me. One of these, two weeks old, asked me to contact my publisher. This one was marked *URGENT*. The second, only a week old, was also from my publisher. This one had *VERY URGENT* written on it. I gave it a couple of days and then I rang him. What he told me persuaded me to leave for Edinburgh straight away. I took the next ferry back to the mainland.

While I'd been in Italy the first printing of the book – one thousand copies – had sold out. A second printing had begun, of a further thousand copies, but interest had risen so dramatically that this had been increased to two thousand and then five thousand.

Several newspapers had contacted the publisher to get interviews with me and an arts programme on radio wanted to do a feature about the book. Suddenly, it seemed, I was a celebrity.

What I wanted was a quiet life. If *The Last Wolf* was successful, then fine, its success would buy me the time to write another book. I told my publisher that I wasn't really interested in a round of interviews and self-advertisements. It was the only occasion on which he raised his voice to me.

'Now look,' he said. 'This is a business we're in here, and the business is to sell books. Right now we're selling lots of them and if we help the process along we'll sell lots more. We can't afford to ignore this, we're going to milk it dry and, like it or not, you're part of the process. You're involved and you're not backing out now. Do I make myself clear?'

'Perfectly,' I said.

Well, I suppose it wasn't so bad having your ego stroked by lots of admirers. I stayed in Edinburgh for a couple of weeks and spoke to editors, journalists and radio interviewers. I was charming and witty and I said all the right things. I was serious when it was clear I was expected to be serious and light-hearted when that was more appropriate. I even managed to be controversial – though only very slightly – just to show that I did have views and opinions of my own.

For example, in a radio interview, a rather earnest young man called Mumford questioned the veracity of some of the historical detail in the book. 'Some of it,' he said, 'just isn't true.'

'What exactly do you mean by that?' I asked, feigning innocence.

'Well,' he said, 'take the date of the death of the last wolf...'

'Yes?' I said.

'Well, it was killed in 1743, wasn't it? Not 1745, as you say.'

Unfortunately this was presented as a query rather than as a statement of fact, so I knew I was on solid ground no matter what I said. Within reason, of course. 'I presume,' I began, 'that your source for the 1743 date is James Harting's book, *British Animals Extinct Within Historic Times*.'

'That's right,' he said, but I knew he was lying. He didn't know what I was talking about.

'Published in 1880,' I added. He looked blank. 'The problem with Harting,' I went on confidently, 'is similar – but in a very minor sense, of course – to that of the calculation of the date of Christ's birth using the gospels as some sort of guide.'

At this point he put on his serious look. 'In what way, exactly?' he asked.

'All written long after the fact,' I said. 'I mean, the last wolf died about a hundred years before Harting was born. He knew the date was around 1743 but he doesn't quote his sources. It might have been 1743 or 44 or 45 or 42.'

'But he says 1743,' Mumford insisted.

'Yes,' I said, 'you're quite right, of course. However, he offers no more evidence for 1743 than I can for 1745.'

'Does that give you the right to change the date, then?'

'But what am I changing it from?' I asked. I let him flounder a little bit on this one, then I stepped in and saved him. 'What I mean is, why do you believe Harting's date is more accurate than mine? If it's just because he lived closer to the date, whatever it was, than I do, then I think you're on dangerous ground.'

'But you're saying then that your date is arbitrary, aren't you?'

'No more arbitrary than his,' I offered.

There was a pause. I sensed that we would move away from

dates and onto some other, more general point.

'So what is the novelist's duty, then?' Mumford asked.

'Oh, to tell the truth, of course,' I replied immediately.

'Even if it means inventing a personal bodyguard for Prince Charlie who never existed historically?'

'Well,' I said, 'I think you're confusing the many types of truth that there are.'

'I thought there was only one,' he responded, far too quickly.

I shook my head sagely – not something that the listeners could witness, of course, but it gave me pleasure. 'No,' I said. 'There's literal truth – dates, names, times, places, numbers, all the so-called facts that some historians love to gather. They prove very little. Other truths are more important…'

'Such as?'

'Well,' I went on, 'how people react to things, what happens in certain situations, the spirit of the age, the mood, the tone of a place and a time, what people feel in their hearts and in their…' – I was about to say 'guts' but this was deemed a rude word on radio at the time – '…in their innermost being…'

'And these things…Are you saying that these things are more important than the facts, is that it?'

'Oh immeasurably so,' I said. 'Immeasurably so.' And, in the pause that followed I winked at him and added, 'Trust me, I'm a novelist.'

Two days later, *The Last Wolf* went into its third printing.

Before going back to Glass I went to see Mr Prospect the taxidermist. He was a disappointed man. Close examination of Charlie revealed him to be much younger than two hundred and seventy years. He was fifty years old at most. However, Prospect had got a friend of his, who specialised in antiques, to take a look at the glass case that Charlie was housed in. The case, it appeared, certainly did date from the late seventeenth century; Prospect's friend could even identify the cabinet maker, a man called Cameron, whose speciality was display cases for stuffed animals and birds.

So who, or rather what, was Charlie? He was definitely a wolf but not a Scottish one. I began to realise that it must have been my father, that noble being, who had arranged for the original wolf to be 'renewed'. Or maybe there was some other story altogether; it didn't really matter. What was clear was that Charlie had been shot perhaps in northern Europe, or had maybe died in a zoo somewhere; he had certainly never seen a Scottish hillside. Not during life, anyway.

And now he was part Alsatian.

Prospect explained that it was the best he could do. The leg that had dropped off was too far gone to be repaired and the likelihood of his getting hold of the leg of a genuine wolf was very slim indeed. So he'd got in touch with a friend at a dogs' home somewhere in the Borders who had supplied him with the left front leg of an Alsatian that had recently been put down. The leg was about half an inch too short and the wrong colour, but these were minor problems and easily fixed. He showed me the result.

Charlie was very much his old self. The snarl was still there and he looked none too friendly but definitely four-legged. And the new leg was fine; there was nothing to show that it was anything other than his own. I congratulated Prospect on his achievement and told him that of course I would have the little plaque removed that asserted Charlie's origin as this was clearly mistaken. I arranged for Charlie to be transported, carefully, back to Glass. But then, when he was on top of his table in the study again I thought I would leave the plaque intact. It looked very good there and it was built in to the structure of the case. There was no sense, really, in spoiling it. So I let it stay.

When I got back from Edinburgh there were lots of letters waiting for me. One of them was from James Redburn who, I had to remind myself, was my nephew, not my son. He asked if he could meet me.

I still had the letter which defined the agreement between Maurice and myself about my relationship with James. I reread it and found that although it was quite clear in forbidding me from initiating contact with James, it contained no provision for the eventuality of James contacting me. So I had to think carefully about what to do. Of course I wanted to meet him, but I didn't necessarily want to *claim* him. Although I despised Maurice in many ways, it was Maurice who had brought James up; I had contributed nothing to his welfare. I decided to write to Maurice first. In my letter I explained that it might be more difficult, in the long run, to dismiss James's attempts to meet me, his uncle, as this would almost certainly make him more curious about what had happened to create the apparent rift in the family. I didn't care what explanation Maurice might give for not liking me – as long as he told me, so that I could go along with the story – but I felt the best plan was for me to write back to James and agree to meet him. I reconfirmed that I would not visit Swordale myself and I would not tell James that I was in fact his father. The terms of the original agreement still stood.

A week later I got a short note from Maurice in which he agreed with what I suggested. A week after that, I met James for the first time.

'So you're my long lost uncle,' he said as he walked in the door, and I said, 'Yes.' And so the relationship began with this first piece of dishonesty and I knew there would have to be more. I wasn't skilled in this and for a few moments I thought of telling him the truth. To hell with it, I thought, he's a man now and he has a right to know. But I'd made a promise and though I had respect for neither the promise itself nor the one promised, I realised that the truth, at this stage, would create more problems than it might solve. 'Yes,' I repeated, 'your long lost uncle.'

I'd expected him to look like me, but he didn't. He was slim, not very tall, and had swept-back fair hair which was already showing signs of receding. He had a vigour and energy that I admired and when he got started he talked with enthusiasm about what he'd been doing for the past few months. He was fresh and interesting and interested and our meeting was a complete success with no awkwardness at all on his part and very little on mine. But I caught myself thinking, now and then, that physically he really did not resemble me at all. He looked like Maurice. He looked very like Maurice. I wondered then if there hadn't been some mistake after all, or something hidden from me for all these years, and that he really was Maurice's son. But this was not possible. Chronology dictated otherwise.

He talked about Greenland. He'd travelled there with the geographical society of his university and he'd fallen in love with white landscapes. He told me that he wanted to go to the Antarctic; he wanted to go to the South Pole; he wanted to be an explorer like Scott and Amundsen. 'Not too like Scott,' I said.

'Oh no,' he said. 'I intend to come back.'

Then he asked me about Maurice, about me and Maurice and again I nearly told him the whole story. I realised that I liked him and I nearly told him everything. But I didn't.

'What's the matter between you and my father?' he asked.

'What has he told you?' I asked.

'Nothing.'

'Nothing?'

'Nothing at all. He says it's between you and him and it doesn't concern me. I've asked him several times but he won't budge.'

'Well,' I said, 'I'm sorry but I can't really tell you, if he won't. I mean, I think I should respect his wishes, don't you?' And then I surprised myself by adding, 'He's your father, after all.'

He thought about this for a few moments and then he said, 'But you don't even talk to one another, do you?'

'No,' I said, 'we don't.'

'But you're brothers, aren't you?'

'Oh yes,' I said, 'no doubt about that. But we've always been very different. I mean, it's not the whole explanation, by any means, but my father, your grandfather, he didn't like me much. I was unreliable, you see, not steady, I was pretty aimless. Maurice was the dependable one – you know, in the Army and all that – and I was off in Paris, being a black sheep. You see, there's lots of things you don't know,' I said, 'and some you should know and some that are best left unknown.'

'I can't agree with that,' he said. 'I can't agree with that at all.'

Of course he was right. It was a foolish thing for me to say.

He left soon after that. I introduced him to Charlie of course, before he went, and I gave him a copy of *The Last Wolf*. It amused me to think that I would never visit Swordale again but at least there would be something of me there. I thought of it as giving Swordale a piece of my mind and I found it gratifying, in a very smug sort of way.

Overall, I was disappointed, not in James but in myself. I seemed to have no passion left. This was my son, whom I'd never seen before, yet I was calm and responsible throughout our first meeting. It was as if I had taken on Maurice's persona – dull, dependable Maurice, Maurice who was sure to do the right thing and not rock the boat. Maybe I was becoming a better person as I got older. Maybe I was beginning to believe my own lies.

There's nothing left. Oh, there's a dozen or so books now and there's Charlie in his glass case still, looking good for another hundred years. But the books are pretty bad. They tell me they're good but they're lying to me. In a year or two no one will read them. And James? Something went wrong with James. Since I first met him some twenty-five, twenty-six years ago, something has contrived to destroy his early enthusiasm for life. He's back on Glass now after a long time away and he's come to see me a couple of times. I've asked him to tell me what makes him so unhappy but he won't say. Maybe he has also realised that there's nothing left. If so, then he arrived at this conclusion sooner than I did. And he shows it in a different way. He's turned into a drunk. He has ceased to care about himself and the more this condition persists the less I care too, about him, about me, about anything, really.

I applaud Charlie, who is the only winner, Charlie who is three parts wolf and one part Alsatian and who never was the last Scottish wolf, neither last nor Scottish. It is Charlie who is proof of the deceitful nature of the strange beings who first killed him and then contrived to ensure his survival.

Alan

Ella visited me once, to tell me she wanted a divorce. I don't know why she bothered to come, really. She didn't have to. Her solicitor was quite clear, she said, that everything was in her favour and the divorce would go through without difficulty. Maybe she came just to rub it in – I'd behaved badly and no one was on my side. I was alone was what she was saying to me, though not in so many words. I was alone and after the divorce I would be even more alone.

There was a screen between us. It reminded me of the chain-link fence I'd put up at Ardkaig with Frank. It was to keep the deer off McEwan's arable acres. He was trying for corn and they all said Ardkaig was too high. No grain above three hundred feet on Glass was what they told him. But he gave it a go anyway and, though the yield wasn't great, he got his crop, without any interference from deer.

I asked her about Frank. There wasn't any emotion involved in the question, it was just a casual enquiry for information. No emotion attached to Frank and none, even, to Ella herself. Well, no, that's not quite true. I'd been inside for three months and had three to go. I hadn't seen her since the trial. I felt nervous when they called me and told me who my visitor was. But I had no feeling, one way or the other, when I saw her. Nothing left, nothing at all. She was pale, a little thinner perhaps. Her hair was longer and had a reddish tint. She wasn't angry, just seemed indifferent, or perhaps I'm confusing my mood with hers.

So I asked about Frank and she said they were still together. Not on Glass, she said. They'd left the island and were living in Craigton. I asked if they planned to get married and she said yes, probably. She didn't seem entirely confident about that. She said they were going to emigrate. Canada or New Zealand. They hadn't decided yet. When I wished her well I was almost being sincere. She'd treated me badly but I'd treated her badly too, no question. I'd no reason to hate her so I wished her well. This meant that, indirectly, I was wishing the same to Frank and that was definitely going too far. I hated the bastard and still do. But for Ella I felt nothing, so I might as well wish her the best for the future. Which I did, and she left.

It was only later I realised that she hadn't asked me about Jessie. But then it was still possible that she didn't know about her.

The Major visited me twice, once in my first month and the second time half way through my sentence, shortly after Ella visited me, in fact. I got the feeling he was desperate to help me and I wasn't really sure why. In the police station in Craigton he'd told me that he felt he had a debt to my father. He also said something about sympathising with my situation, so what did that mean? He took pity on me? Unlikely. He's a good man, the Major, but not given to displays of emotion. Not pity, not from a military man. No, it was almost as if he felt guilty himself in some way, for what had happened. He was apologetic when he told me I couldn't go back to my old job at Swordale. I told him that after what I'd done I'd never expected to go back. If I became keeper at Swordale again the good folk of Ardroy would quickly make their feelings known to him. He said he didn't give a damn what people felt. He was thinking of me, of what I would face, not him. And I believed him, too. He wasn't just making an excuse to fire me.

The second time he came to see me he said he'd got me a job if I wanted it. Ardruie Estate, a hundred miles north, on the mainland. The estate had belonged to Lord Matchwell but he'd sold up a few years ago. The new owner had done a good job of renovating the castle but didn't know much about managing an estate which included a few thousand acres of hill land full of deer and grouse. There was a lot of potential, he said. So they needed someone and was I interested? Well, of course, I said yes. Why wouldn't I? How many men coming out of jail walk straight into a job?

He said the new owner's name was McMurtry. He was Canadian. I asked if Mr McMurtry was aware that his new employee was currently in jail. Did he know what I was in jail for? The Major said he'd told him everything or close to everything. He'd been keen to point out, he said, that I was more sinned against than sinning. That was the expression he used, more sinned against than sinning. So I told him there were things he didn't know about, that I'd done my fair share of sinning too. But he waved this away. 'Who hasn't?' he said. 'Who hasn't? Don't tell me anything more about it.'

He told me that when I got out I should go straight to Craigton. I wasn't keen on the idea but he insisted. He pointed out that I'd have to go to Craigton anyway, to get to Ardruie, so the decision was made for me. He gave me the address of an accountant called MacRae. 'Go and see MacRae,' he said. 'I've made some arrangements, get you started. Don't forget.'

I didn't get a visit from Jessie. This didn't surprise me. Things between us were strained to say the least on the last occasion I saw her. That was when I stayed with her in her tiny flat in Craigton for the two days between tying up Frank on the pier and walking into Craigton Police Station to give myself up. It was clear she didn't want me there and I don't blame her for that. If the police had found out about her involvement she might have been in trouble. But even before that time I knew that our relationship, such as it was, was close to ending.

I'd met her only a couple of months before when I'd gone over to Craigton one time to collect the leather shotgun case I'd ordered from Crerand the Gunsmith. I was just leaving Crerand's when I saw this woman going in to Miss Comlyn's next door. I saw her only for two or three seconds but this sudden sight of her – maybe it was her red hair – stopped me from thinking of anything else but her.

Miss Comlyn sold wool and cotton and everything for knitting and sewing. I turned and pretended to be interested in the displays of yarns in the window. I thought I'd just wait till this woman came out of the shop and I'd say hello to her. But she didn't come out. After a couple of minutes I looked inside and saw that she was actually behind the counter. So she was Miss Comlyn's new assistant, that was it. As it turned out, she was the last one as the old lady died suddenly a few weeks later. Anyway, there was nothing to do but go inside and buy some wool.

Maybe I could make an attempt at an excuse by saying I was overtaken by sudden desire, by momentary passion, that I didn't know what I was doing. But while the first part of that statement is true, the last isn't. I knew exactly what I was doing because I'd done this sort of thing before.

When I was inside the shop I mentioned a special type of yarn I wanted to buy for my mother. Miss Comlyn congratulated me on my good taste. That particular yarn was of very high quality. I said it was my mother's birthday soon and I wanted to get her something special. In fact, I'd read the name on one of the yarns in the window and guessed from the price that it was one of the better ones. Miss Comlyn took some samples from a drawer and placed them on the counter. Was there a particular colour my mother favoured? I said I wasn't sure and I asked her if she had any other colours. She said she'd go into the back store room to check. So I was left alone in the shop with the woman with the red hair who told me her name was Jessie.

Happily, it took Miss Comlyn three or four minutes to find the yarn and by the time she returned I'd arranged to meet Jessie the following Saturday. So I walked back to the harbour feeling very pleased with myself. As I waited for the ferry to arrive I took the yarn that I'd bought, that Miss Comlyn herself had gift-wrapped so neatly for me, and stuffed it into a litter bin.

Before Jessie there was Anna and Caroline and a blonde German tourist called Greta who conveniently was only in Craigton for three weeks. Ironically, in all these affairs it was the Major who helped me out most. The fact that he didn't like travelling to the mainland meant that he frequently sent me over to Craigton on various errands. I picked up deliveries of equipment for the castle or made arrangements on his behalf which he felt were best dealt with in person rather than over the phone. Often I was able to anticipate his needs or even manufacture them and I would offer to make extra trips over to Craigton in my own time. For I had one rule: no affairs on Glass. There had to be eight miles of water, sometimes very rough water, between these women and Ella. And Ella never suspected a thing.

During my time in jail then, I had one visit from Ella and two from the Major. There was one other visitor, just one, and his arrival surprised me, shocked me in fact. It was Christopher Redburn.

I'd met him for the very first time about ten days before the episode with Frank on the pier. I was over in Strongarve and went into West's shop on the corner to get some milk when this man of about seventy came in, slim, quite dapper, in a dark brown tweed suit and neatly knotted dark blue tie. He had a full head of grey hair and a moustache which was black with flecks of white. I'd seen him before, of course, and I knew who he was but I'd never spoken to him. I spoke to him now but only after he addressed me first.

'Is that your Land Rover out there?' he asked.

I said it was.

'So, do you work at Swordale?'

I confirmed that I did. He introduced himself then and when I gave him my name he said, 'McRone? Are you…let me think… are you related to Alexander McRone?'

I told him I was his son and he said, 'Really? Really? Well, I knew your father. A good man.' Then he said there was something he'd like me to do for him, only if I wanted to, of course, and he invited me to come back with him to his cottage.

I gave him a lift in the Land Rover. It wasn't far. His cottage was only a little bigger than mine and Ella's. When we went into the living room, he pointed to the far corner and said, 'There. Meet Charlie.'

It was a bit dark in the cottage – the windows weren't very big – so it wasn't till he switched on the light that I saw clearly what he was talking about. On top of a heavy sideboard there was a glass case with a stuffed wolf inside.

'Fine specimen, eh?' he said. 'Bit of a fright when you see him for the first time. What do you think?'

I said I'd never seen a wolf before so it was a shock to see one now, even one that was dead and stuffed.

'Oh, Charlie's harmless,' he said to me. 'Hasn't bitten me for weeks.'

It was the kind of remark the Major would never have made. No sense of humour, the Major. Doesn't know what a joke is. And here was his brother, so very different. Straight away I began to like him.

He said he knew that James was doing a lot of work getting the castle ready to open to the public. He knew about the Polar Room with its Antarctic Exhibition and so on. He thought that maybe the last wolf to be shot in Scotland – which Charlie was reputed to be – would be an asset, worthy of a room all to himself, perhaps. So he asked me if I'd be prepared to take Charlie with me, back to the castle. Charlie had originally been there, in fact, but had been left to him by his father.

'Quite odd, don't you think?' he said. 'My father left me a cottage with a wolf inside. Do you think there's a message there?'

I said I had no idea.

'Well, neither do I,' he said, 'and I've had a lot longer to think about it than you.'

He seemed very happy to talk. Maybe he didn't have many people to talk to. He spoke about his father again and then about my father. He said, 'I think they got on well together. But then my father seemed to get on better with people he wasn't related to. Often the case with families, don't you think?' Throughout our conversation he asked questions in this way and I'm sure it wasn't just politeness. He seemed to be genuinely interested in hearing my opinion.

I told him I wasn't sure. I said that I'd got on very well with my father, which was true.

'Well, lucky you,' he said. 'Lucky you.'

He asked me if I knew the part my father had played in his father's funeral and I said, yes, I'd heard a little bit about it.

'Of course it was a long time ago,' he said. 'Nineteen thirty-two, a long time ago. How old would your father have been then?'

I reckoned about twenty-four.

'Twenty-four,' he repeated. Then he went off into a kind of dream for a few seconds, a bit like his brother does occasionally. He said, 'I was only a year older than that myself.'

Then he told me the story. I'd heard it before, of course, from my father, but I was interested in finding out if Christopher Redburn's version was any different. Things are forgotten and things change. He told me my father was given the job of carrying the General's regimental sword and helmet in front of the hearse. There was a whole line of cars, black Daimlers, he remembered, behind the hearse as well as a hundred or so mourners on foot. And, at the front of the entire procession, my father, walking slowly and carrying the sword and helmet. It's about two miles from the castle to the cemetery outside Ardroy and they were about half way when it began to rain. It was just a light shower at first but within a few minutes it was raining really heavily, with a high wind, too. This was a sudden isolated squall coming in from the Sound. It lasted about five minutes before the wind calmed and the sun came out. By that time everyone who was walking was soaked and my father, so Christopher Redburn informed me, had lost his hat. He was wearing a dark suit and a bowler hat and the first gust of wind had blown the hat from his head. But he walked on as if nothing had happened. He held on tight to the sword and the helmet and, when they reached the cemetery, he placed them on top of the coffin for the short ceremony at the graveside.

'I was quite dry,' he went on, 'because I'd been in one of the limousines, but your father was soaked through. As he stood there I saw that he was shivering. So when the ceremony was over I made sure he got a lift home in one of the cars. He didn't want to go, of course – not his place and all that nonsense – but I insisted. Didn't want the poor man dying of pneumonia.

'So there,' he said, ending his story, 'is that what your father told you?'

I said that my father's version was pretty much the same. Then I asked him if he knew that the Major had given my father a hunting knife that had belonged to the General, as a thank you for what he'd done.

He smiled. 'It wasn't exactly like that,' he said.

I asked him what he meant.

'I was the one who gave your father the knife,' he said. 'Maurice took a bit of persuading – family heirloom and all that – but I managed it. I remember quite distinctly visiting your father the evening of the funeral to give him the knife. The next day I left Glass forever. Well, so I thought.'

Back to Paris? I suggested.

'No, no,' he said. 'I gave up on Paris, or Paris gave up on me. I went back to London.'

I told him that the official line, which I'd picked up over the years, was that he was based in Paris at that time.

He shook his head. 'I'd been in Paris,' he said, 'but in spite of all the difficulties that London poses, I far prefer it. Never was particularly good at French,' he added. 'Bit of a tricky problem if you want to live in Paris permanently. Anyway...'

He seemed keen to change the subject. He asked me to tell him about what was happening at the castle. There seemed to be little harm in this so I told him as much as I knew. There was the renovation work on the castle itself which was only just starting. The roof needed fixing, and the tower – there was a crack down one side. Part of the lawn by the main gate was to be made into a car park and one of the rooms on the second floor would be turned into a café. And all the pictures in the castle were being sent away for restoration.

'Really?' He seemed very interested in this. 'All of them?' he asked.

I told him that was what I'd heard. He wanted to know the name of the company that was going to do the restoring. I said I didn't know but I could find out for him.

'Well, that would be very helpful,' he said, adding, 'but please ensure that your enquiries are discreet.'

I told him I'd do my best.

I couldn't take Charlie with me then because he wouldn't fit in the Land Rover so I said I'd come back a few days later with the Ford truck. I would bring lots of blankets so we could wrap up the display case and make sure it survived the trip from Strongarve to Swordale.

When I returned two or three days later I had a long wait at the front door of the cottage. I'd brought along McEwan's son, Peter, from the farm to give me a hand. I rang the bell twice and had already decided to leave when I heard someone shuffling towards the door. It opened very slowly and there was Christopher Redburn. He was leaning heavily on the door post and looked quite disheveled. He wasn't wearing a tie and had spilt something on the front of his cardigan. It was one of those heavy knitted ones with leather buttons. It was light green with a darker wet area by the pocket on the left. When he began to speak I realised he was very drunk. His first words to me were, 'Who the hell are you?'

There was an edge of aggression to his tone which I didn't like but when I reminded him who I was and why I was there he softened considerably and invited me in. I told Peter to go and wait in the truck. Christopher Redburn staggered ahead of me into the living room and dumped himself into a chair. It really was like that, as if he'd picked up his body and thrown it so that it landed, not very accurately, in his armchair.

'Not so sure about Charlie now,' he said. 'Might keep'm to myself. What do you think, eh?'

I said it was entirely up to him.

'Well, of course it is,' he said. 'Of course it is. Look, just sit down, will you, eh?' He waved me towards a chair. 'Got to...got to apologise. Not entirely sober, you see. No, I'm far from being sober, actually. Got some bad news...'

I said I was sorry to hear that.

He shook his head. At that moment he looked completely miserable. Then he actually chuckled. 'I'm not very well,' he said. 'Or, to put it more accurately, they're telling me that either I'm not very well or...or I'm *really* not very well.' He shook his head again. 'Do you know what that means?' he asked.

I said I didn't.

'Well, neither do I, and as far as I can make out neither do they. Seems I'm to have more tests and then, when they've got the results of those tests they'll decide whether or not I need to have even more tests. So I said to them, "How many bloody tests do I need?" and...well, let's just say they were non-committal. Would you like a drink?'

I said I was driving so I'd better not.

'Not even just a little one?' He picked up a bottle of whisky from a side table by his armchair and showed it to me. 'Tremendously fine stuff,' he said. 'You know, I haven't touched a drop for...oh, I don't know...twenty or twenty-five years, something like that, so it's pretty much flattened me. Probably feel absolutely vile in the morning. Are you sure?' He held out the bottle again.

Once more I said no.

He poured himself another drink, though it was a small one, and he didn't drink it straight away. He put the bottle and the glass back on the table. 'Maurice, you know,' he went on, 'completely tee-total. Gave it up after his wife died. Gave it up and walked back to the castle. So he told me anyway. No, must have been someone else. Anyway...all the way from London. Hell of a walk, that, don't you think?'

I agreed that it was a long way.

'Well now,' he said and he rested his forehead on the heel of his right hand, his elbow on the arm of his armchair, 'let me think about this.' His eyes closed and nothing was said for some time. I thought he'd fallen asleep and maybe he had for a few moments. But then he shook him himself awake and said, 'Have you got the information I asked you to get for me?'

I said I had. I took a folded sheet of paper from my pocket and handed it to him. He unfolded it and read out what I'd written – company name, address and telephone number.

'And they've got all the pictures, you say?' he asked.

I said that of course I couldn't be sure but that I'd overheard the Major saying something like, Well, we might as well get the lot done.

'Well, that's very helpful,' he said, 'very helpful. Thank you.' He put the sheet of paper on the side table next to the bottle of whisky.

Then he seemed to slip off to sleep again. It was all a bit difficult. I gave him about half a minute and then I coughed loudly. It was enough to rouse him. I asked him what he wanted me to do about Charlie.

'Well, you've come here to take him back to Swordale, haven't you?' he said. He'd clearly forgotten his earlier doubts about Charlie's fate.

I went out to get Peter. It was a bit of a struggle getting the display case wrapped up and onto the back of the truck. I went back into the cottage to say goodbye to Christopher Redburn but he was asleep in his armchair and he was beginning to snore.

So yes, when he came to visit me in jail several months later, it was a big surprise. Especially as he started with an apology. 'When we last met,' he said, 'I was very drunk. My memory of the occasion is a little hazy but yours will be crystal clear, no doubt.'

He was very neat and tidy again, wearing a suit and tie. Though he was perhaps a little thinner than before, he looked well.

He apologised again for his behaviour.

I reminded him that he'd found out only that day that he was ill, so it was understandable.

'Understandable but not excusable,' he said.

Then I asked him how he was. Considering that he looked so well, I assumed he'd made a complete recovery.

'I'm afraid not, no,' he said. 'Three months ago, they gave me six months to live. So I've got three months left. Of course, it's all guesswork really. These estimates aren't always accurate. Who knows, I might stick it out for another four or five months.' He smiled. 'Then again, I could drop dead tomorrow.'

I said I was sorry.

'Oh, don't be,' he said. 'I've had a good life – well, good in bits. There's a few things I regret but not too many. Oh, by the way,' he added, 'those people who say they've got no regrets…well, they're either callous beyond belief or they're lying. I mean, we all make mistakes, we all mess things up occasionally, don't we? But I don't think we should be too harsh on ourselves. What do you think?'

I said that considering he'd had to come to visit me in prison it was clear I'd done more than my share of messing things up.

'Oh, you'll be OK,' he said. 'I've got no doubt about that.'

I thanked him for his confidence in me and then I told him how the Major had fixed me up with a job. He thought about this for a few moments then said, 'Good man, my brother, in some ways.'

I didn't respond to this because I felt he was going to carry on talking, which he did. 'We've had our differences,' he said, 'which you probably know about. We don't talk to each other. Oh, there's good reasons for this, I suppose. But then, after forty odd years maybe we could try to be friends again. But it's not going to happen, I'm sure of that. He's got a long memory, my brother, and he holds grudges. But then I did do something rather nasty to him. Yes, it was mainly my fault. Of course, there's always two sides to a story. He's not entirely blameless but it was me, mainly, definitely me that was in the wrong…'

I pointed out that only a few moments before he was saying we shouldn't be too harsh on ourselves.

He smiled. 'You're a careful listener,' he said. 'And maybe we shouldn't judge ourselves too harshly but we always do, don't we? We have to live with the consequences of our actions and, in my case now, die with them.'

Then he burst out laughing. 'God, that sounded so melodramatic, didn't it. The last thing I want to do now is get maudlin and sentimental. Anyway…'

I suggested that, considering how ill he was, maybe he could come to some sort of reconciliation with his brother. Wasn't that possible?

'He doesn't know I'm ill,' he said. 'In fact, you're the only person who does know. Well, apart from my doctor, of course. And I'd like to keep it that way. You see, if you hadn't turned up on the very morning I got the letter, you wouldn't know either. It's all because I decided to get drunk and spill the beans. Feeling very sorry for myself, I was. Understandable, I suppose, up to a point.'

I suggested it was both understandable and excusable and he smiled. I promised I wouldn't tell anyone.

Then he went on to explain the main purpose of his visit. Again, he was apologetic. 'I'm not here to enquire about your health,' he said, 'or tell you about the degeneration of mine. No, you see, I'd like you to do something for me.'

I nodded and said I'd do my best, whatever it was, but it would have to wait, obviously, until my circumstances changed.

'Oh, that's not a problem,' he said. 'You're out in a couple of months?'

I said it was ten weeks.

'Fine, no matter. Well, look,' he said, 'this may sound a bit odd but what I'd like you to do is deliver a couple of letters for me. One is to James Redburn and the other is to Alice Redburn. Now, I'd like them to be handed directly to James and to Alice, not given to someone else to pass on. Oh, I know it all sounds a bit cloak and dagger and all that but I don't want them to fall into the wrong hands. Do you see what I mean? So I can't send them by post, obviously, and I can't deliver them myself because...well, I've promised never to go back to Swordale – I don't particularly want to anyway. So...so I just need a little help here. I suppose I could leave them with a solicitor...' He shrugged. 'Never liked them much, as a breed. Anyway, do you think you could do this for me?'

I said yes, I'd do it.

'You're an honest man,' he said.

I smiled and reminded him of where we were.

'Well, you're not in here for dishonesty, are you?' he said.

I shrugged. I said it depended on his definition of dishonesty.

He stood up. 'I've left the letters in a package with the people at reception. They said they'd put them with the stuff you collect when you leave. Oh, I nearly forgot. There's one other thing,' he said. 'The ideal time to deliver the letters would be just before my funeral.' He smiled. 'Of course circumstances – yours or mine or both – might jeopardise that. But whatever you do, don't deliver them till after I'm dead.'

I reached Craigton at about three o'clock in the afternoon of the day I was released. MacRae's office was easy to find. When I told him who I was he said, 'Ah yes, yes, Major Redburn gave me some instructions.' Then he handed me an envelope which I didn't open till later when I was on the train north. There was no letter, no message of any kind. Just a cheque for five hundred pounds.

Then I opened the other package, the one left for me by Christopher Redburn. It was a large manila envelope with *Alan McRone Esq* written very neatly on the front. Inside there were three smaller envelopes, not two. There was one for Alice Redburn and one for James Redburn. The third was addressed to me and I opened it straight away. Quite a shock, really. Again, there was no letter inside, no message of any kind. Just a cheque for five hundred pounds.

PART THREE

Capri: 1931

Foster was already halfway through his first bottle of Orvieto Classico when Captain Maurice Redburn and Hester, his wife of ten days, entered the Ristorante dei Amici. They had been the last to leave the ship – Foster and his wife Margaret had been on the first launch – and so were the last to arrive at the restaurant. Everyone was already seated and despite the fact that the Fosters had perhaps the best table in the restaurant – on the covered terrace at the side, with the curve of the island before them, its olive groves and the blue sky above – no one had joined them.

Maurice and Hester looked round but all the other tables were fully occupied. And it was difficult for them now to ignore Foster's loud voice calling to them, 'Over here, old boy! Redburn, old man, over here!' Maurice glanced briefly at his wife. 'Keep smiling,' he said. They made their way over to join the Fosters.

At the start of the cruise it had been recognised that Maurice and Hester were on honeymoon and therefore they might wish to spend most of their time together with no other company than each other. But by the time the *Berengonia* had passed through the Straits of Gibraltar and into the Mediterranean, this tacit accommodation had changed and thereafter they were expected to join in with everyone else in the ship's social activities. It was as if the first three or four days were deemed enough time for a newly-wed couple to get to know each other – in any and every sense of this expression – and then they had to be just like everyone else. They had had their short period of being special; now they had to buckle to and get down to the serious business of enjoying the party. And joining in the communal fun also meant accepting the communal responsibilities. One of these was to take their turn in putting up with the Fosters.

Foster himself – they never found out his first name and he insisted on being addressed as Foss – was in his late forties and seemed to be on leave from a fairly senior civil service post which he never discussed with anyone, tapping his nose and whispering 'Hush! Hush!' whenever the subject of his work was mentioned. The opinion generally held by his fellow passengers was that his leave might well be extended indefinitely as his main activity appeared to be getting drunk. He started with cocktails before lunch, drank the best part of a bottle of wine during lunch and a couple of liqueurs after it. In the afternoon he usually dozed in a deck chair on the sun deck, waking up at about five to make his way back to his stateroom via the bar where he drank a double malt whisky. A shower before dinner freshened him up but also seemed to re-invigorate his thirst which was satisfied only by greater quantities of alcohol than he had consumed earlier in the day.

The men on the ship were divided in their opinion of him. Most did not like him, not because he drank too much but because he couldn't hold his liquor – at the end of the evening he usually had to be helped back to his stateroom. There were a few, however, who rather admired him because, although he was close to fifty, balding and physically in poor shape, he had a young wife who was very attractive, if rather aloof. So they tolerated him, they laughed at his jokes, some of which they genuinely had not heard before, and they accepted the drinks that he bought them, for he was a generous man, particularly when tipsy, and this made up for a lot of his failings.

All the women disliked him. For them there was not just the fact that he drank too much, it was his conduct on the sun deck that disturbed them. In the afternoon, during his doze which could last for anything up to two hours, he snored loudly. Even worse, he snored with his mouth open.

'Have a splash of this,' Foster said as the Redburns sat down at the two vacant places on what was rather a small table. 'Bloody good stuff.' Foster poured wine into their glasses.

'Not for me,' Hester said, but her glass was already full.

'Nonsense, nonsense,' Foster went on. 'You'll love it, love it.' He filled Maurice's glass by which time the bottle was close to being empty. He dumped the last of the wine into his own glass and then held up the empty bottle. 'Garçon! Garçon!' he shouted as he looked round the crowded dining-room. Then he said 'Oh no, no. It's Italy now, isn't it. So what's garçon in Italian, then, eh?'

'Cameriere,' his wife said.

'Is it?'

'You know very well it is,' she said sullenly. 'Do stop making out that you don't know. You can speak Italian perfectly well.'

Throughout this time – the arrival of Maurice and Hester and the ordering of a second bottle of wine – Margaret Foster was a rather forbidding presence, seated with her arms folded and just the hint of a pout on her mouth. When Maurice took his place opposite her she had offered him only the briefest of smiles.

It was her thick red hair, drawn back into a loose bun that attracted her male fellow passengers and proved an object of envy for the women. However, at the start of the cruise the general feeling towards her was one of pity. She appeared to have been saddled with an older man whose main interaction with her was to embarrass and abuse her in public. But after a few days this view hardened. She did not join in with the others even when the opportunity presented itself in the afternoons when her husband parked himself on the sun deck and made it clear he was not to be disturbed. Her manner towards the other travellers was cool and, on occasion, frosty, in contrast to her husband who tried, as hard as his drinking regime would allow, to get along with everyone.

'Well, here we are,' Foster said. 'Splendid place, eh? The most romantic island on earth. What do you say, Redburn?'

'It seems very nice,' Maurice said.

'Nice? Nice? Oh, come along, old man. That's like saying the Taj Mahal is rather pretty.'

'Well, it's rather difficult to say yet. We've only been here twenty minutes.'

'You mean this is your first visit?' Margaret Foster asked and her tone suggested that those who had not been to Capri before were from some other, lesser species.

'That's right,' Hester replied. She was smiling. She gave no hint that she had caught the tone of the question.

Foster said, 'Well, well. The little woman and I come here every year, don't we, darling?'

Margaret Foster nodded.

'In fact,' he went on, 'last year we jumped ship here – all arranged of course – and stayed until the next cruise came along. Had an absolutely wonderful time. Ah, here we are.'

A waiter had arrived with another bottle of Orvieto. He

proceeded to pour. Hester put her hand over her glass. She had not even touched what Foster had originally poured out for her.

'Not having any, my dear? It's wonderful stuff, you know. Wonderful.'

'No thanks,' Hester said. And then, to Margaret Foster, 'How long will we be here?'

'At least till we finish the bottle,' Foster put in and laughed.

His wife ignored this. 'Three days,' she said. 'And though I don't agree with Foss on everything, he's right in recommending this place. It's quite delightful. I'm sure you'll enjoy it.'

'Maurice loves islands,' Hester said. 'He was born and brought up on one.'

'Really? Whereabouts?'

'The Island of Glass,' Maurice said. 'It's in Scotland.'

'How adorable. The Island of Glass.' Margaret Foster repeated the words slowly. 'What a wonderful name. Does it live up to it?'

'Oh yes,' Maurice said. 'Lots of hills and lochs…'

'And the sea,' Margaret Foster said. 'I do love the sea.'

'Lots of that too.'

'All the way round, I shouldn't wonder,' Foster said, raising his glass.

His wife gave him a look of reproach which had no trace of indulgence in it. 'You're just too droll for us, darling,' she said. It was Maurice who winced. She returned her attention to him. 'Tell us more about this island of yours, please.'

'It depends what you like, I suppose. It's a very quiet place. Not very many people.'

'Lots of deer,' Hester said. 'You told me there are lots of deer.'

'That's right.'

'You've seen them? I mean, you have been there, haven't you?' Margaret Foster said to Hester.

'Only one brief visit,' Hester said. 'In the dead of winter. Not so favourable, I have to say. But I like Scotland generally…'

'Too wet for me,' Foster said. 'Need the sun. That's why this place is so good. I say, my dear, why don't you take these two lovebirds on a tour of the island, eh? Tomorrow afternoon, while I'm having my little nap. I mean, you know all the spots, after all. What do you say, eh?' He looked at his wife.

'Oh, we wouldn't…' Hester began, but Foster interrupted.

'The Villa Jovis,' he said, 'the Blue Grotto at the very least, and there are some quite charming little churches...'

'I'd be delighted,' Margaret Foster said but she didn't smile and it was difficult to tell if she was being sincere or merely polite.

In fact, an excursion to the Blue Grotto had already been organised for that afternoon. Hester and Maurice joined in; Foster and his wife returned to the ship.

For Hester the excursion was an unqualified success. The Blue Grotto really was blue and the water was clear. As they sat in the boats at the entrance to the cave there was a great deal of clamour, a lot of argument among the boatmen as to who should go first. But when at last the boat which Maurice and Hester occupied with six others from the ship finally entered the cavern, everything quietened down. The feeling of being in church was added to not just by the stillness but by the high roof of the cave and the mirror-like purity of the water's surface. For Hester the experience was almost a spiritual one. She gazed at the blue walls, inhaled the air which she felt was made out of silver, and she grasped Maurice's hand tightly.

A few minutes later she was back out on the sea again with the rising wind making the surface choppy and unstable. The boat rocked. The boatmen began to call to one another again and the stillness and peace she had enjoyed inside the cave were lost.

Later in the evening, having returned to the *Berengonia*, Hester and Maurice took dinner with Peter Murchison, a wealthy businessman from Birmingham who was on a recuperative cruise having been ill following the death of his wife. Back in their cabin, they found themselves discussing once again the subject of the Fosters.

'I'm sure she doesn't want to do it,' Hester said.

'Do what?'

'Take us on a tour.'

'You're probably right. Anyway, they'll have forgotten by the morning with a bit of luck.'

'And we've been to the Blue Grotto now,' Hester said.

'Oh, there's other places. Foster's probably got an enormous list of them.'

'At least,' Hester said, 'they're a little less boring than Peter Murchison.'

'Oh, Peter Murchison's all right,' Maurice said. 'Think what he's been through.'

'Do rich men always talk about money?' Hester asked.

'Quite a lot in my experience, yes. Especially if they're in the process of amassing great amounts of it.'

'And is he?'

'Oh yes. He's horribly rich. No doubt about it.'

Maurice stepped into the bathroom to change into his pyjamas. He had done this each evening, making sure that he spent enough time out of the bedroom for Hester herself to have changed and be in bed by the time he returned. Then he would switch off the light, get into bed himself and lie still for a few minutes. On the first night he had turned to Hester and found that she was rigid. It was like trying to embrace a plank of wood. He was astonished. This young person, light and supple, who almost skipped about the ship in her eagerness to enjoy the new experience of the cruise, was transformed into something hard and unyielding.

She apologized. 'Give me a little time, Maurice, just a bit more time. It'll be fine, I promise. Really.'

'Of course, of course,' he said. His need to be understanding outweighed his disappointment. He reassured himself that it wasn't unusual for a woman on her wedding night to be shy or even afraid of her first ever sexual encounter, even with someone she loved. It would take time, as Hester said, but he hoped it wouldn't be too long.

But nothing changed on the second night or on the third. Now ten days had passed since their marriage and they had not had sex. Going to bed at night had developed into a nervous, fraught affair. Hester assured Maurice that she loved him, that it would be all right in the end and things would get better. Maurice, whose disappointment had developed into acute sexual frustration, very much doubted this. But one thing was clear: he had no wish to talk about it.

They discussed the Fosters again over breakfast the following morning.

'I'm sure that Margaret doesn't want us tagging along when she tours the island,' Maurice said. 'It's just Foster trying to get rid of her for a while so that he can have a couple of extra drinks in the afternoon. He'd no right to suggest it.'

'But surely that's why she agreed,' Hester said. 'I mean, she's probably keener to get away from him than he is to get away from her. It can't be much fun for her, after all, in the company of someone who's perpetually drunk.'

'I don't particularly like her,' Maurice said.

'Well, neither do I, much,' Hester replied, 'but maybe she's better when she's away from him.'

'It was just a whim,' Maurice said, closing the subject. 'They'll both forget all about it.'

But Foster did not forget. He sought out Maurice and Hester shortly after breakfast and announced that everything was arranged. He seemed even more buoyant than usual. 'You're going to have a wonderful time,' he said. 'Worked out an itinerary for you. Don't worry, not too taxing. The Grotta di Matermania and the Arco Naturale. For some reason neither's on the official excursion list. But it's much better to do these things alone anyway, or with a knowledgeable guide. And the best of it is, you know, that Margaret's got the history of the place off pat, no other way of putting it. Ah, here she is.'

At that point his wife joined them. 'Just telling the Redburns here how well versed you are in the lore of this place,' Foster said.

'It's mostly the Romans,' Margaret Foster said with little emotion. 'It all follows on from them.'

'The Romans?' Hester said.

'Tiberius lived here, you see…'

'Oh, Tiberius, of course!' This from Foster. 'Abandoned Rome and set up house here, by all accounts. Never went back. Can't blame him.'

'Villa Jovis,' Margaret Foster said, whose quiet even tones were in strong contrast to her husband's loud bonhomie. 'That's where he lived.'

'Take them there tomorrow, why don't you,' Foster said. 'But today I've told them you're off to the matrimonial cave.'

Margaret Foster was wearing a mid-calf cotton dress in pale blue and a wide-brimmed straw hat. The hat shaded her face but Maurice thought he detected a particularly deep shadow on her left cheek. A bruise? Surely not. Her leather sandals were practical rather than stylish. Before they set off she suggested to Hester that she might be more comfortable in walking shoes with less of a heel. Hester went back to the cabin to comply. When she returned she was wearing brown shoes and green culottes with a white blouse. Margaret Foster nodded her approval. Though he had not seen service in the tropics, Maurice appeared in khaki Army tropical kit – though minus the sola topi. His brown boots were highly polished. For a moment as Hester rejoined them they all appeared to be examining one another as if unsure whether they were in the right company or not. Then Margaret Foster said, 'Shall we?' and they went down to the launch which was to take them across the bay to the island.

'There's hardly any point on this island from which you can't see the sea,' Margaret Foster said as they reached the edge of the village of Capri barely half an hour later. 'And for most of the time, along the spine of the island, you can see the sea on both sides. At times it's quite breathtaking.'

'You must know the island quite well now,' Hester said.

'Oh yes.'

'How many times have you been here?' Maurice asked.

'Oh, six or seven times, I think.'

In the little space of silence that followed this, Hester said, 'How wonderful.'

Outside the village the road cut through some orange groves. The small dark green trees were arranged in close rows but far from offering shade their claustrophobic grouping seemed designed to manufacture heat. Maurice could feel sweat trickling down his back. Hester was fanning herself with the thin guide book that they had been given on the *Berengonia.* Only Margaret Foster appeared cool, her face partly hidden beneath the brim of her straw hat.

Past the orange groves, they left the main road and headed down a track towards the sea which lay some hundreds of feet below them. Without any form of metalling, the terrain was much rougher than before but Margaret Foster strode on in her now dusty sandals as if she were accustomed to walking along such tracks every day.

They paused at a prominent spot where the track curved inland for a short way and afforded them a good view of a rugged bay which led round to the eastern tip of the island.

'The Villa Jovis is over there,' Margaret Foster said. 'You can't quite see it from here but it's quite stunning. The cliffs are really very high. It must have been a most imposing place from the sea.'

'I've seen a painting of it,' Hester said. 'Rather fanciful, but I imagine there was some truth in it.'

'There's a place,' Margaret Foster went on, 'quite close to the Villa, called the Salto di Tiberio…'

'Salto…isn't that a jump, or something like that?' Maurice asked.

'Sort of. I don't think they really wanted to jump, though.'

'Who?'

'Oh, people that Tiberius wanted rid of. They were taken to this spot and persuaded to jump.'

'Did they land in the sea?' Hester asked.

'Not quite.'

'How awful.'

'I'll show you tomorrow, if you like.'

Hester said, 'I'm not sure that I want to see that.'

'Oh, they've got a railing round the spot now. It's perfectly safe. Can make you a bit giddy, of course.' She smiled. 'Shall we go on?'

When they reached the Arco Naturale, a huge uneven arc of rough stone, Hester was beginning to flag. A blister had started on her right heel. She ascribed this to the unevenness of the surface which made her shoes rub her feet in two or three places. 'I don't think I'm going to make it all the way down there,' she said, pointing to the track's steep descent. 'Or at least, I might be able to go down, but then I can't say that I'd make it back up again.'

Maurice seemed unconcerned. 'We'll go another time,' he said. 'It's not a problem.'

'No, no. Do go on. I'll wait here till you get back. Really.'

'No, Hester, that wouldn't be fair…'

But she was adamant. 'I have a wonderful view,' she said, 'and I shall enjoy just sitting here in the shade for a few minutes. Please, I don't want you to miss the cave because of me.'

Margaret Foster took no part in this debate as to the fate of their little expedition.

Maurice turned away for a moment and took in the view. He had never seen the sky so blue, so utterly devoid of clouds. A day like this at Swordale was impossible, such a deep blue was impossible. And the sea here was also blue, not slate grey, not leaden and brooding as it was at home. Here it was blue and polished up and it sparkled when the sun hit it. He looked at the horizon, ill-defined because of the heat haze. From close to his feet, it seemed, there was blue leading to a thick band of friable white and then up into blue again.

'Maurice?'

He turned back to find Hester already seated on a large rock in the shade of the Arco Naturale itself. She had taken off her shoes and was fanning her feet with the guide book.

'Look, I've got something to read as well. By the time you get back I'll be quite an expert on the island. You'll see. Now off you go.'

Margaret Foster had drawn away slightly. She was a few yards farther down the track in the direction of the cave.

Maurice looked at his wife. For a moment or two he found it difficult to focus on her such was the contrast between the shade that enclosed her and the brightness of the light that struck at everything else. 'Hester?' he said tentatively and it was almost as if the word were new to him.

But she missed his tone. Nor would he have been able to explain it, even to himself. He might have said that the light had played a trick on him and disturbed his usually clear vision; he might have said that his momentary inability to locate Hester in what was, after all, not particularly deep shade, had brought with it tiny indefinable traces of unease, intimations of loss; he might have made all manner of comments about the heat, the beauty of the day and how he didn't really give a stuff about the cave that lay at the end of the track. He might have made any of these comments but he made none and it was Hester who spoke, repeating her cheery injunction, 'Off you go.'

And he went.

Margaret Foster said, 'Do take care, it's rather stony.' Then she moved on. Maurice caught up with her and then adjusted to her pace, which was not slow. At the first sharp bend he looked back but although the stone arch was still clearly visible, Hester was not. He thought of waving but then changed his mind. He felt foolish. Waving was foolish enough but receiving no wave in reply would have made him feel worse. Then he wondered why he felt these things to be important and convinced himself that they were not. He became aware that Margaret Foster was speaking to him.

'I'm sorry?'

'I'm so glad you could come. It really is quite a treat. I mean Foss just won't walk any distance now, even though he's quite capable of it, and he refuses to allow me to go for walks by myself.'

'Would it be entirely safe?'

'Now don't go and take his part, please,' she complained, but she was smiling. 'My Italian's fair and the people here are very friendly, very gentle. The strap broke on one of my sandals once and I was forced to rather limp along until I met a very old man with a donkey cart. He gave me a lift to the nearest village, insisted I join his family for a meal and then delivered me back to the hotel. With my sandal repaired in the meantime, I might add.'

'Well, you can't complain about that sort of treatment, can you?' Maurice said.

'Oh, you can. Well, Foss did. Because I got back late. I still have to remind him occasionally that I'm actually a grown woman and not a child. I think it's because he's older than me that he treats me in that way.'

Maurice decided that he would avoid talking about Foster. He decided he would talk about the view.

'I've never seen the sea so blue,' he said. He thought how inadequate that phrase was for what he wanted to convey which was more deeply felt. His response to the sight of the sea was more than just a few moments of happiness; he was moved; he hadn't realised that the juxtaposition of such simple items as water, rock and light could create something so beautiful. 'I understand,' he began, but the words were more treacherous than the uneven surface of the track. 'I...I think I understand why you come back here year after year.'

'It's my concession,' she replied.

'Concession?'

'It's...' She stopped.

It was the first time Maurice had witnessed indecision in Margaret Foster. She took off her hat and began to fan her face. It was not the heat; she seemed to be embarrassed, as if the completion of her sentence might lead to the breaking of a confidence. Then she added quickly, 'It's his little annual treat to me.' She put her hat back on and set off a bit more briskly than before.

As Maurice followed on behind, he considered what had just been revealed to him. This was little to do with what Margaret Foster had said but what she had done. By removing her hat she had deprived her face of shadow. On her left cheek, there was a bruise, now only partially hidden by make-up which was dissolving in the heat. It was definitely a bruise. Had the revealing of this injury been deliberate or a mistake? Certainly she had returned the hat to her head swiftly as if suddenly aware that she had committed an error but then her actions were difficult to read. Maybe she needed to give him a glimpse, an insight into her troubled relationship with her husband. Maybe it was all an act. She was an intelligent woman who might also use her intelligence to manipulate those about her.

Perhaps the reason she was so stony-faced in the company of Foss was that he alone was not intimidated by her. Each had the measure of the other; they had reached agreement. But then, did this agreement break down occasionally to the point of physical abuse? And here was Maurice, on the edge of learning something new about this woman whom he found attractive but was wary of. He decided to show no further hint of curiosity. If she had something to say, she would have to say it, unprompted.

'Not far now, are we?' he asked.

'I don't think so. To be honest I'm not absolutely sure. About a quarter of a mile, I'd say. The thing is that I've only been to the cave once before. That was the first time we came here and Foss could walk a bit more then. He didn't like the climb back up, though, so we never came again. These days he hardly goes out at all, as you know, unless it's by taxi and that's really not much fun. I rely on others a lot, like yourself and Hester. I'm really pleased you enjoy walking.' She turned to him and smiled.

'If poor old Hester's got a blister, then it might be the end of our walking,' he said, aware that his tone was a little cold. A minute or two later they arrived at the cave.

For Maurice the Grotta di Matermania was a disappointment. It was so different from the Blue Grotto they had visited the day before. It just seemed like any other cave, rather damp and dull even though the Romans had done some building inside it to make it more hospitable. Margaret Foster said that it had been used as a nymphaeum. Maurice had no idea what this might be but decided that a discussion of this particular usage might lead to uncomfortable territory. He just said, 'Really,' with enough surprise in his voice to suggest that he knew exactly what a nymphaeum was and understood in some detail the practices that might have taken place there.

They began the climb back to the village and rejoined Hester about twenty-five minutes after having left her.

That evening Hester and Maurice joined the Fosters for dinner. Maurice would have preferred not to, suggesting that Margaret surely had had enough of them for one day, but Hester persuaded him. 'She particularly invited us,' she said, 'and we should really thank her for taking us on that lovely walk.'

'But you couldn't have enjoyed it one bit,' Maurice said. 'You got a blister and had to limp most of the way back.'

'That was my own stupid fault for wearing brand new shoes on a long walk.'

'Shoes that Margaret Foster persuaded you to put on,' Maurice said.

'Now that's unfair. She didn't exactly pick them out for me, did she?'

'Not as such, no…'

'And anyway, I feel sorry for her.'

'The most unjust of emotions,' Maurice said.

'It's not pity,' Hester replied. 'It's sympathy.'

'Comes to the same thing.'

'No, it does not, and I can't believe you really think so, either. They're two entirely different things. I don't pity her at all; that would be deplorable. I just sympathise with her situation, which, you have to admit, is not of the best.'

'Being married to a drunk, you mean.'

'If you must put it so vulgarly, yes.'
'She must have known,' Maurice said.
'What do you mean?'
'Well, I'd reckon they've been married about ten years at least. And Foster's how old now? Early fifties?'
She shrugged. 'About that, I suppose.'
'So he must already have had a prodigious thirst when they met. You don't reach his state of drinking overnight. It needs years of practice. That's what I mean. She must have known what he was like and she still married him.'
'Perhaps there are some things – even that – which can remain hidden and are only revealed later,' Hester said.
Maurice smiled. 'Well, you know all there is to know about me, at any rate. And I'm easily persuaded. Let's go and have dinner with the Fosters.'

The dinner began well. As usual Foster was the one with the most to say and he treated them all to a string of lively stories which no doubt his wife had heard many times before but she bore their retelling politely, smiling at appropriate moments and even laughing once or twice. Foster revelled in his new audience and related story after story while helping himself generously from the wine bottle. Then, halfway through the fish course, in a voice that was just a little too loud and caused heads to turn at neighbouring tables, he called for a second bottle. For the first time that evening Margaret Foster gave Maurice and Hester an anxious look.
Maurice noticed that the bruise on Margaret Foster's cheek had disappeared. He assumed that the re-application of make-up had been effective. He hadn't mentioned the bruise to Hester and was surprised that she hadn't noticed it. Maybe she had, but decided not to raise the subject.
Maurice felt that he might ease the situation by taking a little more wine than usual himself and therefore reducing the amount available to Foster in the second bottle.
However, this strategy backfired badly when the bottle became empty just before the end of the meal and, to Maurice's horror, Foster called the waiter over and ordered a third.
'Darling,' Margaret Foster began, 'do you really think you

should order another?'

'I couldn't drink another drop,' Maurice said by way of reinforcement.

The waiter was now standing by the table. Foster waved his hand and said to him, 'Come back in two minutes.' The waiter left. Then Foster leaned across to his wife who was sitting opposite him and said, 'I don't care who else does or doesn't want another drink, I do, and I'll damn well order another bottle if I so choose. Is that understood?'

His wife said, 'Perfectly.'

'Good.' He turned to Maurice and, smiling, said, 'Got to keep these damn women in order, you know, Redburn. Turn your whole world upside down if you give them a chance.' Then he waved the waiter over again and completed the order for the third bottle of wine.

The other three at the table remained silent as Foster turned to them once more and brought his now rather errant attention back to his story telling. 'Reminds me of an old chum of mine called Templeton…'

'You've already told that story,' Margaret Foster said.

'What?'

'Templeton going all the way to Caterham on the train.'

Foster looked more than quizzical; he was bemused. It was clear that he was already very drunk.

In spite of himself, Maurice suddenly felt sorry for him and said, 'It was a damn fine story for all that.'

Foster smiled. It was a vague smile. It might have been in response to what Maurice had said or it might have been prompted by some other thought unrelated to any of the present events.

A long silence followed. Foster was breathing deeply like a wounded animal and he was staring in abstraction at the table top on which lay the remains of dessert.

The awkwardness was broken by the arrival of the waiter with the fresh bottle of wine. Foster perked up. 'Ah, excellent, excellent. Plop some into these two glasses,' he said, indicating his own and Maurice's.

'I don't think I'll have any more, thanks,' Maurice said.

'Oh, come on, Redburn, don't be a wet blanket.'

The waiter stood with the bottle poised over Maurice's glass. Maurice shook his head.

'Oh well, then,' Foster said. 'Let's have it here.' The waiter poured him a glass and set the bottle on the table. With a polite nod, he left. Foster picked up his glass, held it up to the light and said, 'Wonderful colour.' Then he downed it in one.

His wife looked as if she were on the point of tears. 'You'll have to excuse me,' she said, rising.

In even tones Foster said, 'Stay where you are, Margaret.'

She sat down again and took a deep breath.

Foster picked up the wine bottle and, without asking, filled Maurice's glass and then his own. 'My dear wife...' he began.

Margaret Foster closed her eyes. 'Oh Foss, please...' she said.

'My dear, dear wife,' Foster went on, 'does not really understand a man's relationship to alcohol, or at least my relationship to it.' He laughed. 'No, you see she thinks I drink too much and I think I don't drink enough. We seem to have no agreement on this point whatsoever and it's rather a shame really. What do you say, Redburn? What do you think, eh?'

Maurice was now sitting with his arms folded across his chest. The other three at the table all looked at him. He found that he still felt sorry for Foster who was clearly no longer in control of his life. He had handed this control over to his need for alcohol. But Maurice also saw that understanding Foster's situation did not make the man any more likeable. He did not like Foster. He almost liked him when he was sober but as he was drunk most of the time this potential for liking him was very limited.

Maurice reached forward for his glass of wine which Foster had filled almost to the brim. He did not pick it up. He merely moved it slightly to one side. 'I think your wife is right,' he said. 'You drink too much.'

Foster's reaction to this news was to look mildly disappointed. Before he could say anything in reply, it was Maurice who added, 'I think Hester and I will retire now. If you'll excuse us.' He stood up.

'But my dear boy,' Foster said. 'My dear, dear boy, the night is young. We've...we've hardly begun...'

'Let them go, Foss,' Margaret Foster said.

Hester smiled at Margaret, a well meaning, understanding smile, and said, 'Goodnight.' She took her husband's arm and they left the dining room which was now nearly empty.

When they got back to their cabin, Hester said, 'What can we do? Oh what can we do?'

Maurice shook his head. 'Nothing,' he said. 'I think it's best we keep out of the picture.'

'But we must do something, surely. The poor woman…'

'It's something she's got to sort out herself.'

'But she can't.'

'Well, maybe so. But if she can't, we certainly can't.'

'But she's suffering so much.'

'I know. But I don't think we should interfere.'

Hester's distress increased. It wasn't clear whether this was from realising her husband was right or from the belief that he was wrong.

Maurice said, 'Tomorrow we can at least spend some time with Margaret, if you think that will help – and assuming, of course, that she wants to spend time with us. But we can't sort out her life for her. She's the only one that can do that. And we certainly can't sort out Foster himself. He's past help, I reckon, well past help.'

'But she isn't,' Hester said. There was still a pleading tone in her voice.

'Quite right. But she's got to do it, whatever it is – leaving Foster or whatever – she's got to do it all by herself.'

'It seems so unfair, that's all.'

'Well, it is. It's very unfair, but that's the way it is.' He began to pull at his bow-tie to unravel it. 'I had a friend once, a very good friend in fact, who got engaged to the most appalling woman imaginable. You could see a mile off that all she wanted was his money. Anyway, we were all very cool towards him about his prospective bride, although we didn't say anything to him directly of course. But then, suddenly, it was all off, and we all breathed a sigh of relief. And I wasn't the only one to tell him how happy I was that the engagement didn't last because I thought she was possibly the worst person in the world for him to marry and he was to be congratulated for avoiding a truly awful fate. And then, of course, it was all on again. They got married. I didn't go – well, I wasn't invited. Hardly any of his friends went because we'd all said such thoroughly nasty things about his new wife. So there you go. I've never seen him since and I've lost a really good friend. All because I expressed an opinion.'

'But you've got a right to be frank with your friends, surely, haven't you?' Hester said.

'Perhaps. But what about Margaret Foster then? First, she isn't a friend – I mean, we only met her a few days ago – and then we don't really know what her relationship with Foster's really like. Maybe this is the way they get on…'

'Oh, that's ridiculous.'

'Well, what I mean is, we mustn't go advising her to leave him or anything like that because suddenly, hey presto, everything might be fine again and she'll tell him how mean we were about him.'

'That seems very unlikely.'

'Well, I agree. But we don't know. We can imagine and we can guess, but we don't know. We don't know what's gone on before. And anyway, maybe she's as much to blame as he is.'

'Oh, how can you say that? You don't believe that, surely?' Hester looked as if what Maurice had said was a personal affront. 'You don't believe that, do you?'

'No, not really. But the thing is that there's rarely one absolute demon and one absolute innocent in cases like these. That's all I'm saying.'

Hester moved to the dressing table. She sat down and took off her earrings. 'Your friend,' she said, looking at Maurice in the mirror, 'is he still married to his abominable woman?'

'Oh yes. And by all accounts they're blissfully happy. And maybe I was wrong about her. Maybe we were all wrong about her. I don't know and now I never will know, for certain, that is. I mean, it's a pity, it really…'

He was interrupted by a knock at the door. Buttoning up his shirt front again he said, 'I bet I know who this is.'

Before he reached the door there came a second, more insistent series of knocks. 'Who is it?' he asked.

'It's Margaret Foster.'

He opened the door and she collapsed against him. She was weeping as he steered her, half carried her towards an armchair. Hester fetched a glass of water.

For half a minute or so she sat in the chair, huddled over, her face in her hands, sobbing. Hester sat on the arm of the chair with her arm round Margaret Foster's shoulders. Maurice stood a few feet away regarding the scene as if from an even greater distance. Margaret Foster looked wretched. Her abundant red hair was now loose and had fallen about her face. Her shoulders were shaking. Maurice began to realise that her distress was the product of a long period of unhappiness rather than some sudden unforeseen misfortune. She looked worn out.

Then she raised her head, drank some water and dried her face with a handkerchief that Hester provided.

'It's the end this time,' she said, 'the absolute end. I mean, I've said it before, I know I have, several times, but this time...it's impossible.'

She sat up. She seemed to have gained some measure of control again. 'He finished that bottle of wine,' she said, 'and asked for another one.'

'Another one?' Hester said.

'I know, it's inconceivable, isn't it. And he was quite, quite drunk by that time, more drunk I think than I've ever seen him. Thank God the dining room was empty.

Anyway, the head waiter came over and suggested that maybe we would prefer the wine to be delivered to our stateroom. Well, Foss went crazy. He absolutely exploded. He got up and actually tried to punch the man. All mayhem broke out.'

'So where is he now?' Maurice asked.

'Still there.'

'What?'

'When I left he was holding them off with a steak knife.' She looked at Maurice. 'I need your help,' she said.

Maurice picked up his jacket and slipped it on. 'Let's see what we can do,' he said.

Margaret Foster stood up. To Hester she said, 'Thank you. Thank you so much. I'm dreadfully sorry I've dragged you into all this but I'm at my wits' end, I really am.'

Hester gave her a hug.

'I think it's best if you stay here, Hester,' Maurice said.

'Really, I'd like to help...'

Margaret Foster said, 'Please, I think your husband's right. I don't want to drag more and more people into this. And anyway, you've been an enormous help already.'

When Margaret Foster and Maurice reached the dining room they found that all the lights had been switched off with the exception of those at the far end from the main entrance where there was a small huddle of waiters. As they entered, the head waiter detached himself from this group and hurried across the floor to meet them. He was a man of about seventy, rather short, with a full head of nearly white hair. Always impeccable in dress and manners, he was clearly flustered by the events of the evening. Maurice noticed that his bow-tie was askew.

'Captain Redburn,' he began, in some agitation, 'he has a knife, a weapon, he's dangerous. I urge caution.'

'Don't worry,' Maurice said. 'Can I suggest that you ask the waiters to leave. If you'd be so good as to remain on hand yourself...'

'Certainly, certainly.' He hurried on ahead of them, waving wildly at the waiters to remove themselves.

When they reached the end of the dining room they found Foster sitting on the floor in the corner, wedged in on one side by the wall and on the other by a trolley on which was spread an assortment of silver cutlery. He was wielding a knife and staring out from his little cubby hole with an expression that seemed to change, moment to moment, from merely drunk to quite insane.

When he saw them approach he said, 'Redburn, old man. What are you doing with my wife, eh? Nothing immoral, I hope?' He laughed.

Maurice smiled. 'What on earth are you doing on the floor?' he asked. 'Not examining the carpet, are you?'

Foster laughed again. 'Damn right. Old Grumpy What's-it here...' He waved the knife vaguely in the direction of the head waiter who immediately jumped back in alarm. '...Old Grumpy thinks it's Isphahan but I'm damn sure it's Baluchi. What do you think, eh?'

'Not my forte, carpets,' Maurice said. 'I'm happy to go along with your opinion on that subject.'

'Won't give me another bottle of wine, you know. Would you credit it? I'm a guest on this damn rust-bucket after all and they should give me what I damn well want, eh?'

'Quite so.' Maurice turned to the head waiter. 'Bring us another bottle, please,' he said. 'With two glasses.'

'Of course.' He retreated quickly into the kitchen.

'Well, you seem to have the magic touch, Redburn, I'll say that. I mean, I even threatened to cut his balls off and he still wouldn't bring me another bottle. Well, well.'

Maurice stepped over to the cutlery trolley and drew it away, repositioning it several feet farther along the wall. This exposed Foster's right hand side. Maurice turned and sat down on the floor beside him. 'You're probably right,' he said.

'What?'

'Baluchi. I remember one we've got at home. Looks a lot like this one. Dark red and black.'

'I told him,' Foster said. 'I told him.' He pointed the knife at the head waiter who had returned with a trolley spread with a white table cloth on which were placed a bottle of wine in an ice bucket, two glasses and a corkscrew. He positioned the trolley well away from his two guests and proceeded, very nervously, to open the wine.

'What a lovely sound,' Foster said as the cork was released from the bottle. 'One of my favourite sounds, you know.'

'I'm sure it is,' Maurice said.

'Now don't get all cocky, old boy!' He laughed. He looked up at his wife who was standing to one side of the head waiter. So far she had said nothing at all to her husband. 'Care for a drop, my dear?' he asked.

'No, thank you,' she said, quietly.

'Great disappointment, you know,' Foster said to Maurice. 'Wife that doesn't drink. Doesn't share one of your greatest pleasures. Awfully sad. Does your...forgotten...forgotten her name, dreadful...Esther, that's it...'

'Hester.'

'Hester. Yes. Forgive me. Does she...imbibe?'

'Not much.'

'But then neither do you. No, you see, that's...what do you say...appropriate...'

The head waiter had now poured two glasses from the fresh bottle of wine but appeared reluctant to deliver them as this would mean getting too close to Foster and his steak knife.

'Give them here,' Maurice said, reaching out both hands.

The head waiter approached warily from one side, as far away as possible from Foster. He handed the glasses to Maurice and then retreated quickly.

In order to accept the wine from Maurice, Foster had to transfer the steak knife to his left hand. Then he held the knife up and looked at it as if unable to define exactly what it was. He gave a shrug and put it down on the floor below his arched knees.

Maurice observed all this very carefully. He put his own glass down and, as Foster took his first long draught of wine, he leaned forward, slipped his hand under his own left knee and Foster's right, and took hold of the knife. He was able to remove it to his own right hand side and then flick it away across the carpet without Foster noticing anything.

Unfortunately however, his attempt to project the knife out of Foster's immediate area was rather too vigorous and it resulted in contact between the knife and the left shoe of the head waiter. In fact, the point stuck into the heel of the shoe – though not the foot itself. This did not prevent the head waiter from looking down, giving a little yelp of surprise and fainting away.

'Dear God,' Maurice said quietly. He got to his feet and went over to where the head waiter was stretched out on the carpet. Margaret Foster was already kneeling over him.

'Poor dear,' she said. 'So highly strung.'

Maurice called to a couple of waiters who were hovering by the kitchen door to bring some water. Then he knelt down on the carpet beside Margaret Foster and discreetly extracted the steak knife from the head waiter's shoe.

A few minutes of intense activity followed during which the head waiter was revived, his feet carefully examined and no wound found. He was helped into a sitting position. He declared he could no longer cope with the dangers of his job and wished to resign. He fainted again. Brought round for the second time he was assured by those in his charge that the dining room could not possibly function without him and his breadth and depth of experience was essential to the welfare of them all, passenger and crew alike. He agreed to reconsider. Finally, he was helped to his feet and ushered from the dining room, shielded from the sight of his deadly enemy the *appalling* Mr Foster.

Who, in the meantime, had fallen asleep.

'Thank God,' Margaret Foster said with great relief when she saw him. 'At least it's over for this evening.'

'Is it?' Maurice asked.

'Oh yes. You'll never wake him now. Once he passes out it's just a case of getting him to bed.'

'How far away is your cabin?' Maurice said. Then he corrected himself. 'Your stateroom.'

Margaret Foster ignored this correction. 'Not far,' she said. 'If we could get him to that exit there – she pointed to the far end of the dining room – it's just one flight down.'

'Well, we'll give it a try, shall we?'

With the help of one of the waiters, Maurice hauled Foster to his feet. He was then dumped, none too delicately, over Maurice's shoulder. There was the occasional mumble from Foster, a growl or two, but he did not wake.

'That's fine,' Maurice said and waved the waiter away. Then, with Margaret Foster leading, they made their way down to the stateroom.

Foster wasn't a particularly heavy man but Maurice was relieved when he was able to unload him onto the bed. He helped Margaret Foster to remove his shoes, his jacket and his tie. As he did so, he couldn't help but notice that the Fosters' stateroom was very much larger and more luxurious than the cabin, Class One, that he and Hester occupied. The bed was an ornate four-poster with a dark red silk counterpane; the carpet was Persian, though Maurice could not have identified the type – he had never seen an Isphahan carpet, nor a Baluchi, at least not to his knowledge. Without meaning to, he said, 'Well, this is a lovely room.'

Margaret Foster said, 'It is, rather.' She looked at her husband, who had started to snore. She added, 'He won't wake now till eight o'clock. Then he'll get up and say what a fine time he had at dinner, not remembering a thing about it. He'll toddle off down to breakfast and wonder why the dining staff are a bit aloof. He'll put it down to the general lack of discipline these days and he'll make jokes about it to anyone who'll listen. Then he'll go ashore, walk round Capri or Anacapri for an hour or so, chatting to the natives in fluent Italian and get back to the restaurant for lunch and start drinking. From then on, who knows what might happen

– he never does; he can't remember anyway. Nine times out of ten it ends like this.'

She looked across at the sleeping, snorting figure of her husband and burst into tears.

Maurice stepped towards her and put his arms round her. For almost a minute she wept on his chest. He found that he was saying, 'There, there...there, there,' and although aware how banal and ludicrous the words were he was unable to manufacture any other phrase more suitable.

As her weeping subsided he began to release her. She moved slightly, as if to separate from him, then slipped her arms up round his neck and kissed him full on the mouth. The kiss lasted no more than three or four seconds before she pushed him away. 'I'm sorry,' she said. 'No, I shouldn't have done that. It was very wrong of me. Please, you'd better...I mean, thank you for helping me, really, thank you, but...you'd better go.'

And a moment later he was outside the door, the lock clicking behind him. He made his way down the corridor. He seemed to be tottering although he no longer had the weight of Foster to contend with. In fact he stretched his shoulder, finding a little ache there and remembered the weight of him; he thought of it and imagined it replaced by the weight of Foster's wife. He stepped through a door and found himself on the promenade deck, standing at a railing with a view of the island. There was only one other passenger that he could see, a man in a white suit, thirty feet away, smoking a cigar and looking out at the lights of Capri. Maurice's hands trembled on the railing. He could not believe what had happened. He could not believe that in the space of barely ten seconds his world had been turned upside down. He could have resisted but he had not and therefore he had betrayed Hester; he had betrayed her *on their honeymoon*. What sort of man would do a thing like that? And already, right now, as he raised his hand to wipe his mouth in case any of Margaret Foster's lipstick remained there, he was involved in deceit.

He stood at the railing for five minutes trying to calm himself down but unable to. He could still smell Margaret Foster's perfume on the chest of his shirt. Disgust and hopelessness were what he felt most and there was another feeling, too. He tried hard not to recognise it but it was there. Unfortunately Margaret

Foster, in her five seconds' worth of kissing, had exhibited more passion than Hester had done in their several unsuccessful attempts at lovemaking. Disgust and hopelessness. And desire.

The following morning neither Foster nor his wife appeared for breakfast. Their absence was noted by several of the company, one of whom – Murchison, the businessman from Birmingham – approached Maurice for an explanation. Maurice informed him, in tones that were curt, if not rude, that he had no idea what had happened to the Fosters. 'Saw you together last night, that's all,' Murchison said, and turned away.

Hester suggested they should visit the Fosters to make sure that everything was all right. Maurice disagreed. He was almost as direct in his response to her as he had been to the earlier enquiry from Murchison. He immediately apologised and then Hester said she fully understood, he'd been through so much with them the night before. Then he said that this did not excuse his rudeness and she said it really didn't matter.

They completed their breakfast in silence. Maurice noted, but made no comment on, the absence also of the head waiter.

It was to be their last full day on the island and Maurice and Hester decided that they would spend at least the morning at the Villa Jovis which they had not yet visited. They joined the first launch to leave the ship and crossed the few hundred metres from the Berengonia to the island on a sea that was flat calm. The water was completely clear and Hester, leaning over the side of the launch, called out in glee as she spotted a fish or some feature on the sea bed. From the village of Capri they took a taxi to the entrance to the Villa Jovis but decided not to engage a tour guide. There were several of these available, all men who looked slightly seedy, wearing crumpled cotton suits that were not quite white. Maurice took Hester's hand and they made their way through the middle of their small gathering, resisting the many invitations that were given in French, German and English, to join the only official tour of the ruin.

The area covered by the Villa and its gardens was extensive so it wasn't long before Maurice and Hester found themselves quite alone. For several minutes at a time they could believe that they were the only visitors that morning.

'Tiberius came here and never left,' Hester said.
'Really?'
'Yes. Even though he was the emperor, he never went back to Rome. He ran everything from here. It says so in the little guide book.'
'It's certainly a beautiful spot,' Maurice said, 'but I don't think I could ever live here.'
'No?'
'No.'
'Too much sun?'
He smiled. 'Everything's so bright and new and...I don't know...to the point of unreality.' He kicked the dust at his feet. 'It's too dry, too parched. I mean, this is a dead place.'
She turned to look at him. 'Oh, how can you say that?'
They had reached the terrace above the Specularium, from which they could look back towards Capri village and the Marina, the backbone of the island and the wall of cliffs which was topped by the plateau where Anacapri lay. The sky again was deep blue, untroubled by even the smallest cloud. Maurice felt that only this blue of the sky was alive and vigorous; all terrestrial colours had been bleached white by the aggression of the light. The natural vegetation had been desiccated by the air to pale greens and yellows; it was reduced to thorny scrub and tough cacti that survived by attacking the environment, not blending with it.
'Is it ever green?' he asked, but Hester, a few yards in front of him now, did not hear the question.
A couple of minutes later, they heard cheering ahead of them. They had descended a flight of stone steps and were following a narrow path which had a smooth rock wall on one side and an iron railing on the other with the sea some hundreds of feet below. As they rounded a corner they found a group of men in brightly coloured clothes – reds and blues – who were shouting excitedly. Suddenly the body of a man was hurled out from among them, rising for a moment over the sea and then plunging down out of sight. A huge roar went up. Hester fell to her knees. 'Oh my God!' she said. 'What are they doing?'
Maurice bent over her. 'It's all right,' he said. 'It's all right...' But he was in shock as well. Still on her knees, she held onto him. He looked down at her, put his hand on her shoulder to raise her

but then looked up again as, with more shouting and laughter another body was pitched over the cliff into the sea. 'It's...It's...They're dummies,' he said at last. 'My God, they're just dummies...'

Hester got unsteadily to her feet. Maurice held onto her and they watched as a third manikin was flung into the sea – all stuffed arms and legs in a bright green costume. After the shock passed and Hester had managed to calm herself, they wondered how they could have thought these were real people, they were so obviously just big dolls in bright clothes.

'Salto di Tiberio,' she said. 'It's the place where they threw slaves to their death. This must be some kind of ritual re-enactment.'

Maurice said, 'Looks pretty barbaric to me.'

'Yes,' she replied. 'I mean, I got quite a fright, quite a fright.' His arm remained tightly round her shoulder.

'Let's go,' he said. 'I don't like this one little bit.'

On the way back to the village of Capri, she said, 'I suppose Guy Fawkes' Night is barbaric, in a way, too, don't you think? I mean, there's not much to choose between burning someone to death and throwing them off a cliff, is there?'

And Maurice said, 'I never thought of it that way before. Maybe you're right.'

They decided to go back to the ship for a late lunch, rest in the afternoon and then return to the island in the evening. This plan would fulfill two objectives. Avoiding the Fosters was the first, and perhaps the more important, but there was also the fact that so far they had always dined on board ship and tonight would be their last opportunity to have dinner on Capri. Ironically it was Foster himself who had supplied them with a list of restaurants; they would have him to thank, in part at least, if they had a pleasant meal. The only potential snag that Hester suggested might intrude was that the Fosters themselves might want to dine ashore as well, in order to avoid the scene of last night's little incident. Capri was not so large that they could be assured of avoiding an embarrassing meeting.

At about one thirty, therefore, they set off in the open launch to cross the half mile or so of still water back to the *Berengonia*. But as they left the marina, they could see a launch moving away from the ship itself and, as the two craft neared one another, they began to recognise some of the passengers on board the landward launch. 'Look!' Hester said. 'Look!' and she pointed out Margaret Foster.

She was standing by the rail and appeared to be looking at Maurice and Hester. In fact the two launches passed within thirty feet of each other, so it was easy for them to see her, even note her expression, which Maurice saw was sombre. He thought of waving, decided against it, then changed his mind and did so anyway. She waved back but her expression didn't change. Her sadness seemed complete and Maurice suddenly felt that he would never see her again. The encounter, the exchange of messages that neither could fully interpret, occupied the space of only a few seconds. The launch that bore Margaret Foster towards land rushed quickly on, trailing its ribbons of water behind it. Maurice thought how easy it would have been to call out to her but he hadn't been able to do that. Even waving had proved difficult. Hester said, 'Well, fancy that.' Then she tugged at his elbow. 'We're here,' she said.

They had been in their cabin for only a couple of minutes when there was a knock at the door. It was the head waiter from the ship's dining room. He was clearly off duty as he was wearing an open-necked shirt and grey flannels. However, the fact that he was not at work did not reduce his usual state of high agitation.

'Captain Redburn, apologies for the intrusion...I believe you have just returned. If you would like me to call back later...'

'Not at all, not at all. Come in.'

'No no no. Not necessary, I assure you. Just to pass on a message, and a letter.'

'A message and a letter?'

'Yes, yes. Oh, I see. Of course. Both from Lady Foster.'

'*Lady* Foster?'

'It seems so, yes. Though they do not like people to know...'

'Lord and Lady Foster?' Hester enquired as she came up to join them at the door.

'That's right. Yes, of course I've known for some time as they have done this cruise before, but I've been sworn to secrecy.'

'Until now.'

For a moment he looked confused. Then he said, 'Ah, of

course, you don't know. They've gone, you see.'

'Gone?'

'Yes. Lord Foster early this morning and Lady Foster just a few minutes ago...'

'We saw,' Hester said. 'She passed us as we were coming back to the ship.'

'Oh, a sad business,' the head waiter said. 'Most regrettable. Of course, you were there. Last night, I mean, and you saw...'

'Yes, I did,' Maurice said.

'Why did they leave separately?' Hester asked.

'Oh, this morning Lord Foster was unwell, quite unwell. The doctor was called at three thirty.'

'Really?'

'Yes. And sent him to hospital immediately.'

'No!'

'Oh yes.'

'She didn't call us,' Maurice said quietly.

'So off he went. Special boat to Naples.'

'And Margaret? I mean, Lady Foster?'

'Arrangements, packing, I think. And now off to Naples too.'

'But we leave tonight, don't we?' Hester asked.

'Yes, yes. But without the Fosters. Their cruise is finished now.' He paused for a moment. 'Very sad.' And then, after another short pause, 'Oh, the letter.' With a slight bow he held out a large white envelope on which was clearly written: Captain and Mrs M Redburn.

'Thank you,' Maurice said as he took the letter.

'Will you be at dinner, sir, madam?'

They looked at one another.

'Probably,' Hester said.

'I will get the chef to prepare a special dish for you as...as a token from us, for your...for your troubles.' With another nod he turned and left.

Hester pushed the door shut. Maurice opened the envelope and pulled out the letter. 'Read it aloud,' Hester asked him, and he did.

Dear Maurice and Hester (if I may be so familiar),

By the time you read this letter I will be well on my way to

Naples to join Foss who was taken ill during the night and had to be moved immediately to hospital. The ship's doctor assures me that his life is not in danger.
However, to be on the safe side he wants Foss to be in a situation where the facilities are better than on board ship. Also, as Foss will probably need a week to ten days of absolute rest, this is best provided in a proper hospital rather than a sick bay.
Foss has had such problems before and although they must be more difficult as he gets older, I do believe he will make a full recovery. I had rather been expecting something like this to happen, actually, as the signs have been there which usually let me know that a collapse is imminent.
So this note is to say goodbye. I'm sorry it's not possible to do so in person but there we are. But this is not just goodbye but thank you as well. You were the only real friends we made on the cruise and I say friends after such a short time because you made it clear – particularly in your actions last night – that you cared, immeasurably more than the others, for your rather benighted fellow travellers. I say thank you, thank you both most sincerely for your good hearts.

Margaret Foster.

'Well,' Hester said, 'what do you make of that?'
Maurice shook his head. 'I don't know,' he said. He handed the letter to her and stepped over to the window. The sea between the ship and the island had a ripple on it now but the ship itself lay motionless. He looked out from the square, salt-encrusted window. In his opinion portholes should be round; he had been on several troop ships before and the windows were not square, they were portholes and they were small and round. But he looked out anyway. He could see the marina and the steep slope where the funicular railway transported its passengers the couple of hundred feet up to Capri village. He could see it moving now, one car going up and one coming down. He imagined Margaret Foster might be in the ascending car but then thought not; if she were going to Naples she would merely transfer, at the Marina, to a larger launch bound for the mainland.

'There's no address,' Hester said. 'Was there anything on the envelope?'

Maurice picked up the envelope which he had laid aside. 'No,' he said.

'What a pity,' Hester said. 'What a pity. What with the rush and everything, perhaps she forgot. I'd really like to get in touch with her again. Such a difficult time for her. When we get back I suppose I could ask the cruise company to forward a letter for me. Do you think they'd do that?'

'Oh, probably. I don't see why not.'

'Good. I shall do that, then.'

And, two weeks later, when they were back in London, Hester did write a letter, addressed to Lady Foster, care of the cruise company. She gave it to Maurice as they made their way to Euston Station where Hester was to begin her journey north to Swordale. Maurice promised to post it for her. Later, as he set off for Woolwich Barracks where he was to be stationed for a week or so, he took the letter from his pocket, tore it into little pieces and dropped it in the gutter.

The Ellsworth Mountains: 1956

The frostbite has led to gangrene which is so far advanced that as they remove Meadway's left boot bits of his foot come away with it. Blackened toe stumps stick out from the disintegration of his green inner stocking. Woods tosses the boot into a corner of the tent and asks James Redburn what the hell they should do now.

They are on their way back from the Ellsworth Mountains where they succeeded in climbing what they believed to be the highest peak, Mount Endurance, at over twelve thousand feet. When they reached the top after a week of walking from Camp 3 they were tired and cold but jubilant. Redburn took a photograph in the couple of minutes of clear weather that coincided with their arrival at the summit. Ten men huddled together and probably smiling underneath their beards and the fur fringes of their hooded jackets. Woods saw the next peak, strangely tall in the few moments of blue sky at their disposal. He took a reading which confirmed that it was two to four hundred feet higher than they were, depending on how far away it was. As the weather closed in with a rush of wind and snow and sudden darkness, there arrived with it a feeling of gloom, a communal despondency that never really left them during their descent to Camp 3.

It had taken too long to get to the top of the mountain; they had used up more than half their supplies in the belief that the trip back – down-hill all the way, as Redburn himself put it – would take less time. But they were wrong. They spent five days and nights in one place, hemmed in by weather that was the worst they had experienced to date, and this place was a frozen rocky wasteland only a few hundred feet below the summit. Every day they recalculated the ration allowance, based on a time, ever more distant, when they would get to Camp 3. Never before had time seemed such a concrete, immovable thing; never before more elastic, stretching further and further from their grasp. It was Meadway, already complaining of pains in his foot, who first began to believe that they would not make it back to Camp 3.

They were down to half rations when they got moving again. A whole day of clear weather allowed them to get all the way down to the base of the mountain itself, with only twenty miles of rock-strewn foothills between them and Camp 3. Morale lifted again and rations, recalculated in their favour, allowed each man an extra portion of soup. But the next day, after only an hour's walking, they were trapped again by a blizzard that lasted until evening. The following morning they set off with the last rags of the blizzard blowing about them but enough light above to indicate that the storm was dying down. They made good progress, although Meadway was now clearly limping and his pain was greater than before.

Two days later, battling through indifferent weather, they reached Camp 3.

Redburn called it a triumph. Fraser was less sure and that evening when he voiced his bitterness about not having climbed the highest peak but some other pile of rocks that no one knew about or cared about, Flood and Cochran agreed. By this time Meadway was clearly in trouble. He had put all his effort and will into reaching Camp 3. On his arrival he collapsed and has been only semi-conscious since.

Redburn and Woods are gagging against the stench that now pervades the chilly tent interior. The stink of Meadway's gangrenous foot is powerful and it sticks to them like paste. It's worse, if anything, than the smell of the penguins at Goose Bay, site of Camp 1. They cleared a space there in the middle of the rookery, pushing back a mixture of pebbles and green penguin excrement with some weathered boards they found on the shore which were relics from a ship that did not survive the winter ice. The penguins complained. It was the laying season and they resented the move, shuffling off with their eggs perched on their feet and turning every so often to slash with their beaks at anything, penguin or human, that got too close. Linton said it was like living on the concrete floor of a public urinal, one that was cleaned maybe once a year. But they got used to it. After a few days it was so much a part of them they didn't notice it any more. But Meadway's foot is different. Weeks later, back in England, Redburn can wake in the morning and be aware, immediately, of this vile smell which suggests his bedroom is carpeted with offal.

Meadway is only semi-conscious, whimpering, it seems, with pain and, in answer to Woods' question about what they can do now, Redburn says he doesn't know. However, he begins to cut away the stocking, slitting it open with a knife from above the calf down to the ankle where it falls apart anyway. He peels it away and it is like skinning a hare; the stocking is as reluctant to detach itself as the pelt of an animal. Eventually he tears it off like sticking plaster, quickly. Woods says, 'Jesus.'

Now the leg is exposed: the bare white bloodless calf, imprinted with the stocking's weave as if finely sculpted in white marble, and the black, disintegrating foot. Meadway groans. He is shuffling about among numberless images, snatches of dreams he cannot concentrate on because of the intensity of the white light inside his head.

Everything is white. Even the penguins, the tens of thousands of them that have colonised the bay and now inhabit his brain, are bleached white, the orange beaks and grey heads of the gentoo reduced to perhaps pale cream at best and monitored only by their shadowy movement. At times they are indecipherable from the sea-birds, the albatrosses and petrels that only Redburn himself can identify with accuracy and pleasure and which now fling themselves around inside Meadway's head, clamouring for attention, competing even with the penguins in the level of noise they generate. For if the unrelenting whiteness is difficult to bear, the noise is completely insufferable. He can hear not just the clacking of the penguins and the calls of the sea-birds but the crack of distant and not-so-distant ice as it breaks from the ice shelf and tumbles into the sea. Rotten, unfertilised penguin eggs explode with a report like the firing of a gun. On their first morning at Goose Bay they counted a dozen such explosions in the space of half an hour before they stopped counting. Meadway can hear them all again and he has begun to count them, too, reaching five or six before his attention founders and he returns to the beginning and says, 'One...'

Wood asks again what they can do and again Redburn says he doesn't know. But he does know. It's three days at least back to Camp 2 where the dog sleds are and a couple of days from there back to Base Camp and the ship. There would be a further day for a helicopter to arrive from South Georgia. So it will take a minimum of six days before Meadway can get the medical attention that he needs right now. In fact Redburn does know what they can do: nothing.

Meadway is dead. His eyes are open and he is breathing and he is dreaming of white things but the decision has been made that he's dead and waiting is all that's left, waiting for the transformation from one state to the next, for the action to catch up with the decision.

Woods says 'Jesus' again.

Redburn covers up the foot, wrapping it in a woollen pullover and laying it down gently. Meadway is inside two sleeping bags, both of which have been unzipped and opened out. Woods now helps Redburn to zip up the inner and then the outer bag so that Meadway is encased in a thick sleeve, right up to the throat. But he has begun to shiver. There is no heating available other than body heat. Placing Meadway on the camp bed with a double thickness of sleeping bag round him is the only way he can be kept warm. They must trap the heat that he himself is generating. But he's still shivering. It's as if the reverse is happening, as if, by imprisoning him with his frozen foot they are inviting more damage, they are allowing the cold to stay inside and populate his body further.

Meadway's mind won't release him from the agonies of the past few days. Whether his eyes are closed or open he sees only the white landscape. Hailstones pierce the skin of his face. There are men roped together like a loose and sagging fence, men moving upwards, each exhausted step a minor triumph. And he's one of them. He's third or fourth down the rope and he's asking himself, as he began to ask all the way back at Base Camp when he started to feel tired, asking why they bothered, what's so special about this cold deserted place that they had to locate the highest point in it and then climb up to the top? This peak in the Ellsworth Mountains has a name which he can no longer remember, or perhaps he's managed to blot it out. He's not sure any more if he has been to the top and is on his way back down or is still supposed to be battling upwards. He doesn't know and he can't bring himself to care. Strength and weakness are words which have lost their meaning. Will, endurance, grit, determination: he has heard these words recently but they've ceased to be real words; they're just a jumble of sounds. For he's beyond urging now, he has given up. His body knows that it won't be able to recover from its several illnesses. It's closing down, bit by bit, and he's becoming separated from each part of it so that no control remains. He feels cold but the cold is in his chest, in his guts, not in his arms and legs which aren't even numb any more; he no longer believes they exist. But he tries to say something and Redburn leans over in an attempt to make out the faint words.

James Redburn carries in his pack a photograph of a ship. Others carry snapshots of girlfriends or wives and, in the case of Liverdale, three small children. But Redburn's photo is of a ship. It's in a small leather wallet that would have allowed him another photograph as well but the left hand side is blank. He's very much in love – or believes himself to be so – with Marina Linnel whom he plans to marry next year. But he hasn't included her photograph, even though he's got several of her. There's only the ship.

It's called the Endurance and it's Shackleton's ship that got stuck fast in the Weddell pack ice in January 1915. The photograph, by Frank Hurley, was taken at night. Hurley placed flares round the ship and set them off simultaneously to illuminate the whole vessel from its ever more solid water-line to the mast tops. It's already a ghost ship, rigging encased in ice, the whole construction resembling a model or rather a trophy, cut out of heavy silver. The ship sits on top of a mound of ice as if it were riding the crest of a wave when suddenly frozen in a moment, an instantaneous denial of time and gravity. But this is just the ice rearing up round it, stronger and ever more forceful so that not even the ship's oak timbers can resist. It was finally crushed by the ice in October 1915 and sank.

So this is the picture Redburn cherishes, a photograph of something noble, romantic and doomed. The other men have not seen this photograph nor has Redburn any intention of showing it to them.

It's black and white, the photograph, but this is not a black and white land, despite what's going on inside Meadway's head which no one else is privy to anyway. Redburn loves the colours. The sky is blue; the icebergs have blue in them and some are so large that they embrace small lakes of shallow water which is translucent aquamarine. The sky is blue, except at sunset when it transforms itself to pink and, sometimes, to orange. Redburn has taken more photographs on the expedition than anyone else; his enthusiasm for the sights of this desolate place, for its many colours, seems boundless. He even admits – to no one but himself – that there's beauty in the green slime of the acres of penguin guano in Goose Bay.

The expedition has one fire-arm, a revolver, which has been used only once so far, to kill the lead husky of the dog team they used when they crossed the pack ice from Base Camp to Camp 2. The dog's name was Oscar, christened by Liverdale after a dog he had had when he was a child. Oscar went lame on the third day after they reached Camp 2 and the following morning he would not get up from his snow hole. Redburn, as expedition leader, took it upon himself to destroy the animal. Woods was annoyed at the waste of a bullet but Redburn would do it no other way. Later Cochran, the cook, took the carcass and skinned it. He cut up the meat and prepared a stew that everyone agreed was the best meal they'd had on the trip so far. Everyone except Redburn, who refused to partake of it. The leftover bones were then thrown to the other dogs who crunched them up within minutes. Everything was used. Nothing was wasted.

There are twelve men in the expedition. Two of them are back at Camp 2 with the dogs. Here there are ten, including Meadway. Woods and Redburn and the remaining seven cram themselves into a tent made for four and discuss what is to be done. Pressed together on the cold groundsheet, they hug their knees as Redburn describes the situation: Meadway is not going to survive but no one can be sure how long it will take him to die. The painkillers carried in the medical kit have nearly been used up and seem to be ineffective in Meadway's extreme condition anyway. Trying to move him is likely to cause him even more pain; staying with him till he dies will jeopardise the lives of the rest of them as they have limited food supplies and must get back to Camp 2 and then Base before more bad weather closes in. Meadway is in pain now and this pain will increase. And Meadway wants to die. This is what he has asked for.

The discussion about what to do takes twenty-five minutes during which the following rules are agreed and written down:

> *1. There is to be a vote on whether or not to carry out the mercy killing of Meadway in order to relieve him of further pain.*
> *2. The vote will be taken by a show of hands.*
> *3. A simple majority will decide the outcome.*
> *4. Abstentions are not permitted.*
> *5. Each of those voting in favour of the mercy killing must be prepared to carry it out.*
> *6. If the vote is in favour of the mercy killing, then the one to carry it out will be decided by the drawing of lots, this draw to involve only those who voted for the action.*
> *7. If the action is carried out, all nine men must agree that they will never reveal:*
> *a) the fact that Meadway was killed.*
> *b) the identity of the one chosen to do the killing.*
> *8. If Meadway is killed, his body will be consigned to a crevasse.*
> *9. These rules will be destroyed following Meadway's death (from whatever cause).*

The vote is taken and is five to four in favour of the mercy killing of Meadway. At this point, Linton, one of the four men who voted against, declares the whole thing barbaric and refuses to abide by the rules already agreed. Redburn says he's out of order. He reminds Linton that when the nine rules were decided, and written down, each man was asked in turn if he agreed to abide by them and every man, including himself, said yes. Linton says he has changed his mind. Redburn tells him he can't change his mind; circumstances do not permit it. He must stick to what he has already agreed. Linton says he doesn't care; he agreed only because he believed that the vote would be no. Woods accuses him of dishonesty, not only towards the rest of the men but to himself. Linton shrugs and says, 'That's how it is, that's how it is.'

Redburn asks again, putting the question to him in full: is he willing to abide by the majority decision reached earlier, i.e. the mercy killing of Meadway and total silence thereafter?

After a delay of several seconds Linton confirms that he cannot condone the mercy killing of Meadway; neither can he agree to keep silent on the matter.

Redburn asks Linton if he can suggest a better approach to the problem.

A long silence follows. It's Flood, eventually, who says that maybe they should think seriously again about just leaving Meadway to die. Redburn is against it; Woods is against it. They argue that it's worse than killing him. He might linger on for a couple of days, in more and more pain as time goes on.

Then Liverdale suggests that they could say to Meadway, quite legitimately, that they are setting off to get help. They could leave him some food, all the remaining painkillers, and tell him they'll be back as soon as possible to pick him up.

'In other words,' Woods says, 'we leave him to die. It comes to the same thing.'

Liverdale disagrees.

Redburn says that help is six or seven days away at best. There's no chance of Meadway surviving that long.

Linton says, 'We need to discuss this.'

'Already discussed,' Redburn replies.

'Discuss it again,' Linton says.

Redburn says, 'No.'

Linton asks for a show of hands to decide whether or not to discuss the issues again. Redburn says he's out of order. Linton tells him to go and fuck himself.

Redburn repeats that it's quite clear that if they kill Meadway, as they have agreed, then they cannot allow information about this action or its perpetrator to go beyond the group. There are mutterings of agreement from the other men, except Linton, who remains silent.

Redburn announces that the way is now clear for the draw to be made to decide who will shoot Meadway. The draw is taken among the five who originally agreed that Meadway should be shot. Five matchsticks are used, one of which is ignited and then blown out. Redburn holds the matches as they are drawn. It is Woods who draws the used match. He looks at it for a moment and says, 'You'd better give me the gun, then.'

The revolver is in Redburn's possession. It is in a small leather bag wedged between his knees in the cramped confines of the freezing tent. He draws it out now and loads it with a single bullet.

He hands the revolver to Woods.

'Anyone want to say anything?' Woods asks. 'Anyone want to say goodbye to him?'

After a short silence, Redburn says, 'Best get on with it.'

Linton says, 'Barbaric, barbaric.'

Woods crawls from the tent. As he does so, air enters that is so cold it feels as if it is made of something solid. As a reminder of how perilous their situation is, it is sudden and irresistible. The eight men remain silent for nearly three minutes. Some of them have their eyes closed. They may be at prayer. Linton has started to shiver. They wait to hear the shot but there is no shot.

When Woods returns, he says that he thinks Meadway has already died. He asks Cochran, the only other with first aid experience, to come to the tent and check. Cochran pushes his way out into the cold. He and Woods return within a further four minutes. Cochran confirms that Meadway has indeed died. Someone says, 'Thank Christ.'

Liverdale says, 'Thank God this nonsense is over. Thank God it's all over.'

Linton raises a hand briefly as if he's about to speak, but then he says nothing.

'If you don't like things you just change them,' Petra Meadway said. 'I had a great-aunt called Mavis and she was an admirable woman, or so my parents thought. In fact, they liked her so much that they gave me her name. I mean...Mavis. Really. Isn't it perfectly vile?'

James Redburn wasn't quite sure if this question was rhetorical or not. He had met the questioner for the first time only three minutes before and her direct manner made him feel uncomfortable. Her voice was slightly too loud.

They were sitting in deep comfortable armchairs in the sitting room of a cottage which was on the outskirts of Hove on the Sussex coast. Summer had arrived suddenly a week before when the temperature had reached eighty degrees. On his way down from London by train, Redburn stood in the corridor by the door with the window pulled down as far as it would open. He stood full in the draught of the air that slid down the side of the train and tore at his shirt. He had to screw up his eyes against the wind but he stayed there all the way down from London, letting the air cool his body. He thought of this figure, eighty, which was well over seventy degrees higher than the temperature he had experienced only five weeks before. He believed that someone or something was being unfair to him, making him so hot so soon after being so cold.

'Oh, it doesn't seem so bad really,' he said, when he decided that a reply was actually required, and he smiled.

'Well, it is. It's an awful name, absolutely awful. So I changed it to Petra. We went there once when I was a child, you see.'

'You went...?'

'To Petra. It's in the Middle East somewhere. It's got famous ruins and all that sort of thing. I was only a child but I liked the name. And I decided that one day I would be called Petra too. Much nicer than Mavis.'

'It's a bird,' Redburn said.

'I'm sorry?'

'Mavis. It's another word for a thrush.'

'Is it? Is it really? Well, I never knew that. Or perhaps someone told me once and I forgot.'

'It might be used more in Scotland than in England.'

'Really? Well, anyway, when I got to twenty-one I said that's it. No more Mavis. It's Petra from now on. And that's how it's been ever since.'

'Didn't...didn't anyone object?'

'Oh, of course they did. My mother and father were absolutely livid. But I didn't care. I just refused to communicate with anyone who called me Mavis. Simple as that.'

'I see.'

'And not everyone disliked it, or rather, disliked me for doing it. Oh no. There were a few who said, well good for you. You know, it's your life and you can call yourself whatever you want. And then there were a few others who objected at first but then came round to it once they saw I really meant it.'

'So you never regretted it, then?'

'Oh, not for a moment. I mean, there were a few problems, of course...'

'Were there?'

'Oh yes. When I met Peter, for instance. No end of confusion there, though I don't really see why there should be. I mean, they're quite distinct names after all, aren't they? Anyway, when we got married it was Peter and Petra Meadway and that was that. People just had to get used to it.'

'I see. I see.'

Redburn hadn't the faintest idea what to say next so he said 'I see' again and took a sip of tea. The woman intimidated him. She had very pale skin and thick black hair cut in a bob that exposed her neck which was slender. He found that he was attracted to her and intimidated by her at the same time and this was an unnerving combination.

The whole situation made him feel uneasy – the clean, tidy sitting room with its heavy furniture, the silver tray with the bone china tea set, the plate of carefully arranged biscuits which he had not yet dared to sample. He was afraid of the order of it all. He was an intruder here, a large, clumsy, overheated object – he could feel perspiration gathering on his forehead and between his shoulder blades.

'I'm sorry about Peter,' he said, realising how lame this statement was, even as he was making it. Then he pulled himself up in his chair a bit and added, 'I mean, it was dreadful what happened to him, dreadful. That is, we were all aware of the risks, but then being wise after the event isn't much comfort. I'm truly sorry for what happened. All I can say, really, is that he worked very hard for us, for the team, you know, and he was totally committed to the expedition, to achieving our goals. His was a great loss, a tremendous blow...'

He stopped talking, leaned back in his chair and hoped that this rehearsed speech had been delivered in a manner casual enough to convince Petra Meadway that it was spontaneous.

She sat quietly for a few moments and then asked, 'Did you like Peter?'

'Like him?' He looked at her face but there were no clues there as to the real intent of her question. 'Well, of course I liked him. Yes, we all...'

'Was he your best friend in the group?' she asked, before he had finished.

'No, no. I can't honestly say that he was my closest...'

'Who was?'

‘My closest friend?’

‘No, his. Who was he really close to out of the whole group?’

‘That would have been…Let me see…’

But there was no one. Meadway was not liked. He was a moaner. He moaned about everything, right from the start. At first it was funny; the others made a joke out of it, called him Meadway the Moaner. But within a few weeks it became clear that he was serious. He complained about the cold, the food, the dogs, the sleds, the tents…he complained about almost everything. He complained especially when he was asked to do something. So when he died, there was regret at the loss of life, the blow to the prestige of the group and the difficulties that would follow from that, but no one mourned him, no one expressed any depth of feeling for him. Meadway had been reduced to an abstract concept and was no longer a person. Things had been easier after he died.

‘Linton,’ Redburn said. ‘Brian Linton. He and Peter got on well. Brian was devastated when Peter died. Well, we all were…’

‘I’d like to meet him,’ Petra Meadway said.

‘Brian?’

‘Yes. Can you put me in touch with him?’

‘Well…of course, yes. I don’t have his address on me at this moment. At least, I don’t think so…’ He took a small notebook from the inside pocket of his jacket which was lying over the arm of his chair. He began to flick through it. ‘Let’s see…’ But there were no addresses in the notebook. It was a diary. There were no addresses in it, even at the end, in the small section headed ‘Addresses’. He knew this but he flicked through the blank pages anyway. ‘No, I can’t see it, unfortunately…’ He looked up. ‘Can I send it to you? I can drop you a line when I get back.’

‘Well…’ She looked at him. ‘I think this has gone far enough,’ she said. He saw that she was sitting with her arms crossed. ‘Whatever it is you’re trying to do – well, I think I know what you’re trying to do – I don’t approve of it. I don’t approve of it at all. You see, I want to know what happened. Not about Peter’s death, exactly – I’m not that morbid – I want to know the details before he died, how he got on with people, I want to know everything about that. Will you tell me?’

James Redburn shook his head slowly. ‘I’m afraid I can’t do

that,' he said. 'No, I can't do that.'

'Why not? Have you anything to hide?'

'Not at all. It's just that there were…well, certain things that happened that were quite unpleasant. It was the decision of the group that we should spare people the details. I think it was a good decision.'

'But I've already said that I'm not interested in those kind of details.'

'Nevertheless…I'm afraid…It's out of the question, really.'

'But don't I have the right to know? Even if, in your opinion, some of the detail is unpleasant. Can't I decide for myself?'

'In this case,' Redburn said, 'I have to say no.'

'I see.' She leaned forward, picked up the teapot and poured out two more cups of tea, without asking him if he wanted any or not. Then she said, 'Peter was a complete bastard, you know, and it's a relief to me that he's gone.'

Redburn added some milk to his tea. He picked up the sugar bowl, selected two lumps with the silver tongs and dropped them in. Cup and saucer in hand he looked across at Petra Meadway and decided that he would say nothing; he would wait for her to continue.

Which she did. 'I'm only saying this,' she said, 'because you must have reached the same conclusion, the same unpleasant conclusion. I mean, you were together, all of you, for…five months, was it?'

'Seven.'

'Seven months. There you are. So you knew what he was really like, didn't you?'

Redburn sipped his tea.

'He was lazy,' she went on. 'He was lazy and selfish. He got hugely enthusiastic about things but then gave up on them when he saw that a bit of effort was needed. Our life together was just a series of things that never got finished. And I'm convinced he was unemployable. I mean, he left the Army after three years – I'm amazed he lasted that long. God knows what he would have done if he hadn't gone on your expedition. Couldn't stick at anything, you see. No stamina, physical or mental. Of course I never said this to anyone involved in the expedition. I mean, no one asked me, for a start, and then…well, there was the chance of getting rid of him for six months, maybe even for good. It got to the stage when I even wished for that. We'd already separated, you know.'

'I didn't know that,' Redburn said, happy to be able to say something at last. 'No, I didn't know that. I'm sorry.'

'Don't be. I haven't told you the worst yet.' She reached down to the table. 'Look, you haven't had a biscuit. Don't you want one?' She picked up the plate and offered it to him. He took a chocolate biscuit and immediately regretted this as the coating began to melt beneath his fingers.

'He started to get violent,' she went on.

'Violent? With you, you mean?'

'Yes.'

'Good God.'

'He broke my nose once,' she said.

'No, I can't believe it. That's awful…' He looked at her. He looked at her face.

'Oh, I'm fine now,' she said. 'But there were black eyes, too. And occasionally other bruises.'

'I'm sorry,' he said. 'I'm so sorry.'

'You keep saying that,' she said, 'and you needn't, you know. After all, it was nothing to do with you.'

'No, but…'

'He was a coward, you see. He only got violent when people couldn't hit back. I imagine that was a side of him that you never saw.'

'No, no, I didn't.'

'But, in a way, I think that might be what killed him, or influenced his death, anyway.'

'How do you mean?'

'Well, he was taking on something that was so much bigger and stronger than himself. I mean the place, the conditions and so on. When they began to hurt him and when he knew there was nothing he could do about it, I imagine he just gave up. What do you think? Tell me. Could this be some of the unpleasant detail you wish to spare me?'

'Well…' He had finished the biscuit by this time but was left with the problem of the chocolate on his fingers. With his left hand he reached for a handkerchief, then changed his mind. He sucked the end of each finger. 'You might be right,' he said. 'Peter did decline quite rapidly. But then the conditions were bad. Well, actually, no, they were worse than bad, they were appalling, the worst I've ever seen and I've spent some time in these kinds of places before. But...but yes, you might be right,' he said. 'You might be right. He succumbed very quickly.'

'So why do you do it?' she asked. 'Why do you do it if conditions are so bad? Why do you go there?'

'Me? Me?' At last he took the handkerchief from his pocket and wiped his fingers dry. He put the handkerchief away and sat for a moment staring down at the tea things spread before him on the table. 'Why do I do it?' he said quietly.

And an hour later, in Brighton station, sitting in the train waiting to leave, and then, some time further on, trundling through the Sussex countryside, he continued to examine this question that Petra Meadway had asked him and to which he had given a bland answer of no value and already forgotten.

London: 1931/32

Maurice Redburn was not fond of cities. He'd lived in three and visited several more. Once, he'd tried to count them but reached twenty and gave up. Of the three he'd lived in, two – London and Edinburgh – he'd gone to by choice but the third – Paris – he'd been taken to when choice of any sort was not open to him. He'd woken up in a hospital bed at the beginning of October, 1918, and over the next few days he discovered that the hospital was in Paris, in the 10th Arrondissement. He also found out that he'd been unconscious for a total of thirty-six hours but that he had no broken bones and would almost certainly make a full recovery. He was told he was very lucky and could expect to rejoin his regiment in the Royal Artillery, within a few weeks.

He didn't regard the prospect of returning to the Front as being lucky but duty persuaded him that he should do it. He rejoined his unit to the sound of cheering but this jubilation was not related to his return. It was the morning of November the eleventh and the War had just ended.

It was the noise of cities he disliked most and what it derived from: the constant movement of people and objects along channels less and less able to accommodate them. It was an irony that during the War there hadn't been so much city noise. He could remember seeing columns of people, in the countryside and in the towns and cities, columns of people and trucks and horses and artillery, walking slowly, heads bowed as if ashamed of the sky, dejected, weary and quiet.

Now he was in London again, stationed at Woolwich where he'd joined the Army in 1916. And it was noisy. Had London been as noisy then, during the War? He couldn't be sure. There were more vehicles now, certainly, and more people too, particularly here in the City, the City inside the city. What was the other name they used? The Square Mile? Yes, that was it. He thought of what his father owned on Glass – twenty-five acres of grounds at the castle, a few acres of foreshore, sixty-five arable, a hundred of forestry and five hundred, or thereabouts, of moorland. That came to a bit over a square mile and was valued at...well, he had no idea, really, none at all, though his father probably did. But this square mile he was about to set foot in as he left London Bridge and headed along Gracechurch Street towards Cornhill, this Square Mile was worth countless millions of pounds. And that was only the property and didn't include what was held in safes and vaults. For how many banks were there here? He didn't know. He wondered if anyone knew, if anyone had ever gone, street by street, and counted, one, two, three...

No, he'd far rather be spending time at Swordale than here, treading the hard pavements of a gigantic anonymous city. And it would be easy, in fact, to put this right. He could just turn around now, make his way to London Bridge Station and take a train back to Woolwich. He could easily get leave of absence as his father was seriously ill. Then it was just a case of taking the overnight sleeper from Euston to Inverness. He could be in Swordale in twenty-four hours from now, thirty-six at the most, where he would rejoin Hester, his wife of only five weeks, who had gone ahead a couple of days before. And there was his father, who had perhaps less than four weeks to live and who desperately wanted to see his favourite son before he died. There were two people who wanted him or needed him and he was going to deny them both. He was going to stay here, in this place that he loathed and, he feared, turn himself into a person to be loathed.

The offices of the cruise company were in Cornhill, housed in a five storey building not far from the Bank of England itself. The doorman made a deep bow as Redburn ascended the short flight of steps to the main entrance. Redburn couldn't say if this was the doorman's usual habit or especial deference to a man in uniform. But the uniform probably helped, Redburn felt, and he was glad he was required to wear it. He felt comfortable in uniform. The reactions it prompted in others were often to his benefit.

As was obvious now. The receptionist summoned a clerk to accompany him to an office on the sixth floor. 'James Manning Salisbury' was the name declared by the brass plate on the door, followed by 'Director, Mediterranean'. Quite a large area to direct, Redburn caught himself thinking as the clerk knocked on the door. On hearing a slightly weary 'Yes,' the clerk opened the door a foot or so, stuck his head round it and said, 'Captain Redburn to see you, sir.'

'Thank you, Geoffrey, yes. Invite the captain in, please.'

The door opened wide and Redburn strode in, hat removed and trapped under his left arm.

'Captain Redburn.' Salisbury rose and came from behind his desk to greet his visitor in the middle of the office. They shook hands and Salisbury returned to his seat. He indicated a chair to one side and invited Redburn to sit down.

Salisbury was fiftyish, Redburn guessed. He was wearing a dark grey three-piece suit whose waistcoat bulged with the strain of enclosing his overlarge stomach.

'I believe you're recently back from our three-week jaunt in the Med,' Salisbury said when both men were seated.

'That's right, yes.'

'And I hope it was all you expected it to be. Perhaps more, in fact.' He smiled.

'Oh, certainly, yes. It was excellent all round.'

'Good, good. And your wife...she enjoyed it too, I hope?'

'She did.'

'Splendid, splendid. I'm always glad to meet satisfied customers. So...so what can I do for you today, captain?'

'It concerns Lord and Lady Foster,' Redburn said.

'The Fosters. Ah yes. Now that reminds me...but, no, I'm sorry, please go on.'

'Hester and I...' Redburn began, 'That's my wife, Hester...'

'Yes.'

'...we met the Fosters during the cruise and unfortunately we witnessed the...the onset of Lord Foster's illness. It was all most upsetting. Well, for Hester and myself, of course, but principally for Lady Foster...'

'Well, indeed.'

'And, as you probably know, they had to leave the cruise in Naples. I believe Lord Foster was taken to hospital there...'

'That's right, yes. He was.'

'But unfortunately they left so abruptly that we weren't able to exchange addresses. We did get a note, actually, from Lady Foster, but understandably it was very brief...'

'Well, yes.'

'...and my wife is particularly keen to renew acquaintance with Lady Foster so I'd be very grateful if you would...' He paused as he extracted a letter from an inside pocket of his jacket. '…if you would send this letter on to Lady Foster.' He reached over and placed it on the desk in front of Salisbury. 'I realise you can't give me her address directly so this would seem to be the proper way…'

Redburn stopped when he saw Salisbury's rather grim, stony expression. 'Is there some sort of problem?' he asked when ten seconds of silence had passed.

'Oh, none at all,' Salisbury said, as if snapping out of a daydream, 'but tell me…are you saying you haven't had any contact with the Fosters since they left the cruise?'

'That's right.'

'I see. I see.' Salisbury sat back in his chair. 'I regret to inform you, Captain Redburn, that Lord Foster…I'm afraid he didn't survive his illness.'

'Ah.'

There was a long pause during which Redburn thought hard about this information. Salisbury was astute enough to allow him to do this.

'So when did he die?' Redburn asked.

'Oh, I think it was within a day of leaving the ship.'

'So he died in Naples?'

'Yes.'

Redburn said, 'Poor Lady Foster, all alone in Naples with a dead husband. Not exactly pleasant.'

'Well, no.'

'If we'd known – I mean, Hester and I – if we'd known Foster's condition was so serious we would gladly have left the cruise ourselves in order to…to…'

'I can assure you, Captain Redburn,' Salisbury interrupted, 'that the company did everything in its power to assist Lady Foster.'

'Oh, I'm sure you did.'

'We ensured the safe transportation of the body back to England and I believe that Lady Foster's sister was at her side in a matter of…well, hours…'

'I see. So this was, what…three weeks ago?'

'A little over three weeks, yes. I believe the funeral was held two weeks ago, in Highgate.'

'Highgate?'

'That's where they live. Well, where Lady Foster now lives.'

'All the more important, then, that this letter gets to Lady Foster as soon as possible.' Redburn pointed to the envelope on the desk.

'Ah, the letter, yes. Well now, it may not actually be necessary, Captain Redburn. You see, I think…' Salisbury opened a drawer and drew out an envelope which he pushed across the desk where it joined the one Redburn had placed there. '…I think you'll find all the information you require in here. You see, yours is not an uncommon request and one we are always happy to discharge. In fact, only a matter of half an hour ago, someone else asked me to do exactly the same thing. None other than Lady Foster,' he said, 'with a request to forward this letter to you.'

Redburn was nothing if not disciplined. He didn't open Margaret Foster's letter until about thirty minutes later when he was sitting in a tea shop on the Strand. In fact, he waited until his tea had arrived, had been poured and he had buttered a scone and taken a first bite, before he drew out the envelope from his jacket pocket and slit it open using the stem of a teaspoon.

My dear Maurice and Hester,
I owe you a great apology for taking such a long time to attempt to get in touch with you. You were both so kind to me during the Berengonia *cruise that I was determined to contact you again. Alas the events of the past three weeks have rendered many of my plans untenable, as I will explain below. It was only yesterday that I realised that in the haste that attended my departure from the* Berengonia, *I failed to ask for your home address. Nor did I, in my brief note to you, indicate my own address. Consequently I have had to approach the cruise company to forward this letter to you. I hope it arrives safely and finds you both well.*
The 25th of last month seems like such a long time ago now. Any attempt to recount what happened that day now seems superfluous, given the events that followed. I will merely record that it was one of the most unpleasant days of my life and I pray that I will never experience another like it.
Foss passed away in Naples only a few hours after arriving at the hospital there. As you can imagine, I was completely

shocked. Foss had experienced problems like this before but none had been particularly serious. None had required hospitalisation. He had always seemed to me to be remarkably robust and he was so very young – only forty-seven. However, the doctors in Naples, who, I may say, were extremely helpful and understanding, pointed out that the years of excessive drinking had not only damaged Foss's liver but weakened his heart as well. He died of a massive heart attack.

Of course, I was frantic. I thought of you both immediately but the Berengonia had already left Naples. I could have cabled the ship but I decided that this would have been an entirely selfish act on my part. What did I expect you to do? That we had become such good friends in such a short space of time did not warrant any further intrusion in your holiday. I reminded myself that it was more than a holiday, it was your honeymoon. After all, nothing more could be done for poor Foss and, as for myself, my sister Claire arrived from Paris within two days and was the greatest support to me.

The cruise company made all the arrangements for Foss to be transported home to London. I believe they were duty bound to do so but nevertheless everything was arranged meticulously and my journey back home was not at all as unpleasant as the circumstances might have dictated. Of course, I am talking about my physical comfort only. I was worried about the funeral arrangements and meeting Foss's family, some members of which I had still to meet for the first time. I was glad that Claire was with me to share some of my concern.

However, now that Foss has been laid to rest and Claire has returned to Paris, I find myself in this big, draughty house in Highgate Village with a great silence round me as well as large amounts of time I must endeavour to fill.

My first duty – to myself, I may say, to keep myself active and busy and prevent me from brooding – is to re-enter the world of society, linking up again with those friends whose friendship I have neglected over the past few years. I must also communicate with those new friends I have made recently. Of the latter, I can assure you, you are at the top of the list.

Consequently, I hope you will forgive my silence and accept my invitation to visit me sometime here in London where you will

be made most welcome.
With sincerest best wishes,
Margaret Foster.

There was an address and telephone number. Redburn thought of phoning but decided against it. He finished his scone and tea and requested the bill. As he was paying it he asked the waitress how to get to Highgate.

Redburn had assumed, from Margaret Foster's use of the term 'village', that Highgate was indeed that, a village on the outskirts of London. However, as he made his way up Highgate Hill from the Underground Station, he realised that this place bore no resemblance to what he would have termed a village. On Glass there were several villages, each a grouping of twenty or thirty cottages with hills beyond and streams running to the sea.

Occasionally a flock of sheep might be driven down the main street of Strongarve to the high pasture to the west, though the term 'main street' was too grand an expression for the narrow thoroughfare which could be crossed in only three or four strides from the gate of the primary school to the front door of the post office.

Highgate may well have been a village in the past but it was now being overtaken by the outward spread of the metropolis. To either side of Highgate Hill there were tens, if not scores of streets and Redburn had no idea which direction to take.

He enquired of three people, none of whom knew of the street he was looking for. The fourth didn't know either but suggested he should return to Highgate Station and ask there. There might even be a map.

There was no map but he was directed up the hill again. After fifteen minutes of walking he was in Pond Square and from there he got further directions from a newspaper seller. A further five minutes' walk took him to the Fosters' house on Southwood Lane.

A maid informed him that she would enquire as to whether her ladyship was free to see him. She showed him into a large reception room with dark, wood-panelled walls on which were hung portraits of – he guessed – the Fosters' ancestors. They were mostly nineteenth-century paintings with one or two perhaps even earlier. All were of men, many of whom were in uniform.

The poses were formal; there were no smiles; there was a great deal of facial hair on display. Redburn decided they were all Foss's relatives, not Margaret's, though he had no reason to support this idea. The whole array reminded him of the portraits in Swordale – dark, forbidding renderings of old, self-important men. Maybe he'd be up on a wall somewhere himself one day.

Margaret Foster was wearing black and it suited her, he thought, as it accentuated the whiteness of her skin. She was pleased to see him but surprised at the timing of his arrival.

'How on earth did you find me?' she asked.

'I got your letter,' he said.

She held her hand out to him and he took it briefly before they both sat down.

'My letter?'

'The one you left at the cruise company.'

'But...but that was only this morning.'

'That's right. I know. I missed you by about half an hour. I went there with the same intention as yourself.'

'Leaving a letter, you mean? For me?'

'Yes.'

'Well, how bizarre.' She smiled. 'What a coincidence. I mean, the same morning...'

'Quite.'

'So, do you still have the letter? I mean yours to me.'

'Well, I do, but it's a little superfluous now, don't you think?' He took it out of his pocket and held it in front of him.

'Not at all. I would very much like to see it.' She reached out a hand. He rose, stepped across the six or eight feet that separated their armchairs and gave it to her.

She placed it on the arm of her chair. 'I'll read it later,' she said. 'I look forward to it.'

'I was sorry to hear about Foss,' he said as he sat down again.

'Really? Oh, Maurice...May I call you Maurice?'

'Of course.'

'And you must call me Margaret. So...so you were sorry to hear about Foss, were you?'

'Well, of course I was.'

'No, no, no,' she said. 'No. Do you remember all that business in the dining room and so on? On the cruise, I mean.'

'Vividly.'

'Well, suppose I said to you that what you witnessed was Foss at his worst...You'd be inclined to agree, I suppose?'

'It was all very unpleasant, certainly.'

'Well, indeed it was. But now, suppose I said that, in fact, that was Foss close to his best.'

'I'm not sure what you mean.'

'What I'm saying is that in public he could usually hold things together – not always, as you saw, but most of the time. And people made allowances for him. You know, "Good old Foss, a bit drunk tonight, overdid it rather, but a good chap at heart..." All that sort of thing. Do you see what I mean?'

'Up to a point.'

'Well, I can assure you that he didn't deserve any sympathy. None. None at all. He was quite horrible to me nearly all the time. At best he was patronizing and condescending and at worst he was boorish and abusive. And violent.'

'But he never hit you, surely?' Redburn asked. 'Not you.'

She smiled and shook her head. 'You don't know the half of it,' she said.

'He hit you? Really? No.'

'Do you remember our little walk on Capri?'

'Yes, I do.'

'I had a bruise on my cheek, if you remember.'

Redburn took a few seconds to answer. 'Yes,' he said, 'I do remember.'

'A jewellery box did that. Luckily I was some distance from him so I didn't get the full force.'

'My god...'

'Oh, Foss was a typical alcoholic – charming when sober and a complete beast when drunk. I mean, he only hit me when he was drunk but as that was most of the time, he hit me rather a lot. I did manage to avoid him some of the time, but not always. Of course, the next day, he was always surprised.'

'Surprised?'

'By the bruises. "You've got a black eye," he'd say to me in the morning. "However did you get that?" So I'd tell him and he'd refuse to believe it.'

'He had no recollection of it?'

'None at all. To the point that he managed to convince himself I'd taken a lover who used to beat me. So we'd go away on a cruise and when I still got bashed about he'd suspect that this imaginary lover had followed us and was on board. Latterly he was quite befuddled most of the time, even when sober.'

'My god,' Redburn said. 'I didn't realise things were...quite so bad.'

'Well, why should you? I mean, you only knew us for...what was it...three weeks? Two?'

He shook his head. 'I'm not sure. Two, I think.'

'Well, there you are. But then there was that awful scene in the dining room.'

'It was unpleasant, certainly,' Redburn said, 'but I assumed that particular incident was exceptional.'

'Well, it wasn't.'

'I see.'

There was silence for a few moments and then she stood up. 'You'll stay for lunch?'

'Well...'

'Of course you will. And, in the meantime, we'll have some tea.' She stepped over to the door and called for the maid. When she had completed her instructions she returned to her seat.

'I haven't said this to anyone,' she began. 'I mean, since Foss died I've been surrounded by all his old cronies and, as you can imagine, some of them are as fond of the bottle as he was. And lecherous, too. I've had one proposal of marriage and two other invitations which were, shall we say, a little less formal. Beastly people. And his relatives. Oh my god, his awful, awful relatives. You've no idea...Anyway, clearly I couldn't say this to any of them but I'll say it to you: I'm glad Foss is dead. In fact, I'll go further: I'm really, really glad he's dead. Now, that's a terrible thing to say, isn't it?'

After a few moments Redburn said, 'I don't think anyone could blame you for feeling that way, considering what happened to you.'

'Well, I have to take at least part of the blame myself.'

'How can that be?'

'Well, simply that I knew what I was letting myself in for when I married him.'

'You mean, he was like that back then too?'

'Yes. Oh, not quite as bad as he was latterly but he was already drinking heavily. He was occasionally abusive…'

'But you still agreed to marry him?'

'Yes, I did.'

'You loved him, then?'

She smiled and then she laughed out loud. 'Loved him? My god, Maurice, my god. How old are you?'

'Thirty-two.'

'Really? Same as myself. Well, and you saw action in the Great War?'

'Yes.'

'And you've been a soldier ever since?'

'That's right, yes.'

'For a man of such experience you still display a rather naïve view of the world, don't you think?'

'I'd rather say,' he said, 'that I still retain some faith in people.'

'Really? Well, any faith you might have in me is misplaced. You see, my marriage to Foss was more of a commercial arrangement. Foss was rich and I was poor. He wanted an attractive wife and I wanted money. On one level, you could argue, it was perfectly civilized.'

'So how did you meet?' Redburn asked.

'Music hall brought us together,' she said, smiling. 'Now, there's a shock for you.'

'Music hall?'

'My parents, you see. They were in the business. Lawrence and Flora Milburn. Lo and Flo. Ever hear of them?'

He shook his head. 'I'm afraid not, no. I went to the music hall once, a few years ago. Didn't like it much, so I didn't go again.'

'Well, I don't blame you. Very over-rated. But I had little choice myself, being born into it, as it were. My father played the piano and my mother sang. And I sang too, from the age of about five onwards.'

'You're a singer, then?'

'Was. And I wasn't that good, actually. I suppose I was a bit of a novelty when I was a child and then, as I grew up, I…well, let's just say I made sure I took full advantage of all my positive qualities. I just made sure I looked good. I could do that. That was easy. And I found that lots of people – lots of men, that is –

came just to look at me rather than hear me sing. I had lots of admirers.'

'And one of them was Foss?'

'Yes. One evening after the show I was presented with the biggest bouquet of flowers I'd ever seen. And they were from Foss. Little, plump, bald-headed Foss. He was fifteen years older than me, completely besotted and determined to make me his mistress. Well, I said no, of course. But he was nothing if not persistent. More flowers arrived. There were flowers every night for…oh, three or four weeks, I think. And champagne. I refused to drink with him but he brought more bottles than even he could drink so I gave any that were left over to my father who sold them to a friend of his in the wine trade. Who knows but Foss might have wound up buying the same bottles again. The flowers I took to a local hospital who were very grateful. I think I almost acquired sainthood at that point.' She smiled again. 'Yes, that phase worked out quite well, all round.'

'Except for Foss, presumably.'

'Oh, I don't know. I think he knew he was being toyed with and he rather enjoyed it. But of course I knew I'd lose him if it went on too long.'

'So you were already…you had a plan?'

'Yes. One day I said to him, "We need to talk." "Oh, I agree," he said. "But not here," I said – we were in my dressing room, backstage. Actually, "room" is a very grand word for what was, in fact, little more than a broom cupboard. Very very cramped. Foss loved it, of course, as it meant he was practically sitting on top of me. But I said, "Book a table at Fortnum's. Afternoon tea, tomorrow at three thirty. A quiet table." Well, he did it, of course. And I made sure I was looking my best and I kissed him on both cheeks, engulfing him in perfume, and tea was served and it was all very civilised. And then I told him my plan. It was quite simple, really. I said I'd marry him and I'd educate myself so that I could behave like a lady and we'd live in style. Well, he was shocked. Didn't say anything for a while and then he said, "No, it's just not possible." So I thanked him for the tea, stood up and walked out. But I knew that wouldn't be the end of it.'

'All part of the plan,' Redburn said.

'That's right. But I had to be careful, you see, not to give in too early. Anyway, I heard nothing for a few days and then the flowers started arriving again and I sent them back, all of them. And then, after a few more days I got a note asking me to have tea with him again at Fortnum's. Another talk. But this time he said maybe we could do it after all. "Get married, that is," he said. And I said, "Is that a proposal?" to which he replied, "Yes." So I told him to go away and make the arrangements and not come back till everything was fixed. And he said, "Is that an acceptance?" And I said, "Yes".'

'So you got what you wanted?'

'Yes, and a lot more besides.'

At this point the maid arrived with tea. Two or three minutes were occupied with pouring, stirring, the offering of cakes. When they were alone again she said, 'So, do you think I'm a terrible woman?'

'Oh, there's no doubt about it,' he said, smiling.

She said, 'You're laughing but I can tell you're shocked.'

He sipped his tea. 'I'm surprised, certainly.'

'I'm sure you are. But here I am, a daughter of the stage who's now a lady – well, in title, shall we say – and I'm a rich widow as well.'

'And are you happy?' he asked.

'What a shocking question.'

'Really? What do you mean?'

'Don't you know that's the rudest question you can ever ask anyone?'

He smiled again. 'I thought your aim was to be candid. Surely it's the kind of question that fits the tone of the conversation so far.'

'Well, that's true, I suppose.'

'So. Are you happy?'

'Being a rich widow? In one sense I am,' she said.

'Just one?'

'I'm not being abused. That's the most important one. But what about you? Are you happy?'

'Oh, I think so, yes.'

After a short pause she said, 'Not an entirely convincing answer. Where's Hester? Is she in London?'

'No, she's in Swordale.'

'Ah, the Island of Glass.' Her tone was faintly mocking. 'So you're in London by yourself?'

'Just me and a few thousand others in Woolwich Barracks. But I'll be posted to Edinburgh in a few weeks.'

'And Hester will join you there?'

'I hope so, yes. But my father's unwell at the moment and she offered to look after him – well, make sure he's looked after properly, that is. So she's up there in Swordale for the time being.'

'I see.' She placed her empty cup and saucer on the table that sat between them. 'She's very pretty, isn't she?'

'Yes, she is.'

'And devoted to you. Completely so.'

'I'm very lucky, yes.'

'But you don't love her, do you.' This was presented as a statement rather than a question.

To his annoyance he found he had to look away. 'What a remarkable thing to say,' he said, though there was no irritation in his tone. 'Of course I love her. After all we're...we've only just got married.'

'Well, precisely,' she said. 'A difficult time. Getting to know each other, or trying to. And it was very clear to me on the trip, on the cruise, that she's...how can I put it...she's a bit of a disappointment to you in some areas.'

He stood up and then leaned over to place his cup and saucer beside hers on the table. Again there was no anger in his voice when he said, quietly, 'I think I'd better go.'

'Not staying to lunch?'

'No, I don't think so.'

'Well, that's a pity.'

'I'm not sure why I came here,' he said.

'Oh, Captain Redburn...' she said quietly, 'Maurice...' Once more her tone edged precariously close to mockery. 'Don't lie to me. Don't lie to yourself. You know exactly why you came here.'

He set off towards the door but had to pass close by her chair as he did so. She caught him by the wrist.

'Go if you must,' she said, 'but I know, and you know, that you'll be back.'

General Arthur Redburn, Maurice Redburn's father, who was

now at Swordale being looked after by Hester, had declared some years before that there would never be a telephone in the castle in his lifetime. Decrees came easily to the general – it was a word he used frequently to describe his decisions – and when he issued them there was to be no debate, only compliance or, in the case of his sons Maurice and Christopher, even when they ceased to be children, submission. This particular decree was superfluous because few of the islands had telephone links with the mainland. The first telephone on Glass was not to arrive until 1937, by which time the general had been dead for five years.

In earlier times his decrees mostly concerned his immediate family and the management of the castle household. Later in life he expanded their range to encompass humanity as a whole. For the world was changing, he believed, and not for the better.

Surely he wasn't the only one who could see that? 'Before the war...': this was a phrase he used when beginning many of his pronouncements and it was followed by the recounting of facts designed to prove how much better things had been then, how greatly inferior they were now.

But Hester actually liked the old man, despite his decrees and his grumpiness and his occasional rants. With Hester he was calmer, softer, more malleable. For she cared for him well, assisting his nurses to wash and dress him, feeding him when he lost the use of his right arm after a stroke. Christopher, who had arrived in Swordale from Paris a few days before she had, told her, a week into his stay, that she was doing too much, that she should leave everything to the nurses, but she said that he always asked for her and, anyway, she was very fond of him. This was an emotion that Christopher could not understand in relation to his father who, he assured her, was the embodiment of evil. 'He made my childhood hell,' he said to her, adding that he, Christopher, had only returned to Swordale because he was broke and had nowhere else to go. The only compensation – apart from meeting her, of course – was that, with his father ill and confined to bed, he could roam the castle at will and do pretty much as he pleased. She told him she felt he was being unkind; he told her he was being generous, for she had not experienced his father as he had.

But the question of a telephone was a problem for Hester. She had expected to be able to communicate directly with Maurice, to keep him informed about his father and to hear, from him, what his plans were, when he would be posted to Edinburgh and when she could join him there. For that's where he was to be stationed, wasn't it? But instead of picking up a telephone and placing a call, she had to rely on letters. And she wrote lots of letters – one long letter every day – but received few in return. Maurice was not a good correspondent, even with the woman he'd married only a few weeks before. And she could not understand this. He had military duties, of course, but surely a few minutes each evening could be devoted to writing her a paragraph or two. Those few letters she did receive said very little; they were more like telegrams than letters. Between greeting and valediction there was a very small amount of information and nothing of his plans other than an indication that he was likely to stay in London for a few weeks yet. He always assured her he would write at greater length soon. It became clear to her that 'soon' usually meant within a week or ten days.

Maurice was also affected by the absence of a telephone for he disliked writing. Most of his day was spent at a small desk in a small office where he compiled reports on insignificant subjects of no interest to him or, it seemed, to anyone else. The idea of spending more time, in his off-duty hours, at another desk writing letters was not attractive, even if these letters were to Hester. So the making of a telephone call would have been much simpler and much more effective. It would have helped, too, with one other big problem.

He longed for Hester's voice to tell him what to do, not for the words she would use – for this was a subject he couldn't possibly discuss with her – but through their tone of reassurance. He was sure he would be able to draw strength from it.

Right now he needed strength to say no, but he said yes. He returned to Highgate four days after his first visit. He'd telephoned Margaret Foster to tell her he wanted to see her. He tried to detect a note of smugness in her voice but there was none.

She opened the door herself and said, 'Come in.' Just that; no further greeting. And she wasn't wearing black this time. Something in pale blue, modern, whereas the black dress of his first visit, as well as being funereal, had suggested an earlier age, Victorian.

'You were right,' he said.

'Yes, well, let's not dwell on that, shall we.' She closed the door behind him. 'I've given Ellie the afternoon off,' she said, 'so there's no one here but us.' She led the way upstairs and she took him into a large bedroom with a four-poster bed draped in pale blue satin. It reminded him of rooms at Swordale. She closed the curtains but there was light from the corridor through the open door. 'Not my room,' she said. 'Not Foss's room either. Another room. Our room.' Then she took off the pale blue dress and placed it carefully over the back of a chair. He watched as she undressed completely and stood before him quite naked. She smiled and seemed to be trying not to giggle. She pointed at him as he stood there in the same pose he'd held since he entered the room. She pointed at his uniform and said, in mock-confidential tones, 'Actually, Maurice, it's your turn now.'

As Hester was several hundred miles away on a Scottish island she was unlikely to hear of Maurice's infidelity but even so he realised he needed to be on his guard. He didn't want to be in the situation where a friend, spoken to in confidence, might find it impossible to resist spreading some gossip. But then he had few friends and anyway, he never felt the need to talk. The idea of confessing your improprieties to someone, or boasting about them...well, it was silly, a sign of weakness. No, you just got on with things and prepared yourself to live with the consequences.

But his brother, Christopher, was very different. Here was someone who couldn't hold anything in. Words poured out of him. Getting him to keep a secret was close to impossible. In Christopher's view, people had to be told. Everything. As Maurice was to find out a few weeks later when he travelled north to attend the funeral of his father.

He'd been in London for about two months when the telegram arrived to tell him his father had died. It was the morning of a day when he had arranged to visit Margaret Foster. He rang her to explain why he couldn't come to see her.

'You poor dear,' she said. 'I'm so very sorry.'

'Yes,' he said. 'Thank you.'

'I know how close you were to him.'

'Yes, well, that's right.' There was a pause. He wasn't quite sure how to continue. He decided to stick to practical matters. 'So you'll forgive me,' he said, 'if I don't see you today.'

'Of course, of course.'

'I'll head up to Euston straight away. Should be able to get a train to Edinburgh and change there. I mean, rather than wait till tonight for the sleeper to Inverness. Might save a few hours.'

'Yes...'

'Not that it actually matters much, I suppose.'

'Well, you need to be there...'

'Yes.'

'And how long...I mean, have you any idea how long you might be away?'

'Very difficult to say. I've got two weeks' leave but I can always extend it if need be. There'll be quite a lot of things to sort out.'

'I'm sure...'

'But I'll be in touch.'

'Write to me.'

'Actually, that might be a bit difficult.'

'Really? But there must be a post office on your island, surely.'

'Oh yes. Of course there is. But it's a tiny place, remember. The word "village" really does mean village.'

'I don't follow you.'

'Highgate Village,' he said.

'Oh.'

'How many people? Twenty thousand? Fifty thousand?'

'I've no idea.'

'No, well...the entire population of Glass is three hundred and seventy. And everybody knows everybody else's business. I'm sure the postmistress can tell you exactly who's been writing to whom for the past ten years.'

'Phone me, then.'

'Not from Glass, I'm afraid. There aren't any phones on the island. But I know I'll have to go over to the mainland occasionally so I can ring you from there.'

'Promise?'

'Promise.'

'Good. Good.'

He had to settle for the sleeper after all. He discovered there was no time to be gained by leaving for Edinburgh straight away. There was no onward connection that day so the choice was to go to Edinburgh, stay in a hotel overnight and join the early train in the morning or just wait for the sleeper service and go straight through. He opted for the sleeper.

He sent a telegram to Hester to tell her when he'd be arriving. Then he thought of ringing Margaret Foster again and suggesting they meet for lunch. But he decided against it. He'd said his goodbyes and didn't want to undo them. He cleared up some of his office work, packed and then made his way into town.

Hester met him on the pier as he disembarked from the ferry. She was crying and continued to cry as he embraced her and tried to calm her down. Christopher was there, too. Maurice's greeting to his brother, whom he had not seen for several years, was stiff, formal. Just a handshake and a nod. No affection.

They made their way to the castle in the black and cream Daimler that had belonged to the General. It was a big, growly beast of a car which pitched and bounced along the undulating coast road and then the pot-holed drive to the castle itself. Maurice noted that much repair work was needed.

Christopher drove while Maurice and Hester sat in the back. Hester was still weeping, inconsolable.

'Hester,' Maurice said, placing his arm around her shoulders as she sat forward, her head in her hands. 'I know you got very close to the old man but you must…try and be calm.'

Hester shook her head, her face still obscured by her hands.

'Hester…'

But she was still in tears when they reached the castle. When they got out of the car, Maurice held her shoulders and looked at her. No, this was not just the death of his father, there was something else troubling her for sure. 'Whatever is the matter, Hester?' he asked.

'It's not about your father,' she said and she pulled away from him and ran inside.

So, within fifteen minutes of arriving on Glass, Maurice learned of his wife's infidelity with his brother. His reaction to this news was to say nothing for half a minute, which was too long for Christopher.

'Say something, for Christ's sake, Mo.'

'Well, what do you want me to say?'

'Aren't you even angry? No, you're not angry. I can't believe it. You're actually...'

'Getting angry wouldn't be of much help,' Maurice said.

'At least say something. Do something or say something...'

For privacy's sake the three of them were in the billiard room on the first floor. It was a large room, lined with dark oak paneling and with a single billiard table rather isolated in the middle.

'You know, father always wanted to get another of these,' Maurice said. He was standing at the balk end of the table, his hands resting on the polished wood above the cushion.

'What?'

'Another billiard table. I asked him why and he said that the room was big enough for two...'

'Mo...'

'Ridiculous idea, of course. So, this...' He looked at Hester, then at his brother. '...this attachment. Do you see it as being permanent?'

'God almighty. Do you know how ridiculous you sound?'

Hester said, 'No.'

'No?'

'Not a permanent attachment, no.'

'I see. So...I take it you agree?' he said to his brother.

'I want whatever's best for Hester,' he said. 'Her wishes are paramount and I'll fall in with whatever she decides.'

'Very noble,' Maurice said. He turned to Hester. 'What about our attachment, Hester? Do you want a divorce?'

She'd started weeping again. She shook her head. 'No,' she said, 'but I imagine you do.' Then she added, 'Please forgive me, Mo. I don't deserve it but please forgive me.'

Maurice knew that this was the moment when he should step forward and embrace his wife. He should forgive her. She was suffering horribly and he knew he was greatly to blame. He should forgive her and show her that he cared for her. He knew he should do this and he also knew that he couldn't.

Christopher knew it, too. He said, 'You know, you're a poor excuse for a husband, Mo.'

'And you're somewhat wanting as a brother,' Maurice replied.

Over the next few days, up to and beyond the funeral of General Redburn, Maurice made arrangements within the castle whose aim was to make it unlikely for him to meet either Christopher or Hester. The castle was a big place with more than fifty rooms. Maurice had counted them when he was a child and had reached a number he could no longer remember. So it wasn't impossible for all three to live in this huge, draughty, echoey building without meeting each other for hours at a time. Maurice took a room on the second floor but spent a great deal of time in his father's study at the top of the building, in the square tower. He went there on the pretext of sorting out important documents but the main purpose was to isolate himself in a place that was inaccessible. He climbed the staircase his father had had made and entered the study via the trapdoor which he closed and locked behind him. Only once, on his second day back in the castle, did someone strike the underside of the trapdoor to summon him from exile.

This was Jane, one of the maids, who nervously apologized for disturbing him but told him that a Mr McArdle had arrived to see him.

At first he was unsure who McArdle was and then he remembered: the undertaker. Of course. Yes, he'd come over from the mainland to finalise arrangements for the funeral in two days' time.

'Show him into the Salmon Room, would you?' Maurice said, his face looming above her from the open trapdoor. 'Bank up the fire and give him something to drink.'

'Yes, sir.'

'Oh, and go and find my brother. He needs to be there, too.'

'Yes, sir.'

The trapdoor closed.

Maurice understood the need for a meeting with the funeral director but found all the minor details of the arrangements to be tedious. The general was already sealed in his coffin which had been placed on the deal table in the middle of the old kitchen on the ground floor. The grave had been dug. McAlister, the grave-digger, fearing the hard frost that was forecast, had done his digging while the earth was still soft. And the Reverend Newarke would conduct the service and no doubt select some words of praise for his departed parishioner and laird. What more was required?

He'd witnessed funerals in France during the war, hasty affairs attended by those whose concern for the newly dead was outweighed by their fear of the still living. Once he'd attended a funeral in a field, a funeral that had lasted barely three minutes, the coffin lowered quickly, words read out at speed and earth filled in with the assistance of all seven mourners. The dead man was a farmer and he'd died of a heart attack in a town twenty-seven miles away. His last wish, so Maurice was informed, was to be buried on his farm, and his daughter had insisted on this. But the farm lay close to the front line so there was the risk of enemy fire; there was the risk that those gathered at the graveside might themselves die in the act of mourning. So all was haste and rush and a weeping daughter bundled into an army vehicle to be transported at speed away from the enemy lines.

Maurice learned later that the farm had indeed been hit by heavy artillery fire, the farmhouse destroyed and the farmer violently disinterred by a direct hit on the grave. At the end of the war the daughter had been accused of collaboration with the enemy. She was tried and convicted and shot. Maurice didn't know where she'd been buried.

So he had little appreciation for the supposedly delicate aspects of funeral arrangements, even for his own father. A body was a body, flesh in decay, nothing to love or care for any more. But he knew that there had to be a bit of a show. The islanders expected it, even if he found it meaningless.

But McArdle had come from the mainland, as requested, so deserved some respect. He declined the whisky on offer and talked about limousines. How many would be required? Christopher pointed out that there were fifteen members of staff living at the estate, several with other family members who would certainly want to attend the funeral. Some of them were elderly and not in the best of health.

'Five limousines, then?' McArdle suggested.

'Ten,' Christopher said.

'Ten? Ten?' Maurice looked at him in disbelief. 'Ridiculous idea.'

'Everyone in the castle will want to be there,' Christopher said calmly. 'Better to have too many limousines than too few.'

'Even so…'

McArdle said, 'How many, in total, do you expect will need to be accommodated, if I may ask?'

The Major shrugged.

McArdle was a small, obsequious man in his black suit. He was about fifty years old, Maurice guessed, but portly and bald already. He held his black bowler hat tightly by the rim in hands that were slim and unblemished, hands that had never held a spade or a hammer. Or a rifle. Maurice found himself unable to warm to the man. Yet he was no doubt good at his job, efficient, organised…

McArdle said, 'Your gamekeeper, Mr McRone, has asked a favour.'

'Really? He asked you?'

'Pending your approval, of course. He would like to carry your father's helmet and sword in front of the cortege.'

'I see. Well, I don't see why not…'

'I believe that of all the estate employees he was quite close to your father.'

'You could say that, yes.'

'He said it would be an honour for him to perform this duty in memory of your father.'

Maurice stood up. 'You must forgive me, Mr McArdle,' he said. 'I find it very difficult to concentrate on the matter in hand, important though it is. I'll be pleased to fall in with whatever arrangements you arrive at with my brother…number of limousines and so on. And yes, I agree to McRone's request. Now, if you'll excuse me…'

He left the room without a handshake of farewell for the undertaker who, already on his feet, bowed to the departing figure.

When Maurice was gone and the door was closed behind him, Christopher said, 'Please forgive my brother, Mr McArdle. He's been under a great deal of strain.'

Maurice made his way to the old kitchen on the ground floor where his father's coffin was. There had been some concern about sealing the coffin before Maurice's arrival. Would he want to see his father one last time? But Maurice had said no. He might have added, but didn't, that he'd seen more than his fair share of dead bodies and didn't want to see any more. Nevertheless, the previous day, shortly after his arrival, he'd spent some time sitting by the coffin.

And this is what he did now. He wouldn't be disturbed here while, as everyone liked to believe, he was paying his respects to his father. But, as with his intermittent retreats to the study in the tower, it was more an attempt to isolate himself. For, though he knew the general had favoured him above his brother, he didn't like his father much. Too interfering, too demanding. And his treatment of Christopher was uncaring to the point of spitefulness. Of course, given the recent revelation about Christopher's conduct, maybe his father had been right. What Christopher had done was unforgivable. But Maurice realised he was not without blame himself. In effect he had abandoned Hester. And, was it right to demand fidelity from someone he had, in turn, betrayed? No, it was a mess and, as he sat a few feet away from his father's body, he found himself wondering what his father would have done in these circumstances. And the answer was simple: almost certainly he'd have made things very much worse.

He heard voices in the front hall. Christopher was bidding McArdle goodbye. He heard a car starting up and then wheels crunching on gravel. He rose, placed a hand briefly on the coffin lid and left the room. He found Christopher a minute or so later, back in the Salmon Room.

'Shall I tell you what we decided?' Christopher asked.

'Don't bother,' Maurice said. 'I'm really not interested.'

'You know, I really don't understand you, Mo…'

'Fine,' Maurice said. 'I don't expect you to.'

'I know I've behaved badly…'

'So you've said.'

'But I mean…the funeral and everything…we really need to agree on…'

'I agree,' Maurice said, interrupting. 'I agree with whatever you've arranged. There.'

Christopher shook his head. 'OK, OK,' he said. Then he added, 'I'll be leaving immediately after the funeral. The same day, if possible.'

'Back to Paris?'

'No, no. Back to London.'

'London?' Maurice said. 'I thought you were living in Paris.'

'Well, I was but I ran out of money.'

'Really? Well, the old man might have left you something in his will.'

'I doubt it.'

'You may be right.'

Maurice walked across the room to look at the glass case, hung above the heavy sideboard, which contained a replica, taken from a cast of the original, of a thirty-six pound salmon caught by their grandfather in 1893. It was the display that gave the room its name.

'Do you remember that?' Maurice asked, pointing to the display case.

'What?'

'The fish, the salmon.'

'Remember? What do you mean? It was caught before we were born. You know, Mo, you've got this intensely annoying habit of veering off into something completely...completely irrelevant.'

'Irrelevant? You think so?'

'Yes.'

'I was just thinking...Father was disappointed he never caught a bigger one.'

'Competition, eh?' Christopher said. 'Even between generations of the same family. Anyway, Grandfather didn't catch that fish.' He pointed to the display cabinet.

'What do you mean? Of course he caught it.'

'No, it was Kincaid who caught it.'

'Kincaid?'

'You don't remember him?' Christopher said. 'Well, I'm surprised, Mo. He was the water baillie. Died...oh, ten years ago or thereabouts.'

'Of course I remember Kincaid,' Maurice said. 'Lived in Shore Cottage.'

'That's right. I had a chat with him once. I was only eight or nine, I think. But anyway, he told me the story about catching the fish. And it tells us a lot.'

'Does it? About what?'

'Oh, about the family, our relationships with other...shall we say...lesser people. And about Grandad, too, the main thing being that he didn't catch the fish.'

'So Kincaid caught it, did he?'

'Yes. Kincaid hooked it,' Christopher went on. 'He played it till it was exhausted and then he handed the rod over to Grandad who just had to hold it steady for the ten seconds or so it took Kincaid to grab the gaff and drag the poor thing from the water onto dry land.'

'So, isn't that how it happened then? And still does, as far as I know.'

Christopher shook his head. 'You know, Kincaid showed me a cutting – very proud he was, too – a cutting from the Dalmore Herald: "Monster Salmon Caught on the Droy." Something like that. All about Grandad catching this huge fish. And no mention of Kincaid. And he had a photo of Grandad with the fish which was taken by a photographer invited over from the mainland just to take that one picture. Grandad and the fish. No Kincaid. And I remember he was so proud that Grandad had seen fit to give him a copy of the photo. He told me what a generous man the Major was.'

Christopher turned to the display case again and examined the deep body of the three and a half foot long salmon with its hooked upper and lower jaws and its dead eye. 'And here we are,' he said, pointing to the small brass plate on the frame, '*Salmon weighing thirty-six pounds, caught on the River Droy by Major Galvin Redburn on March the fourteenth, eighteen ninety-three.*'

A silence of several seconds followed this. Then Maurice said, 'So what's your point, Christopher?'

'It's the deceit of it,' Christopher said. 'This family's good at deceit. All of us. Oh, me included. I don't excuse myself.'

'I should hope not,' Maurice said as he left the room.

In a spirit of compromise, Christopher had ordered seven luxurious limousines for the funeral so that all the castle staff could be accommodated. However, half a dozen of the staff decided to walk. They were followed by a group of fifty or sixty men from the village of Ardroy. The entire column of cars and people was led by Alexander McRone, the gamekeeper, in black coat and bowler hat, bearing before him the general's helmet and sword.

Only one of the three principal mourners – Hester – showed any emotion at the graveside. She wept during the Reverend Newarke's address – 'He does bleat on,' Christopher commented later – and broke down again when she added her tiny handful of soil to that which was tossed into the grave by the mourners when the service was over.

Sixty-five people went back to the castle after the funeral for sandwiches and drinks. It was Christopher who counted them. He was convinced that most of them just wanted a dram. There was whisky for the men and sherry or lemonade for the women, who numbered four, including Hester. 'Women don't usually go to funerals here,' Maurice explained to her.

In mid-afternoon, when it was already beginning to get dark, the wind freshened and the sky quickly clouded over. McArdle and his men with their hearse and seven limousines were already on the pier in Ardroy waiting for the ferry when it became clear that a storm was on its way. By four thirty any hope of the ferry's arrival was gone. The strip of sea that separated Glass from the mainland was as full of rage as some of the Reverend Newarke's sermons. An ocean-going liner would have struggled to make headway against the ferocity of the storm. For the Eilean Dubh, even though it was large enough to accommodate nine vehicles, crossing the Sound was out of the question. Those on the pier didn't even wait for word from the mainland; it was clear there would be no ferry that day.

Back to the castle came McArdle and his slow procession of shiny black cars. Maurice had rooms made up for the men so that they could stay overnight. McArdle himself was profuse in his thanks and embarrassed at the inconvenience he'd created, inconvenience not just to Maurice Redburn and the castle staff but to the Stephensons on the mainland. The senior member of the family, James McWilliam Stephenson, recently dead at the age of ninety-seven, would remain unburied for a further day.

The island's isolation during the storm also ensured that Christopher could not leave. He decided he could at least keep clear of Maurice for the remainder of his stay and then get on the first ferry that made it to the island.

Which arrived at 2pm the following afternoon. With the storm reduced to a few tattered clouds and waves subsiding into indifference in the Sound, the Eilean Dubh pushed its way across smoothly and added an extra trip in early evening to ensure that all traffic to and from the island was catered for.

Christopher left on the first ferry as he'd promised.

'What do you want me to do, Maurice?'

'Maurice? Why so formal? Didn't you use to call me Mo?'

'I don't know. It doesn't seem right any more.'

'Doesn't it?'

'No.' She shook her head. 'I don't know why. Distance,' she added, 'in all its forms.' She paused. 'If you want to divorce me, I won't stand in your way.'

'Divorce?' Maurice said. 'No, no. I don't think so.'

They were in the Salmon Room which, over the winter, Hester had been using as a living room. It was the only room on the ground floor which always had a log fire laid each morning.

'Let's sit down, shall we, at least,' Maurice suggested.

They sat on either side of the fire, Hester in the armchair that had been occupied by McArdle only a few days before.

'I'll do anything you want,' Hester said. 'Do you want me to leave?'

'Where would you go?'

'I'm sure I could find somewhere.'

'I doubt it,' Maurice said.

'Maybe I'm more resilient than you think, than perhaps you allow me to be.'

'I'll always be grateful for the way you looked after Pa. You certainly showed some tenacity there.'

'I always thought you were close to him but actually you didn't like him much, did you?'

'Was it that obvious?'

'You and Christopher both. But then...I don't know...from what Chris told me, maybe it was inevitable.'

'He favoured me, you see,' Maurice said. 'Pa, I mean. And, even when I was quite young, I could see how unfair that was. I didn't complain, of course. A bit difficult when you're being given the best of everything. But I felt for Christopher in a way, though Pa was right, to an extent.'

'Right to treat Christopher as he did?'

'No, I didn't mean that. No...right in his assessment of Christopher's character – wayward, feckless, not very practical...'

A long pause followed and then Hester said, 'I'm sorry, Mo. I've offended you in the worst possible way. It was despicable of me. And I'm truly ashamed.'

'You were lonely,' Maurice said. 'You were experiencing a loneliness that I created for you.'

'Don't make excuses for me, Mo, please.'

'Oh, I'm not, I'm not. I'm just saying that I'm at least partly to blame. I mean, sending you up here to this huge empty place in the middle of winter. I can't blame you for wanting to leave.'

'I didn't say I wanted to leave.'

'No? I inferred...'

'No, I asked if you wanted me to leave. Tell me and I'll go.'

'I don't want you to leave.'

'Right.'

'But I don't want to keep you here against your will.'

'I've got no wish to rejoin Christopher, if that's what you mean.'

'Well, that's not what I was thinking about, but nevertheless...I'm glad you said it.'

Another silence.

'So I'll stay here, then?'

'Yes, for the time being. I've got to go back down to London, of course, but then I'll be up in Edinburgh soon. I know they've been dragging their feet a bit on that but it's still the plan. I'll look for a house. I mean, we could look together...you wouldn't mind staying in a hotel for a couple of weeks, would you?'

'No, no. Of course not.'

'Good, good.' He stood up and walked across to the nearest window. There was a view of the village with the hills beyond and, to the right, the sea, still not quite settled into placidity. 'I'd rather be here than in London,' he said.

This last statement was a lie. The remainder of his stay at Swordale was devoted to preparations for leaving it. He had to get someone in to manage the estate in his absence, put plans together for the farm, the hill land, the grouse moor, the fishing, the general upkeep of the castle and grounds. It took him three weeks to do this and then he set off back down to London.

On the way he considered his options. Hester had said he could divorce her if he wanted to. Would Margaret Foster marry him? Did he want to marry Margaret Foster? It was worth thinking about and he thought about it a lot. Of course, she'd never live at Swordale. No, if they married he'd be committed to city life – not London necessarily but somewhere large and noisy. Abroad, perhaps. Is that what he wanted? The choice at present seemed to be with Hester in Edinburgh or with Margaret Foster in London. It wasn't a difficult choice.

He phoned Margaret Foster on the evening he got back to London. 'Maurice,' she said, 'well, Maurice, I thought you'd forgotten all about me, but look, I've got a few people here right now and it's really…really rather…could you…do you think you could call back in the morning?'

He rang at 11am but Ellie told him that Mrs Foster was unavailable. Perhaps he could try later? He rang at one o'clock and she was there.

'Maurice,' she said. 'Where are you?'

'I'm back in London.'

'But you didn't call.'

'Well, I was on Glass. No phones, remember.'

'But you said you'd call. I mean, from the mainland.'

'I was on the island the whole time.'

'The whole time?'

'So much to do,' he said. 'You wouldn't believe…'

'But you said you'd call.' It was almost a whine. 'And you didn't.'

'I'm sorry. Really I am. It was just…very hectic. Lots of people wanting lots of different things…But look, I'm…can I come and see you? There's a few things I'd like to talk to you about.'

'What sort of things?'

'Well, to do with us.'

'You sound very serious, Maurice.'

'Well, I don't mean to. It's just that I'd like to talk to you about us, about our future.'

'Our future? But what's to discuss? You're a married man, Maurice. That pretty much takes care of things, doesn't it?'

'Things can change,' he said.

She took a few moments to consider this, then said, 'Now,

Maurice, please don't tell me you're thinking of abandoning Hester...'

'No, of course not. It's just that I think she's quite keen to end the marriage herself.'

'You *think*?'

'She's clearly not happy. Neither am I.'

'So you're keen to do a swap, is that it?'

'That's a very cold way of putting it, Margaret.'

'But that's pretty much how it is, isn't it?'

After a short pause he said, 'Yes, it is. I'd rather spend the rest of my life with you than with Hester, certainly.'

'Oh, Maurice...'

'Can we talk about this? This evening?'

'This evening's a bit difficult.'

'Tomorrow, then.'

'No, not tomorrow, not tomorrow...'

'So when, then?'

He could hear her breathing. For a few moments that's all he could hear.

'Margaret?'

'It's difficult right now.'

'Difficult?'

'Things have got complicated. Oh, Maurice, why didn't you keep in touch? Why were you away so long?'

'Three weeks? Is that so long?'

'A month, Maurice. Nearly five weeks. I thought you'd forgotten all about me.'

'Oh, come on, Margaret, don't be silly. I thought about you every day. Every single day.'

'And how was I to know that?'

'For goodness' sake, Margaret, I told you I couldn't contact you.'

'You said you would. You said you'd phone.'

'But I told you, I just couldn't get to the mainland.'

'I can't see you again, Maurice.'

'What?'

'I can't see you again.'

He considered this information for several seconds and then asked, very calmly, 'Why not?'

'Because I'm going to be married.'

Another pause. 'Married?'

'Yes.'

'Christ. Married...What do you mean, married?'

'I'm...I know it's all happened very quickly...'

'Quickly? I'll say quickly...Christ...One of Foss's old buddies managed to persuade you, did he?'

'Good God, no. Not one of those...'

'Then who?'

'His name's Peter Murchison.'

'And who's he?'

'Don't you remember? From the cruise.'

'Peter Murchison? No, no...oh, wait a minute...businessman from Birmingham? Is that the chap?'

'Yes, that's him. He got in touch...'

'Got in touch, asked you to marry him and you said yes. And that's that.'

'No, Maurice, it wasn't at all like that.'

'Listen, Margaret, Hester and I had dinner with him a few times – more out of pity than anything else – and I can say without hesitation that he's the most boring person I've ever met.'

'That's hardly fair, Maurice. He wasn't well then. You knew that. You both knew that.'

'That doesn't excuse him,' Maurice said. 'So, when's the wedding? All arranged already, is it?'

'We haven't fixed a date yet. Within the next month or so...'

'Cancel it.'

'No, I can't do that.'

'Come on, Margaret, there's still time. Cancel it. I mean, you don't love him, do you? It's been only two minutes...'

'Maurice, there's no point in you...'

'Oh, hold on a minute,' Maurice said. 'I remember him a bit better now. Quite rich, isn't he? No, no, I'm wrong. He's very rich, extremely rich. Well, well, well, the old priority comes to the fore again.'

'Now you're being spiteful and rude.'

'Well, how do you think I feel? I go away for a few days and when I get back, everything's upside down. How can things change so quickly? What on earth were you thinking?'

'He's a good man, Maurice.'

'A good man. Is he?'

'Yes, he's...he's right for me.'

'Ah yes. Maybe that's more accurate. And I'm wrong for you, am I?' After ten seconds of silence, he repeated, 'So I'm wrong for you, am I?'

And she said, 'Goodbye, Maurice,' and hung up.

When he received his long-overdue posting to Edinburgh four weeks later, Maurice left Woolwich and London hoping that he would never have to return. Edinburgh represented a new start. It was spring. The hyacinths and daffodils and, later, tulips were flowering in Princes Street Gardens and he strived to fill himself with hope. He wrote to Hester inviting her to join him so that she could inspect some houses which might be suitable for them. His posting was for two years initially, with the prospect of extension. They might as well be comfortable. He was aware that his Army pay would not cover their expenses but he had some considerable income from Swordale Estate; he wasn't poor.

As they had agreed, he booked her into a hotel for a month so that she would have plenty of time to look for a house.

He decided to forget Margaret Foster. Of course, he couldn't forget her; he thought about her every day. But he didn't ring her and he didn't write to her. However, she did enter his life once more. About five weeks after their last phone call, he read a notice of her marriage in *The Times*. Consequently that particular episode in his life, if any further confirmation were needed, had come to an end.

But three days before Hester was due to arrive in Edinburgh he received a letter from her saying that she would not be coming because she was unwell. And she was unwell because she was pregnant.

PART FOUR

Glass

Over the years a code had evolved. The Major knew that five or six sharp raps in quick succession on the underside of the trapdoor, followed by a muffled cry involving words probably referring to the presentation of a meal, could safely be ignored for five minutes or so. The next series of knocks would be of the same intensity in terms of sound, but of longer duration – perhaps a dozen knocks in all. The words that followed would still be indecipherable, warped by wood and air and the Major's well developed ability to mishear, but were of a higher pitch, indicating a greater sense of urgency. At this point the Major would know that he had a couple of minutes at most before he would have to descend. This second alarm also demanded acknowledgement and he would do this by stamping his right foot on the floor twice. The third and final summons involved the use of no instrument other than voice. There was no more knocking; there was just the word 'Mo!' repeated three or four times at such a high, piercing volume as to be inescapable.

He knew that today would be different. He felt that events might occur during the course of the morning that would result in permanent change to the way he lived. And this disturbed him. He disliked change. No, that wasn't quite true: he disliked sudden change. There was that business with McRone, for example. That was a single event which altered many things in the space of a morning. It affected the arrangements at the castle – he lost a gamekeeper and his assistant at the same time. But that was a minor issue. More important was the fact that it changed his relationship with his own son, James. This wasn't just because they disagreed about how the incident should be handled but because there was a definite shifting of power. James was in charge now, that much was clear, though to be fair, James still deferred to him in certain matters. However, these matters were of little or no significance. He might be consulted on the layout of a room or the colour of the wallpaper, but never on the use of the room itself. Even the gardens, there were changes to the gardens. He came to realise that he could stop now, give up, retire, whatever the appropriate phrase was, he could withdraw from his involvement with the castle and no one would really notice.

Nevertheless, it seemed that he was needed right now and it was a pity that today of all days, the day of his brother's funeral, things were starting off so badly. The signs were not good. The underside of the trapdoor was not being tapped or knocked, it was being battered; he could see it being jarred upwards by the power of the blows from beneath. And the voice, the repetition of his name, had gone beyond insistence, further even than urgency; it was clear that something was badly wrong.

He pulled up the trapdoor and looked down. 'What is it?' he asked of his wife who was standing on the third step of the stepladder with the usual broom in her hand. From this angle it was inevitable that she should look tinier than ever and this impression was reinforced by the fact that she was wearing black, a black coat and gloves and a small black pillbox hat with a veil. He was struck also by how frail she was, and how vulnerable. He wondered where her strength came from. She was breathing heavily from her exertions. 'Oh, do come down, Mo,' she said. 'You've got to sort things out.' He could see genuine distress in her eyes and he heard it in her voice. For the first time for a long time the condition she was in affected him deeply. He pondered these three words – frail, vulnerable, distressed – and suddenly thought, I mustn't lose her, I'd be lost without her. Then he realised how selfish this thought was. He said, 'Now come on, Alice, I'll be right down. Whatever it is, we'll fix it in no time.'

She held onto the stepladder as he came down, slowly and carefully. 'Of course, you won't allow stairs to be put in, will you,' she said. 'It'd be much safer.' It was an old subject, one that she couldn't help raising whenever they found themselves here, in this configuration of bodies, attached to an uncertain construction of wood and metal, she holding, he ascending or descending, neither in control. To her astonishment he said, 'Oh, I don't know. Maybe it's time for a staircase after all. Maybe James can arrange it.'

They went down, slowly, to the ground floor, the Major following his wife, her descent marginally quicker than his. The staircase was newly carpeted and the Major still had to get used to the feel of it beneath his feet, the give in the thick maroon pile which lent to his steps a certain instability. On the third floor landing they passed the encased wolf and Alice Redburn placed her hand momentarily on a corner of the cabinet to steady herself.

The undertaker, MacMillan, was waiting for them at the foot of the stairs in the hall. He was a tall man whose expression managed to be sombre and kind at the same time. Beside him stood James Redburn, clearly agitated, fiddling with his bowler hat. It was James who spoke first. 'We're late,' he said, pointing to his watch and dropping the bowler hat in the process. 'We're already fifteen minutes late as it is.'

'Such a simple thing,' Alice Redburn said, more to herself than to anyone else. 'Simple, really.'

'MacMillan,' the Major said, 'do you know what all this is about?'

'Some of it, Major,' MacMillan said. 'Some of it, at least. Your wife, Mrs Redburn...she wants...' He paused and looked across at Alice Redburn for confirmation of some kind but there was none. She was looking at the floor as if troubled by some huge guilt.

'What does she want?' the Major asked.

'She wants me to open the coffin, sir...'

'She...what?'

'I don't know what all the fuss is about,' Alice Redburn said. 'I mean, it's quite simple, surely...'

'I have explained, sir...'

The Major butted in. 'You want MacMillan to open the coffin?' he said to his wife. 'What on earth for?'

'Surely,' she began, 'surely...I mean it's quite simple, isn't it? It's got a lid after all.'

'But...but why?' He looked at her in astonishment and confusion. 'I mean, you had a chance...we all had a chance...to look...'

'It seems such a simple request,' she said. 'I don't understand the difficulty...'

'But it is difficult,' the Major said. 'I mean, these things are screwed down...' He turned to the undertaker. 'Aren't they?'

'I've tried to explain, sir,' MacMillan said, 'that it's too late now to open the coffin. It's been sealed. There's a process...'

'Oh, I know that, I know that,' the Major said. He looked at his wife. 'Don't you see,' he said to her, 'it's too late. It's just too late. I mean...but why this sudden need?' He saw that she was almost in tears and again he was moved by her obvious distress. He stepped to her side. 'Alice,' he said gently. 'Alice.' Then he turned to the undertaker. 'Look, give us a couple of minutes, will you?'

'We're already late,' James Redburn said. 'We're already late and there are people waiting.'

'Then they'll have to wait a bit longer,' the Major said, with sufficient irritation in his tone to dissuade any further discussion of the issue. 'Come along, dear,' he said and put a hand on his wife's shoulder. They left the hall, going through a door to the right of the staircase. This door was now marked 'Private' and it led through to the small extension where they had lived for the past twenty years.

In the living room Alice Redburn sat down in one of the large flowered armchairs and started to cry. She pulled a handkerchief from her sleeve and wiped her eyes and nose several times over the space of a minute or so while her husband looked on silently, unable to decide what he might do. He couldn't remember the last time he'd seen his wife so upset and he realised that his ability to offer comfort – if he had ever had such a thing – was now lost. But when she appeared to be gaining control again, her tears drying up, and she had begun to blow her nose noisily, he managed to touch her shoulder and say, 'Alice, whatever is the matter? I mean, why on earth do you want them to open the coffin?'

She wiped her nose one last time, tucked her handkerchief away and said, 'I got a letter.'

'A letter?'

'From Chris.'

'From Christopher?'

'Yes.'

'I see,' he said quietly. He sat down in the vacant chair next to hers. They were now sitting at an angle to one another, rather than opposite, but close enough for their feet to touch.

'It was delivered yesterday...I mean, last night, in fact.'

'Last night?'

'It was delivered by hand. That is...' She retrieved her handkerchief and dabbed at her nose again. 'Alan McRone came here and delivered it by hand. He came here because...well, he came over at Chris's request. Alan, you see, went to visit...to visit...no, it wasn't Alan was it, it was...Oh dear...' She began to weep again, wiping her eyes quickly in irritation at her inability to convey the meaning she sought.

'Alice, please,' the Major said, employing the soft tones he rarely used and only to his wife, 'calm yourself, please. Just take it slowly.' He leaned forward and raised a hand as if about to stretch across and take hold of one of hers – the closeness of the two armchairs would certainly have permitted this – but he didn't complete the movement. He sat back again and said, in more even tones, 'You've had a shock, I can see that. Just...just start from the beginning.'

'Yes, yes,' Alice dried her eyes and consigned her handkerchief to her sleeve again. 'Yes, well,' she began, 'you see, Christopher went to see Alan McRone in jail and asked him if he would deliver a couple of letters...'

'So there's two letters now?'

'Yes. One to me and one to James.'

'Ah.' This small sound had more than a hint of understanding and resignation to it.

'You see,' Alice went on, 'Chris knew he was dying and he wanted someone to deliver these letters because he couldn't do it himself. He couldn't come to Swordale, you see. He made a promise and didn't want to break it.'

The Major exhaled deeply. 'Very noble, I'm sure.'

'And he didn't want to post them because he wanted to be sure that only I got to see mine and only James got to see his.'

'He didn't want there to be any chance of me intercepting them, you mean?'

Alice said, 'I think...I think that's it, yes.' Then she added, 'Oh, Mo, this is dreadful, dreadful...'

She looked as if she was about to burst into tears again but the Major said, 'No more weeping, Alice, please. I can't...I mean, I don't blame you for any of this, obviously, so just tell me all about it. Just tell me, please.'

She got up and went over to a very fine rosewood sideboard which was only a few feet from her armchair. She picked up an envelope that was lying on top and took it to her husband. She held it out to him and said, 'This is the letter. I think you'd better read it.'

He shook his head. 'No,' he said, 'I don't want to read it. I don't even want to touch it. You just sit down and tell me what's in it. Of course I'm pretty sure it'll be a work of fiction like everything else he wrote.'

'Oh, Mo, how can you say that?'

'Very easily. It's what he did for a living. People tend to forget that. He made up stories. I don't think he ever managed to master the difference between fact and fiction.' He paused. 'But look, go on, tell me.'

Alice sat down again. 'He says in the letter,' she began, 'that he had an affair with Hester...that is, your first wife...'

'I'm perfectly aware who Hester was,' he said.

His tone startled her. It was the first time in their many years of marriage that he had directed towards her a sarcastic remark.

Aware of this himself, he added, very quickly, 'I'm sorry. No, I shouldn't have said that. I'm sorry. Please go on.'

She composed herself and continued, 'Chris had an affair with Hester and she became pregnant and gave birth to James. So...so Christopher is James's father, not you. And then, because you wanted to keep the scandal secret, you agreed – I mean, both of you – that James wasn't to hear about this until one of you died. The promise made was that the survivor would tell James about his real parentage.'

She saw that her husband had begun to smile. It was only just recognisable as a smile, wry and unbelieving. She went on, 'And, well, he came to believe that you wouldn't keep your part of the bargain so, as he knew he was going to die, he decided to write to me and to James explaining the situation. That's...that's the gist of it.'

After a short pause he said quietly, 'I see.'

Alice looked at him, waiting for some further response which was not forthcoming. At last she said, 'Please say something, Mo. I can't stand this.'

'Well, it's all nonsense of course,' he said.

'Nonsense?'

'Yes. I mean, the poor man was never exactly right in the head and I imagine his final illness must have completely unhinged him. The whole story's complete rubbish.'

'The letter,' Alice said quietly, 'well, dates and facts and so on, I don't really know of course but...let's say it's very persuasive.'

'Oh, I'm sure it is. Look at all the people who bought his ridiculous novels. But that doesn't mean to say there's any truth in it. Just bear in mind that he went to Paris in 1929 or 30, something like that, and that was the last anyone saw of him till he turned up in 1950. So he couldn't possibly have had an affair with Hester because he never even met her.'

'Well,' Alice said, 'I know all this happened before I met you, Mo, but if things didn't happen as Chris says in his letter, then why on earth did you two not get on?'

The Major shrugged. 'Oh, there were plenty of other reasons for that. It's a very long story, and dull too. All to do with childhood, our father and so on. Not something I really want to talk about. But look, more to the point...' He sat forward in his chair. 'What's all this got to do with opening the coffin?'

'It's in the letter,' Alice said.

'Ah, this confounded letter...'

'Chris has asked for something to be placed in the coffin beside him, to be buried with him.'

'I see. And what is it exactly?'

'Oh, it's quite small...well, fairly small...light, certainly. Very light. You see I could have...I mean, I could have done it yesterday perhaps but, well, I didn't know anything about this sealing business...'

'Alice...'

'Seems such a fuss. I mean...'

'Alice...'

'Yes?'

'What is it? Tell me what it is.'

'Well...' She rose from her chair. 'You won't like it, Mo. You won't like it at all. But anyway...' She stepped over to the sideboard again and opened the top drawer. She took out a long cardboard tube and handed it to her husband. 'It's this,' she said. 'He wanted it to be placed in the coffin beside him.'

The Major took hold of the tube but made no attempt to open it. He examined it as if it were of a class of objects he'd never seen before.

'There's a painting inside,' his wife said. 'Well, a copy of a painting. You can open it if you wish.'

He located the end with the white plastic disk. He removed the disk and slowly pulled out the rolled-up sheet of paper that was inside the tube. Holding one edge in his left hand he carefully unrolled it with his right until he had revealed the photo-reproduction of the portrait of his first wife. 'Well, well,' he said quietly. 'Hester.'

Although the corners of the copy curled inwards, her face was wholly visible. He adjusted the position of his hands to rid the picture surface of glare. He looked at the portrait for some time and said nothing. Alice Redburn said, 'I think James must have sent it off for restoration with all the others. Chris found out about it and contacted the company separately to ask for a copy. And when the men arrived with all the paintings, this tube arrived, too. And it was addressed to poor Chris but of course he was already dead, so…so…and then in his letter he asked if…if the painting could be placed beside him in the coffin. That's if I got the letter in time, of course. D'you see?'

The Major allowed the portrait to roll itself up again in his hands. He sat now with the tube and the rolled-up picture both lying across his knees. 'I'm sorry, Alice, but it's quite impossible,' he said. 'Completely out of the question. You heard what MacMillan said, the coffin's sealed and that's that.'

'Surely, Mo…'

'No, it's not possible, it really isn't.' He stood up. He placed the cardboard tube and the portrait on the armchair. 'Now, let's get back to the others.'

'But, Mo,' Alice said as she got to her feet, 'don't you think…'

'Alice, it can't be done, and there's an end to it.' He opened the door. 'So now, please, let's go back. Please.' He extended a hand to her and, as she came to his side he took hold of her elbow gently. 'Let's go,' he said. 'They're waiting.'

They returned to the hall but there was no one there. James and MacMillan the undertaker were in an adjoining room, on the other side from the private quarters occupied by the Major and

Alice. It was a large sitting room with a view of the sea.

The Major said, 'It's all right, MacMillan. I think we've resolved that issue. No need to open the coffin, you'll be glad to hear.'

'I am glad to hear it, Major.'

'So, let's get on with it, shall we?'

'Yes, certainly…'

'Just a moment,' James said. To MacMillan he added, 'Could you leave us for a couple of minutes? I'll let you know when we're ready.'

'James, for goodness' sake,' the Major said. 'You were the one complaining about the delay. Hadn't we better get on?'

'Not just quite yet. I'm sorry, Mr MacMillan, but we'll need another few minutes.'

MacMillan's gesture was one of acceptance, not irritation. 'As you wish,' he said and he left the room.

'This had better be good,' the Major said.

'Oh, it's not good,' James said. He was standing near the door. 'It's not good at all. You see, while you were out of the room we had a visit from Alan McRone.'

'Did you indeed.'

'Yes. And he gave me a letter.' James took an envelope from his inside pocket and extracted five hand-written pages.

'Ah, a letter from Christopher, I believe,' the Major said.

'Yes, it is. How did you know that?'

'Alice got one, too. Didn't you, dear?'

Alice nodded.

'And I'll tell you what's in it, if you like,' the Major went on. 'It's all some nonsense about him being your father and not me.'

'That's right, yes. So it's nonsense, is it?'

'Oh, complete rubbish, I assure you. I mean, if you've ever read any of his dreadful novels you'll have gathered that my brother was a bit of a fantasist.'

'So it's complete fantasy, is it?'

'Certainly. I hope you're not giving it any credence.'

'Well,' James said and he began to re-arrange the pages in his hand, 'there's two things to think about, I'd say.'

'Really?'

'Yes. First, it would explain why you and he never spoke to each other for the best part of forty years and second, it's very detailed indeed about the events of 1931, 1932 and so on, round about the time grandpa died.'

'Chris wasn't even here then,' the Major said.

'What do you mean?'

'I mean precisely what I'm saying: Christopher wasn't at Swordale then. He went off to Paris some time in the late 1920s and we never saw him again – well, I didn't, anyway.'

'So you're saying he never even met Hester?'

'Exactly, yes. Why he should come up with this ridiculous story, I've no idea.'

'Well, if he wasn't here,' James said, 'there's something that needs to be explained…'

'And what's that?'

'Something the decorators found the other day.'

'Who?'

'The decorators. In the Polar Room. They were stripping the walls. They came across some kind of inscription on the plaster…'

'An inscription? What do you mean?'

'Well, they took off about three layers of wallpaper and when they got down to the plaster there were some names written there, with dates.'

'Dates?'

'Yes. One from 1895 with a few names below it and one from 1931. November the 10th, or perhaps the 12th. But definitely November, 1931. There were names there as well. Murchison, for example, the gardener. Remember him?'

'Murchison? Yes, of course…'

'And a few chambermaids and, I don't know…a butler or two perhaps. And then, Hester Redburn and C. M. Redburn.'

'C. M. Redburn,' the Major repeated.

'It's got to be Christopher, hasn't it?'

'Well…' He made a non-committal gesture with his right hand. 'I suppose…a scribble on a wall, you say?'

'Yes. They did it in 1895, then in 1931. Got as many people as possible to sign the wall, then papered it over.'

'I don't really see what you're driving at,' the Major said.

'I'm sure you do. I'm talking about the real relationship between Christopher and Hester. Christopher wasn't here when I was born but he was here about a year earlier. He got here at the end of 1931 and stayed for three or four months until Grandfather died.'

'No, no,' the Major said abruptly and he waved the suggestion away. 'No, you've got it completely wrong there, completely wrong...'

'Are you saying that he didn't even attend grandpa's funeral?'

'That's right, he didn't. I mean, how could he be so unfeeling that he didn't even come home for his father's funeral?'

'But he did,' James said. 'I'm sure of it. He told me about it himself.'

'Oh, well, that's hardly conclusive evidence, is it? I mean, it's just as trustworthy as that ridiculous letter.'

'And what would you say if I could actually prove that Chris was here in 1931?'

'Well, that's quite impossible.'

'I'm afraid you're wrong,' James said. His smile was brief and without warmth. 'I can certainly prove it. Just wait here. I'll be back shortly.' He left the room.

The Major shook his head.

'Oh, Mo,' Alice said. 'Please tell me the truth. I mean about Chris and Hester. I won't think badly of you, you know. I'll never change what I think of you, of course I won't...but you need to tell us exactly what happened. You do, really. For James's sake.'

'I've told you,' the Major said. 'I've told you.' He stepped away from her and walked across the room to the main window from which he could see the expanse of Ardroy Sound, the surface of the water wrestling with itself as a breeze gathered force from the north. 'I refuse...' he said. 'I refuse to...' But he never completed the sentence.

A few moments later James returned. Alan McRone accompanied him.

'Major...Mrs Redburn, good morning,' McRone said.

The Major turned from the window. 'Alan,' he said, 'well, it's good to see you again.' To James he said, 'How on earth can Alan help? He wasn't even born in 1931.'

'I'm aware of that,' James said. 'It's about his father.' He turned to McRone. 'I remember hearing the story about your father carrying the regimental helmet and sword in front of the hearse at my grandfather's funeral. That's what happened, wasn't it?'

'General Redburn's funeral,' McRone said. 'Yes, I heard that story many times.'

'And is there anything else you remember about it?'

'Well, there was that business with the bowler hat. You know, he was wearing a bowler hat and it got blown away in the wind. Took them a while to find it…'

The Major said, 'James, please, I've heard that story too, and believe me, I didn't need to hear it again because I was there. Yes, Alan's father did carry Pa's sword and helmet and yes, his bowler hat was blown from his head. I can vouch for all of that because I was there and I saw it. So what's the point of all this?'

To McRone James said, 'Do bear with us, won't you. We're having a bit of a family argument here and I'm sorry to involve you but this really is very, very important.'

McRone looked round at the three figures before him. 'Yes,' he said. 'I can see that.'

'So, this is the question,' James went on, 'can you recall, from what your father told you, who was present at the funeral?'

'Well,' McRone said, 'of course, that's quite a difficult question…'

'Of course it is,' the Major said. 'This is ridiculous…'

'Please,' James said, 'let's just get to the bottom of this, shall we? So…' He turned to McRone again and said, 'Please, do your best.'

'Well, let me see, there was John Murchison – he was the gardener – and Mrs Niven…and there was…'

'Actually,' James interrupted, 'I was thinking not so much about the castle staff but the family – I mean, our family. Did your father ever mention who the principal mourners were?'

'Oh, I see what you mean. Well, there was the Major here, obviously…and there was the Major's wife…' He looked across at Alice. 'Pardon me, I mean the Major's first wife.'

Alice waved away this comment. 'Don't apologise, Alan,' she said. 'I'm not that sensitive.'

'Go on,' James said.

'And there was the Major's brother, of course…'

'You mean Christopher? The man we're burying today?'

'Well, yes…'

'No, no, no,' the Major said in even tones which expressed

neither anger nor irritation. 'No, you're mistaken, Alan, or your father was. I mean, it's quite natural, of course, for you or your father to assume that Christopher was there at the funeral. After all, it was a son's duty to be present.'

James said, 'Are you sure, Alan? I mean that your father actually said that Christopher was there? We just need to know the truth.'

McRone looked from James to the Major and then back again.

'That's all we can ask of you,' the Major said. 'Just tell us the truth. Are you sure your father mentioned Christopher or are you just assuming he did?'

'Well now...' McRone paused and then went on, '...there's the question of the hunting knife.'

'Hunting knife? What hunting knife?'

'Well, it was decided that my father should receive something, you know, as a thank you. I mean, not just for what he did at the funeral, walking in front of the hearse and so on, but because he was...because he and the General got on very well. So he got the General's hunting knife, as a kind of token, a memento and, well, it was Mr Christopher Redburn who actually presented him with it.' He looked at the Major. 'With respect, Major, I believe you weren't very keen on the idea but your brother insisted. And it was him who came and handed it over. The same evening as the funeral. My father was already in bed. He got a chill from the soaking he got – so he told me, anyway, and he was quite ill for a few days, in fact. But that first night he got a visit from Mr Redburn who gave him the hunting knife. I've still got it, actually.'

McRone looked at the three people before him, none of whom seemed capable of responding to this information. 'Is that it?' he asked. 'Is that what you wanted to know?'

James said, 'Yes. And thank you very much for that. You've been very helpful. Very helpful. We can let you go now. Thank you.' He stepped over to the door and opened it. 'Kindly tell MacMillan, will you, that we'll be with him shortly.' McRone left the room and James closed the door.

'Well, then,' he said as he rejoined the Major and Alice, 'that seems pretty clear, doesn't it?'

'Nothing of the kind,' the Major said.

'Oh, come on, please. Why have you kept this a secret for so many years? Why didn't you tell me? Why are you so reluctant to admit to it now? I mean, don't you think I've got a right to know who my father is?'

'And who has been a father to you? Can you tell me that? Who's been a real father to you? Me or that wretch out there in his coffin?'

'Oh, Mo,' Alice said. 'Please, Mo...'

'Why do you want to change everything now, after all these years? Couldn't it all have been left in peace?'

'No,' James said. 'Not something like this, not something like this.'

Alice said, 'Can we at least bury the poor man now? We need to...to get on. I mean, there are people waiting.'

'You're right,' James said. 'Let's go and do it. We can carry on this discussion later.' He made his way to the door.

The Major walked over to an armchair by the window and sat down.

'Mo,' Alice said, 'aren't you coming?'

He was sitting side on to them but didn't turn to look. 'No,' he said, 'I'm not coming.'

'What?' This from James. 'But you've got to come.'

'No. No, I'm not coming. Tell them I'm ill. Tell them anything you like. I don't care. I'm just not coming and that's final.'

'Mo, please...' Alice took a few steps towards him and then stopped. James approached and put his arm round her shoulders. 'Let's go,' he said quietly. 'Best to leave him, I think. Let's go.' Together they turned and he steered her gently towards the door.

About the Author

David Shaw Mackenzie (www.davidshawmackenzie.com) is from Easter Ross in the Highlands of Scotland. His several careers have led him to various parts of the Middle East, Latin America, Spain and Italy. He now lives in London with his wife, Rachel. These days he spends his time mostly writing fiction and painting pictures of trees.

He is the author of two novels, *The Truth of Stone* (short-listed for the Saltire Society Best Scottish First Book Award) and *The Interpretations*. His short fiction has appeared in many literary magazines and anthologies, including *New Writing Scotland*, *Stand*, *Edinburgh Review*, *Chapman*, *News from the Republic of Letters* and three editions of 'Best Short Stories' anthologies.

More Books From ThunderPoint Publishing Ltd.

The False Men

Mhairead MacLeod

ISBN: 978-1-910946-27-5 (eBook)
ISBN: 978-1-910946-25-1 (Paperback)

North Uist, Outer Hebrides, 1848

Jess MacKay has led a privileged life as the daughter of a local landowner, sheltered from the harsher aspects of life. Courted by the eligible Patrick Cooper, the Laird's new commissioner, Jess's future is mapped out, until Lachlan Macdonald arrives on North Uist, amid rumours of forced evictions on islands just to the south.

As the uncompromising brutality of the Clearances reaches the islands, and Jess sees her friends ripped from their homes, she must decide where her heart, and her loyalties, truly lie.

Set against the evocative backdrop of the Hebrides and inspired by a true story, *The False Men* is a compelling tale of love in a turbulent past that resonates with the upheavals of the modern world.

'...an engaging tale of powerlessness, love and disillusionment in the context of the type of injustice that, sadly, continues to this day' – Anne Goodwin

The Oystercatcher Girl

Gabrielle Barnby

ISBN: 978-1-910946-17-6 (eBook)
ISBN: 978-1-910946-15-2 (Paperback)

In the medieval splendour of St Magnus Cathedral, three women gather to mourn the untimely passing of Robbie: Robbie's widow, Tessa; Tessa's old childhood friend, Christine, and Christine's unstable and unreliable sister, Lindsay.

But all is not as it seems: what is the relationship between the three women, and Robbie? What secrets do they hide? And who has really betrayed who?

Set amidst the spectacular scenery of the Orkney Islands, Gabrielle Barnby's skilfully plotted first novel is a beautifully understated story of deception and forgiveness, love and redemption.

With poetic and precise language Barnby draws you in to the lives, loves and losses of the characters till you feel a part of the story.

'The Oystercatcher Girl is a wonderfully evocative and deftly woven story' – Sara Bailey

The House with the Lilac Shutters

Gabrielle Barnby

ISBN: 978-1-910946-02-2 (eBook)
ISBN: 978-0-9929768-8-0 (Paperback)

Irma Lagrasse has taught piano to three generations of villagers, whilst slowly twisting the knife of vengeance; Nico knows a secret; and M. Lenoir has discovered a suppressed and dangerous passion.

Revolving around the Café Rose, opposite The House with the Lilac Shutters, this collection of contemporary short stories links a small town in France with a small town in England, traces the unexpected connections between the people of both places and explores the unpredictable influences that the past can have on the present.

Characters weave in and out of each other's stories, secrets are concealed and new connections are made.

With a keenly observant eye, Barnby illustrates the everyday tragedies, sorrows, hopes and joys of ordinary people in this vividly understated and unsentimental collection.

'The more I read, and the more descriptions I encountered, the more I was put in mind of one of my all time favourite texts – Dylan Thomas' Under Milk Wood' – lindasbookbag.com

Changed Times

Ethyl Smith

ISBN: 978-1-910946-09-1 (eBook)
ISBN: 978-1-910946-08-4 (Paperback)

1679 – The Killing Times: Charles II is on the throne, the Episcopacy has been restored, and southern Scotland is in ferment.

The King is demanding superiority over all things spiritual and temporal and rebellious Ministers are being ousted from their parishes for refusing to bend the knee.

When John Steel steps in to help one such Minister in his home village of Lesmahagow he finds himself caught up in events that reverberate not just through the parish, but throughout the whole of southern Scotland.

From the Battle of Drumclog to the Battle of Bothwell Bridge, John's platoon of farmers and villagers find themselves in the heart of the action over that fateful summer where the people fight the King for their religion, their freedom, and their lives.

Set amid the tumult and intrigue of Scotland's Killing Times, John Steele's story powerfully reflects the changes that took place across 17th century Scotland, and stunningly brings this period of history to life.

'Smith writes with a fine ear for Scots speech, and with a sensitive awareness to the different ways in which history intrudes upon the lives of men and women, soldiers and civilians, adults and children'
– James Robertson

Dark Times

Ethyl Smith

ISBN: 978-1-910946-26-8 (eBook)
ISBN: 978-1-910946-24-4 (Paperback)

The summer of 1679 is a dark one for the Covenanters, routed by government troops at the Battle of Bothwell Brig. John Steel is on the run, hunted for his part in the battle by the vindictive Earl of Airlie. And life is no easier for the hapless Sandy Gillon, curate of Lesmahagow Kirk, in the Earl's sights for aiding John Steel's escape.

Outlawed and hounded, the surviving rebels have no choice but to take to the hills and moors to evade capture and deportation. And as a hard winter approaches, Marion Steel discovers she's pregnant with her third child.

Dark Times is the second part of Ethyl Smith's sweeping *Times* series that follows the lives of ordinary people in extraordinary times.

'What really sets Smith's novel apart, however, is her superb use of Scots dialogue. From the educated Scots of the gentry and nobility to the broader brogues of everyday folk, the dialogue sparkles and demands to be read out loud.' – Shirley Whiteside (The National)

The Bogeyman Chronicles

Craig Watson

ISBN: 978-1-910946-11-4 (eBook)
ISBN: 978-1-910946-10-7 (Paperback)

In 14th Century Scotland, amidst the wars of independence, hatred, murder and betrayal are commonplace. People are driven to extraordinary lengths to survive, whilst those with power exercise it with cruel pleasure.

Royal Prince Alexander Stewart, son of King Robert II and plagued by rumours of his illegitimacy, becomes infamous as the Wolf of Badenoch, while young Andrew Christie commits an unforgivable sin and lay Brother Brodie Affleck in the Restenneth Priory pieces together the mystery that links them all together.

From the horror of the times and the changing fortunes of the characters, the legend of the Bogeyman is born and Craig Watson cleverly weaves together the disparate lives of the characters into a compelling historical mystery that will keep you gripped throughout.

Over 80 years the lives of three men are inextricably entwined, and through their hatreds, murders and betrayals the legend of Christie Cleek, the bogeyman, is born.

'The Bogeyman Chronicles haunted our imagination long after we finished it' – iScot Magazine

A Good Death

Helen Davis

ISBN: 978-0-9575689-7-6 (eBook)
ISBN: 978-0-9575689-6-9 (Paperback)

'*A good death is better than a bad conscience,*' said Sophie.
1983 – Georgie, Theo, Sophie and Helena, four disparate young Cambridge undergraduates, set out to scale Ausangate, one of the highest and most sacred peaks in the Andes.

Seduced into employing the handsome and enigmatic Wamani as a guide, the four women are initiated into the mystically dangerous side of Peru, Wamani and themselves as they travel from Cuzco to the mountain, a journey that will shape their lives forever.

2013 – though the women are still close, the secrets and betrayals of Ausangate chafe at the friendship.

A girls' weekend at a lonely Fenland farmhouse descends into conflict with the insensitive inclusion of an overbearing young academic toyboy brought along by Theo. Sparked by his unexpected presence, pent up petty jealousies, recriminations and bitterness finally explode the truth of Ausangate, setting the women on a new and dangerous path.

Sharply observant and darkly comic, Helen Davis's début novel is an elegant tale of murder, seduction, vengeance, and the value of a good friendship.

'The prose is crisp, adept, and emotionally evocative' – Lesbrary.com

The Birds That Never Flew

Margot McCuaig

Shortlisted for the Dundee International Book Prize 2012

Longlisted for the Polari First Book Prize 2014

ISBN: 978-0-9929768-5-9 (eBook)

ISBN: 978-0-9929768-4-2 (Paperback)

'Have you got a light hen? I'm totally gaspin.'

Battered and bruised, Elizabeth has taken her daughter and left her abusive husband Patrick. Again. In the bleak and impersonal Glasgow housing office Elizabeth meets the provocatively intriguing drug addict Sadie, who is desperate to get her own life back on track.

The two women forge a fierce and interdependent relationship as they try to rebuild their shattered lives, but despite their bold, and sometimes illegal attempts it seems impossible to escape from the abuse they have always known, and tragedy strikes.

More than a decade later Elizabeth has started to implement her perfect revenge – until a surreal Glaswegian Virgin Mary steps in with imperfect timing and a less than divine attitude to stick a spoke in the wheel of retribution.

Tragic, darkly funny and irreverent, *The Birds That Never Flew* ushers in a new and vibrant voice in Scottish literature.

'...dark, beautiful and moving, I wholeheartedly recommend' scanoir.co.uk

Over Here

Jane Taylor

ISBN: 978-0-9929768-3-5 (eBook)
ISBN: 978-0-9929768-2-8 (Paperback)

It's coming up to twenty-four hours since the boy stepped down from the big passenger liner – it must be, he reckons foggily – because morning has come around once more with the awful irrevocability of time destined to lead nowhere in this worrying new situation. His temporary minder on board – last spotted heading for the bar some while before the lumbering process of docking got underway – seems to have vanished for good. Where does that leave him now? All on his own in a new country: that's where it leaves him. He is just nine years old.

An eloquently written novel tracing the social transformations of a century where possibilities were opened up by two world wars that saw millions of men move around the world to fight, and mass migration to the new worlds of Canada and Australia by tens of thousands of people looking for a better life.

Through the eyes of three generations of women, the tragic story of the nine year old boy on Liverpool docks is brought to life in saddeningly evocative prose.

'...a sweeping haunting first novel that spans four generations and two continents...' – Cristina Odone/Catholic Herald